THE
PRESIDENT'S
ASSASSIN

Also by Brian Haig

Secret Sanction
Mortal Allies
The Kingmaker
Private Sector

THE
PRESIDENT'S
ASSASSIN

BRIAN
HAIG

WARNER BOOKS

NEW YORK   BOSTON

Copyright © 2005 by Brian Haig
All rights reserved.

Warner Books

Time Warner Book Group
1271 Avenue of the Americas, New York, NY 10020
Visit our Web site at www.twbookmark.com.

Printed in the United States of America

First Printing: February 2005
10   9   8   7   6   5   4   3   2

Library of Congress Cataloging-in-Publication Data

Haig, Brian.
     The president's assassin / Brian Haig.
          p. cm.
     ISBN 0-446-57667-0
     1. Drummond, Sean (Fictitious character)—Fiction. 2. Politicians—Crimes against—
Fiction. 3. Attempted assassination—Fiction. 4. Presidents—Election—Fiction. 5.
Political campaigns—Fiction. 6. Washington (D.C.)—Fiction. I. Title.

     PS3608.A54P74 2005
     813'.6—dc22   2004010404

With love to:
Lisa
Brian, Patrick, Donnie, and Annie

ACKNOWLEDGMENTS

A lot of exceptional people had a hand in this novel. Luke Janklow, the world's greatest agent and truly a friend to treasure. Everybody at Janklow, Nesbit who labors every day to make their writers' lives rewarding and fulfilling. Rick Horgan, my editor, my friend, and the bane of my existence because of his unmatched eye, because of his bothersome integrity, and because he just won't allow an unresolved plot point or flawed personification to linger. Mari Okuda and Roland Ottewell, copy editors and friends—or perhaps alchemists—who magically turn a pig's ear into a purse. And to everybody at Warner Books, from Larry and Jamie and Jimmy down, who treat publishing not as a business, but as a wonderfully fun way to make a living.

A few special observances: Chuck Wardell and Pete Kinney, who not only loaned me pieces of themselves to construct Sean Drummond, but also, in this book, loaned me their names; and Mike Grollman, a friend, a talented writer whose day will come, and a great sounding board.

THE
PRESIDENT'S
ASSASSIN

CHAPTER ONE

SETTLING INTO THE BACKSEAT OF THE CAR, I MENTIONED TO THE ATTRACtive young lady seated beside me, "That's a lovely pistol you're carrying."

No reply.

"The accessorized holster's nice, too."

"Well . . . they're FBI issue."

"No kidding. Ever shoot anybody with it?"

"Not yet." She gave me a brief glance. "You might be my first."

From her accent she was from the Midwest, Ohio, someplace like that. From her tone and demeanor, she meant it. Neither she nor the gentlemen in the front smiled, offered hands, or appeared in any way pleased to have me as a passenger.

So to break the ice, I said, "I'm Sean Drummond."

She said, "Keep quiet."

"Nice morning, isn't it?"

She gave me an annoyed look and stared out the window.

"Where are we going?" I asked her.

"I'm trying to think. Shut up."

"That's not what I asked."

"Well . . . you're not paying attention to the answer you're getting."

We were in the backseat of an unmarked black sedan with two plainclothes types in front. I said, "You guys know where we're going?"

The one in the passenger seat glanced sideways at his partner. "Yeah."

As I mentioned, I'm Sean Drummond, an Army major and a JAG attorney, and for all I knew these three were goombahs and we were on our way to the nearest marsh for a quick whack. Well, probably not—though I think the lady was tempted. We had just departed the front gate of CIA headquarters and turned right onto Dolley Madison, headed west toward McLean. No lights or sirens were turned on, but the driver kicked it up to about seventy, which I regarded as interesting fact number one.

I knew the lady's name was Jennifer Margold; I knew she was a special agent from the D.C. Metro Field Office of the Federal Bureau of Investigation, and probably she wouldn't be in the backseat of this car were she not good at something. Early to mid-thirties, shoulder-length coppery hair, slender, and as I mentioned, attractive—not beautiful, more like pretty in an interesting way.

She looked bright, and wore a dark pantsuit with practical pumps, light on the makeup, and heavy on the bitchiness, if you ask me. Also, for fieldwork Fibbies prefer what she was not wearing: bulletproof vests, blue windbreakers, and baseball caps. I regarded this as interesting fact number two. Her eyes, incidentally, were a sort of frosted blue, like chilled cobalt.

I should also mention that I wasn't attired in a uniform or

anything, but a blue serge suit, which was both stylish and appropriate, as my current assignment had nothing to do with the Army or law. Actually, I was new to this job. In fact, I wasn't really sure what my job was. I said to the driver, "I'd really appreciate it if you'd pull over at the nearest Starbucks."

He laughed.

I said, "Come on, guy. I'll buy. You all look like mocha latte types."

Agent Margold replied, "I told you, shut up."

Anyway, I was on loan—or maybe banished—to something innocuously titled the Office of Special Projects, part of the Central Intelligence Agency, though I wasn't working at the Langley headquarters but somewhere called an offsite—a nondescript large red-brick warehouse in Crystal City with a sign over the entrance that read "Ferguson Home Security Electronics."

You'd think that would be enough of a front, but the Agency has a classified budget, which is an invitation for extravagant idiocy. Three or four red delivery vans were parked out front, and there were actually a few guys whose job it was to drive them around all day, and even more guys who were supposed to pop in and out and pose like customers. There was even a receptionist out front named Lila to handle the occasional rube who dropped in looking for a home alarm or something. But she's okay. She's very friendly. Also, she's really pretty.

The CIA is really into this smoke-and-mirrors stuff. I mean, how much simpler would it be to just slap up a sign that read "VD Clinic"? No more vans and no more phony customers, and for sure there'd be no casual foot traffic. I actually submitted this recommendation on my second day on the job. But I already knew the response. These people have big-time image issues. For an agency charged with national security, they're really insecure.

Anyway, after only a mile or so we turned left onto a street called Ballantrae Farm Drive, a sort of suburban block filled with Pepsident monstrosities. McLean, if you're interested, is one of Washington's more elite suburbs, with no shortage of posh enclaves for the rich and privileged. Still, I could picture a Realtor taking a prospective couple to this block saying something like, "But since you said money is no object, I wanted to be sure you saw this lovely neighborhood."

We continued our drive down the street and eventually we reached a cul-de-sac, and it wasn't hard to guess that the big shack with the three Crown Vics at the curb was our destination. Two guys in suits stood guard at the front entrance, and they weren't holding welcome signs.

You saw that house and you knew—all red brick with tall, thick Corinthian stone columns in front, slate-roofed, and if I had to estimate, about fifteen thousand square feet of interior grandiosity and pomposity, pool out back, cabana, and all that.

We climbed out of the backseat, and one of the guys in suits promptly approached. He seemed to know Special Agent Margold, because he said, "Everybody's inside, Jennie. It's ugly. Director's still ten minutes out." He handed her a clipboard and she signed in, name, time, date, whatever.

Presumably he was referring to Mark Townsend, the head of the Federal Bureau, which told you these clowns were also Fibbies. Not that I have anything against the FBI. I actually admire what they do and how well they do it. It's *how* they do it. A lot of FBI types are lawyers and accountants, and when you turn them into law enforcement agents you get this weird culture and this sort of hybrid personality, or maybe a hyphenated personality. They're so insufferable, they better be good.

Also, jurisdiction's always a touchy issue with law enforcement types. Aside from the aforementioned government sedans and federal agents, I saw no ambulances, no ME wagon, no forensics van, nor had anybody strung up any yellow crime scene tape. This was interesting fact number three.

Interesting fact number four was the absence of uniformed or local cops, the usual first responders. So whatever occurred inside that house was being kept strictly federal, a synonym for serious, and was being handled low-key, which often rhymes with messy, or, more often, embarrassing.

Margold handed the clipboard back to the guy, who asked me, "Who're you?"

"Building inspector."

He did not respond. I asked, "You the termite guy?"

He smiled tightly. "I'd like to see your ID before you sign in."

Actually, when I was pulled out of the shower by a 7:09 A.M. phone call from my boss, the only instructions she could offer over an open line were to be sure not to sign the crime log, and nobody but Agent Margold was authorized to know my true identity. She also mentioned that to preserve my anonymity, I should curb my tart tongue and watch my manners, whatever that means.

In my few short weeks with these clandestine types, the one thing I'd learned is that what is said rarely is all that is meant. You have to read between the lines. Don't sign in means we don't want you getting subpoenaed later. Don't identify yourself means it would be inconvenient to have a witness on the stand recalling your presence. So I was being neither coy nor rude when I told him, "Seriously, if I show you my ID I'll have to kill you."

He said, "Seriously . . . if you don't, I might kill you."

Agent Margold stepped in and informed the guy, "He's authorized. I'll keep an eye on him."

"He *has* to sign in, Jennie."

"Trust me, he doesn't. If you get backlash, refer it to me."

She stared him down with those icy blue eyes, and reluctantly he allowed us to pass. Whatever happened inside this house this fine spring morning had these people so tightassed it would take a month of Metamucil to clear their pipes. But we progressed together, she and I, up the driveway and then along a walkway to the grand front entrance. She paused at the doorway, slipped white paper booties over her shoes, slapped latex gloves on her hands, and, speaking out the side of her mouth, said to me, "It's apparent that you have authority issues. If I get the slightest problem from you, Drummond, I'll slap your ass in handcuffs and have you carted out." She handed shoe covers and gloves to me and added, "Stay beside me, keep your smartassed mouth shut, and don't touch a thing. You're here to observe, period."

Goodness. I tucked my tail between my legs and replied, "You're right. I'm glad you brought this to my attention, and I'm truly sorry. You have my word, I'll be more responsive, helpful, and obedient."

Actually, I didn't say that. I slipped on my booties and gloves and asked, "You going in first?"

And without further ado, we entered a cavernous foyer with white marble floors and, to the left, a sweeping curved stairway, and on the ceiling above, a massive crystal chandelier. As I was here to observe, period, I also took note of the oriental chest against the far wall, the handwoven Chinese rug centered neatly in the foyer, and the corpse about five feet from the door.

The corpse—a female, late twenties, and in admirable physical shape, ignoring her present condition. She was dressed in a nice navy blue suit with a plain jacket and short skirt and was lying on her back, hands clutched at her throat with her knees bent and her legs spread wide apart, so you could see her pink undies; though modesty was no longer a concern for her. Both the position of her hands and the halo of blood around her head suggested she'd been shot in the throat. The blood looked dark, indicating an artery had been nicked, and the fact that it was only partially dry that she'd gotten it around the time I should've been having my morning joe.

She looked like a broken rag doll that had gotten caught in a big wind and tossed on her butt. But that's not what happened— she'd taken a frontal shot from a slug with enough throw weight to fling her five feet through the air.

I don't think Ms. Margold missed the corpse, though she ignored it and walked on. Also, she had either been in this house before or had been briefed on the layout, because she led me straight through a large living room and directly to the dining room, and more corpses.

More precisely, an elderly man and woman were seated at each end of the dining table, slumped forward, facedown in the soup—or to be completely precise, their faces were in soup bowls, filled with Cheerios for him and Frosted Flakes for her.

The man was about mid-sixties, white-haired, attired in a gray pinstriped light wool business suit, white shirt, and shiny black tasseled loafers. An expensive black leather briefcase was parked beside his left foot, like he was about to leave for work, though obviously that didn't pan out. The woman was about his age, red-haired, and she wore pink pajamas under a blue silk dressing gown, as if she expected to be eating in front of strangers, though from the scene at the table, probably not the strangers who dropped by.

Agent Margold moved directly to the male victim's body, felt his neck very briefly, and backed off. I noticed, to our right, nearly in the corner, two agents leaning against the wall who did not seem to be doing much of anything. But maybe they weren't supposed to. She suggested to them, "What . . . maybe two hours?"

The heavier one nodded. "An ME's on the way. But yeah . . . when we arrived thirty minutes ago, he was still real warm. Time of death between six and seven o'clock. Closer to six, I think."

She walked around and examined the room a moment. The table was long and thick, custom-made obviously, able to seat about fourteen. The room itself was expansive and expensively furnished, and the lady of the house was a finicky housekeeper and possessed good decorating taste, or she hired good help. Fresh bouquets of flowers rested on the fireplace mantel and a large centerpiece sat on the middle of the table, suggesting, I thought, that she and the hubby might've entertained recently.

But maybe they weren't husband and wife. You have to be careful about assumptions at a murder scene. The dead guy could be her lover, her tax accountant, or her killer. Also, the two gents by the wall kept glancing at the male corpse and largely ignored the woman. As a general rule, all corpses are relevant to a crime, and perhaps not in life but in death, all bodies become equal. Yet in most multiple murders, one corpse is the main event and the rest are simply victims of the three Ws—wrong place, wrong time, wrong company. I wondered if the young lady in the foyer was their daughter.

We all contemplated the corpses for a moment. Margold asked, "Who was the first responder?"

Again the heavier guy responded, "Danny Cavuso. Works out of the Tysons Corner cell. Because of proximity to the residence, the Tysons office is on standby for problems. A telephonic check was supposed to be made every morning when Hawk left for work. When no call came by six-thirty, a call was made here. No answer. So Cavuso was dispatched."

"Alone?"

"Andy Warshuski from his office was his backup. The front

door was unlocked. They swept the house and grounds, and called in the incident. When we arrived, they left together."

"So they're the only two who departed the site?"

"Except the killers."

"Keep it that way. Complete quarantine. Nobody departs unless I say so."

He replied, "Already got that word," and she returned to her visual inspection, leaving me to ponder interesting fact number five. Perhaps she was worried about forensics getting disqualifying foot- and fingerprints from everybody who entered the house. Or perhaps I was missing something important.

Anyway, lawyers are not forensic experts, but eight years of criminal law does afford a few skills and insights. The right side of the man's head had a small entry hole—dead center in the temple—and though I couldn't yet observe an exit wound, the gray-and-red mess splattered on the expensive wallpaper suggested the bullet had passed through cleanly. I moved around a bit, formed a mental image of the male victim alive and seated upright. The shot had been fired flat and level, I decided, as if the shooter positioned the gun right next to the guy's temple, and boom. But more likely the killer had taken the shooter's crouch and fired from a distance, which accounted for the level trajectory. The lady of the house had taken her bullet in the right rear quadrant of her neck. From the debris splattered messily across the near side of the table, the shooter had stood slightly to her right rear with the weapon sighted slightly downward. I made a mental note to think about that.

That the bullet had passed cleanly through the male's head rather than ricocheting around the skull, as so often happens, suggested a powerful weapon. And from the way the lady back at the front door had been flung backward, you knew it was more than a .22, certainly, though I thought the size of the entry wound in the man's temple indicated something smaller than a .45.

I walked around and visually checked the exit wound of the male victim. The whole side and rear quadrant of his skull was missing, too large a hole for a .38, unless the bullet had been a hollowpoint or been modified in some nasty way to boost the tissue damage. The bullet had to be lodged in the wall—good news for the ballistics folks.

Also, the attack had come as a complete surprise to the couple at the table. That was obvious. Neither victim had tried to stand up or fend off the attack, or had even acknowledged their killer. Like, "Could you please pass the sugar, Martha," then— *bang*—"Auugh." No, actually, more like, "Martha, could you pass another slice of that delicious toast?" "Of course, dear, and would you—" *bang*, *bang*, Augh, Augh.

Special Agent Margold appeared to be in a hurry, because after only a cursory inspection, she asked, "How do we get to the basement?"

The skinnier agent said, "Back by the kitchen. Second door on the right. Ben Marcasi's down there."

She glanced at me and said, somewhat curtly, "Come along."

So I came along.

We went through a short passage to the hallway and found the second door on the right. As we walked, I tried to piece together why the Agency was on the hook for this thing, and more selfishly, was Sean Drummond on the hook for anything? From the looks of things and the presence of the Bureau I ruled out the ordinary stuff: burglary, drug deal gone sour, and so on. In fact, what happened inside that dining room looked like an execution. There had been no conversation between victims and killers, no argument over money, no vengeful message, no negotiation, not even an exchange of good-byes.

Generalizations, like assumptions, can be misleading, yet it's a fact that executions nearly always are the tradecraft of mobsters and drug gangs. Both like to regard murder as just business, a swift and elegant way to settle a dispute, end a partnership, or terminate a misbehaving employee. But wiseguys would bring in only the Feds, and drug gangs might draw in the DEA but should not concern the CIA. A blown witness-protection thing? That could involve the Agency if the victim was a witness in an international terrorism case, I guess. So that was a possibility. Or was the dead guy at the table a CIA employee? Maybe this was some weird courtesy thing between federal agencies: Hey, one of your guys got whacked this morning—want to come see?

I smelled coffee as we passed the kitchen. For some reason, the odor sent a chill down my spine. Not three hours before three people awakened, never realizing they were dressing for the last time, sharing their final breakfast. Sad. So I followed Agent Margold down the stairs and into the basement, and at the bottom of the steps she yelled, "Ben! . . . Ben! . . ."

"Back here," a voice replied.

The basement was large with a high ceiling, essentially a spacious, open room with tan wall-to-wall, no sliding doors, no exterior entrances, not even windows. It was more casual and sparsely furnished than upstairs, and there was a feeling like it didn't see much use, but in the far right corner I spotted a tidy pile of toys; an Erector set, two balls, a toy truck, and so forth.

Like that, the couple upstairs were no longer clinical clue magnets; they were now Grandma and Grandpa, they took the grandkiddies to the Smithsonian and remembered all their birthdays, and their murder became more than an incident: It became a tragedy for some family and a matter of more than passing interest for me. Wondering if Margold's mood reflected some personal connection, I asked, "Did you know these people?"

She faced me and said, "Open your mouth again and you're gone."

We were getting along famously.

Anyway, we proceeded to a door and entered a small room that, from the condition of the drywall and unmarred whitewash, appeared to be a recent addition.

A heavyset middle-aged male stood in the middle of the floor, running his hands through his balding hair, and he turned to face us as we entered. The absence of other living beings in the room indicated this would be Ben. The room—small and claustrophobic, because in addition to Ben were some ten wall-mounted video monitors, a high-tech communications console, a brown Naugahyde lounge chair, and a single bed in the far corner. Also, strewn here and about, three additional corpses.

Nearest to the door and us sat a young woman who had taken three or four slugs on the right side of her body. She was seated in an office chair at the commo console, her body pitched to the left, her right hand stretched toward the console, and it struck me she might've been reaching for something when she got popped. The other two corpses were males, late twenties and mid-thirties, wearing wrinkled gray suits and more bullet holes.

The younger of the two men had removed his jacket and was prone on the bed, and if you ignored the small hole in his right temple and the splatter of skull viscera on the far wall, the expression on his face was weirdly placid and content—arms crossed, feet crossed; his sleep had turned permanent without so much as a whimper.

The second male corpse was seated on the lounge chair, jacket slung over the chair back, eyes wide open, and his expression, not placid, was a mixture of shock and agony. His fingers were clutched at his throat, just like the lady at the door, where he'd also been shot. If you didn't know better, you'd think he'd had a heart attack. In a way he had. They all had.

Another thing got my attention. The dead guy on the bed had removed not only his jacket but also a holster containing a Glock automatic. A matching holster and Glock pistol were still hooked to the belt of his dead partner. I eliminated my CIA employee theory and leaned toward the blown witness thing. "Who are these people?" I asked Margold.

Margold was busy feeling the neck of the young lady at the console and said, "Shut up" to me, and then to Ben, "Roughly same time of death as the others."

"Yeah." After a long moment, he noted, "Nearly simultaneous."

"Same weapon as upstairs, right?"

"Uh . . . maybe. Same caliber. I'm thinking a thirty-eight."

"About. Had to be a silencer."

"Had to be," he agreed. After a moment, he said to her, "Can you reconstruct yet?"

"Yeah . . . it's pretty straightforward. Who's at the front door?"

"June Lacy." He added, "Been with us three years. From upstate Minnesota, I think . . . engaged to get married next week."

"Uh-huh. What time did Hawk's driver arrive?"

"Same time every morning, 6:15. Name's Larry Elwood. Anyway, Larry'd pull into the driveway, leave the car idling, come to the front door, and June, or whoever was on shift, took over from there."

Agent Margold was examining a clipboard on the console, apparently a security log, because she said, "The entry's right here. Six-twenty, Elwood arrived." She looked at Ben. "'Took over from there'? What's that mean?"

"The team had a morning routine. June would roust the

Hawk out. She'd escort him out to the car, and Elwood drove him in. The Hawk liked to be at his desk at 6:45 sharp, even on Saturdays. You can tell by the condition of the house the man was a stickler . . . We got serious heat if we threw him off schedule."

"So that's what happened," Margold replied after a moment. "Elwood—at least someone who *looked* like Elwood—pulled into the driveway, came to the door, rang the bell, only this time, when Lacy answered, she took it in the throat." She added, "Nothing arbitrary about that throat shot. Drowned out her warning."

Ben nodded. "I just reviewed the tape. The car pulled up at 6:20. Like you said—five minutes late. And you're right, a guy who looks like Elwood walked directly to the front door. Obviously, the cameras only canvass the exterior, though."

"Yeah, well . . . it's fairly obvious what happened inside. After he killed Lacy, he stepped inside, capped the Hawk and his wife, then rushed down here and did these three." She pointed at the bank of monitors. "Let's see the tape."

I didn't think it was that obvious, but Ben raised no objections, nor did I. Ben moved to the console, pointed to one of the monitors, pushed a few buttons, and rewound till you could see the time was 6:19. He pushed play, and after about thirty seconds a shiny black Lincoln Town Car with impenetrably darkened windows crossed in front of the house and pulled up the driveway, not stopping till it was nearly to the garage door. A male got out, walked to the front of the car, then you lost him for a few seconds as he crossed the front of the car, but he reappeared as he headed up the walkway to the entrance. The camera lost his image again when he walked under the overhang supported by the concrete columns. So you couldn't observe what happened at the door, though from June Lacy's corpse, you knew *what* happened, just not how.

The driver, Larry Elwood, wore a dark suit, was heavyset and black. One of those silly chauffeur's hats with a visor obscured his face. Also he walked slowly, almost haltingly, and slightly hunched over, like he had a stomach cramp or was trying to work a kink out of a bum leg. Or perhaps as though he was hiding his face, disguising his physical appearance from the camera.

Margold picked up on it, too, because she asked Ben, "You're positive that's Elwood?"

"Looks like him. Hell, though, I'm not sure of anything."

I suggested, "Maybe there was more than one of them."

Ben asked, "Who's he?"

I asked, "Who're you?"

"Ben Marcasi." He turned to Agent Margold and again asked, "Who the hell's he?"

Margold looked at me. "I thought I warned you to keep your mouth shut."

"Right. Just, you know . . . forget what I said."

But obviously she couldn't forget what I said. She informed me, "Ben's Secret Service . . . the deputy chief of the White House security detail." She waved an arm around. "This house falls under his supervision. These are his people."

Goodness. It all came into focus—the poop was hitting the fan, and clearly they knew it. What wasn't at all clear was *who* had died upstairs, and what I was doing in range of the splatter.

So to clarify that first point, I asked, "And the dead guy upstairs . . . Mr. Hawk?"

"A code name. The deceased male upstairs is Terry Belknap . . . White House Chief of Staff." But she obviously wasn't interested in providing more insights or information. She asked me, "Why do you think there were two shooters?"

"Did I say *only* two?"

"I don't . . . uh, okay, two or more. Why?"

I allowed her a moment to digest her own question before I

suggested, "You understand that the couple upstairs were shot nearly simultaneously, right? He was facing his wife and he took it in the right temple. The geometry suggests his shooter fired from the living room entry into the dining room. Had the same shooter nailed Mrs. Belknap, the bullets would've struck her in the front or possibly left frontal lobe. But the Mrs. was facing the Mr. and she took it in the rear left quadrant of her neck. Ergo, a second shooter popped her from the kitchen entry into the dining room."

Agent Margold nodded and said, "You could be right. But there are—"

"Not could be . . . It's a fact."

"All right . . ."

"That's two shooters who gained entry. If they found a way to get two inside, why not three? Or four? Lacy opens the front door and takes it in the throat. Two, three, or four guys race in. One moves to the living room, one to the kitchen. The third and maybe the fourth sneak down here."

Margold said, "Let's entertain your theory for a moment. They've got some kind of signaling device—radios maybe—and as you suggested, they launch their attacks simultaneously." She walked over to the dead guy in the lounge chair. "He's armed, he's alert, he's facing the door . . . he gets it first. Then her, before she can push the central alarm," she said, indicating the dead lady at the commo console. "The sleeper, he's harmless . . . he gets it last."

"Nope," said Ben, shaking his head. "Not only are cameras covering the whole exterior of this house, there's also motion detectors. No way you could get even *one* person approaching undetected. Couldn't happen."

After pondering Ben's blanket assurance, I asked, "No blind spots?"

"Glad you asked—none. Cameras cover the full backyard, the house flanks, and there's two roving cameras mounted high on the columns in the front that give you a panorama of *everything* approaching this house." He pointed at the monitors. "You saw yourself—driveway, lawn, street out front . . . everything's covered."

I noted, "I saw a blind spot against the front wall of the house."

"Well, yeah. The cameras had to be mounted on the columns. But we were aware of that. So that space is covered with movement sensors."

"Radar or light beams?" I asked.

"Radar. I oversaw the security architecture and installation myself. One detector spaced every five feet. Foolproof."

Wrong answer, Ben. I asked, "And what happens when two or three bodies breach a beam simultaneously?"

"That's imposs—"

"Like, they're walking in a line, so they all hit the beam at once?" I knew the answer, actually. But sometimes the Socratic method works best.

Ben paused. He then gave the only answer he could give. "Theoretically, you might get one alert."

"So this Elwood guy pulls into the driveway—and one, two, or three other guys are inside the car with him. He gets out; they get out. They stay low, using the car as a visual screen from the cameras till they get to the blind spot by the garage door. They get right against the front wall of the house, inside the blind spot, and move in lockstep with Elwood." After a short pause, I added, "And because the folks down here observe what they think is Elwood moving alone on the walkway, they assume it's him making the movement detectors go off."

17

The room was suddenly quiet. I asked, "Is that a possible scenario?"

Poor Ben looked like he just understood he was about to have a big career problem. "I . . . I don't think so."

Margold looked at me, then at Ben, then at the three corpses in the tiny room. She said, "Ben . . . we better check."

So we trudged back upstairs, through the long hallway and the spacious foyer, past poor Lacy's body, and onto the front entry. Neatly trimmed bushes and shrubbery were up against the front wall of the house, and there was a thick strip of mulch separating the bushes from the well-manicured lawn. But once you knew what you were looking for, and at, the disturbances in the garden mulch jumped out at you. Ben bent forward at the waist and gawked. After an awkward moment, he insisted, "That proves nothing. Could've been a gardener or a wild animal made those tracks."

I suggested to Margold, "They're footprints. You should definitely get molds before it rains."

Margold's nostrils sort of flared. "I'll decide how to do my job, if you don't mind." She contemplated the mulch, then pointed at me and snapped, "You . . . let's have a word."

We walked, she and I, to the end of the driveway, far enough to be out of Ben's earshot. She studied my face and asked, "Who the hell are you?"

"Nobody. Forget I was here. Now, if you'll please tell your people to give me a lift, I'd like to go back to my office. Incidentally, it was really swell working with you. Tough case. Best of luck."

"Look . . . in case you haven't noticed, six people are dead inside that house. Including the White House Chief of Staff."

"I noticed. Do I need to walk out of here?" Okay, I was being a little over the top. And maybe Margold's testiness that morning was justified, as she had obviously been shoved in front of a moving train. But she had rubbed my face in the crap, and what goes around, comes around.

She said, "You're staying. Don't pretend otherwise."

Also, I was thinking on my feet. I had no idea why my boss dispatched me to this gig, and if I stayed I'd only sink deeper into the muck. Mrs. Drummond had not raised a complete idiot, and I now knew that what had happened inside that big house was the form of execution subtitled a political assassination. Mention that phrase in the CIA and people go all pale and sweaty on you. The next thing you know, some idiot named Oliver Stone's making a movie with a character named Drummond. I said, "You're the FBI. You're great—handle it."

Ms. Margold ignored me and began talking about the seriousness of this thing and so forth. I tuned her out.

In fact, I was sure this was why my boss had ordered me to keep a low profile. The Agency did not want to be within ten miles of this thing. Actually, the Agency headquarters was only two miles down the road, so I should walk fast.

Apparently Margold saw she had lost my attention, because she swallowed and said, "Okay, I get it. Look . . . well, I'm sorry if I was . . . a little brusque earlier."

"A little *what*?"

"Okay . . . I was rude. Nothing personal."

"Bullshit. You're worried because you've got the murder of the year on your hands. The Lord of the Feebs will be here any minute, and you caught the rap. You're supposed to show you're on top of this thing and explain what happened here, yet for some reason no ME or forensics people have arrived, the first guys on the scene are standing around with their thumbs up their butts, Ben's worried about covering his ass, and it suddenly struck you that you're all alone with your ass on the line. So I say something bright and enlightening, and you decide I might be helpful. Also, you'd like somebody to help catch the crap when it flies. Thanks. Get me a ride out of here."

Her jaw muscles tensed a bit, but she kept her cool. Actually, she smiled. "You're more alert and intuitive than I gave you credit for, Drummond."

"Are you going to get me a ride?"

"But you're not leaving."

"Wrong. Says so in the federal statutes—CIA handles assholes outside, FBI handles assholes inside. It's yours."

I spun around and was starting to walk away when she warned, "You better hear about the note before you take another step."

I stopped, but did not turn around. Actually, I knew I should not have stopped. But knowing what you should do and *doing* what you should do are two very different things. I could feel her eyes on my back.

She mentioned, "It was found on that oriental chest in the foyer. The initial entry crew immediately transported it to our lab for analysis."

Okay, now I had a millisecond to decide—did I really want to hear about the note? This was Washington, the one place where in fact what you don't know doesn't hurt you. But having seen all those bodies, I was curious. Boy, was I in a fix.

Then it was too late as she explained, "To paraphrase the words read to me over the phone, this slaughter was a warning. 'You can't stop us. There will be others, and the President will be history in the next two days.'"

"History?"

"Their word, not mine."

That awkward phraseology aside, it occurred to me that my options had just dwindled. The assassins could be foreign terrorists, and that would definitely involve the Agency, so I should stay or I'd be in hot water. Or they could be homegrown idiots and staying would implicate the Agency in a domestic legal matter, and also put my ass in the sling. The only clear fact was that the people who found a way to bypass the security in this house, murdered six people, and beelined out of here were legitimately bad hombres, skilled, bold, and smart. In fact, Mrs. President might think about calling a few term life agencies to see who offered the most affordable rates for a few days of additional coverage on Mr. President.

Margold was thinking along the same lines and said, "This thing might be beyond domestic. You're as involved as I am."

Not so. At least, not yet.

She added, "The Director could get here any second. He's expecting a full and comprehensive briefing. Trust me, he's not a man you want to disappoint with half-assed results."

"All right. I'm here in an advisory capacity." I reconsidered and said, "Actually, I'm not here. The instant your boss shows up, I'm out of here."

She nodded, but did not reply.

In retrospect, I should have heeded the old warning: Never test the depth of water with both feet. But it was already too late.

CHAPTER TWO

WE STEPPED BACK INSIDE FOR ANOTHER VISUAL AND MENTAL SWEEP OF the surroundings. First, however, I took a moment for attitude adjustment. I was annoyed at being back inside this house, annoyed at being blindsided by my boss, and most of all, I was annoyed at Ms. Margold. Had Miss Tightass not kept the motive and victim profiles from me in the first place, we wouldn't have to go through this again. For the record, I've seen death, destruction, and corpses in my Army and legal career, and I'm not queasy. Yet it is something I've never grown used to, and a rerun is in some strange way worse than a first run.

But you have to focus at a murder site, and I noted first the absence of a peephole on the front door. There were lines of small side windows to each side of the door, and I suggested, "Possibly she never saw his face."

"What? Oh . . . Lacy . . . You mean Elwood's face?"

"Yeah. Look here. If he stood close enough when he rang the

doorbell, even if she peeked out the side window, she could only observe the side of his body."

Margold walked over and peered out the window to confirm the accuracy of this observation.

I obviously did not need to explain why this point was relevant, even important. The driver, Larry Elwood, was at that moment our only identified suspect. But there were no living witnesses and Elwood's face wasn't on the videotape in the basement, which left open the possibility that the gentleman we observed on film stumbling up the walkway was an impostor. The fact that June Lacy couldn't recognize Elwood's face at the door would leave his status ambiguous. Solving crimes is about inclusion and exclusion; Larry Elwood could still go either way, and we were back to roughly five billion UnSubs—FBI-speak for Unknown Subject and normal-speak for haven't got a clue. I mentioned, "Make sure your forensics people take fingerprints from the doorbell buzzer."

"I've already made a mental note of that."

"Incidentally, where's the car? And where's Elwood?"

"Missing. We've confirmed that Elwood left the motor pool at five-thirty, headed this way. An APB's out on him and the car."

"It's a big city."

"No, Drummond, it's a small city. New York and L.A. are big cities."

Ironically enough, I get a little pissed when sarcasm is used on me, and I replied, "Great. Then you'll have no trouble finding them."

"Actually . . . the car's equipped with a specially coded satellite navigation system that also works as a locator."

"Easier still."

"But it's apparently been disabled."

"Isn't that a surprise."

"Yeah, actually." She looked at me and said, "Only a handful of people are aware of the existence of that locator system. A very small handful."

"Not as small as you thought."

I took a knee and regarded June Lacy's body again. Her left hand covered the bullet hole, and the exit wound was hidden beneath her, so it was impossible to confirm whether the same caliber bullet did her as the others.

My eyes shifted to her face. June Lacy wasn't beautiful or even pretty, really. Her face was too roundish and her features were flat and ordinary, though she was striking, I thought even captivating, in a way that caught you by surprise. It took me a moment before I put a finger on it. She had a noisy innocence, a serenity of spirit, a sort of pleasant simpleness, not of the mind but of the soul, where it counts. Hers was that kind of happy girlish face found peeking out from the third row of a church choir, or at curbside during the Memorial Day parade, hand over her heart, having not the slightest doubt that this is the greatest country on earth, that the world is populated by knights and dragons; she stands with the knights, and is just so damned proud to be part of it. I'm not that type. Perhaps I once was, but no longer. Actually, for a moment I felt guilty and even a little soiled in her presence. More than that, I felt terribly sad and, in some strange way, deeply angry.

Ben had mentioned she was a Minnesotan, and indeed, Special Agent June Lacy emerged from a Nordic gene pool; her hair was silvery blond, her skin fair and unblemished, and her eyes were a sort of Baltic Sea pale blue. She was a slumber party habitué, never the prom queen though always in the court, the girl everybody entrusted with their most embarrassing secrets, though she wouldn't be among the elite Secret Service were she not also bright, ambitious, and adventurous.

No doubt, in some small town in northern Minnesota everybody was real tickled that little June with the pretty blond pigtails was now a handpicked bodyguard for the President of the United States. Every year the high school principal probably informed the incoming frosh that if you cracked the books and kept the wrong sorts of noxious substances out of your nose, a desk in the Oval Office might be a stretch, but a seat on Air Force One wasn't, because one of our fine students did it, and doesn't that make you all proud?

Clearly, a walk in Lacy's footsteps would no longer be the galvanizing inspiration it once was.

I glanced up at Agent Margold, who, incidentally, looked like the class-valedictorian-school-president-most-likely-to-succeed type. "She never had time to react."

"Don't feel sorry for her, Drummond. Had she been on her toes this would never have happened."

A priori, I couldn't argue that point, nor did I try. In my experience women tend to be harsh about other women. Whereas I, a male, was a bit conflicted. It's no longer PC to regard men as the protectors and females as the protected, implying as it does a relationship of the stronger and the weaker. We're all interchangeable and androgynous these days—all sensitive, caring creatures, who share cooking duties, child-rearing, and thankfully not childbirth or monthly periods. I even remember to put down the toilet seat at a lady's house. But I was raised an Army brat and spent my life on Army bases, where the fifties are eternal. Point is, I find it a little difficult to get my arms around all the contemporary mantras on these things, and I was very pissed that somebody put a bullet through June's throat.

I noted the sparkly engagement rock on her finger. Two more weeks and the knot would've been tied; the bridal gown surely was fitted and bought, the church reserved, the RSVPs collected—the guests wouldn't even have to change their travel plans, just their moods and wardrobes. I was tempted to adjust her skirt for dignity's sake, but Margold and her pals would probably get lathered up and cite me in a report or something.

I squeezed June's shoulder, stood up, and informed Margold, "Let's reconstruct."

"Fine. You start."

"All right. At 6:15, Lacy's probably waiting in the foyer for Elwood to arrive. Maybe she's seated on a stair—the guys downstairs announce through her earpiece that Elwood's headed up the walkway—*ding-dong*, she walks to the door, opens it, some guy's holding a pistol, and before she can speak or react, *bang*—no, not *bang*, but *pssssht*—a bullet passes through her throat. Right?"

"Right. Had to be a silencer."

"She flies backward. Two, maybe four guys enter, and . . . and . . ."

"And what?"

"Maybe not all the killers were men."

Margold gave me a weird look. "Yeah . . . possibly. You're thinking they brought along a woman to stay at the door and talk so the Belknaps would hear a feminine voice and not suspect anything amiss."

"It's a possibility we need to consider."

She looked down at Lacy a moment. "Interesting theory. Wouldn't that presuppose they knew a female agent would open the door?"

We both allowed that vagrant thought to hang for later. Margold suggested, "Next one shooter goes into the living room, and one or two more sneak downstairs to the basement. One remains here by the door. Say it's a she . . . she goes straight to the kitchen and gets into position . . . she gives the signal and they all open up." She faced me. "Like that, right?"

"Be careful with the exact numbers. Say two to four, and wait till forensics and ballistics confirm the exact count." I added, "Where are the spent shells?"

"You're thinking they used catchers on the guns?"

"If they used silencers, that means automatics, and that means the shells should've ejected. Tell your forensics people to look under every rug and inside every crevice. Of course, I doubt they'll find any."

"Right."

We returned to the dining room, where the two agents still loitered against the wall. Margold looked at them and said, "You two getting paid for sitting on your asses?"

The heavy one said, "Ah, don't bust our balls. We've sealed it off and we're waiting for forensics. Just following the manual and making sure we don't contaminate the site." After a moment he added, "You'd be well-advised to do the same."

Margold shook her head and began walking around the table.

I asked, "Why aren't the ME and forensics here already?"

The skinny guy said, "We were ordered to avoid locals. No quality control or evidence transfer issues." After a moment, he added, "So the teams have to come all the way up from Quantico." He shook his head. "Welcome to Washington. They're caught in traffic. About five minutes out."

Margold was moving around the room, testing out the shooters' positions, I guess to confirm my theory about a second gunman. She looked at me and said, "I'm done. Anything else?"

"Uh . . ." There was something. But what?

She looked at her watch and asked, again, "Are you done?"

I studied Mr. and Mrs. Belknap. We were overlooking something, I was sure. I said, "Ben mentioned Elwood arrived at 6:15 every morning."

"Yeah. And he came five minutes late this morning."

"You should think about that five minutes."

"On my list already."

"Also . . . well . . . Belknap probably had to wake up at five . . . maybe five-thirty, so he could shower, shave, dress, and have breakfast."

"What's your point?"

"You married?"

"No . . . why?"

"Ever been married? Cohabited?"

"No, I've . . ." But apparently I had struck a sensitive nerve, because she snapped, "If you have a point, get on with it."

"Conjugal habits, Agent Margold. The guy's an early bird; she didn't have to be. How'd they know these two get up and eat breakfast together?"

I was sure she got my point, but she did not acknowledge it. In fact, she said, "Let's go back to the basement. Now."

She stopped halfway down the stairs, turned to me, and whispered, "No more of those observations in front of the others. Obviously, if the killers knew how to skirt the security, and obviously if they knew about the security room in the basement, and . . . I'm not stupid, Drummond. Inside knowledge, right?" She looked me in the eyes and added, "But don't confirm that to anybody. Understand?"

I didn't understand. But I did appreciate that there was more here than met the eye—either a cover-up or not everybody in this house was trusted, or this lady had a few bats in her attic.

Ben had also returned to the security room, where he was replaying the tape of Elwood over and over, like if he watched it enough times the past would change and he'd still have a career. I sort of felt sorry for the guy. The killers had not played fair; they had found the kink in Ben's armor, and broken it off in Ben's butt.

The rule of thumb in his business is that guarding moving targets is the tough part. Home truly is a man's castle, and when you construct a deep moat around it, and you man the ramparts with stouthearted souls, it should be safe and impenetrable.

Should be. Unless the moat becomes your worst enemy. From the moment that black limo pulled into the driveway and entered into the castle proper, so to speak, it was accepted by the watchmen in the basement for what it appeared to be and in fact was not. The system instills confidence, nullifies distrust, and erases the wariness. June Lacy didn't die because she was careless, June Lacy died because her bosses told her to trust the electronic moat to do her work for her.

Every Washington institution plays by its own rules, and the Secret Service has a less forgiving mentality than most. Ben was headed for an early pension, unless he was a wicked bullshitter, in which case he'd end up handing out tickets at the White House tours office. But it was better than the cold morgue drawer where his team and the hapless Mr. and Mrs. Belknap were headed.

Anyway, Margold and I nosed around and gave the basement security room another once-over. Nothing new jumped out, though I concluded that Margold had probably hit the mark about the progression of death—the guy in the chair got nailed first, the lady at the console got it second, and then the sleeper.

If you had perfect intelligence and time to consider and plan the assault on this room, that's exactly how you'd do it; says so in the manual, neutralize the most imminent threats first. But that was exactly the point; the shooters didn't have time—they burst open the door and shot. I looked around for stray bullets that had struck a wall or the furniture. None. One shot, one kill . . . with the exception of the lady at the console, who took three slugs on her right side. I spent a moment examining her more closely. Her right arm was stretched out, she was in easy reach of the panic button, and it struck me that her killer had coldly used the impact of the bullets to drive her back, to prevent her from reaching it.

Very impressive.

Too impressive. I mentioned to Margold, "It's likely they used fiber-optic filament cameras. Slip it under the door, and you know what lies behind the closed door."

She nodded. Then she bent over the corpse on the bed. She was beginning to explain, "This guy must've pulled the night shift, and—" when her cell phone went off. She answered, "Margold . . . uh-huh . . . I understand, George . . . right." After a moment, she said, "No . . . well, we're almost wrapped up . . . Uh, yeah, we can be there. Ten minutes."

She punched off and appeared distracted. Finally she looked at Ben. "I've gotta go. Forensics and the ME will be here any minute. Agent Jackson's in charge till they get there." She looked at me. "The Director got diverted en route. We're heading to his location."

"We?" I shook my head. "Your boss, your case, your nightmare."

For the second time she smiled. "Is It? Did I fail to mention we're meeting at the George Bush Center? Isn't that a CIA facility?"

I stared at her, then I turned to Ben and said, "Give us the tape with Elwood arriving." A fresh thought hit me, and I asked Ben, "Did you view the portion with Elwood departing?"

"Uh . . . no. I . . . I hadn't thought of that."

"Provide that, too."

Margold looked at me and said, "Good catch."

"Right."

We went back upstairs, and halfway up I grabbed her arm and suggested, "You should think twice about allowing Ben free rein of this house."

"Meaning what?"

"For one, he's a potential suspect. Inside knowledge got out, and Ben certainly knew the layout."

"What's two?"

"There's going to be a witch hunt, and Ben was in charge of this operation. He should never have been permitted to tamper with the evidence before you arrived. But this is now your watch. Cover your ass."

"I . . . I should've thought of that."

She was right. She should have.

She returned to the dining room to inform Agent Jackson he had the football and to eject Ben from this house.

Ben rejoined us at the front door, handed Margold the tapes, and said to me, "Look . . . don't draw hasty conclusions. There's no proof there was more than one killer."

"There was more than one, Ben. Get used to it. If it's any consolation, I'll be sure to pass on that the security was nearly adequate."

"Gee . . . thanks."

"Think nothing of it."

"Yeah. I won't."

On our way to the car, Margold said to me, "This what you do for the Agency . . . reconstruct crime scenes?"

"Nope."

"Then how'd you . . . how'd you put it together?"

"Oh . . . well, I used to kill people."

She shook her head. "Seriously."

"All right, I'm a criminal lawyer."

She rolled her eyes and said, "That's why I hate working with you CIA people. You're all compulsive liars."

I smiled.

She said, "Get in the car."

And the problem with the FBI is they're all compulsive skeptics. Before I went to law school I was in Special Ops, I did do this for a living, and it does afford a certain familiarity with method and technique.

On a more becomingly modest note, I saw the disturbances in the garden mulch before we ever entered the house. Margold should've paid better attention when she was slapping on her latex mitties and telling me what an asshole I was.

She informed the driver, "We've got five minutes. Don't make me late. Move."

He stomped on the gas, and we peeled out down Ballantrae Farm Drive, mini-mansions whizzing by on the left and right. Halfway down the block, a long convoy of vans and dark Crown Vics passed us going the other way. Margold whipped out her cell phone and spent two minutes giving instructions to her contact in the forensics team, telling the technicians what to collect—foot molds in the garden, spent shells, fingerprints on the doorbell buzzer, whatever. She ended the conversation saying, "Yeah . . . okay . . . we'll both find a time later for you to get our shoe molds."

She punched off, sat back, and stared out the window, apparently searching her brain for anything she had overlooked. This was a lady with a world of bad news on her shoulders, and she was not carrying it well, in my view. I asked her, "Are you the case officer?"

"Nope. That would be Special Agent Mark Butterman. A good man, one of our best."

"He one of the guys back at the house?"

"Those were initial response guys. Butterman lives halfway to Baltimore. He's in that big convoy."

"Well, why were you sent?"

"Same reason you were sent."

"Because you're witty, charming, and brilliant?"

She eyed me for a moment and then said, "You can figure out a crime scene, but you can't figure this out?"

"Enlighten me."

"They need two sacrificial assholes to take the fall in the event this thing doesn't work out and the President dies."

CHAPTER THREE

ON THAT VERY INTERESTING AND DISTRESSING NOTE, WE PULLED TO A STOP at the entrance of the Central Intelligence Agency.

Margold said to the driver, "Wait here," then to me, "You can relax now. You're home."

"Yes, home sweet home." Though in fact this was not my home.

A word about how I wound up here. The winter before, my former boss, a two-star named Clapper, the Judge Advocate General, decided it would be in somebody's best interest if Sean Drummond took a long sabbatical. I was a Special Actions Attorney, a cryptic title that suggests little—in fact is meant to suggest nothing—but I was part of a small and select cell of judges, lawyers, and legal assistants that attend to the legal issues of those people and units engaged in Top Secret operations. It is a shadowy world, and it was our job to keep the lights turned off.

I spent eight years prosecuting and defending criminal

34

cases, and I wouldn't confess this around the water cooler or anything, but I love the Army and I actually liked my job. In fact, I was sort of hoping the Army had misplaced my file, or some clever clerk had said, Hey, this Drummond guy, he's good at this, and I know this sounds really novel, weird even, but what if we left him in place: great for the taxpayer, great for Drummond . . . works for everybody, right?

Exactly—the Army never thinks that way.

Actually, I think General Clapper wanted a break from me, which is understandable. I can wear on bosses. So I was loaned to this civilian law firm for what was supposed to be a year, a big white-shoe outfit in D.C. filled with Ivy League types, former politicians, and other stuffed shirts. I think Clapper was hoping the stuffiness would rub off, and we could sit around afterward, sipping sherry and talking opera and fine wines, and we'd really bond. As if that wasn't bad enough, certain members of this firm were hip deep in shenanigans, and the JAG officer I replaced— a she, as it happened, and a dear friend—was murdered. So I was enlisted by her sister, a City of Boston ADA, to help bring down the murderer, who was on a killing spree and terrorizing D.C.

But our investigation led us into the middle of a very sensitive and vital CIA operation, and I was dragged into this same building and had my arm nearly twisted out of its socket. The CIA wanted to protect its operation, I wanted everybody involved in my friend's death to pay. They thought they had a deal, I didn't, and everybody I wanted to pay, paid. Happy ending, right?

Right—there are no happy endings with the federal government. The CIA was impressed with my cleverness, my deviousness, and particularly my ruthlessness. My Army boss was not, notes were compared, and here I am.

In short, Clapper got what he wanted—me out of his hair.

The CIA got what it wanted—an employee on somebody else's dime. And nobody cared to ask what *I* wanted. But there are worse places to be, I guess. At least the work seems fairly interesting.

Also, I got the girl, Janet Morrow, and for her role in this affair, she got to be a big celeb up in Beantown and was elevated to deputy district attorney, so her life and mine have gotten quite busy. She now has to oversee the combined caseloads of some thirty criminal attorneys. I supervise only myself, but that's an exhausting and full-time job. So we see each other on the occasional weekend, and we've both got a foot on the brake, because we know this is no way to build a relationship.

Also, I ended up with a full rack of Brooks Brothers suits and sports coats—courtesy of the law firm—so I look richer and classier than I am, and I blend in really well at the CIA.

Anyway, now a CIA employee awaited at the front entrance, a suave and polite gentleman who even opened the door for Agent Margold, smiled at us both, and said, "Hi. I'm John, from the Director's office."

Margold said, "Hi, John."

And he paused for a moment, until I also said, "Hi, John." How did I get involved with these people?

He nodded. "I hate to rush you, but things are chaotic topside." But John was also curious and he asked me, "How bad was it?"

"How bad was what?"

"The killings. You just left the Belknap murder site, right?"

"Well . . . how are things over here, John?"

"Hectic. Everybody's bouncing off walls, rumors flying. So what'd you see?"

"Dead people."

"Yeah, right. How'd they get it? Shot? . . . Gassed? . . . What?"

I looked John in the eye and said, "Six good people are dead and it is absolutely none of your fucking business how."

Margold smiled.

John scowled. But he swiftly cleared Margold and me through security, and then escorted us through the lobby to the elevator, up three floors, and down a hallway and into an empty conference room.

"Wait here," he informed us. "The bosses are meeting in the Director's office. The other participants should all be here shortly."

He departed without saying who they were, which was annoying and probably intended to be. I have that effect on people. But the Director John referred to was James Peterson—head tuna of my food chain. And you can bet that what was happening upstairs in his airy top-floor suite was a food fight, though the particular genre of this game was dodge the banana. To continue with the bad food metaphors, Belknap's assassination was the hot potato the bosses were flipping from lap to lap, hoping it would stick to somebody else's department, service, agency, bureau, or whatever. For sure, everybody was going to get a piece of the action, but in D.C. it is called getting The Lead. When things go south, as so often happens, The Lead has the center seat at the congressional inquest and everyone else shovels the crap in their in-box. I smiled at Margold. "Five bucks says it's yours."

She shrugged but did not take my bait. After a moment she did say, "Tell you what. Let's make a deal."

"Bad idea."

"Why?"

"Because you have nothing I want."

"Not a trade. A deal."

"Go on."

"I'll watch your ass if you watch mine."

"It takes a deal to watch your ass?"

She stared at me, and I wondered for a moment if I was about to be reported to the PC Bureau for Impure Ribaldry or something. But she said, "Come on, Drummond, we could be good together."

"Good at *what* together?"

She smiled. "Well, you strike me as a guy who knows how it works. You keep me apprised of what's happening here, and I'll fill you in on our side. I'm not looking for glory or credit. I just want to survive this thing."

Could I trust her? Absolutely not. But in these situations you don't say no, you play all sides against the middle. I said, "You've already seen how good I am. How good are you?"

"I'm . . . well, I'm a little out of my depth on this one."

"There is no depth on this one."

She held out her hand. "Jennie, from Columbus, Ohio, thirty-five years old . . . Ohio State undergrad, psych major, master's and Ph.D. in Applied Psychology from Johns Hopkins."

I raised an eyebrow.

"Oh, I'm very smart." She smiled again. "Eleven years on the job . . . three in Detroit working the bricks, three more years on the bricks in the Big Apple . . . the last five I worked in the Behavioral Science Unit at Quantico as an instructor and profiler."

"Is that why you're involved in this case? Profiling?"

"No. Three months ago, I was promoted to Senior Agent in Charge, or SAC, for National Security, at the D.C. Metro Office." She looked to see if I had any further questions. I didn't, and she said, "Now, you. Quickly."

But before I could reply, the door burst open and a line of people began filing in, two women, the rest men. Everybody had their game faces on, like they had all been airbrushed of emotions, self-doubts, or confusion. Facial expressions aside, you knew their sphincters were the size of pinheads.

First to enter were the heavies, Mark Townsend, Agent Margold's esteemed Director, and behind him the aforementioned James Peterson, ringmaster of this gathering of egos.

I took a moment to examine these two. Townsend was tall and slender, stringy-looking actually, with a long narrow face, a gray brush cut, and an odd, wide-eyed, unblinking stare. Peterson was short, chubby, dark-haired, blubbery-lipped, and a bit sanguine in appearance.

Actually they looked a little like Abbot and Costello, though neither man was to be taken lightly, and you knew at that moment neither was in a jovial, lackadaisical, or chummy mood.

Townsend, to his credit, was not a political hack, but had actually scaled the ranks on hard work, merit, and performance. Thus he personified the full corporate ethos of his Bureau: incorruptible, humorless, a stickler for details and punctuality, lacking compassion or forgiveness for sins, oversights, or errors. Understandably, the White House and the Bureau field hands were terrified of Mark Townsend. This had something to do with Agent Margold's bitchiness that morning, I surmised.

Peterson was more relaxed, more personable, more reasonable, and certainly more amiable. But he had spent six years as the incumbent honcho of the Agency, a near record of survival, so his charm was illusory and his footwork was mythical. Mr. Peterson did not evoke terror, but he did promote coyness and a healthy sense of insecurity.

Anyway, I was so distracted by the entrance of Les Grand Pooh-Bahs that I entirely failed to notice the gent who followed three steps behind them, before Margold elbowed me and whispered, "My boss."

So I looked, and it turned out I knew the guy, George Meany.

In fact, George was the former fiancé of my current squeeze, Janet Morrow, and he and I had worked together on the murder of her sister Lisa Morrow. More precisely, George Meany had been conducting the government cover-up, so "worked together" is a term with interesting and generously loose ends. Also, I had gotten in the way of his attempt to rekindle his romance and passion with the lovely Miss Morrow. I had the impression George held some resentment about that.

I wondered if he knew I was now doing his former. By the same token, I wondered if the lobby metal detector had been checked recently.

But maybe I had nothing to worry about. Maybe George had put it all behind him, us, and the instant he laid eyes on me he would rush across the room, throw his long arms around my shoulders, and say, "Sean, Sean, you great guy you. Gee, I really missed you."

In fact, George was the ambitious type, and when we bagged the killer, he had stolen full credit, made a big name for himself, and, as present circumstances indicated, landed a big promotion out of the deal. From that angle, the guy owed me big-time. I just wasn't betting George would see it that way.

Anyway, Townsend and Peterson moved to the front of the room, and the underlings all began taking seats. There was a bit of confusion and jostling, because the session was too rushed for namecards, and, impromptu or not, in the celestial capital of the world's mightiest nation, where you sit defines who you are. I took a chair against the wall and tried to pretend I wasn't there.

George Meany bagged the seat closest to the front, right beneath his boss's nose, close enough that he wouldn't have to strain his neck to get his nose up his boss's butt. By the way, this wasn't musical chairs; the name of this game was avoid the hot seat. Ergo, the Bureau had La Lead and Monsieur Meany had his pudley on the chopping block. I directed a finger at Margold. She tried to ignore me.

Our host, Director Peterson, allowed everyone a moment to get organized, settled, and so forth, before he cleared his throat and said, "We have a lot to get done and very little time. Most of us already know each other, I think. Still, we should begin by identifying ourselves."

I saw Meany's eyes scan the faces around the table, and when he got to me he did not appear surprised or even displeased by my presence. Actually, I had the sense he *expected* me to be there. George correctly pronounced his own name, and announced to all concerned, "As the Assistant Director in Charge, or ADIC, of the D.C. Metro Office, I will head this investigation. I just want to thank all of you in advance for whatever help and assistance you can offer. We have tense and busy days ahead. But we are all professionals. I'm confident we'll work well together."

Everybody nodded at George, acknowledging this masterpiece of bullshit. The federal government hasn't got a clue how to work together—not well, not otherwise. Still, it was good form to state it, and equally good form to recognize the sentiment.

The gent across from George went next; he was named Charles Wardell, he represented the Secret Service, and he looked fidgety and edgy. Mr. Wardell had come to hear how his Service screwed up and to assure everybody it would not happen again. Nobody at that table offered to trade places with him. His team already had minus six on the scoreboard and couldn't even hope to break even.

The lady to Meany's right appeared hesitant, and I thought at first that she was seized with shyness; eventually I understood she was waiting to be introduced. When nobody stepped into the breach, she said, "Nancy Hooper . . . Special Assistant to the President."

Regarding this la-di-da title, there are many special assistants to the President, most of whom are superfluous stamp lickers. But Mrs. Hooper was not superfluous, innocuous, nor, I gathered from the expressions around the table, a welcome presence. She was the President's public relations guru, consigliere, and hatchet person. She informed us, "I'm here, obviously, to provide political guidance and oversight."

Nobody corrected her, but the expressions around the table said, Bullshit. She was here to make sure the buck stopped in this room.

Her hair was dark and curly, and the rest of her was tall, skinny, and lanky, with piercing brown eyes and a hooked nose, which lent her a weird resemblance to a featherless parrot. I recalled seeing her on the tube a few times. She had struck me as pushy and glib, but bright, with a quick mind, a facile tongue, and she went straight for the kneecaps. Her admission to this conference room did not signal happy sailing ahead.

Next went the guy across from her, Mr. Gene Halderman, an Assistant Secretary of Who-Gives-A-Shit from the newly minted Department of Homeland Security. Gene appeared to be in his late twenties, Armani suit, blow-dried hair, and I wondered if he'd wandered into the wrong room. Certainly he was the youngest person at the table, he was from the youngest department, and he didn't get the dress code.

I was really hoping somebody would send Gene out to get coffee. But maybe he was a whiz kid, maybe I underestimated him and we were lucky to have him in our midst.

Anyway, Gene Halderman made it through his introduction without stuttering, which was a hopeful sign. He then looked down the table, directly into George's eyes, and said, very earnestly, "And you can expect the full cooperation of my department in this matter. We are facing a dire national emergency. We will not let you down, George."

Nobody laughed, but a few people coughed into their hands. Mr. Halderman's secret was out—he was an idiot.

Next went the little old lady seated to the left of Mrs. Hooper and directly across from me. She said, "Phyllis Carney, Office of Special Projects here at the CIA." As I mentioned, she was old, white-haired, thin-framed, at least seventy, pushing eighty, and you looked at her and wondered what she was doing here—on active government duty—and not down in Florida, the Elephant's dying ground, parching her skin and whacking little white balls into little empty holes. But you had to know that nobody dodges the federal age ax unless they possess some supernatural talent or skill, or a loving and influential nephew on the Senate Appropriations Committee.

I wasn't sure which applied to Phyllis Carney, nor did I—nor would I ever—have the balls to ask. It happened that Phyllis was my boss, the same lady who had arranged for my assignment to her organization, and the same lady who dispatched me to the den of death this morning. I was still wondering why, and something told me I was about to find out.

Agent Margold went next. Her comparatively low title drew a few unimpressed stares, and then moi. I failed to mention my Army rank, which wasn't a deception but an optional protocol for military officers serving as interagency exchange students. Though, in truth, even in the Army nobody takes a JAG officer's rank seriously, especially JAG officers. Anyway, I was the only person in the room lacking a rarefied title and responsibilities, and I was sort of hoping somebody would send me out to fetch coffee.

But now I knew all the players, and I found myself wondering about the heavy mix of national security officials in this room. I had observed no sign or evidence that what happened at the Belknap residence this morning was more than a domestic murder. Obviously, somebody knew something that hadn't yet been shared or divulged.

But Peterson was moving things along; he fixed us all with a grave stare and said, "At around 6:20 this morning, Terrence and Marybeth Belknap and four Secret Service agents were coldly murdered. Terry and Marybeth were close friends of mine. They were fine people. I'm sure they were friends to several of you in this room."

Several heads bobbed up and down. The Belknaps weren't my friends, or even my acquaintances, but I recalled those toys in the basement and did feel a pulse of sadness. Then I thought of sweet little June Lacy with the bullet through her throat and felt a burst of genuine regret.

He cautioned, "You've all seen or heard about the note. So you know we're facing a serious emergency. In the event you're wondering, the FBI has the lead. Speaking for the country's intelligence agencies, I pledge our full assistance until the killers are found and stopped." Having dispensed with the pieties and pro forma claptrap, he faced Townsend and said, "Mark, I'm sure you have some thoughts to add."

"A few thoughts, yes." Townsend stood, tapped his watch, and informed us, "In forty minutes, Director Peterson and I will brief the President. We will therefore listen to Special Agent Margold's preliminary report, and then leave it in your hands to get this investigation organized, up, and running. The hourglass has been overturned, ladies and gentlemen. The killers promised more murders within the next two days. Whether they have the capability or not, we must take this seriously. In fact, some of you around this table might be targets. You should take a moment to think about that."

He paused very generously to allow us that moment.

No eye contact was made, and nobody gasped, fled from the room, or passed around final bequests, but clearly this was an unwelcome reality—a few people at this table might think twice before putting a down payment on a condo in Florida, or even buying a full gallon of milk. No doubt Peterson and Townsend had rosy bull's-eyes on their prominent backsides. Mrs. Hooper, because of her prestigious portfolio and high public profile, could well be morgue bait. But the rest of us appeared to be free and clear, except as target practice.

In a world of haves and have-nots, being a have-not is not always a bad thing.

Anyway, the mood was set. Six people were dead, murdered, and it was up to Margold to explain how, and then for all of us to figure out why, and by whom.

Townsend pointed at Margold and said, "Proceed."

CHAPTER FOUR

MY NEW PAL JENNIE SPOKE FOR FIFTEEN MINUTES. SHE USED A FELT-TIP marker and wallboard to create a visual of Terrence Belknap's home and security systems, took everybody through the arrival of the government car, through the perp's walk up the pathway, then through the trail of death from the front door to the basement. She was indeed very bright. She spoke articulately, minimized the FBI jargon, knew which details were important, had good recall, was organized and succinct, and she had a pleasant voice. Wisely, she did not speculate, or even elaborate beyond the facts.

She finished up by saying, "We in the FBI classify murders into two broad categories: organized and disorganized. This might sound generic, even oversimplified. It is not. It's a very complicated judgment and we draw many inferences and discoveries from those classifications. Unquestionably, this was an organized killing."

From my observation of the faces of the players around the table as she spoke, nearly everybody had listened attentively, raptly, even apprehensively. Mrs. Hooper fell into none of these categories, tapping her pencil on the table, yawning, totally bored and disconnected. She put down the pencil and asked, "Is there a relevance I'm supposed to draw from that observation?"

"Well . . . it has great pertinence to those involved in the hunt for the murderers," Jennie replied. She paused. "Here's what's noteworthy to you. During my years in the Behavioral Science Unit, I observed over three hundred murder sites and studied countless others. This killing . . . it's one for the books . . . flawless intelligence, preparation, and execution. This operation was planned weeks in advance. We should expect . . . well, whatever they have planned over the next two days, expect the same pattern."

"The leopard doesn't change his spots. Tell us something we don't know."

Jennie nodded. "All right. Here's what's curious . . . even alarming. It is axiomatic in our business that political assassins are disorganized. Their motives may be myriad, but their profiles and patterns are not. They are nearly all social losers, frustrated individuals, of low intelligence and ability. They fixate on the target and the statement they want to make. They take only elementary precautions to avoid evidence and witnesses, to create an escape plan, to avoid detection. In fact, nearly all political assassins *want* to be identified. Irrelevance is the mental hell they're trying to escape."

"All right, what was their motivation?"

"There's no way to know. Not yet."

"At what stage will you know? After the President's dead?"

Set aside the nasty tone, and Mrs. Hooper had posed a pressing and beguiling question. Jennie replied, "If they have a message, they'll choose the time and place to convey it." She added, "Personally, I'm not sure they have a message."

"And what would you call the note they left?"

"I haven't read it. I'm not prepared to analyze it."

"But you know what it said."

"I heard a summary. It didn't sound like a message. It sounded like . . . like an announcement—a taunt."

She was right, it did. I mean, they open the game by capping the President's right-hand man, and then leave a note that reads, *Up Yours, more to follow, then the big guy himself.* These people had big egos *and* brass balls. But gosh, wouldn't we all look bad if they got away with it?

Surveying the faces around the table, Jennie asked, "Other questions?"

After a moment, Townsend asked, "How long were you in the house?"

"Twelve minutes, sir. Two sweeps."

"Twelve minutes?" Those unblinking eyes regarded Jennie for a full ten seconds. The effect was unsettling, almost creepy, like staring at a dead fish and waiting for it to speak. But eventually the lips parted and he said, "That was an impressive analysis for such a short time."

"Thank you, sir. Mr. Drummond here was invaluable. He figured out there was more than one killer, and he pointed out a number of other clues I might have overlooked."

"That's why we have teams," Townsend replied. "We all bring something to the party." He then said, "You have some speculations and leads, I assume."

"I do."

"Proceed."

"We believe the killers had a detailed understanding of the security. They knew how to circumvent the security systems, they may have known a female agent would answer the door, and apparently they knew Terrence and Marybeth Belknap breakfasted together." She paused, then added, "They knew exactly how to deploy themselves in order to kill everybody in that house efficiently and simultaneously."

Mr. Wardell of the Secret Service didn't like the direction she was going and said, "I hope you're not implying that one of our people might be involved."

"I implied nothing."

"You'd better not."

Jennie nodded. Though of course she had implied exactly that, and Mr. Wardell worked up a little steam. "Look . . . before anyone jumps to a bad conclusion, the Secret Service has been officially guarding the President and his people since 1902. Can anyone here name a single instance of betrayal?" He looked at the faces around the table and added, very insistently, "No federal agency matches our vetting and security procedures."

For a moment the room was silent. Then Phyllis Carney commented, "Charles, I don't mean to be contrary, but really . . . we at the CIA take a backseat to nobody when it comes to safeguarding against traitors and betrayals."

It took a moment before we all realized the sound we heard was Charles Wardell's balls rolling around on the floor. He said, "I . . . I didn't mean to imply that our systems are airtight."

Margold nodded appreciatively in Phyllis's direction and said, "Anybody with knowledge about the security at that house needs to be put under a microscope immediately."

Townsend turned to Wardell. "Provide that list to Meany this morning. And for impartiality's sake, the Bureau will handle the interrogations and investigation."

Poor Mr. Wardell did not look happy to carry that word back to his beloved Service. He was realizing, of course, that the crap was about to rain on the American praetorians and there was not a big enough umbrella to hide under. At least he could look his peers in the eye and claim he fought the good fight.

Townsend glanced back at Margold and asked, "Further leads? Speculations?"

"Well, the driver, Larry Elwood, and the location of his car have to be targets of immediate and primary interest. Elwood is a suspect, obviously. However, his car arrived five minutes late and his face is not visible on the videos. This could imply his car was hijacked and the man on our tape is an impostor. Also, the car is a mining site for forensics."

"Good point." Townsend turned to George Meany. "What are we doing about the car?"

"An APB has been issued."

"Not enough. Scramble helicopters and notify every local jurisdiction to conduct a street-by-street search. Put out a description to every tolltaker in the five-state region. Assume they changed plates. Focus on the car model."

George was furiously scribbling all this down on a notepad.

Townsend studied him and said, "By nightfall, every black Lincoln Town Car from Baltimore to Richmond better have been stopped at least a dozen times." To underscore that, he added, "My official car included. If I don't get stopped and searched, I'll have somebody's head."

Jennie suggested, "We should also send agents door-to-door in the Ballantrae Farm neighborhood, asking if anybody saw anything this morning."

I suggested, "In any of the weeks leading up to this morning. The killers no doubt staked out the Belknaps' house well in advance."

Townsend looked at Meany and commented, "It's an exclusive neighborhood. Strangers would be noticed."

Actually, anybody not in a Brooks Brothers suit and a hundred-thousand-dollar luxury car would stick out like a purple banana on that block.

Meany needed to get a point on the board and suggested, "Also, every police district and sheriff's department from Baltimore to Richmond should be told to report any murders, killings, or serious incidents to us immediately. We can't afford a delay in notification."

My personal feelings about George aside, he was smart and competent, and it was a timely suggestion. Washington, D.C., is an annual contender for the murder capital, and a relevant murder could easily get lost or misplaced in the city's embarrassment of riches. Following up on George's thought, I asked, "Exactly what is everybody outside this room allowed to know?"

I thought for a moment I was going to be asked to leave. But Peterson shook his head and said, "Leave it to Drummond to drag the elephant into the room."

George Meany chuckled. Jennie smiled, and everybody else stared at me. I take a bit of getting used to.

But apparently this question fell into Mrs. Hooper's basket, who said, "I haven't decided. For now, Terry Belknap is at home with the flu." She glanced at Peterson and Townsend and instructed them, "You two go brief the President. I'll let you know."

Power is a weird thing. Theoretically and on paper, the Directors of the FBI and CIA are higher in the food chain than some lady who came to town on her boss's coattail and did not need permission from Congress for her corner office in the West Wing. Yet this brief exchange cleared up any messy confusion about who was who in the pecking order. I really missed the Army, where everybody has their rank on their collar. The rank doesn't always tell you who's actually in charge, but it does tell you who can and who can't screw you.

Anyway, they both nodded and departed, and Jennie Margold and I exchanged troubled looks. As soon as the door closed, Jennie addressed Mrs. Hooper and asked, "Are Drummond and I missing something? The White House Chief of Staff's dead. You can't hide that."

It was an interesting question, and apparently a provocative one, because for a moment it just hung in the air. Then Phyllis, my boss, said, "It's . . . well, it's a little more complicated than that, I'm afraid. We probably should have seen this coming."

"Why?"

"Well . . . the bounty." She studied a spot on the wall for a moment. "Somebody has offered a reward of one hundred million dollars to whoever murders the President of the United States."

Shit.

CHAPTER FIVE

On that bizarre note, George Meany looked down the table and said, "I have calls to make. Take fifteen minutes to freshen up, then we'll decide what comes next."

The room swiftly emptied, except for Phyllis and me. Phyllis pretended to ignore me while everybody filed out, then I was hard to ignore. She said, "It sounds like you did a splendid job. Jennie Margold was very complimentary."

"Agent Margold was preoccupied with the ton of shit on her shoulders. I had nothing better to do."

"Yes, I'm sure. But I'm glad you gained her trust and confidence."

"Really? Why?"

Phyllis approached this question with the delicacy it deserved. "Surely it is no secret that the FBI and our Agency occasionally fail to communicate in a . . . well, a timely and effective manner."

"I had no idea."

She forced a smile. "Must I actually explain this to you?"

"Yes."

"All right. In addition to assisting the investigation, I expect you to be a conduit of information. Pay attention to what the FBI is learning and relay that back to me." She added, "Of course you can feel free to selectively pass on any information from our shop that might help the Bureau."

"Define 'selectively.' "

"Use your judgment."

"Bad idea. Spell it out for me."

"All right. We're all on the same team, and we're interested in the same goal. I don't really care who gets credit for success. I do care greatly about who is blamed for failure. Understood?"

I nodded.

"Good. Any other questions?"

I had been waiting for this moment. "Why me?"

"Why not you?" After a moment she mentioned, "I read your classified Army file before I decided to bring you over here. You've had an interesting and varied career, Sean. Five years with the Special Forces, hunting and killing terrorists. Eight as a criminal lawyer, handling the most sensitive kinds of cases. My people are analysts or field operators . . . they have no investigative or killing experience." She looked me in the eye and asked, "So again, why not you?"

Well, I was new to the job, I wasn't actually a CIA employee, I didn't have a clue how the Agency was supposed to help, how it operated internally, not to mention a federal statute called Posse Comitatus, which prohibits military officers from engaging in domestic law enforcement activities. Also I hadn't voted for, nor did I even particularly *like* this President. But deductive logic aside, I could think of only one impelling reason it should be me—I was the perfect scapegoat.

But perhaps I was being overly cynical. Skepticism's healthy, but is only a hop, skip, and jump from the abyss of paranoia, which is not. Really, it boiled down to trust, and the question was: Could I take this lady at face value?

I recalled what I knew about Miss Phyllis Carney, whose job title, incidentally, was Special Assistant to the Director. There was only one special assistant in these parts, and lumping two spoonfuls of sugar into the boss's coffee wasn't the duty description.

I knew she had fifty-three years in the Agency and had climbed, scratched, and clawed her way from a secretarial stool to her current exalted perch. This made for an interesting and exotic résumé, I'm sure, not to mention a skillset including such archaic talents as stenography and garroting. Given the span of her service, she had played in some rough games and tilted against the big leaguers, or as the boys in the ranks say, she'd seen her share of the shit. She was either quite good at what she did or monumentally expert at dodging blame. Probably both.

Regarding her personal life and habits, I was aware she had once been married and her husband had either died or they were divorced. So there was no family left in the picture, no distractions from her work, and no complicating loyalties. Actually she was quite charming, bright, and clever, and her speech, manner, and dress were old-fashioned in a way that was disarming and faintly seductive. In her presence, in fact, you actually had to remind yourself that nobody survives half a century in her line of work who can't yank the lever on the scaffold and walk away whistling.

I recalled the words she had used to welcome me to this organization: "We only handle high stakes in this shop, Sean. We're usually the last resort and only occasionally the first resort. The problems that come to us are either too hard or too sensitive for the organization at large to swallow. Although not physically dangerous, our work can be professionally hazardous." I had replied, "Piscem natare doces," and she had stared at me a moment before she snapped, "I'm not teaching a fish to swim. I'm warning a cocky fool to be careful." She smiled pleasantly and added, "Latin minor, Smith College, class of '48."

Phyllis was not universally known, though I had come to discover that she was known individually by nearly everybody in the Agency, an important and worthy distinction. Like most big organizations, the CIA is a collection of duchies and princedoms run by big egos, a briar patch of conflicting agendas and reciprocal paranoias, with high walls you can't see but that you can definitely stub your toe on. Mentioning you work for Phyllis Carney was like waving an E-ZPass. Now she asked me, "Is there a compelling personal reason that would preclude you from handling this?"

"Several. George Meany—you might recall that he and I had a few issues."

"Yes, I recall that . . . Watch your back around George."

"Two—I'm not qualified for this job."

"Nobody is *qualified* for this job. I can't recall an instance where someone placed a bounty on our President's head. Can you?"

"All right . . . I don't trust you."

After a moment, she said, "I see." After another moment, she said, "I have to place a call to the office to inform everybody to lock up their sensitive materials and take three days off. And you look like you need a cup of coffee."

Actually, I needed a new job. But I left and found Jennie in the snack bar, slathering jam onto something that looked like a breadish acorn when I approached her from behind and asked, "What's that?"

She did not turn around. "A scone. It's an English breakfast treat."

"No kidding. Like an English doughnut?"

"Spare me the bad doughnut jokes, please." After a moment, she said, "You're really *not* from the Agency, are you?"

"Why?"

"Well, you wear a suit that costs too much, you're bright and cocky, so you're three-quarters of the way there. But you're not arrogant . . . or sneaky. I don't think you're even sly."

I studied the back of her head. "How long have you worked for George Meany?"

"A few months."

"What happened to we'll watch each other's asses?"

"Oh . . . *that* . . ." She began squeezing a tea bag into a cup. "Did you take the deal? I don't recall hearing it."

"All right—it's a deal."

She had left her blue jacket on the chair in the conference room and I could now observe that hers was indeed an ass worth watching. Also she had a wasplike waist, slender hips, and if I had to guess, a 38D cup, or maybe DD, although what's in a letter? Of course, I was already seriously involved with a significant other. Sort of. But from a purely professional standpoint, I was reassured to observe that Agent Margold was not only brainy, she was in tip-top shape, she could probably chase down your average badass, and in an emergency I wouldn't herniate doing the fireman's carry. Also she smelled good, sort of lemony, so she probably practiced good hygiene. Clean bodies, clean minds. But maybe not.

Anyway, she stirred her cup for a few seconds, avoiding conversation. Eventually she said, "Actually . . . George requested you this morning."

"Did he?"

"He said you knew your way around."

"Is that all he said?"

"He also mentioned he had worked a case with you before. He said you showed good instincts. That was it."

Was that *it*, or was George setting up Act Two so he could slip me the weenie? If so, where and how did Ms. Margold fit into that scheme? I grabbed a foam cup and pushed a lever that gushed coffee out of a big vat. I asked, "Did you know about the bounty?"

"Nope. It's interesting, though."

"You mean it's interesting if it's not on you."

"That's exactly what I meant." After a moment she asked, "Do you think the money's behind it?"

"I think it's one possibility. We slap bounties on the heads of Aideed, bin Laden, and Saddam, and now somebody decides to turn the tables. Poetic retribution. Right?"

We diddled with our coffee and tea.

"It would be really remarkable," she said.

"It would be the ultimate screw-you. They announce that they intend to whack our President and they do it."

She finally said, "We have to be careful here. Lesson one at my classes at Quantico, I always stressed the dangers of reverse causality."

"Good point. But you don't have to worry about that with me."

"No?"

"I keep protection in my wallet."

She rolled her eyes. "I'm referring to the trap of circuitous logic. Bad things always come in threes . . . A woman has triplets, therefore the babies are bad."

"Sounds reasonable."

I think she was regretting she'd called me bright. But as if his ears were burning, George Meany suddenly materialized beside us and grabbed a foam cup. With a sideways glance at me, he mentioned, too nonchalantly, "Well, Drummond, I see we'll be working together again."

"Small world."

"Isn't it?"

"Too small."

He ignored that and asked, "So what do you think?"

"About you?"

"About this."

I looked him in the eye and said, "I think, George, that you've got about forty-eight hours to get to the bottom of this or your career's toast. You'll go down as the Agent in Charge who failed to prevent a presidential assassination. What do *you* think?"

He did not answer that loaded question; instead he changed the subject and asked, "Incidentally, how's Janet? I hear you two have become an item."

"Great. She turned thirty last week. What a party we had. She got into her birthday suit, and I got into my birthday suit, and . . ." I looked at George and said, "Is this . . . well, an insensitive topic for you?"

Apparently so, because he said, "Fuck off," and walked away.

Jennie stared at his back. "What was that about?"

"Nothing." Though in fact it was about a great deal. Prior to his reassignment to D.C., Meany was an agent in Boston, where he and the lovely Miss Morrow had worked together on several cases. Love and lust bloomed, they moved in together, got engaged, and then Georgie Boy screwed her to break a big case

59

that got him glory, a promotion, and a career shift to D.C. As if that weren't enough—both literally and figuratively—the guy tried to screw Janet again after her sister was murdered. But Janet was far too nice a person to tell George what an asshole he was.

I'm not a nice person. Besides, somebody had to remind this putz that there is a price when you screw friends and lovers. Also, I was sure Georgie had something up his sleeve regarding yours truly, and I wanted to get in the first blow. Actually, George was slick and resourceful, and I might not get in a second shot. I said to Jennie, "We'd better get back."

"Yeah, we better."

While we were walking down the hallway she advised me, "Don't antagonize George. A lot's riding on his shoulders. He doesn't need distractions."

"Probably not."

"This case is bigger than whatever there is between you two."

"You're . . . well, thank you for pointing that out."

"You have to rise above personal issues. Think of the country. Get this under control."

"Exactly what I was thinking."

"Also George Meany's a small-minded, vindictive prick. He'll find a way to really hurt you."

Goodness.

So we reentered the conference room. The players were all back in their seats, but apparently there'd been a little reshuffling, and Mrs. Hooper was now directly across from Mr. Meany, and Messrs. Halderman and Wardell now sat closest to Jennie and me. If poor Gene Halderman made another idiotic remark, he'd be sitting in the parking lot. I made a point to sit next to the exit.

Mrs. Hooper kicked things off, saying, "Let me size up this

problem for you. Seven months out from the general election, can you imagine a worse time to have this crisis? Do you all understand what I'm saying?"

I think we were all wondering when Mrs. Hooper thought there *was* a good time, but we collectively nodded and tried our best to appear attentive and sensitive to her problem. We were civil servants getting our marching orders from our political masters. It's always interesting and often informative to hear what the politicos are thinking.

She continued, "The President's schedule over the next four days includes a campaign sweep through the South. These are key battleground states. This is a neck-and-neck campaign. The election will turn on who wins there, and we cannot cancel or even reshuffle these appearances." She added, as though the guy were an afterthought, "The Vice President has scheduled appearances, some of which we can cancel, some of which we cannot."

I said, "Did it occur to you that the assassins might know the President's schedule? In fact," I added, "maybe they started the killing this morning because they knew the President would be vulnerable for the next two days."

Mrs. Hooper stared at me a moment, then replied, "I don't believe that's an issue. Some events are publicized, but the details and security arrangements are strictly need-to-know."

I reminded her, "So was the security plan for Belknap's house."

She did not appear to welcome or embrace this insight, but Wardell picked up on it and said, "The advice of the Secret Service is to bury the Vice President in cold storage till this thing blows over. Also, cancel *all* public appearances for the President over the next few days, or until this thing becomes clearer."

She replied coldly, "I told you that's not in the cards."

"That's an official recommendation, incidentally."

"You're on record."

"I'll follow up with a paper copy of our recommendation after the meeting."

"I'm sure you will."

Having gotten the pissy ass-covering out of the way, Wardell explained for all our benefits, "We can and will beef up the security details, but no way can we provide double coverage of everybody in the administration."

Mrs. Hooper thought about that grim warning a moment. "After this meeting's over, I'll give you the names of the people we want double-covered. Offhand, the President and Vice President, obviously, and certainly the Secretary of Defense."

It went without saying that Mrs. Hooper would also make the final scrub. But nobody was impolitic enough to mention that, including me.

Wardell informed her, "Double coverage of the President and Vice President was initiated at 0730 this morning. We don't do the SecDef, he has a CID detail. But I'll be sure to pass the word."

Meany chose this moment to ask a good and timely question. He said, "If you double the coverage, Chuck, what are the odds?"

"That depends. Our defenses and techniques are set up primarily to deter, hinder, and prevent the very type of single assassin Agent Margold described—nuts, weirdos, and ego-deprived idiots. There's a strong historical basis . . . you know, Lincoln, Garfield, JFK, the attempts on Ford and Reagan . . . All those assassins were lone nutcases. So our agents study profiles of these people and we train them to react to the modus operandi of that kind of individual."

He looked around for a moment to be sure we all understood this significant point. "We're dealing here with a highly trained team. Maybe two people . . . maybe a dozen. We can and will vary the President's movement patterns and protection pro-files . . . But if he's out in the open, if he's pressing flesh and smooching babies—"

"If it's a manpower issue," Meany interrupted, "we'll supple-ment your people with our agents."

"It is a manpower issue. But our agents operate as teams. Throw untrained people in the mix and it would cause prob-lems." He looked at George and emphasized, "The best thing you can do is find and eliminate the threat before it gets to that point."

Mr. Wardell was nobody's fool—the ball had just been shoved into Meany's court.

But to further amplify that point, Wardell added, "We'll han-dle the defense, you handle the offense. But let's be perfectly clear—this game won't be won on defense."

Mr. Wardell had now covered his beloved Service's ass up, down, and sideways, and three Sundays from Monday.

I waited for Meany to boot the ball into someone else's court, but he stared at the wall, perhaps contemplating the ef-fervescent career that once was his. Phyllis broke the somewhat strained silence and asked, "Back to Drummond's query, Mrs. Hooper. How *would* you like this handled publicity-wise?"

Instead of responding, Mrs. Hooper turned to Mr. Meany and asked, "How sure are you that this is about the bounty?"

"We're not sure of anything. The motive is unknown at this time. Even the note could be a ruse."

"For *what*?"

"Belknap's murder could have been about Belknap, period. He was the highly public CEO of a major Wall Street firm before he joined the administration, and he made enemies by the bushel. The Secret Service has a thick file of death threats against him. Right, Chuck?"

BRIAN HAIG

"It's true," Wardell replied. "The Hawk was not a popular man."

George hypothesized, "The note could have been left to throw us off track." He studied the tabletop a moment before he added, "We have to keep an open mind."

Mrs. Hooper thought she saw a straw here and immediately reached for it. "All right. Tell me about the other possibilities."

It suddenly struck me that George had been fishing for just this opportunity. He smiled at her and replied, "I'll tell you what I think. If they were serious about killing the President, there wouldn't be a warning."

This glimmer of hope brought Mr. Wardell forward in his seat. "Go on."

George said, "They'd be stupid to alert us. Their job becomes more difficult . . . more risky."

Mrs. Hooper asked, "Then what's the point?"

"The point?" Clearly George was enjoying his moment, showing his brilliance, dispersing profundities to the washed and unwashed. He looked at all our faces, then back at Mrs. Hooper. He said, "Footballers call it the trap play. We distract ourselves trying to protect the President, and they use the diversion to escape."

I had already considered George's theory, and already discarded it. Threatening the President's life was anything but a distraction; it was a magnet for the largest dragnet in history. But if George wanted to sound stupid, I wasn't going to contradict him.

Still, this was getting a little too open-ended for everybody's comfort level, so Jennie chose this moment to explain, "My boss may be right. Or he may be wrong. Here's what we *do* know— or at least can *reasonably* postulate at this stage. They're American. At least, from the idiomatic expressions, whoever wrote the note is American. And they have professional-level abilities and equipment."

"Great," said Mrs. Hooper. "I put out to the American people that some unknown group of professional assassins is hunting our President. Just great. Do any of you see where I have a problem with that? What do you think the public reaction's going to be?"

Indeed, we all saw her problem, and we all worked up appropriately pained expressions that were, of course, completely phony. That was her problem, and like all professional bureaucrats, we intended to keep our noses out of her in-box, and were sorely wishing she'd keep her nose out of ours.

Our problem was getting a handle on this thing when clearly the bad guys had a head start, momentum, and presumably a plan. I had the feeling Jennie was right; the killers knew exactly *what* they were going to do and *how*. The scheme would unfold at their pace and tempo. Unless they made a stupid mistake or miscalculation, if the President stayed out in the public, there was a good chance we'd still be playing catch-up when the big caisson rolled down Pennsylvania Avenue.

Anyway, the meeting dragged on, partly because clueless people tend to be talkative, and partly because George was enjoying the sound of his own voice. The decision was made to issue a public statement saying the White House Chief of Staff and his wife had been murdered and the circumstances and cause were under investigation, which at first blush appeared to be an attempted burglary gone askew. I must've missed something in this discussion, because it struck me that the only people who wouldn't be misled by this silliness were the killers.

Further, it was decided the task force would operate out of Ferguson Home Security Electronics, because it was centrally located and a secure facility; because it contained all the necessary communications and intelligence systems; and because nobody suggested a better place. Actually, Mr. Halderman helpfully volunteered the use of the newly constructed Homeland Security Information Analysis and Infrastructure Protection Office, and that drew a few chuckles. Nobody could even remember all the adjectives. It sucks being the new guy.

But finally Meany appeared to recognize that we were wasting precious time, while the opposition was not. He informed us, "Agent Margold's preliminary observations suggest a two-pronged approach. This was an inside job, so we will turn over every stone to find that leak. And we will look on the outside to find our perpetrators."

Right. This was sound and logical reasoning. Everybody nodded to acknowledge George's wisdom.

He continued, "I suggest three major efforts." He nodded in the direction of Charles and said, "Agent Wardell will be responsible for the cocoon of security around the administration." He pointed at Jennie and announced, "Agent Margold will direct the team investigating the murders." He smiled at me and said, "Drummond will head the team looking for any international connections . . . specifically, who put the bounty on our President's head, and whether there are international ties."

I said, "I have a question."

He studied my face, suspecting I was going to say something nasty.

Rather than disappoint George, I asked, "What are *you* going to do?"

"Glad you asked, Drummond. I'll oversee the overall operation. It's my philosophy to power down—to put direct responsibility on my subordinates. It encourages initiative . . . and accountability."

This sounded like an excerpt from some New Age management text. But nobody missed the subtext here. In Washington jargon and practice, accountability means shit flows downhill. George was going to be sure everybody had a little skin in the game, and if the ship hit an iceberg, the captain of this good ship wasn't going to be waving bon voyage from the forebridge to the crew in the life rafts. There would be no life rafts. If George had his way, there would be no survivors.

I glanced at Jennie. She rolled her eyes.

CHAPTER SIX

THE SIGN ON THE FRONT DOOR OF FERGUSON HOME SECURITY ELEC-tronics declared, "Closed for inventory and product liquidation."

Yet the parking lot was already filled with official-looking cars and unmarked vans, and guys and gals wearing fretful expressions and blue and gray suits were parading in and out of the entrance.

It struck me that the locals might find all this activity a little distracting, uncharacteristic perhaps, even mysterious. To belabor my aforementioned point, had they pursued my quirky yet ingenious suggestion to make this a VD clinic, the sign could read, "Incurable airborne gonorrhea discovered—enter at invitation only." For sure this would explain the odd visitors with stricken faces, and nobody was going to be sniffing through the garbage or absently wandering into the building.

I was happy to see Lila, our receptionist, seated at her desk, disguised as usual as a sexy front-desk clerk. She looked up as I entered, but I detected no hint of recognition on her face. To my surprise, she said, "All right, pal . . . stop right there."

"What?"

"Hands where I can see them. Remove your ID slowly. I have a gun under this desk—it's pointed at your balls."

"But, miss, I'm a CIA bureaucrat. I have no balls."

She laughed.

I leaned across her desk and in all seriousness said, "If you haven't received the warning, there *is* a guy running around town impersonating an FBI agent. He's got real-looking creds, he's armed, and he's dangerous."

"I hadn't heard."

"He's using the alias George Meany, and if he shows up here and flashes his creds, you *should* blow his balls off."

She laughed again and informed me, "Special Agent Meany arrived nearly an hour ago."

"And did you at least kneecap him?"

"Please. He was very nice and charming. Also cute. Is he married?"

"No. But you're married."

"Oh . . ."

She laughed again. Women are such bad judges of men.

But appearances aside, Lila was a smart and perceptive lady. Which was a prerequisite for her job, since she belonged to the Agency's security service, and probably knew ten ways to kill me with her eyelashes. She signed me in, commenting, "I hear you had a fun morning."

"I had an *interesting* morning."

"It's sure getting weird around here."

"It was weird here before this morning."

She shrugged and said, "Phyllis is in her office with Mort. She wants you to join her right away."

So I left Lila, and by the door that led into the converted rear warehouse I noted that some tidy and efficient soul had already installed a bulletin board showing the temporary residents where to set up, and where to sit, who'd be on whose team, who'd have what phone numbers, and, more helpfully, the phone numbers for some nearby pizza and Chinese delivery joints. I hate to sound incorrigibly sexist, but when women have the reins, the little things do get taken care of.

Also I observed a bunch of temporary partitions that appeared to have been hastily erected to divide the equally temporary occupants into roughly three groups: Agency employees, Feds, and Homeland Security bureaucrats.

I should mention that in the federal culture, walls are the foundations upon which you build trust, teamwork, and fluid communications. Just kidding.

I walked through the maze of cubicles and walls without seeing anybody I knew, found Phyllis's crib at the rear of the building, and entered. She nodded at the heavyset man seated comfortably in a chair in front of her desk, whose face I only vaguely recognized. She said, "I believe you two know each other."

Not really, though I did recall being briefly introduced to Mort Silverman around my second day on the job. He was short, bald, and broad of girth—fat, actually, a gent of Jewish descent with an elegant Bronx patois who handled Middle Eastern affairs for the team. I was not really sure what this meant, and the Office of Special Projects does not really encourage its employees to give a shit. Unlike me, Mort was a regular CIA employee, and his official title was project officer, as was mine, so we were roughly equal in rank.

Anyway, the three steaming cups of coffee on the desk suggested that Phyllis had already been notified by Lila that I was in the building, and further indicated that Phyllis was laying it on thick.

She apparently read my mind, because she offered me a seat with an ingratiating smile and then ordered Mort, "Tell him what we know."

Mort handed me a slim folder stamped "TOP SECRET—Sensitive Sources," followed by the usual string of initials indicating sources and collection methods and the compartments you'd better belong to if you open the file. I wasn't in any of the right clubs, but with the White House Chief of Staff decomposing on a morgue slab, protocols were falling by the wayside, fast. Mort asked me, "You heard about the bucks on the President, right?"

"Where do I sign up?"

"Hey, pal, if I knew, why would I be sittin' here?"

Ha-ha. Phyllis stared at us, I'm sure thinking that men have a really neat sense of humor.

Mort informed me, "Inside the folder's what we know. Read it when you get time. It's like a mystery novel with the back half missing. Thing is, we learned about it only a few weeks ago."

Agency people are great folder builders, and I flipped it open and scanned the cover page, an abbreviated guide to all that followed. Essentially, we had first learned of the bounty not through any of the sophisticated collection means listed on the cover, but an announcement on Al Jazeera, the Arabic-language news channel. Details to follow.

I looked at Mort. "This is for real?"

"Real as it gets."

Phyllis chose this moment to say, "It does look implausible, doesn't it? It was aired three or four times before the night shift at the counterterrorism cell noticed. Of course, we got them to remove it from the broadcast."

Mort said, "Yeah, but it was prime time over there and Al

Jazeera's on satellite—Middle Easterners, Americans of Arab descent, Indonesians, Pakistanis . . . its audience is huge. Plus Arabs are big-time bullshitters, and these days they all got a cell phone, so word spreads fast around the souks and tea rooms."

Naturally, I asked, "And how did Al Jazeera learn about it?"

"Back it up a bit," Mort replied. "There was a Web site posting the offer and reward."

"A Web site?"

"Yeah. Called www.killtheprez.com."

"This is a joke, right?"

"That's what we thought. At first. After this morning, I might think differently." He handed me a color page. "What do you think of this?"

I took a moment to study it, apparently a reproduction of the Web page under discussion. The background was pink, the print a crazy mixture of fonts, colors, and writing styles, reminiscent of one of those old-style circus posters, with floating balloons and clownish little figures dancing around the page. It certainly looked like a joke, or like somebody so contemptuous of this President that even an offer to assassinate him deserved to be treated facetiously.

I next read the offer, splashed in bold blue letters across the top: "KILL THE AMERICAN PRESIDENT AND EARN $100,000,000 UNTRACEABLE AMERICAN GREENBACKS."

Beneath the heading was the inevitable small print, laying out the "contest" rules and requirements, of which there were three: The claimant had to communicate his plan in advance; a unique "killing signature" was required for authorship verification; and to receive the grand prize the claimant had to remain anonymous and above suspicion.

I looked up at Mort. "How do you communicate your intentions in advance?"

He bent forward and pointed at a line near the bottom. The line read, "payoff@intercon.com." Mort said, "That address."

"And with that address can't you find who's behind this?"

"We tried. That address is linked to an anonymous e-mailer, and probably that one links to a daisy chain of five or ten more anonymous e-mailers."

Mort somehow sensed I didn't have a clue, and talked me through it. "It's not all that sophisticated. The e-mail is automatically forwarded to an anonymous e-mailer—sort of like a blank mailbox—where it happens again, and again. Like jumping through ten black holes." He directed my attention to the bottom of the page where seven or eight languages were listed—Russian, Spanish, Arabic, even Yiddish. Mort said, "Click your cursor on one of those, and it directed you to the same Web page, only it was in that language."

"We're talking past tense?"

Phyllis said, "The Web site was closed two days after the Al Jazeera broadcast."

Mort commented, "Al Jazeera's news manager told us they were tipped off by a phone call. Wouldn't say who. Can you believe that asshole quoted me the First Amendment?" He looked annoyed.

I asked, "Who shut down the site?"

"The owner."

"Do we know why?"

Phyllis looked at Mort and said, "The prevailing theory at the time was that he pulled the plug before the joke caught up with him."

"What's the current feeling?"

Phyllis regarded the Web page. "It's possible he got one or two viable offers. Probably there was an exchange of e-mails, the prospective killers forwarding their plan and the recipient somehow verifying he had the money. It's also reasonable to assume that some kind of arrangement to get the reward was worked out. Of course, we have no idea what."

"I see."

Phyllis leaned toward me. "But I think we'd all agree that one hundred million is a large . . . well, an almost incredible figure." She added, "We limited the knowledge as much as possible. The Secret Service was informed, of course, and the White House."

Mort added, "And don't assume it's Arab money. Could be a pissed-off Saudi prince, Colombian or Mexican drug lords, a foreign government, some U.S. billionaire who finds this President politically disagreeable . . ." He frowned and let the list of disturbing possibilities drift off.

Phyllis informed me, "Certainly you can appreciate why we've tried to keep this under a tight lid. This bounty . . . well, it's an almost insurmountable temptation, isn't it? That kind of money can fuel a lot of wicked ambitions."

True enough. I don't believe *everybody* has a price, but a hundred million bucks can leave stretch marks on a lot of consciences. I mean, there are guys in New York who, for a few thousand Georges, will pump ten slugs into whoever you name. For a hundred million they'll wipe out Manhattan, with Queens thrown in for a bonus. But back to the discussion, I said, "It smells like a hoax."

She stared at me a moment then replied, "Drummond, you might find this hard to believe, but you are not the only bright person in this organization. Consider this—what matters is not what you or we believe but what others believe."

She had a point. I suggested, "This might be a good time to ask other international intelligence agencies what they know about this."

"Catch up. An hour ago, a message went to all our station

chiefs to visit their counterparts and ask around. Given time differences, this kind of sweep normally takes about twelve hours to complete."

"And I'll be informed, right?"

"Trust me."

No comment.

There was a knock at the door, and it opened. Jennie stood in the doorway and asked, "Can I steal Sean for a moment?"

Nobody seemed to mind, so I stepped out and followed her through the maze of partitions to a side room allocated as her temporary office.

Directly outside her office and behind a gray metal desk sat an elderly woman, heavyset, with frizzy brown hair surrounding a face that was round and cherubic, like a jolly, chubby angel. We paused momentarily for Jennie to introduce me to Elizabeth, her executive assistant.

Elizabeth looked a little frazzled and clearly was not enjoying her new and uncertain environment. We exchanged pleasantries, then she asked me, "Where do I get paper and supplies in this madhouse?"

"Got me."

"How do I get my phone connected?"

"Plug it into the wall?"

Elizabeth pointed at the wall. "There is no phone socket out here."

"Good point."

"So . . . ?"

I shrugged.

Elizabeth said, "You work here, don't you?"

Jennie informed her, "He's my partner for this case. But he's a typical male, Elizabeth."

For some reason Elizabeth found this very funny. Personally,

I considered this remark both rude and sexist, rooted as it was in an old, false, and demeaning stereotype. I suggested to Elizabeth, "See Lila out front. She knows everything."

As we entered Jennie's office, she looked at me and said, "Okay, we've had a couple of breaks."

"Go on."

"We found the limo."

"And did we find Larry?"

"Larry, too. The limo was discovered in the woods, maybe three miles outside Culpeper, Virginia. Larry Elwood was in the front seat."

"Should I be an optimist?"

"It wouldn't look right on you."

"Right."

"Unfortunately, the car and Larry were incinerated."

Unfortunate for us, but even more unfortunate for Larry, I thought. Yet for some reason I was not surprised by this revelation. "Okay, details."

"The car was spotted by a helicopter from the Culpeper Sheriff's Department. The pilot saw the smoke, called it in, and the local fire department promptly responded. Everything was already toast."

"Fast fire."

"Very fast. The car, the car's interior, and Elwood were soaked with gasoline. But Elwood was beyond caring, having already been shot in the head several times. Incendiary grenades were used for ignition, at least five, some taped to the underside, along the gas tank, all rigged to explode simultaneously. This wasn't amateur work."

"Eliminating all forensic traces and evidence, right?"

"And our key suspect."

"So Larry's probably not an accomplice."

"Don't be hasty. Could be you're right, and he and the car were kidnapped. That would assume the killers knew the car type and plate numbers, as well as Larry's route and morning routine. Leading back to our insider theory. Or could be Larry was part of the scheme, they recognized he was an obvious lead and decided to eliminate him before he compromised them. In that case, they're really brutal bastards."

I thought the morning murders already established that.

"Another thing," she continued. "You recall that Peterson ordered Chuck Wardell to give us the names of everybody involved in the Hawk's security detail?"

"Okay."

"They maintain three shifts for the Hawk's residence. The shift we found this morning—the dead shift—that's the B shift. The C shift was supposed to come on duty at 1300 hours. They all showed."

"And the A shift?"

"D shift. There's no A shift—don't ask." So I didn't and she continued, "We've accounted for everybody but one agent. Guy named Jason Barnes. Since he went off duty yesterday at 1300 hours, nobody's heard from him."

"Maybe he left town."

"Maybe. His supervisor's next door. I thought you might want to be there."

"Good. Let's talk to him."

We proceeded to the office next door, where Agent Mark Kinney was seated at a table swilling a diet Pepsi. He was roughly my age, bony-faced, dark-haired, retreating hairline, fit, and from all outward appearances, an everyday Joe, which I'm sure fit nicely with his job description.

As we entered the room he looked up with an expression I

judged to be slightly pissed off and distrustful. I know that look. I get it a lot.

Jennie handled the introductions as we fell into chairs directly across from Agent Kinney. We all shook hands. Jennie smiled and in a friendly tone advised him not to regard this session as a threatening or antagonistic interrogation. She suggested he should look upon this as simply an amiable and innocent background chat between three federal officers.

Kinney polished off his Pepsi without a word.

They then chitchatted about topics small and large—family, Washington, and why Dallas always kicks the crap out of the Redskins. So we learned that Agent Kinney had a wife and 2.3 kids, twelve years in the Secret Service, he couldn't wait to get out of house duty and back on the travel squad, and other useless trivia. This is called establishing rapport and loosening up the subject. I call it wasting time.

There are two broad schools of thought regarding interrogation methods. The one in vogue down in Quantico these days is called, I think, the Lawrence Welk technique. Klieg lights, rubber truncheons, and demeaning or harsh questions are passé. Play soft music, avoid frightening gestures, establish a collegial relationship, and be sure to treat the target with the same courtesy and respect with which you'd like to be treated. If I understand this method correctly, the subject eventually thinks he's in a dentist's chair and opens wide.

A lot of experts and supposed studies advocate this technique. In my view, if you want to save time and get the truth, a friendly knee in the nuts is always a useful way to start off. Metaphorically, of course. Except sometimes.

Anyway, the run-up to this soft sell takes a while, but this guy made his living guarding windbags, and he showed the patience of Job until Jennie, in a tone meticulously modulated to be nonthreatening and nonpatronizing, mentioned, "Listen, we've managed to contact everybody in your team except"—she glanced at her notepad—"except Agent Jason Barnes."

"Jason? Well, that's odd."

"Yes. Isn't it?"

"Yeah . . . it really is. You've tried his home number?"

"A team was even dispatched to his home . . . in Springfield, right?" Kinney nodded, and Jennie informed him, "He's not there. Nor is his car."

"I've got his cell number and pager number in my pocket. Maybe if—"

"Ditto. We're getting his electronic answering service."

"Well . . . hmmm. That doesn't make sense."

"Maybe there's a simple explanation. Could he have left town?"

"Jason wouldn't . . . I mean, it's SOP . . . He'd have to inform me, and it wouldn't be like—"

"But he's single, isn't he?"

"Yes . . . but—"

"So it's springtime. Maybe he's shacked up with somebody." He chuckled. "Not a chance."

"Why? He's a normal, healthy heterosexual, isn't he?"

"Listen, Jason Barnes is so clumsy with the ladies, it's laughable. Also he's a very devout Christian. I'd bet my month's pay he's not shacked up."

Wisely, Jennie changed tacks, and put the onus on Kinney. She smiled pleasantly and said, "Uh . . . well, look, I'm shooting in the dark here. Help me get to know Jason."

"Get to— Wait a minute. Is he suspected of something?"

Clearly, Agent Kinney knew this wasn't a friendly session, and clearly he knew Jason Barnes was possibly a big problem for him. He was Barnes's boss, and if his trusted subordinate had helped whack the man and wife they were guarding, in addition to four of his comrades-in-arms, Agent Kinney was going to have an ugly notation on his next evaluation.

Also I thought Kinney was probably a decent guy and even a good leader. Displaying loyalty down is always an admirable trait in a boss—except now.

So I lied. "We need to ask everybody if they saw anything suspicious over the past few days. Maybe if we knew a little about Barnes it would help us track him down."

Kinney looked at Jennie, then at me. He said, "Check his file."

"It's on the way over," Jennie replied. "But we're in a bit of a hurry here. Give us a shortcut."

I thought, for a brief moment, that Kinney was going to mumble into his cuff link, "Agent in peril . . . send help."

Instead he said, "All right. For starters, he's incredibly bright. Grew up in Richmond. Father's a judge . . . I think, a federal judge. Jason's a VMI grad, and he spent three years as a Marine infantry lieutenant. Excellent record as a Marine. Excellent record as an agent. Personally and professionally, the guy's clean as a whistle."

In fact, Mr. Kinney's brief biography exposed more about Jason Barnes than he probably knew or possibly intended. As an Army brat and as a soldier, I had several times lived or been stationed in the South. When I get tired, my childhood drawl sometimes slips through, and I still pick politely at corn bread and pecan pie, which I hate, but you don't insult the natives.

Broadly speaking, the South of my childhood produced two types of white southern male. First was the shitkicker, product of an agrarian culture, pickup trucks, and Waylon Jennings; if they learned how to add and spell, they aspired to attend Ole Miss, or Bear Bryant U, where pigskin, beer tasting, and frat partying were regarded as serious, taxing majors.

And second, the southern aristocracy and pretenders thereof, who sent their kids to old-line, top-drawer schools like UVA, Duke, William and Mary, and VMI, to be followed by at least a few years of military service, which they were expected to regard as part privilege and part obligation. I had worked with and for a number of these southern gentlemen turned officers, and it appeared Jason Barnes fell into this more exalted category.

Anyway, Jennie said to Agent Kinney, "Thank you. That's helpful. How long have you known him?"

"Since he entered the Service. Two years."

"Hobbies . . . personal habits . . . ?"

"Church, gym . . . that's about it. He doesn't smoke, drink, gamble, or swear. I'm nearly positive he's still a virgin. I'm telling you, he's a Boy Scout."

"So you consider him . . . incorruptible?"

"Yeah—I suppose I do."

"Money problems?"

"Not likely. His family's well-to-do, and Jason's frugal. Also, I don't think money means much to him . . . He's really into this spiritual thing."

"Uh-huh. Career problems?"

"Promoted just last month. A year ahead of his peers."

"Peer problems?"

Bingo. Agent Kinney stared at the table a moment, then said, with evident discomfort, "He's . . . he's awkward socially. Okay? A little stiff and intense, I guess. He's very detail-oriented and by-the-book. It gets on some people's nerves."

Jennie said, "Describe socially awkward."

Kinney took a moment, I think searching for a charitable way to couch this. He said, "Like a lot of incredibly bright people, he's not particularly good at relating. I just don't think he finds most people interesting." He looked at Jennie, and pointedly not at me. "You know how some bright people can be, right?"

Jennie did not respond to his question, but instead asked, "Mental stability?"

"As sane as you or me." Apparently he realized this was a statement loaded with weird possibilities, because after a moment he added, "But ignore my personal view. We all undergo a psych screen before we're even accepted to the Service."

"I'm aware of it," Jennie replied. "Have you seen the results of Jason's screening?"

"As his supervisor, I was allowed to view it."

"Please recall for us what it said."

"I told you he's bright. About a 160 IQ. No abnormality, no mental disorders. A footnote from the psychologist referred to what he termed Jason's mental rigidity. It wasn't a criticism, though. In fact, he predicted that Jason would be unusually diligent and dedicated."

"That was all?"

"A few father-son ego issues. Nothing abnormal."

I asked, "And how does Jason Barnes feel toward his Commander in Chief?"

He looked me dead in the eye and said, "Secret Service agents have no personal feelings toward the President, Mr. Drummond."

This was the proper response, of course—blind loyalty to the position, not the man—and it was bullshit.

I didn't want to upset Agent Margold's interrogatory game plan, but the clock was ticking, and thus far this guy was jerking us off. So I said, "Bullshit." He stared back at me. "You described Barnes as a Bible thumper, moral and righteous. And a genius. He's judgmental, isn't he?"

"All right." After a moment, he smiled and replied, "You asked, so I'll tell you. This President—he owned Jason the instant he had that first White House prayer breakfast. We'd all take a bullet to protect the guy, because that's our job. Jason would throw his own mother in front of this President." Only later would we learn how true that was, but after a moment he suggested smugly, "But that's not what you wanted to hear, is it?"

Jennie and I exchanged glances. We had gone through our checklist of sins, vices, and human flaws, and nothing Kinney had said made our senses tingle. She turned back to Kinney and asked, "Well . . . how do you account for his disappearance?"

"I can't." He looked at me, and then at her. "Hey, I know what happened at the Hawk's house this morning. And you think there was a leak or inside help, and maybe you suspect Jason was the source. Wrong. Jason Barnes is one of the most dedicated agents and purest souls I've ever encountered. I'd stake my career on it."

He already had bet his career on it. In fact, it seemed like the appropriate moment to reinforce that point, time to give him the metaphorical knee in the balls. I informed him, "If it turns out you're wrong, and you've given us no indications as to how or why, the Director of the CIA will forward a letter to the President citing you as both an idiot and a danger to his personal health."

He stared back at me.

Jennie had also concluded that her kindler, gentler side had failed to foster a spirit of genial openness. She seconded my threat, and then one-upped it: "Lying to or misleading a federal officer is punishable under code 1001. If I discover you withheld, I'll charge you with aiding and abetting a felon." She added, more sweetly, "Now take a moment to consider whether you want to add or correct the record."

The cockiness drained from Agent Kinney's face and although, as I said, he was struggling to be a good leader, the loyalty-down thing suddenly became a heavy cross to bear.

Eventually he insisted, "I told you the truth." After another moment of reflection he added, "There was a time . . . six or seven months ago . . . when Jason was experiencing a bad time."

"Meaning what?" Jennie asked.

"He became . . . emotional . . . moody."

I asked, "Why?"

"I don't know why."

True to her trade, Jennie leaned forward and said, "Describe moody."

"Just . . . Look, I don't know—distant, bothered, impatient . . . a little emotionally unstable."

"And did you ask him what it was about?"

"Yeah, I asked. But Jason's an incredibly private person. I gave him a month off to relax. He came back fine."

Jennie thought about this a moment. She asked, "Had anything happened at work?"

"No, nothing to do with the job. It was something personal."

Jennie looked at me as she asked Kinney, "Anything else?"

"Nothing."

I said, "Thank you. You may go. But if you think of anything you missed, call us or we'll have your balls."

The second he was out the door, Jennie asked me, "Well . . . what do you think?"

"I think Agent Jason Barnes sounds like the ideal bodyguard for your national leader, your bank, or your virginal daughter. A religious zealot, pure of heart, devoted to God and country, probably never had an impure or ribald thought in his life."

"You're right. He doesn't sound like a suspect."

When I did not comment on this observation, she added, "Among my duties, I'm the FBI liaison to the Secret Service. I work with them all the time. I coordinate our joint operations and my office processes their background checks. Physically, mentally, and emotionally, they're an extraordinary group. But they're not all angels." She added, "Barnes does sound like a model agent."

"Sure does. Put an APB on him and get a search warrant."

"Get— I'm sorry?"

"Nobody's *that* perfect, Jennie. He's hiding something."

"I haven't got a clue where you're coming from."

"Think about what his boss just told us."

"His boss just told us he's a golden boy. And I know for a fact he passed a number of very rigorous background checks."

"So did I. And so did you." I looked at her and added, "I know what I hid. Would you care to confess what you forgot to tell the background checkers?"

She thought about this a moment and then she replied, "Are you forgetting probable cause?"

"He's on the security detail and he's missing."

She shook her head. "I could maybe twist that logic to justify an APB on the basis of a threat to his security. A search warrant has to be vetted by Justice, though. I'll be laughed out of the building."

"Good point."

"Tell me about it."

"Be sure to mention the very alarming phone tip you just got from the anonymous caller."

"We don't play it that way, Sean. This is the FBI."

"Wow . . . the FBI. After the President's dead, be sure to put that on your résumé."

"There's no need for sarcasm."

"Nor is there a need for excessive moralism. Play this one any way that works, Jennie."

"If one of the murder weapons turns up in his home, we'd be . . . in fact, the whole case would be—"

I reminded her, "You don't have a case to protect. A team of possibly professional killers is hunting the President of the United States—focus on the problem at hand."

In response to her still hesitant expression, I added, "These people aren't playing by the rules. These people know no rules. In this game, color outside the lines, or you lose."

CHAPTER SEVEN

JENNIE PLAYED IT THE WAY THAT WORKED, AND THE POWERS THAT BE GAVE us the search warrant for Jason Barnes's home in Springfield.

Springfield was a mere eight miles away, but it was rush hour, Washington traffic, and speed was critical. Jennie therefore ordered a helicopter, and voilà, one dropped into the parking lot, we climbed aboard, and off we went into the wild blue yonder. The pilot followed I-95 South to the Springfield exit, turned right, and we flew at low altitude over the endless patchwork of red-brick townhouse communities that is Springfield.

I haven't got a clue how the pilot picked the right complex, but he obviously did, judging by the several dark sedans that had cordoned off a landing pad and the agent who approached Jennie and me as we alit on the tarmac.

It turned out he was Special Agent Mark Butterman, the case officer, mid-fifties, long and thin, salt-and-pepper hair, leathery face, a suburbanized Marlboro man in a gray suit. He walked and spoke with a confidence I hoped wasn't misplaced, was too old to be wet behind the ears, and I recalled Jennie mentioned that he was handpicked because he was one of the Bureau's best and brightest, so somebody had a head on their shoulders. This was not the right opportunity for some youthful, overeager, promising stud to show he could cut it (or not). But it happens.

Jennie introduced us, and we shook. I knew Butterman was having a particularly crappy day, though he remained friendly and appeared unperturbed by the pressure.

Anyway, Agent Butterman knew time was precious, and he launched immediately into a fast-paced update on the progress of the investigation. To wit—hundreds of samples and particles had been vacuumed and collected from the Belknaps' house, and forensics was concentrating all its resources on that haul, though there had been no significant breakthroughs. Nor, from his tone did he expect any.

It turned out Mrs. Belknap was a big la-di-da in the D.C. social circuit, and her home was an endless gathering place for the rich and pompous—book clubs, political fund-raisers, and what have you. Throw into that mix some fifteen Secret Service agents who roamed freely around the home, two maids, three yard people, repairmen, and whoever, and enough fingerprints, hair samples, fiber samples, and DNA traces had been lifted to populate New Jersey.

On a more upbeat note, my tip regarding the disturbances in the garden had panned out; they were footprints, three different shoe sizes and types, two male, and one that appeared to belong to a tiny-footed, narrow-shoed female.

Also the preliminary ballistics tests were wrapped up, indicating that four different, though identical, caliber pistols were used, implying either a quartet of killers or a remarkably talented duo of ambidextrous shooters. Which landed us at the present.

Regarding the here and now, he informed Jennie and me, "The super let us in. Seven agents are inside right now. It's small. Barnes lives alone. Shouldn't take long."

The clock was ticking, and he led us to, and then inside the townhouse, a modest two-floored, brick-fronted, faux colonial job. I wandered around for a moment.

Butterman was correct; the place was small, though not cramped, and for a bachelor pad, almost comically neat and tidy. The furniture was a sort of mix of modern and traditional, with colors and patterns that seemed to match the curtains, that matched the wall colors and the carpet, and so forth. Actually, there were no colors or patterns—everything was pure white. I said to Jennie, "What's that smell?"

"Lemon Pledge."

"Lemon what?"

"Scented furniture pol— Oh . . . you're kidding."

Right. Also I was making a point. Regular guys don't live like this, if you know what I mean. Jason's furniture didn't look cheap or expensive, and the art pieces were framed posters—a European cityscape I couldn't identify, an old movie poster I also didn't recognize—that indicated nothing about the tastes of the inhabitant, beyond a serious preference for Wal-Mart. Jennie noted, "He doesn't seem to live above his means."

Butterman concurred with her assessment and informed us, "He rents. Nine hundred and twenty a month, according to the super. Cheap for this area. He drives a used Mazda 323 he bought two years ago for eight grand."

I suggested, "But how he lives today might not be how he wants to live tomorrow."

"The ambition of every criminal mind," Butterman agreed. He added, "No liquor in the house, not even a Bud in the fridge. A teetotaler. No porn, no old magazines or even newspapers. He doesn't even have a TV. And if he keeps weapons here, they're gone. The guy lives like a monk."

Actually, as we wandered around, I was starting to wonder if anybody actually did live here. The place was clean as a whistle, so sterile and pristine I expected a Realtor to pop up from behind a couch. To the right was a tiny living room, connected to an even tinier dining area, and what is termed an efficiency kitchen—ordinarily an oxymoron, though in Jason's case it proved to be a stunning understatement. The counters were clean, bare, and scrubbed, and I detected no clutter, no dirty dishes, not even watermarks in the sink. I peeked inside his fridge and everything was dress-right-dress, a perfectly linear parade ground of milk cartons, yogurts, salad dressings, a cornucopia of low-cal, low-fat, and low-flavor goodies. I felt guilty in the midst of all this order, cleanliness, and health consciousness.

Four guys and gals in blue windbreakers were milling around the ground floor, not aimlessly, though clearly nobody appeared to be sure what they were searching for. This was my bright idea and I didn't have a clue what to look for. There would be something, though. Jason Barnes was not the benighted saint his boss thought he was. I was sure of it. Maybe.

Jennie said to me, "Upstairs."

So up we went, and at the top of the stairs was a narrow hallway that twisted to the right, and three doors. We opened the first door and it was a tiny bathroom that smelled like a pine forest, with precisely folded, freshly laundered towels, a spotless mirror, and a toilet you could eat off, were one inclined to do such a stupid thing. Did anybody actually live in this house?

I stepped inside and looked around a moment. A narrow closet was hidden behind the door, and it struck me that this would be the perfect hidey-hole for Jason's darkest secrets and filthiest habits. I swung it open and peeked inside, expecting a blow-up doll to fall out, a corpse, something. There were six shelves, and not a square inch of free space. Laid out on the shelves was a veritable armory of medicines, nasal sprays, antibacterial soaps and shampoos, skin care ointments, and various medical salves, balms, preventatives and devices, from enemas to ear wax cleaning solvents. There must've been three hundred bottles and vials and tubes, all neatly arranged, a harem of things to make sure you smelled good, slew galaxies of germs, and never experienced a constipated moment, or even ringworm.

Jennie, who was more familiar with these things, whistled. She said, "Here's where his money went."

"Hypochondriac?" I suggested.

She eyed the supplies a moment. "Aside from the aspirin, Band-Aids, and antibacterial ointments, these are all preventatives and body cleaning aids. Not a hypochondriac. Still, this is a little . . . odd."

"More than a little."

We backed out, and the next door led to the master bedroom, where two agents were busily defacing another temple of neatness. A massive and very ornate carved crucifix hung over the bed. The third door led to another, tinier bedroom that had been transformed into a compact office. Jennie said, "In here."

A female agent was already pulling books off shelves, and she faced us when Jennie asked her, "Anything interesting?"

"Depends what you mean by interesting." She elaborated, "Mostly horror novels and religious books. Lots of Stephen King and Anne Rice—all that spooky stuff. He's got the full Tim La-Haye series . . . Armageddon and all that. I don't know how he sleeps at night."

I smiled at the agent and said, "Did you see anything called *How to Whack a President?*"

She smiled back. "Do you recall the author?" She added,

"There's some military manuals on weapons and munitions. I don't know if that means anything. Leftovers from his military service, I guess."

I regarded the manuals a moment. Actually, they meant nothing except that Mr. Neatness had one flaw—he was a pack rat. Big deal. I was still carting around a lockerful of manuals issued to me during my basic infantry officer training. But I had a good reason: I could run out of toilet paper someday. You never know.

Jennie commented, "It's never that easy. But you usually learn a few things about people from their reading habits."

I said, "Like what?"

She asked me, "What's on your bookshelf at home?"

"Let's see . . . the collected works of John Donne, Shakespeare's tragedies . . . of course, all of Oprah's picks . . ."

She rolled her eyes. Why wasn't I being taken seriously?

On the wall across from the bookcase hung the usual vanity assortment—a VMI diploma, an officer commission, a few military awards, all of which were low-grade I-showed-up-for-work-on-time medals. In the middle was a presidential photo with a handwritten inscription that read: "To Jason, thanks for your service." Well, we'll see.

Not present were any items or paraphernalia of a personal nature—photographs of Mom and Dad, photo albums, desk trophies, mementos, or even any old letters or bills. By itself this meant nothing. Collectively I thought it meant a great deal.

Jennie was nosing through book titles. She said, "I'll tell you what's discordant. Here's this highly intelligent guy with a tightly ordered, disciplined mind. Yet his reading tastes run toward chaos, make-believe monsters, and destructive visions. It's contradictory."

"And what do you make of that contradiction?"

"Let me think about it awhile."

I advised the agent, "Be sure to flip the pages on the books."

I walked to Jason's desk, sat down, and began browsing through drawers. Every pen, stamp, and paper clip was in the proper place, no loose change, no stray papers, no trash, no clutter or debris whatsoever. The order and cleanliness was manic and implied something. I mentioned, "The future Mrs. Barnes is one lucky lady."

The agent said, "The future Mrs. Barnes is going to go nuts. I did the kitchen earlier. The inside of his silverware drawers are labeled—you know, dinner forks, salad forks. His glassware and plates are shrink-wrapped inside the cabinets. The guy's garbage looked folded."

I glanced at Jennie Margold. "Your expertise is head cases."

"He displays classic anal compulsive tendencies certainly. Clearly he's neurotic. It's even possible he's bacillophobic. Though I—"

"He's what?"

"Fear of germs."

"Why didn't you say so?"

She smiled. I love a woman who appreciates my bad jokes. She said, "I'm talking unnecessary fear. The type who boils his toothbrush every morning."

You can never tell about people. It's interesting. I observed, "So here's a guy who wakes up every morning wondering if this is the day when he has to take a bullet for his boss. You wouldn't think he'd sweat the small stuff."

This got a big laugh out of the agent, though Jennie emitted a groan. She continued, "He's an only child, most likely. A very strict upbringing. Military college and his three years of Marine Corps life probably amplified his imprinted habits. It could relate to the paternal issues Mark Kinney cited. An overbearing father he's still struggling to placate and please. Freud would—"

"Excuse me," I interrupted. "The crime—does this relate to the crime?"

"Oh . . . right." She nodded at me, somewhat surprised. "You know your stuff. Obviously, you remember that I classified the Belknap murder as an organized crime. Well, organized crimes are the product of neat, orderly, compulsive minds . . . and—"

"Like Jason Barnes's mind?"

"Ostensibly. He could fit the personality profile." She added, "So would a million other males in this country."

"And females."

"Not really. Serial and mass killing are forms of aggression peculiarly suited to males."

"Oh please."

"I'm not making this up. It's a statistical fact. Do you know there are only two or three female serial killers in prison today?"

"Well . . . maybe women don't get caught."

"You mean women are smarter."

"Women are sneakier."

"I think you mean more clever." She smiled.

We returned to the perplexing puzzle of Jason Barnes. Jennie said, "Let me suggest this. It's early to hypothesize, but an only child with a demanding mother or father, neatness becomes a way to please. Only children tend to be oversupervised, neatness is a visible barometer of obedience, and there's no sibling around to blame for the mess."

I made a mental note to tell my big brother he owed me big-time. What a nit-picking idiot he'd be had not little Sean been around to pin all the raps on.

She continued, "It can be deterministic. They're instinctively neat and orderly, but when they feel guilt about something— tiny things—some revert . . . become obsessive . . . insufferably compulsive. They feel they can expunge or make amends by ordering and straightening up their external environment. A lot of these people, later in life, they end up on couches."

Interesting. But she was right, you have to be careful, it *was* too early to reach conclusions. At that moment, we had a suspicion of an inside leak, and a missing agent. I mean, how stupid would we look if Jason showed up in the morning, explaining he had met some hottie in a bar who invited him over to straighten her pantry and iron her undies? Also, a few impressions scavenged from the surface barely scrape the emotional density of a full-blown person. Still, we were starting to tease out a few characteristics about the increasingly peculiar Mr. Barnes. You never know.

"We should take his Rolodex and address book," I informed Jennie. I added, "And get the phone company to give us his records." I pointed at his desktop computer. "You've got people who can unscramble this hard drive, right?"

She nodded. "They'll work all night, if need be."

"Need be."

She stared at me.

"Am I being too—"

"Are you ever. Back off. Our people know how to handle this."

"Oh . . . sorry."

"I understand. You want to catch these people. We all do."

Then she thought of something else and turned to the agent leafing through books. "Go to the master bedroom, collect Barnes's shoes, and send them to forensics immediately." She looked at me and said, "We'll compare them to the foot molds from the garden. Yes . . . no?"

"Good catch."

Jennie's cell phone rang again, she punched on, identified herself and then listened. She looked and sounded exasperated.

"I understand . . . right . . . when . . . uh-huh, and where?" After a moment, she said, "The helicopter's in the parking lot. I'll be there inside twenty minutes."

She punched off and stared at the floor a moment. She said, "Wait'll you see this."

CHAPTER EIGHT

STRAIGHT AHEAD AND THROUGH THE HELICOPTER'S WINDSHIELD, WE OB-served three or four columns of dark smoke curdling up from 495, Washington's notorious beltway, and below, a long and frustrated parking lot that snaked its way back to northern Virginia.

The pilot twisted around in his chair and yelled back to us, "No place to land. When I get low, jump out. Watch the skids."

He tugged back on his throttle and the machine swooped down about five feet off the ground and loitered. I leaped first and landed on a small patch of grass, turned, and saw Jennie hurtling into me. I had just enough time to get my hands out, and she landed in my arms. A nearby cop was staring. I asked, "What happened here?"

He replied, "Man, you won't believe this. Some asshole fired at a car." He pointed a finger at a mangled wreck leaking black smoke near the front of the tangled pack. "There—that thing . . . Used to be a BMW 745i, if you can believe it. Just started crashing into other cars. Everyone was doing about sixty-five . . . and you got this."

I saw that in addition to the wrecked BMW, "this" included some fifteen cars ranging from dimpled to mangled, a collage of shattered safety glass, torn steel, and ripped and dented people. Looking badly shaken, the cop remarked, "Probably just road rage . . . but holy shit."

Three county fire trucks, ten ambulances, and a fleet of marked and unmarked police cars were squeezed onto the outer median, lights flashing, radios squawking, the whole nine yards. To my right rested a crunched-up blue Ford Escort, where an emergency crew manhandled a Jaws of Life apparatus. An old woman howled in agony, and two emergency aid workers leaned through the car window and fought to plug an IV into her arm. To my left were several dazed people seated on the backs of ambulances, their shirts and dresses stained with blood. Above circled three news helicopters, broadcasting this corpus of destruction and misery.

Twenty yards from the BMW, I noted a clump of cops, in the midst of which stood a man looking singularly self-important, cell phone in one hand, the other waving around, directing an invisible symphony or something. It was George Meany, and understandably, he was not displaying the gestures or body language of a happy man. I asked Jennie, "Why are we here?"

"What?" She appeared distracted.

"How do we know this was caused by our friends?"

"I . . . what?" She was peering in the direction of the old lady who'd been fighting the emergency aid people. I followed her eyes and saw that the woman was now slumped forward, quiet and still, the fight gone out of her. The rescue team was catching its breath and the medical techs were repacking their kits. Jennie took a step in the direction of the car, and I took her arm. "Don't. She's beyond help."

"But—"

"I know." I squeezed her arm. "Focus on finding her killers. Now, why are we here?"

Jennie took a long swallow and said quietly, "Let's go ask."

We joined Meany, who ignored us and continued to chat on the phone. Above the cacophony I caught snatches of George's conversation, and clearly the tone was neither cordial nor pleasant. Actually, George looked a little panicky, like a guy being told it was his ass on the line. For a brief instant I almost felt guilty about disliking him. He said, "That's right, sir." He wiped some perspiration from his upper lip. "No, uh . . . yes sir . . . of course, sir." He hung up and announced, "What a fuckin' nightmare."

Jennie asked him, "How do we know it was them?"

Meany licked his lips, pointed, and said, "That black BMW over there . . . the plate check says it belongs to Merrill Benedict."

Nobody said anything. Nobody needed to say anything. Merrill Benedict was the White House spokesperson, the poor soul thrown into the daily mosh pit called the White House press corps to look and sound like he was answering questions he wasn't answering. About forty, slight of build, sandy-haired, a bit of a dandy, but nice-looking, and boy, was the guy a gold-star bullshitter. I asked George, "Dead?"

"That's what being torn in half will do to you, Drummond."

Jennie said, "So he was the target. And all the rest of these poor people were . . . were . . ."

I looked at her. Her face was drained of color and her eyes looked cloudy and unfocused. All this misery and chaos was getting to her, was in fact affecting us all. But you have to swallow your feelings and put on a game face, or you scare the shit out of the public. I said, "The clinical expression is 'collateral damage.' " I added, "But I don't think that fits this."

"No?" asked Meany, looking at me a little incredulously. "Well . . . what does it fit, Drummond?"

"I don't think this was random carnage. I think the killers intended something spectacular."

George shook his head derisively. "Just what I need. A half-baked theory from a half-assed lawyer." He smiled—or more accurately, sneered—at me and added, "If you don't mind, Drummond, I'll make up my own mind after I hear from the professionals." Now I remembered why I disliked this guy.

Jennie, however, had heard what I said and asked, "Why? Why would they . . . I just don't . . . I mean, I don't see . . ."

There was no answer, yet. I replied, "We should think about that."

And for a brief moment we did think about it. Clearly there were a thousand easier and less conspicuous ways to murder Merrill Benedict—an ambush in his driveway, poison in his toothpaste—any and all of which could've been accomplished without witnesses, without complications, and without this indiscriminate brutality. But I was sure that was exactly the point—the decision to murder Merrill Benedict in plain daylight, in the densest traffic, at the worst possible hour was meant to ignite an atrocity, to provoke awe and revulsion. Throw a stone into water, and you know you'll get ripples. Unbelievable.

"Seven dead, so far," Meany muttered, a bit stunned. "Twenty-two more injured, several critically."

Actually, eight dead and twenty-one wounded as of a moment ago, but the devil's not in the details in a nightmare like this. Meany commented, "Thank God it was rush hour. No children."

"Think parents, " I replied. No need to spell out that there were a lot of kids waiting for Mom or Pop to come swinging through the door, who were instead about to find a glum-faced D.C. detective bearing bad tidings on their stoop. I caught Jennie's eye, and she turned away.

I looked at George and asked, "Witnesses?"

"What?"

"Witnesses, George?"

"Oh . . . well, the police are collecting statements." He said to Jennie, "That lady over by that ambulance . . . the blue skirt, over there?" He pointed and we saw her. "She thinks she saw something. Make yourself useful and see what the cops are getting out of her."

The lady in question was already being interrogated by a pair of detectives. Jennie flashed her fed creds and asked the duo to take a powder. Actually, I was a little surprised when the detectives put up no fight and complied. Then again, the conditions on this highway weren't normal—not with this level of carnage, not with a federal notice to report all serious incidents immediately, and certainly not with feds falling out of helicopters. It was beginning to dawn on the locals that what happened here was something much worse than a simple case of road rage gone berserk.

Jennie asked the lady's name, Carol Blandon; her age, sixty-one; her address, Montgomery, Maryland; and so forth. We didn't care about her personal info, but it's important to assess a witness before you get into it. With a shaky hand, Mrs. Blandon held a bloody bandage over her left eye, and clearly she was distressed and a little out of focus. But she appeared lucid enough, and she sounded reliable, albeit a bit crabby, which, given the circumstances, was understandable. In a soothing and respectful tone Jennie finally asked what happened.

"Oh, I . . . well, I was in the third lane . . . you know, of the four lanes. I was . . . I think I was . . . maybe, three cars behind that black car over there." She stared for a moment at the wreck that was once poor Merrill Benedict's BMW. "I was listening to the radio . . . I don't remember what, and . . . and, I . . . well, I saw this man stand up in his car and stick his upper body out of the moonroof."

This was a very significant point. I asked, "You saw him stand up?"

"I suppose he might already have been standing when I looked. What's the difference?"

"You're right. No difference." Actually, the difference was that Mrs. Blandon just went from being a key witness to a contextual witness in court, assuming we got to that point.

Jennie asked her, "Do you recall what he looked like?"

"No. It all happened very fast."

Jennie then asked Mrs. Blandon, "Do you recall the make of car?"

"I . . . I don't know."

"Color, number of doors, SUV, sedan . . . anything? It would be helpful."

"It was on the inside lane and the cars in between obscured my view. I couldn't tell you anyway . . . I'm not good about that."

Jennie and I exchanged glances. I said, "Well, just tell us what happened."

"All right, this young man was sticking out the top of the car. It was an odd sight. I remember thinking it was some high school kid . . ." She shook her head. "Then he had something on his shoulder . . . not big . . . a tube of some sort and it belched fire."

I said, "Not a gun . . . a tube?"

She stared at me a moment. "Yes. A tube. And then . . . then, oh my . . . well, then everything turned crazy, and I *had* to stop looking. Cars were banging into each other . . . I hit the brakes, and I got slammed from behind . . . and . . . and . . . oh, sweet Lord, it was awful."

I drew Jennie off to the side, out of Mrs. Blandon's earshot. I informed her, "She's describing a shoulder-fired antitank weapon. The guy fired out the sunroof because the backblast needs to escape or you get fried."

Jennie nodded and pointed at an exit ramp about a hundred yards from where we stood. She said, "That's probably where they escaped. They fired, exited, and drove off like nothing happened."

"Right. Maybe somebody who drove on, or somebody already in the hospital, got a better look at that car. We should find out."

She put her hand on my arm and said, "I'll ask George to tell the cops to ask around. We'll also ask the local TV and radio stations to request public assistance."

Jennie's cell phone rang and she backed off and answered it, leaving me to thank Mrs. Blandon for her assistance. I overheard Jennie say, "Yeah . . . uh-huh. What? . . . oh, shit . . . you're kidding."

She rolled her eyes at me and said into the phone, "No . . . I don't mean, *literally*, you're kidding." She paused. "All right, just tell me everything you *know* . . . Okay, fine—everything you *think* you know."

She listened for another two minutes, intermittently prodding the agent on the other end, then said, "I see." After another moment she said, "At least an hour. Our helicopter's gone. No. I can't . . . Well, just call Mark Butterman. See if he can get over there. I want that place swept clean."

She hung up, drew a few breaths, and then informed me, "You won't believe this."

Surveying the surrounding carnage, I replied, "Try me."

"Justice Fineberg walked up to the front door of his large and lovely Bethesda home at 7:00 P.M. and it exploded."

"*Phillip* Fineberg?"

"Yeah. Know anything about him?"

"A bit. But how . . . I mean, doesn't a Supreme Court justice have a security detail?"

"The Supremes have their own security people, a mix of retired cops . . . some retired Bureau types . . . double-dippers. My office handles their clearances, reviews their procedures, and coordinates joint matters." After a pause, she added, "They're a good outfit. But they're not bodyguards. They just weren't expecting . . ."

"What?"

"The on-scene investigator's not sure." She added, somewhat annoyed, "I'm so tired of dealing with agents with law degrees. Ask a simple question and you get ten conditionals. You know what I mean?"

Right. "Well, what did he tell you?"

"The security agent who drove the justice home said the explosion happened at the front entrance. Little damage to the home. Even the doorway's intact. Fineberg was the only casualty."

"Shrapnel marks?"

"Yeah . . . like that. Some sort of fragmentary device, he thinks. The device nearly blew Fineberg in half."

I considered that a moment. "The explosive device was placed outside the door."

"In fact, it was." She looked at me and said, "You're on a roll . . . Want to take a stab at the rest of it?"

"Sure." I asked, "Was there a security system at the house?"

"An electronic system. Sensors inside, cameras outside—all

very sophisticated . . . supposedly tamperproof. Since 9/11, all the Supremes have them."

"Do the cameras record or just view?"

"Record. Tapes are kept for twenty-four hours, then taped over."

"Surely the killers reconnoitered in advance."

"That would make sense." She thought about that and came to the appropriate conclusion. "We'll review the tapes and see if we can pick them out."

"After what we saw this morning, we should consider the possibility that they knew the security routine . . . possibly even the security setup in advance."

"Bad assumption," Jennie replied. "The Secret Service and the Supremes' security detail are different organizations."

"With a hundred million dollars, think about what you can buy. Or who."

"All right . . . I won't rule it out as a possibility."

I tried to re-create how it might have happened, thinking about how I would do it. "When you review the tapes, you might see a delivery drop earlier in the day. FedEx, UPS—something."

She shook her head. "Not possible."

"Of course it's possible."

"All mail and packages are collected and screened for explosives and poisons. Even the stuff delivered to their homes. Standard precaution since the anthrax and ricin attacks."

"Did I say the bomb was *in* the parcel?"

"Oh . . . you mean—"

"Yeah. As the delivery person dropped off the package, he—possibly she—planted the explosive device somewhere near the front door."

"How?"

"Like, they bent over, one hand placed the package by the door, and the other inconspicuously put the bomb in place."

She considered that and then said, "That could work, couldn't it?"

I nodded. "It's an ideal ambush site. Fineberg had to be stationary at least a few seconds to unlock the door."

"I . . . I hadn't thought of that."

"If there are bushes by the door, maybe the explosive device was hidden there. But you said it nearly blew him in half."

"The agent reported the explosion went off around waist level."

"That doesn't make sense. A normal explosive device or mine would blow off his feet, possibly his legs." I considered this for a moment, then I thought about the antitank weapon used here, and a really weird thought popped into my mind. "Unless it was a Bouncing Betty."

"A Bouncing Betty?"

"A type of military mine."

"Tell me about that."

"They're fairly common . . . small . . . hard to detect with the naked eye, especially when camouflaged. You stuff it into the ground and it sticks up about two inches. When it's triggered, a small explosive goes off, the detonating device pops about three feet into the air, and then goes off."

"Wouldn't Fineberg have to step on the mine?"

"They come out of the factory pressure detonated. But they can be modified into tripwire- or even command-detonated devices."

"So it would—"

"Yes—it would. A guy's up the street watching. The second Fineberg's hand touches the knob, up pops Mr. Nasty."

"Jesus—how do you protect against something like that?"

"I think that's exactly the point."

"What am I missing here?"

"Their note—we can't."

She nodded. Then she suggested, "But there's something important—something we're overlooking. I'm not thinking . . ." She glanced in the direction of the ruined BMW, then said, "Anti-tank weapons . . . Bouncing Bettys . . . this is military hardware we're talking about."

"And . . . ?"

"And where did these people get their hands on these things? Right?"

Right.

Jennie then rushed off to inform Meany of the newest disaster, our guesses about the weapons used, and what this might mean in terms of fresh leads and whatever.

Left with nothing better to do, I withdrew my cell phone from a pocket and turned it on for the first time that day. The little window informed me that somebody in the 703 area code had called about ten times. Incidentally, the CIA, like the Army, is big on reporting chains and timely communications. Of course, as a lawyer, I'm accustomed to working and operating alone, making my own decisions, accountable to nobody but my clients and the court docket. I was having a little trouble getting back into this chain of command thing.

I decided to get this over with and called Phyllis. On an open airwave, I was no doubt engaging in an egregious heresy of some sort. But with three helicopters broadcasting overhead, and a Supreme Court justice splattered across the front of his house, confidentiality was the least of our worries, in my view.

Phyllis sounded a lot annoyed and wasted a few comments reminding me I wasn't the only one working this case, and so on. Then she listened patiently as I unloaded the latest. She asked a few questions, some of which I could answer, and some of which I couldn't. Finally she commented, "Well, I can't recall a worse evening."

I nearly replied, "How about 9/11?" The CIA hadn't exactly ended that day parading down Constitution Avenue draped in victory laurels, as I recalled. But maybe she had a point. By the evening of 9/11 the worst was over, except for the shock, funerals, cleanup, and revenge. These guys weren't through. In fact, the worst could be yet to come. I commented, "Well, the morning wasn't so hot either."

"The morning was just the entree."

"Right." I suggested, "We should probably anticipate another hit to start off our day tomorrow."

"It would be a mistake to expect these people to be predictable. They haven't been yet."

"Would you care to wager?"

"No, I would not." She changed the subject and noted, "This is all very mystifying. It's obvious why they assassinated Merrill Benedict, don't you think?"

"I think it *looks* obvious. Like Belknap, he's a confidant of the President, and given his job . . . Well, there's going to be a big hole at the White House morning press briefing tomorrow."

"Indeed. Now, what about Fineberg?"

Good question. Connections are important in any criminal case; they're irreplaceable when they're all you have. So I considered her question and it was a bit tricky.

Justice Phillip Fineberg wasn't close to anybody I knew of. And though it pains me to speak ill of the dead, here goes; the man was a prick. He was about seventy, a legal egghead plucked two Presidents back from the faculty of Yale Law, and every President since has cursed the choice. The press generally characterized him, somewhat delicately, as cantankerous and iconoclastic, journalistic code words for a robed asshole. He browbeat and terrified every lawyer unfortunate enough to appear at the highest court, even those arguing a case he favored.

The American Bar Association could raffle tickets to pee on his gravestone. Also his legal opinions were irrational, and he was famous—or infamous—for writing contrarian dissents insulting to both the minority and majority opinions. His eight brethren would dearly love to get this lug in a back alley and lump him up good. Except somebody beat them to the punch.

In truth, Fineberg's murder would be a source of quiet jubilation in many quarters, and made no sense I could see.

Phyllis repeated, "Well? Is there a connection? Or was he just a target of convenience?"

"I don't think there's a specific connection."

Apparently I was being tested, because she snapped, "Think harder, Drummond. This city is filled with targets. There has to be a reason they chose him. Right?"

"Right."

"I didn't give you this assignment to spectate. These killers aren't stupid. You can't afford to be."

So I thought harder. I suggested, "Maybe Fineberg was a decoy."

"For what?"

"To sow doubt and confusion. To mislead us and force us to waste time and precious resources chasing down an empty path. You know—"

"Yes . . . possibly." After a pause she observed, "Also, there are many prominent people in Washington, our ability to protect them is limited, and by forcing us to spread out, it gets easier for them."

"Right." The lady was on, and I went into the listening mode.

She added, "They're forcing our hand. This makes three

important officials in one day. We can't very well dissemble any longer, can we? We're going to have to disclose what's happening to the public."

"Maybe we should have done that earlier."

"Don't be naive. There was a very good reason we chose to handle things this way."

"To avoid embarrassment?" I offered.

"Oh please. What nobody could in good taste confess this morning. What we all wanted to avoid—hysteria. Every person in this town with a hint of an impressive title is going to beg for protection. Somebody has to perform the triage."

"Go on."

"A lot of feelings are going to get hurt, and a lot of enemies made. Understand—with an election, the President wanted desperately to avoid that."

Made sense, I guess. I was reminded of the cold war days, when a select handful of people in the Pentagon were issued special passes to be flown out of the city on the first whiff of an incoming nuclear attack. They would ride out the great cataclysm inside a hollowed-out mountain somewhere not even God knew about, to emerge, I guess, after the Geiger counters stopped having heart attacks. It was the ultimate get-out-of-jail card, the modern equivalent of a ticket to Noah's Ark. For the rest of us, it was an official stamp of expendability. Fortunately, the big one never came, so there were no hard feelings—as if anybody would've been left to feel bad anyway.

Not so this time. The President was involved in a touch-and-go election campaign, plenty of people would remember, and he already had enemies by the bushel. I said, "Got it."

"I shouldn't have to explain these things to you."

Right.

It's never pleasant getting your butt chewed by the boss. But

I didn't really want to get into it with this lady, who might lace cyanide into my cigars or something. And for the record, if you'll pardon the pun, the lady was dead-on. Bodies were piling up, and Sean Drummond's singular contribution was to explain how. What mattered was why, and from there you might get to who.

I asked her for an update on the bounty, and she informed me that no progress had been made, though reports were still filtering in from around the world, and she would let me know. In other words, piss off.

She closed by informing me that Jennie, Meany, and I needed to be back at the Incident Command Center in time for a nine o'clock session of the oversight cell.

I began to wonder if this day was going to end.

CHAPTER NINE

THE 9:00 P.M. SESSION OPENED WITH AN OVERVIEW FROM A PLUMP AND pasty-faced Bureau pathologist, who brought along a number of visual aids to jog our imagination and encourage discussion. The information wasn't all that helpful, really. But I guess it's good for morale to allow everybody a moment in the sun.

Also, the day had been long and grueling, the hour was late, and a pathology lecture is a lot like a sixth-grade sex ed class— it's all in the pictures.

At least the bureaucrats seemed to be catching up to the killers' frantic pace, and there was no unseemly melee as everybody tried to figure out who sat where. Name placards had been prepared; legal pads, sharpened No. 2 pencils, and even bottled waters were arranged. The same players from the morning session were present and accounted for, excluding my big cheese, James Peterson, who I guess was lurking in the shadowy corridors of Langley plotting something. More likely, he was exercising his option to keep his distance from this thing. Smart guy.

In fact, I was a little astonished to see Director Townsend drumming his fingers on the end of the table and watching the mass assemble. But it made sense, I guess. With the White House Chief of Staff, the presidential spokesperson, a Supreme Court justice, and assorted others filling drawers at the morgue, taking in a Kennedy Center musical was probably not the best of ideas. Still, I think it said something about the man that he did not keep his bureaucratic distance, that he was staying in the thick of things, and if—or, as it now looked—*when* the shitstorm hit, he was going to be front and center, with no prophylactic layers of bureaucracy for cover.

Also, I was relieved to see that Mr. Townsend did not appear pissed, distraught, or even moody; he actually looked collected and impassive, as though this was just another day, another investigation, another job to be done. Of course, it wasn't. But good leadership is four-tenths being there and six-tenths looking the part.

Anyway, the day had been a scorcher—literally and otherwise—and nobody had changed clothes, or showered, and the room was windowless, so it smelled a little ripe, though that was the least of our worries.

In fact, two minutes into it, everybody was stone-cold sober, stealing glances at their watches and waiting for Dr. Death and his nasty pictures to go away, when he got to something I found interesting and useful.

We had finished reviewing the anatomical donnybrook at Belknap's house and a new corpse flashed onto the screen: an aged and scrawny body sprawled on his left side across his front porch.

One glance and you knew this guy had scribbled his last illegible dissent. The doc pointed at the slide and said, "See here how Fineberg was blown nearly in half. Really the only thing holding him together is his spine. Even a layman can detect from the severity of trauma that his death was virtually instantaneous. Until the autopsy's complete I won't venture the exact cause of death . . . but see here." He pointed at a fresh slide. "The right side of Fineberg's body, the hollowed-out side, took the brunt of the blast."

There followed a number of lavish close-ups of Phillip Fineberg's oozing entrails, exposed rib cage, and so on.

"The depth of the tissue damage," the doc continued, "and the heavy accretion of gunpowder on Fineberg's skin suggests the device exploded, we estimate, within three feet from his body. Of particular interest, judging by the angle of the entry wounds, the device was some three feet off the ground when it exploded. This is curious, yes? The explosion occurred at approximately the same height as the doorknob."

He paused to allow everybody to consider this novel possibility. Mr. Gene Halderman of Homeland Security was thoughtfully stroking his chin, no doubt thinking, "Ah-hah—the old bomb in the doorknob thing."

The doctor then said, "But when we found no trace of brass, or even brass enamel, we ruled that out. The device dispensed hundreds of particles composed of iron bauxite, a mixture of tiny pellets and some coarser pieces with sharp, uneven edges, perhaps from the shell of the device. What this means, we don't know. We do bodies, not bombs. So we've forwarded shrapnel fragments and powder residue over to—"

George Meany suddenly pushed back his chair. "Wait!—hold on a minute . . ." He regarded the picture a moment before he informed the good doctor, "From what you're describing . . . I think . . ." He paused until he had everybody's undivided attention. "That . . . that sounds like a Bouncy Nancy." His eyes roved around the table, and in response to the confused expressions he added, "If you're unfamiliar with this device, it's . . ." and proceeded to give the unwashed and unknowing a brief description of Bouncy Nancys and how the weapon matched the damage inflicted on Fineberg, and so forth.

He summarized by saying, "Incidentally, I should mention another suspicion I've been toying with. Regarding the Merrill murder, the police investigators were of the opinion that a rifle was used to send his car out of control. I looked at that car—it was pretty banged up, and had caught on fire. Hard to say for sure, but I suspect an antitank weapon might've been used."

George was scoring big-time points with his boss, Director Townsend, who sat nodding and wide-eyed throughout.

Mrs. Hooper stared with newfound awe and admiration at the deductive wunderkind.

Gene Halderman leaned back in his chair, hands sweeping through his pompadour, no doubt thinking, "Wow. When I grow up . . ."

Jennie shot me a bemused smile. I smiled back.

That George. What can you do?

George said, "In fact . . . I think . . . Well, this might be a new and very critical lead. How did these people get their hands on controlled and sophisticated military hardware?"

Nobody had a ready answer to that question.

After a moment Townsend asked, "Did you serve in the military, George?"

"No . . . I entered the Bureau out of college."

"And your apparent familiarity with military munitions, how did you come by that?"

"I try to stay up on things, sir. I recall reading about mine types. And as the doctor was describing the judge's injuries, it struck me th—"

"Were you aware I was a Marine platoon leader in Vietnam?"

"Yes . . . I think I knew that."

"That I still carry shrapnel in my left hip? In fact, it might interest you to know the shrapnel came from the very device you're trying to describe."

"I'm sorry to hear that. Is it painful?"

Those unblinking eyes regarded George. "Bouncy Nancy? The proper nomenclature is a Bouncing Betty."

George glanced very briefly at Jennie Margold, who had become curiously occupied dislodging something from under a fingernail. Then he returned his boss's stare. "I misspoke." After a moment he added, "Of course I meant a Bouncing Betty."

"Of course you did." Those dead-fish eyes turned to me. "Drummond, right?"

"Yes sir."

"You were at the crash site?"

"I was."

"And you were briefed on Fineberg's death?" The question was obviously rhetorical, and he offered, "Maybe you have other observations you'd care to share with us—that is, to share directly."

Phyllis's eyebrows rose. I cleared my throat. "Well . . . actually, Agent Margold discovered another important connection."

Jennie looked up from her fingernails. Townsend replied, "Proceed."

So I did. "During our search of Jason Barnes's townhouse, we discovered a small batch of military manuals on his bookshelves. I thought nothing of it, actually."

"Yes?"

"But at the crash site, Agent Margold recalled that one was the Army field manual on the Light Antitank Weapon, or LAW."

"Is that so?"

"Another was the field manual on military mines."

For a moment you could hear a pin drop. Actually, it was the sound of two tons of shit hitting the floor. Chuck Wardell lurched forward in his seat. "There could be a thousand perfectly innocent explanations for that."

Phyllis responded quickly, saying, "No doubt there could be. But shouldn't we focus on the one that's not at all innocent, Charles?"

"I . . . I can't believe this," Wardell stammered. "Jason Barnes is a fine and loyal agent. He has no motive, and . . . and I . . . I won't sit here . . . and . . . and let you people . . . let you lynch him . . . and . . ."

His convoluted syntax aside, I actually admired Mr. Wardell's effort to cover Barnes's ass. In a ruminative moment it struck me that were it my gilded ass up in the air, I shared no tribal loyalties with anyone in this room, and nobody was going to rush to my defense. I glanced at Phyllis, but she appeared to be preoccupied staring down Mr. Wardell. I looked at Jennie, and she nodded and smiled. She was really nice. I smiled back.

I really needed to make a few friends. If we didn't start making progress, pronto, this thing would turn ugly, and I was the lowest-ranking person on this team. As a rule of thumb in Washington, it's always lonelier at the bottom than the top.

Anyway, before it turned really pissy, Director Townsend asserted himself and informed Mr. Wardell, "Nobody's lynching Jason Barnes." Everybody nodded—there were no hasty lynchers in this room.

After a moment Townsend emphasized, "Absence of evidence is not necessarily evidence of absence. Everything I've heard is circumstantial." Again, everybody nodded and a modicum of equanimity was restored. He then looked around and asked, without even a hint of irony, "Can anybody tell me what we know about this Jason Barnes?"

Jennie-on-the-spot was apparently prepared for this pointed question and she swiftly and efficiently recounted the observations we had picked up at Jason's home, his personal quirks and habits, and so forth. Wisely, she did not reveal or even imply that Jason was an exact match for the type of compulsive, organized killer we were looking for, mollifying Mr. Wardell, for the moment. She reached down to her briefcase and said, "I made copies of his Secret Service personnel file. Why don't I distribute them?"

She walked around the table, dropping folders, and everybody began leafing through the professional life and times of Jason Barnes. Mr. Wardell was nobody's idiot and refused to retreat into a consent of silence, mumbling things like "steamroll" and "rush to judgment," and whatever.

Like prison records, apparently, the longer you serve, the thicker the book. With only two years in His Majesty's Service, the info on Barnes was sparse, factual, and not all that illustrative, or even enlightening—Caucasian, male, age, academic degrees, height, weight, and so on. Also included inside the folder were the annual ratings from his boss, Mr. Kinney, which I took a moment to examine. They were, as he had indicated, universally exceptional.

Interestingly, because of his Marine service and "remarkable potential," Jason had bypassed the traditional initial stint of investigative duties and been assigned straight to protection details. He had twice won the highly coveted Agent of the Month award. Also there were commendatory letters from various administration personages complimenting the agent's extraordinary work and diligence on a trip to California and another to some African country.

On paper, this guy was so conscientious, professional, and shit-hot he didn't even need a bulletproof vest.

I took a moment to study his photo. Jason Barnes was fairly good-looking, actually—high cheekbones, smooth complexion, thin lips, and eyes that were deepset and light blue, or possibly gray. His hair was brown and short, with every strand in place, and I wondered if he had AstroTurf in his DNA. Even his eyebrows looked plucked and neatly combed.

On the surface, this was a guy who could get his share of the ladies into the sack. But attractive bone structure aside, something about him didn't sit right. He was *too* well-groomed, and as a result, a little strange-looking. In a well-lit room, women with less than five beers in them would look carefully at Jason Barnes and take a pass.

Sounding surprised and distressed, it was Mrs. Hooper who broke the studious silence. She held Barnes's photo aloft. "I know this guy. From Belknap's house." She unhappily added, "I've spoken to him a few times."

I mentioned, "And I hope he remembers them as warm and pleasant conversations."

She stared at me like I was weird.

But seriously, I—actually, we all—needed to open our minds a bit. With only suggestive evidence, with no scintilla of anything substantive, we had slipped the noose around this poor schnook's neck. The more circumstantial the case, the more somebody needs to tamp the breaks and sniff for the bullshit. I'm good at dubious.

In truth, Jason Barnes had led an honorable, in fact an exemplary life—military college, three years as a Jarhead, Secret Service—all in all, a life dedicated to the trinity of God, country, and family. Also, crime originates in the mind, and what was missing here was the why—as in, *why* would this gilded paragon of red-blooded American goodness become a homicidal maniac?

Or was there another side to Jason Barnes, a shred or shard burrowed so deeply that his supervisors, peers, and a shrink entirely missed it? Was he a split personality, half Mr. Goodbar and half Simon LaGreedy? As a member of the Secret Service, Jason had surely been apprised of the bounty on his boss's head—all that cash, for whoever had big enough brass balls to collect it. Possibly. However, nothing in his life pattern suggested money was the flame that lit his wick.

Of course, people change. Daily proximity to all that power and money can wear on the soul, the mind, and the spirit. The poor schlep gets up in the morning, drives his crapped-out Mazda to the manor house, and then squats in a cramped and dreary subterranean cell, through the cameras observing the Lord and Mistress upstairs entertaining the glitterati, gleaming Mercedeses stacked out front, people in tuxes and evening gowns guzzling the bubbly, trading political fixes, and plunking $50K checks into the coffers of the Grand Old Party.

Or had Jason Barnes experienced some spastic metamorphosis? Some galvanizing revelation that sent him caterwauling into a homicidal rage?

I mentally ran his life backward. His father was a judge, and had in all likelihood filled his son's head and heart with lofty notions about equality and justice. He was raised in Richmond, a bastion of southern culture, largely bypassed by the carpetbaggers, which was both a good and a bad thing. Having once spent a few weeks in Richmond on a case, I recalled it as one of those cities with a quaint, almost small-town feel and insular, tight-knit neighborhoods. Being a prominent judge's child could not have been easy for little Jason Barnes. Army bases have that same close-knit aura, and as a colonel's kid, I remembered the way other kids and their parents looked at me when I did bad things. Boy, did I remember.

Also, we knew for a fact that Jason was a pious man whose adulthood had been cloistered in monasteries to high ideals and patriotic virtues. We had uncovered his monkish lifestyle, and witnessed his quirky appetite for neatness and order, so the obvious question now seemed to be: How deep and how wide did that go?

In the enlightened words of somebody, it's not the cynics who ignite revolutions, it's the disillusioned idealists. Perhaps Jason Barnes took a long and disquieting peek behind the curtain of the counterfeit reality, at the pulleys and levers behind the spin machine, at the money that greased the machinery, at the full hypocrisy of democracy, so to speak, and maybe . . . well, maybe Jason decided that somebody needed to clean up this mess. Maybe.

Both motives sounded reasonable: greed, the oldest engine of dirty deeds; and rage, the nectar of history's most appalling crimes. Yet neither rationalized the sheer extravaganza of killing. A pious man on a moral crusade doesn't massacre innocents, and a greedy man has his own reasons to be circumspect in his actions. The contradictory extremes made no sense, unless we were missing some connecting line between the victims. And if Jason's motive was money, why leave that leading note at Belknap's home? And why put Fineberg and Benedict in the morgue?

The catch with a bounty is you have to be alive, free, and clear to cash in. And it is drilled into the thick skull of every Marine infantry lieutenant in Tactics 101 that surprise is a decisive advantage, not to be wasted through error or careless judgment.

It made no sense that Jason Barnes would identify his intention, his mission, and his target.

And just as I was mulling those vexing issues, Director Townsend won the booby prize. He looked up and mentioned, "According to this form his father is Calhoun Barnes." He looked around the table. "*Judge* Calhoun Barnes?"

Jennie replied, "His supervisor mentioned his father's a . . . a federal judge, I believe."

Director Townsend put down his folder and blinked a few times. "Doesn't anybody here appreciate the monumental significance of that fact?"

I looked at Jennie, but she had suddenly pushed back from the table and was whispering furtively into her cell phone.

The other faces around the table were clueless.

The name struck a bell with me for some reason that, unfortunately, I couldn't put my finger on. Something.

Townsend folded his hands in a temple and informed us, "Calhoun Barnes was on the President's short list for the next Supreme Court opening. That fact was leaked to the press and widely disseminated."

All of a sudden it came back to me.

The light apparently flipped on for Mrs. Hooper as well, who uttered, "Holy shit. This guy is Calhoun Barnes's kid?"

"It appears that he is," Townsend replied, also sounding not overly pleased.

But before we could probe more deeply into that dark revelation, Jennie punched off her cell phone and bent forward. She announced, "That was Roy Ellington from forensics." She added, "During our search of Barnes's townhouse, Sean and I forwarded his shoes to the lab for comparison with the foot molds taken from Belknap's garden. We have a perfect match."

George had been quietly sulking and he came out of his funk. "Tell us about that."

"Jason Barnes's running shoes correspond exactly to a set of prints found in the garden, and some partial dirt tracks located inside the house."

George asked the obvious. "Then Barnes was at the house this morning?"

I asserted my lawyership, replying, "It means his shoes were at the house."

"Shoes don't walk without feet in them," George insisted.

Jennie reported, "The lab also discovered traces of the mulch on his shoes. Apparently, afterward, he returned home and changed, before he disappeared."

Mr. Wardell commented, "Look, before everybody . . . well . . . the shoeprints . . . I mean, Barnes worked at that house, and—"

"We considered that, Chuck," Jennie informed him. "But Barnes made a mistake."

"Meaning what?"

"The Belknaps entertained last night. According to the security log, Mrs. Belknap had her yard service tidy up before the party. The grass was cut, the garden was raked, and a fresh layer of mulch was applied around 4:00 P.M.—three hours after Barnes's shift ended."

"Yes, but . . . I . . . I know I sound . . . well, stubborn but—"

"If he returned after his shift," Jennie persisted, "to chat with a colleague, whatever . . . it's not listed in the security log."

"Maybe they forgot to log him in."

Director Townsend said, "But it's unresolvable, isn't it? That whole shift is dead."

We all nodded at this unimpeachable truth.

But what Wardell, in fact, what everybody, excluding Townsend, Mrs. Hooper, and I, failed to yet appreciate, was why—as in *why* Jason Barnes might feel impelled to murder the President, his spokesperson, and a Supreme Court justice.

Mrs. Hooper had apparently heard enough. She announced, "It's time to put out an advisory to all federal employees. They should vary their daily routines and their routes to and from work." She paused and looked around the table at the security professionals. "Does anybody disagree?"

Nobody disagreed.

I pictured a bunch of federal employees the next morning kissing their wives, husbands, and kiddies good-bye, wondering if they should be kissing their own asses good-bye. Washington was not ready for this.

Townsend turned to George and somewhat gruffly said, "You've got until morning to discover where these military munitions came from."

George nodded.

Phyllis added, "And perhaps you can ascertain what other weapons or munitions they got their hands on."

Townsend acknowledged this sage advice with a nod and said, "That would allow us to assess what they could reasonably do, our risks, what we need to protect against."

We all thought about that a moment. If the killers had Stinger antiaircraft missiles, Mr. President better stick with trains. If they had more antitank missiles, even the Oval Office was no longer safe. If they had anthrax or a suitcase nuke, we should *all* be thinking about an excuse to leave town.

Townsend turned next to Jennie and ordered, "Send somebody to Richmond. I want Mrs. Calhoun Barnes interrogated tonight." He added, very forcefully, "Our challenge is to match the speed of our investigation to the velocity of whatever the killers are planning. The federal government does not have a reputation for quickness.

I challenge all of you to overcome that. Oh—and by morning I would like to have some idea who his co-conspirators are."

It was interesting that he said "his co-conspirators," as though there were no longer any doubts or equivocations about what Jason Barnes had been up to that day. Inside this room Barnes was now The Man.

I wasn't so sure about that. In my view, the problem with the FBI is they spend all their time catching criminals, whereas I, a former defense counsel, spent a good part of my career getting them off. It's all about mindset.

As an old criminal law prof used to impress upon us, remember the fifty-fifty rule: Anytime you have a fifty-fifty chance of getting it right, there's a 90 percent probability you'll get it wrong.

Director Townsend looked in my general direction and said, "Drummond, you figure that one out."

Right.

CHAPTER TEN

ON THAT UNHAPPY NOTE, THE OFFICIAL PART OF THE MEETING ENDED, and everybody broke into small knots, tidying up loose ends and exchanging whatnots.

Meany, I noticed, was buttonholed by his boss, Townsend, and the loose knot they were transparently tying was George's ass. They stood in the far corner, George, stiff and erect, arms at his sides, occasionally recoiling as his boss spoke with his chin jutted forward, hands locked on his hips.

What I would've paid to overhear that discussion.

Mrs. Hooper of the White House was trapped in the other corner, having her ear bent by frisky little Gene Halderman, who was still struggling to find a purpose, useful or otherwise. The loose end they seemed to be wrestling with was how to break this shower of bad news on the unsuspecting public. I couldn't wait for the morning news shows to see the spin they put on this one. I pictured the anchor saying, "The White House this morning announced that in collaboration with the D.C. mayor's office all government officials are strongly encouraged to participate in a traffic management experiment and to vary their routes to and from work." Pause. "In other local news, local stores have reported an unexplained rush on bulletproof vests and armored cars."

Mr. Wardell had not budged from his seat, and nobody was dropping by to tie knots, trade hints, or even offer bromides. I think it was dawning on him for perhaps the first time that his beloved Service had two feet really sunk in the doo-doo. He was thumbing through the folder on Jason Barnes, rubbing his forehead, and I've seen shell-shocked soldiers who looked more with-it. In fact, he was probably wondering how much worse this could get. Worse, Chuck. Given how much Barnes knows about the security force and procedures protecting the President, your worst nightmare.

I also stuck around for a few minutes to get my marching orders from Phyllis, which did not start off convivially. I mean, did she say, "Well, Sean, what a very impressive display of detective work, both at the Hawk's house and on the beltway, and I apologize for my earlier nastiness, because you're really some guy"? No, she withdrew a cell phone from her purse, showed me how the on button functioned, and called to my attention the career benefits of checking in often. The lady was pissed, I could tell. She even threatened to make me produce written reports. I'll take the poisoned cigar, thank you.

As I mentioned, I'm not an easy man to have working for you. I actually felt a genuine spike of regret for the difficulties and anxieties I had caused Phyllis, and I silently vowed to do better.

In fact, I assured her, "Will do," hoping she didn't see my crossed fingers.

She nodded knowingly and patted my shoulder. "Better do."

"Anything else?"

"Only this. Mort has been combing through the reports pouring in from our station chiefs. It seems word about the bounty was known more universally than we thought."

I nodded.

"But," she continued, "nearly every international intelligence institution discounted or dismissed it—just as we did. They concluded it was a joke or an elaborate hoax."

"And their thinking now?"

"They think we have a very big problem."

"And they're glad it's not their problem."

"Actually . . . they're worried it might be their problem."

"Meaning what?"

"They're desperately hoping none of their people put up the money, and none of their native criminal enterprises or terrorists are trying to collect it."

Right. America had changed since 9/11, and the rest of the world was experiencing a jolt of dislocation, not to mention anxiety adjusting to the new reality. It's like waking up one morning and discovering your generous, happy-go-lucky next-door neighbor with that frisky Lab just moved out, a grumpy gun collector moved in, and his three Dobermans are pissing all over your wife's prize rhododendrons. It's a little scary. You really don't need your kids tossing eggs at his front door. The Pentagon was probably lit up like a Christmas tree.

Phyllis droned on a bit longer about the activities of our friendly counterterrorist people, who, she assured me, were working around the clock to figure out where all the known and suspected terrorists in America were at that moment, what they were up to, even scrubbing the immigration files to see if anybody dark and moody had sneaked across the border in the past few months.

Some interesting leads and developments were being considered, and they were still beating the bricks, hustling their sources, and squeezing their stoolies. But nothing had popped, so far.

I wasn't optimistic. In truth, the intelligence agencies are so fragmented and compartmentalized, one hand never knows what the other's doing. Often, one hand doesn't know what *it's* doing.

Another annoying reality was that my Top Secret clearance was so pathetically limited I could barely peek into my own desk drawer. This sucked. Intelligence agencies are so risk-averse that information is never released until it's been checked six ways from Sunday, massaged, dry-cleaned of conjectures and assumptions, and stuffed with so many maybes, possiblys, and on the other hands that you aren't even sure about the date at the top of the memo. So you find out on Friday about the terrorist attack coming on Saturday, only it was last Saturday. The point is, you have to see what's working when it's still called soft intelligence, because usually by the time it hardens, it's irrelevant.

Phyllis, on the other hand, had so many initials and suffixes attached to her clearance, she could sniff the Director's undershorts.

Also it went without saying that the counterterrorist folks were targeting most of this gumshoe effort at Arabs, or, more broadly, those who practice the Muslim faith. This had become the venerable convention, and while it is politically incorrect in our tolerant nation to even allude to terrorism as a religious cause or crusade, try walking onto an airplane these days thumbing through the Koran. Right.

Yet it struck me that the people doing these killings probably weren't Arabs, jihadists, anybody who gave a rat's ass about Allah, or even anybody who glanced toward Mecca, except to watch a cool sunrise. This felt too secular and, in a way, either too personal or not personal enough.

But I didn't confide this thought to Phyllis. When you tell smart people obvious things they conclude you're not smart.

Anyway, we finished up, and I decided I should exercise my discretion and pass these latest updates on to Jennie. So I walked out the door, and to my surprise, George grabbed my arm and muttered, "You and I need to have a word—in private."

I stared down at his hand.

Two seconds of awkward silence passed before he released his grip and stepped back. He drew a few breaths, smiled, and suggested, in a more suspiciously polite tone, "I just think we need to have a confidential discussion."

"Fine."

George led me down the hallway and around a corner where we were out of everybody's earshot and, more curiously, everybody's eyesight. He spun around and we ended up face-to-face, about a foot apart. He looked coiled and pissed off, and I wasn't sure if he was going to throw a punch or kiss me. For the record, I preferred the punch.

But George did neither. He gave me a hard stare and said, "Do I have to tell you how much I dislike being set up in front of Townsend?"

"As much as I dislike having my observations plagiarized?"

George was neither faintly embarrassed nor even interested in this accusation of rotten behavior. He said, "Look, I know it was her."

I yawned. "Busy day, George . . . bodies piling up. We through?"

George was obviously acting on an angry impulse, and it

took a moment for his wits to catch up with his mouth. He offered me a chummy smile. "Look, Sean, I know you and I have a . . . a complicated relationship."

"What's complicated, George? We don't like each other."

"I like you."

I stared at him.

Even he laughed. "All right. But I admire you. I actually envy your sixth sense, and your understanding of the criminal mind."

"Should I say thank you?"

"You should consider it. You owe me a big one. I requested your assignment to this task force."

"How very generous of you."

My sarcasm hit the mark, because he replied, "It was, believe it or not. You'll get good exposure if you do well."

"I'll bet. Last time, I got *you* promoted, as I recall."

"There'll be plenty of credit to go around this time. Don't worry about it."

In fact, I wasn't worried about it. I thought of June Lacy, missing her wedding and her life; about the bodies on the beltway; about the newly deceased Supreme Court justice; and it struck me that the point where anybody should get credit was long past, regardless of how this turned out.

George, however, thought differently and informed me, "She wants my job. She's scheming . . . she's deliberately undermining me."

"Why would I give a shit?"

"Well, that's the spirit. You shouldn't. In fact, that's what I'm warning you. Back me up, and I'll back you up. You're a smart guy, right? Smart guys don't end up on the losing team."

"Warning me?"

He sort of smiled. "I wouldn't want you to get confused or to misconstrue my meaning."

"Or what?"

The smile evaporated. "Get your head out of your ass, Drummond. I'm offering you good advice, and a good deal. Help me out, and I'll help you out. I'd just like an early heads-up on what she's up to—any discoveries. I don't need surprises."

I don't really like threats. And I definitely didn't like George. Also I doubt it escaped him—it certainly didn't escape me—that this was the second time a woman had come between us, so to speak.

Maybe if I watched more soap operas I'd have a better idea how to handle these things. Maybe not.

I said to George, "Thanks for the lecture . . . advice . . . whatever." In other words, fuck you.

He started to say something, but apparently thought better of it, spun around, and left.

I walked back to the conference room, where I saw Jennie speaking quietly into her cell phone. She saw me and punched off, but I must've looked guilty or something, because she asked, "Was that about me?"

"I don't know what you're talking about."

"You're a lousy liar."

"That really hurts, Jennie. I'm a lawyer."

She laughed. "Cut it out."

"All right, truth—George wanted to know if I thought you liked him. I think he's . . . you know . . . a little infatuated with you."

She poked my shoulder. "He told you I'm a scheming bitch. He warned you to watch your ass around me. Right?"

I suppose I looked a little surprised.

She laughed. "I told you—I'm smart."

"But I—"

"Look, it's not the first time. Meany began playing this twisted game the day I started working for him."

"Why?"

She considered my question. She said, "How well do you know George?"

"I never drop the soap when we shower together."

She laughed.

She took my arm, an intimate gesture that surprised me, and began leading me down the hall. For some reason, my thoughts drifted to Janet up in Boston, and I felt a twinge of guilt I clearly did not deserve. I mean, this was perfectly innocent—just two professional colleagues who coincidentally had a few different glands, having an innocuous conversation in the hallway of a government building. Her attractiveness aside, our relationship was entirely professional, we both had enough on our agendas, and any thought of sex was trouble.

Agent Margold, incidentally, smelled great, no longer lemony, more lavenderish, which is actually a big turn-on. I mean, there's something about flowers and sex, like chocolate syrup and ice cream. Why else do guys bring flowers to dates? Right. Jennie remarked, "George has a reputation in the Bureau. He's a great agent, resourceful, diligent, and clever. He's broken some big cases, and it's been noticed by the powers that be."

I sensed that she didn't expect me to comment, and I didn't. She continued, "It's gone to George's head. He's become . . . obsessed with his own success. Driven."

"Go on."

She said, "When the SAC job opened a few months ago, it was between me and a more senior agent. The other agent was already assigned to the D.C. office, was popular with the rank and file, and he knew the local ropes. Through the grapevine I heard he badly wanted the job." After a moment she added, "I let it be known I wasn't interested."

"Why?"

"The other man was a great agent, I thought he deserved it, and I thought he'd do a great job. Of course, George was the real reason."

"Again, why?"

"Wrong chemistry . . . it wouldn't work."

"Again—why?"

"Let me finish. John Fisk got the job. About a month later he died."

"Natural causes or line of duty?"

"What's natural for our business? He walked into a sniper's crosshairs."

"I don't recall hearing about it."

"You wouldn't. He was at a conference in San Francisco. Big news out there, page four in the *Post* here."

"Oh."

"Here's the irony—the conference topic concerned policing techniques to handle the recent spate of sniper killings. He walked out of his hotel for breakfast, and somebody with a long-range rifle put two shots through his forehead."

"I'll bet that livened up the conference."

"Not really. John was supposed to give the keynote that morning."

"Big hole in the agenda."

"And in John."

"Right, and in John. But to whack a cop at a cop convention . . . that's— Did they get the guy?"

"Still at large." She added, "But we have a strong suspicion who was behind it."

"I have an alibi for that weekend."

She punched my shoulder again. "Prior to John's assignment to D.C., he led a Long Island unit that specialized in mob cases. He broke some big ones that really hurt them."

"I thought offing feds and cops was sort of taboo with the goombahs. Isn't it supposed to be bad for business or something?"

She nodded. "Yes, we make it very bad for their business. But they make exceptions. What we think was something John did, somebody perceived as personal." She shrugged. "Anyway, we'll find them—and we'll get them. Murdering one of us is something *we* take personally."

It struck me that the mob and FBI are in some ways similar, like yin and yang, both being sort of fraternal organizations with distinct cultures, and a taste for what the mob calls revenge and the Bureau calls justice. It's interesting. Back to the subject, I said, "So you ended up with the job after all?"

"And with George." She smiled faintly. "You don't say no to Director Townsend if you want a future in the Bureau."

"I'll bet. What happened?"

"What happened?" She paused as though this was awkward. "Coming from the Behavioral Science Unit, I'm regarded as an outsider. I'm out of the mold. They're mostly lawyers, former cops, and accountants. I'm neither fish nor fowl, *and* there've been some transference issues."

"Meaning what?"

"Well . . . I got this job because John Fisk was murdered."

"They can't hold that against you."

"Consciously, they don't. But subconsciously, it's a factor and a fact." She added, "I don't blame them."

"Sure you do. They're assholes."

She laughed. "I'm a shrink, Sean. I've been trained to view people and situations with clinical detachment. It's a perfectly natural response, really—a common form of grief, actually." After a moment she added, "And yes, they're all assholes."

But in retrospect, a few disconnected pieces and loose threads fell into place. Like the pair of agents at Belknap's house that morning twiddling their thumbs. Or the peculiar reticence of the agent who refused to give Jennie a full and comprehensive explanation about Fineberg's murder. It was reassuring to learn they weren't just idiots and incompetents. It was disturbing to learn they were sandbagging Jennie Margold, my putative partner. This was a little scary. I asked her, "What's Meany's role in this?"

"He perceives me as a competitor."

"I see."

"Do you?" she asked. "I'm now one of the five highest-ranking women in the Bureau. At thirty-five, I'm the youngest. There are only three female SACs, the Bureau has an awful reputation with feminists, a clique of females on the Hill are pressuring for reform . . . and, by the way, two high-level assistant directorships are scheduled to open next year."

I said, "And George is undermining you?"

"Destroying me."

"Like . . . how?"

"Every trick in the book—isolation, cutting off my information flow, spreading rumors, stealing credit for my work. He's very clever." After a moment she confided, "He's making my life hell."

In fact, George had made my life very difficult for a few weeks and I hadn't even been working under him. But basically, set aside his vanity, ambition, and penchant for treachery, and George wasn't such a bad guy.

We had passed through the exit and were now outside in the parking lot, standing beside Jennie's shiny black government sedan. Somewhere nearby, a helicopter was waiting to whisk us off to Richmond and Mrs. Calhoun Barnes. It was an ideal night for flying—a beautiful evening, not a cloud in the sky, lots of glittery stars, the air still and humid. Also nearby, somebody, perhaps named Jason Barnes, was plotting another murder.

We stopped walking, and she continued to hold my arm, and it became, well . . . a little distracting. Between this case and her diabolical boss, Jennifer Margold was under crushing pressure. She looked nonplussed, but I wondered if it was getting under her skin. The sexes tend to handle these things differently. Men get grouchy, and/or they drink a lot, or they climb up on a watchtower with a sniper rifle. Women feel compelled to be nurtured, they need physical contact, reassurance. It all goes back to the womb, I think. I'm not really good at reading women. I said, "You're smarter than him."

"Perhaps."

"Outthink him."

"In this game, the fox sometimes beats the owl."

She pulled my arm and turned my body, and we ended up facing each other, about a foot apart, maybe less. Her breath smelled cinnamony, and a cool breeze blew the hair off her forehead. She smelled and looked yummy. The woman was in distress and was vulnerable, which surely accounted for the spasm of protective machoism I was feeling. We looked into each other's eyes and I realized I was attracted, a little infatuated, and curious to see where this was going. But I was already involved, and of course, mixing office politics and sex is a recipe for getting doubly screwed.

I recalled a woman friend once informing me that what makes men different from women is simple: A woman wants one man to satisfy her every need, where a man wants every woman to satisfy his one need. Not true—simply not true. But true enough.

She said, "This is my problem . . . not yours. I'm telling you because . . . because, I don't want you getting cut down in the crossfire."

"I can take care of myself."

She smiled. "Still . . . watch your back."

"No problem. I've handled George with one arm tied behind my back."

I had the sense that my mucho-machoness wasn't selling, but she said, "Oh yeah. Over a woman . . . right?" When I failed to reply, she said, "Is it . . . I mean, are you . . . still involved?"

"Are you?"

"Well . . . call ahead for Saturday nights."

"I meant, anybody special?"

"Me? You know, the occasional billionaire bachelor . . . a few Nobel prizewinners. The problem with D.C. is you never meet anyone interesting." I think she was kidding and maybe replying in kind to my maladroit evasiveness. She squeezed my arm. "What about *you*?"

"Oh . . . me? Well, it's a little complicated."

"Complicated?"

After a moment I said, "She's not exclusive." I added, "So . . . I guess, I don't have to be. Right?"

"I don't know your arrangement."

"Well . . . neither do I."

Which raised the ever-evocative question—was it a good thing? Actually, Janet's career, my career, and the time and distance between Washington and Boston were in the middle, we both knew it, and neither of us had taken a single constructive step to rectify it. That said something, I think. Ours was a sometimes thing, leaving me too much free time, too much freedom, and we all know idle hands become playful hands.

Of course, I'm Catholic, and coital loyalty and that till-death-do-you-part thing are big with us. So is the obvious corollary, the get-it-all-out-of-your-system-first thing. I said, "Don't worry about it."

"Why would I be worried about it?"

"Oh." Had I misread a signal here?

She smiled. "We're partners. Partners should know a little about each other, right?"

"Right. So . . . are you a cream and sugar in your coffee person?"

"Tea person, Earl Grey preferably. No additives."

"Blood type?"

"A pos. Yours?"

"Ice water."

She laughed.

Anyway, a mass murderer was running around Washington, her boss was cutting her throat, mine wanted to throttle me, and there I stood, lightheaded and giddy, making an idiot of myself.

Time to change the subject, and I said, "Richmond."

"Right. Judge Calhoun Barnes, what do you know about him?"

"As your boss said, he was on the short list for the next Supreme Court opening."

"Why is that past tense?"

"He died."

"Oh. Well, he must've been a good judge."

"Judges are always in the eye of the beholder. The profile I read on him described him as a law-and-order fanatic, ultraconservative, a strict constructionist, brutal on criminals. Great guy,

if you're a prosecutor. A monster, if you're the accused, or repre-
senting the accused."

She looked at me and asked, "Do you know how he died?"

"I do."

"Don't keep things from me."

I smiled. "Find out when we get there."

CHAPTER ELEVEN

AS I SAID, IT WAS ONE OF THOSE PERFECT NIGHTS TO FLY, CLEAR SKIES IN every direction, silvery moon, no wind or choppiness, and it was smooth sailing as we left Washington in our wake.

I was becoming very intrigued with the woman beside me, and as I knew virtually nothing about her, this was a little presumptuous and possibly premature. When somebody dissects criminal minds for a living, you have to wonder.

After we got comfortable, I said to her, "Tell me why you decided to become a shrink."

After a moment, she smiled. "As in all shrinks are nuts and what's a nice girl like me doing in a strange place like this? Isn't that what you're asking?"

"Exactly."

"Watch it, pal."

I smiled. "I would think it's very challenging to remain sane when you study the criminal mind. Doesn't it—"

"Get to me?" After a moment she said, "You know the hardest part? Putting yourself in the frame of the victim. That comes with the job. You have to see and observe a crime from both angles."

Having prosecuted and defended, I also had experienced that part of the job, albeit with a bit more healthy detachment than allowed in her field. So I had an idea where she was coming from. It sucked.

She continued, "The easier part is understanding the criminal. I know this sounds . . . maybe a little abnormal . . . but for a trained psychiatrist the criminal mind is endlessly fascinating. The things they do, how they do it, why. Also you bear in mind that it's for the greater good. If you don't answer those questions, you can't find them, you can't catch them, and you can't get them off the streets."

I said, "I knew a shrink in the Army. A little offbeat, but basically a good guy. Over a beer one night he told me that after sessions with the real nutsos, he thought of home, his wife, his kids, and that brought him back."

"A professor of mine called it the anchor that keeps the ship from drifting. Being single, I think about my parents, about my childhood in Ohio."

"Mom and Dad must be proud of you."

"Mom and Dad are dead. Car accident, when I was thirteen. They left one night to get some groceries, it was snowing, and they never came back."

"Brothers? Sisters?"

"None. But my parents were both wonderful. Dad was an executive at a food company, an up-and-comer. Mom, she was just Mom. He was tall, handsome, and brilliant, and she was beautiful and charming. Dad read to me every night, and Mom fixed my boo-boos."

"Good memories."

"The best." She smiled. "Now I'm going to sleep. Keep talking if you like. I'm going to stop listening."

I catnapped until the bounce of the machine setting down jarred me awake. Through the window, I could see that we were in a large, lit parking lot in the middle of Richmond proper and, more happily, that we hadn't crashed. I don't particularly trust things without wings that fly. I checked my watch. Nearly midnight.

Through the window, to our left, and about forty yards off in the distance, I noted the distinctive roof and columned portico of the Capitol Building of the Commonwealth of Virginia.

I recalled from some high school state history class that this building was regarded as an exemplar of neoclassical Roman architecture, planned by Thomas Jefferson, who had also designed the University of Virginia, erected Monticello, invented a bunch of furniture, drafted a constitution, was a Secretary of State, a President, ran a plantation, and raised a family, or possibly two. I can barely find time to do my laundry.

Jennie's head rested comfortably on my right shoulder, and I gently nudged her awake. Her eyes opened and I informed her, "We're here."

"Where's here?"

"Maybe where it all began."

"Do you really believe that?"

I replied, "I believe in Chekhov's rule."

"The Russian writer?"

"Same guy. If a gun is revealed in Act One, it must go off in Act Four. The gun already went off—it's time to go back to the first act and find out why."

She sat up and stretched. She said, "I'm going to confess something you might find . . . a little strange."

"You like me?"

She punched me. "Not that strange." She said, "I hope we're wrong. I truly do. I'd hate to think one of the good guys turns out to be a bad guy."

Nice sentiment, although I really hoped she was wrong. If we didn't get a break soon, the federal government was going to be depopulated, and Ms. Margold and Mr. Drummond were going to be standing on somebody's carpet explaining why we let that happen. Surely she knew that. I said, "Get your stuff. Let's go."

About thirty feet from the helicopter, a shiny blue Crown Victoria and a shiny young man, who introduced himself as Special Agent Theodore "call me Ted" Baltimore, awaited us. Ted jumped into the driver's seat, we climbed into the backseat, he twisted around and informed us, with true southern surliness, "Buckle your seat belts."

I said, "Wha—"

"Don't you argue with me, sir. Bureau policy. Buckle up or the car ain't movin'."

I felt a strong urge to choke Ted to death. But Jennie said, "Thank you, Agent." She buckled up, glanced at her watch, and asked, very nicely, "You live here, Ted? In Richmond?"

"Sure do."

"Like it?"

"Yup. Born hereabouts. Home for me."

"I'm glad to hear that, Ted." After a moment she added, "You have eight minutes to deliver us at Mrs. Barnes's front door. Eight and a half, and I'll have your ass shipped off to the northern tip of Alaska."

"You're kiddin', right?"

"It's late, I'm tired, and I'm having a really bad day."

The stakes and the pecking order apparently crystallized in

Ted's mind; he punched the accelerator and burned rubber out of the parking lot. We took a right and then a left and another right and then we barreled at high speed down a wide boulevard filled with office buildings. Ted asked Jennie, "All right with you, ma'am, if I flip the lights and siren?"

She said, "Yeah, great idea—wake everybody up." I made a note to remember that Ms. Margold woke up a tad on the moody side.

"Yee-hah," squealed Ted, reaching out the window and slapping a light on the roof.

I leaned forward and asked Ted, "You go to Ole Miss?"

"Hell no!" He laughed. "That school ain't good for nothin', 'cept, sometimes, maybe football." After a moment he added, "Alabama U—better football, better parties, and better women."

"Right." And there, in a nutshell, was the mentality of the young, virile southern male. Ted yelled, "Hey, what the hell y'all got goin' up there in Washington? A goddamn war, sounds like."

So, having nothing better to do, Jennie and I took turns giving Ted a watered-down version of the killings, withholding the juicy parts, like why and who, which wasn't difficult, since the who remained an open question, and we had not a clue why. That could change in the next hour, or it might not. But it hadn't changed yet. Anyway, everything we informed Ted about he could get off the morning news, and when we'd concluded our little duet, Ted commented, "Sheeeit."

Having lived in the South, I was aware this amorphous expression actually meant, "Well, that's a sizable issue, and I sympathize with you." It can also mean, "Sounds like you're utterly fucked."

Anyway, having gratified his curiosity and established a spirit of mutual bonhomie, I asked Ted, "Did you know Judge Barnes?"

He scratched his head and thought about that. He said, "He

was federal. Had a few cases got worked up to his level. Never testified myself. Heard his reputation, though."

"And what was his reputation?"

"A good judge. Hated criminals. Heard he was a fine man, too." He added, "Damned shame what happened."

Jennie asked, "What did happen?"

I suggested to Ted, "Why don't you take a stab at that?"

"Sheeit."

In this case, I believe the aphorism meant, "Forget it, pal."

"Suicide," I informed Jennie. "The judge hung himself."

"Not exactly," Ted corrected. "The man shot *and* hanged hisself."

Jennie asked, "Simultaneously?"

"Hard to do sequentially," Ted replied with a rare, thoughtful expression.

Jennie asked, "Is that possible?"

"Guess so."

"But . . . how?"

"Seems he got hisself up on a stool, slipped a rope 'round his neck, and put his granddaddy's revolver in his mouth. Pulled the trigger and kicked at the same time."

"That's unusual," commented Jennie.

"Yup," replied Ted. "A meticulous man. Don't see many like that these days."

No kidding, Ted.

Jennie turned and asked me, "Do we know *why* he killed himself?"

"That's what we're here to find out."

We had just departed a business section and entered a long and obviously prosperous urban boulevard. Homes of considerable size and grandeur closely bordered the sides of the street, grand manses from another time and another era, when Richmond was widely regarded as the Rome of the South. Times change, the Old South is gone, the New South has risen, and Atlanta and New Orleans have long since eclipsed Richmond as business, cultural, and political epicenters. Richmond has become a backwater, but it remains a lovely, even pleasant place, while Atlanta now has all the character and charm of L.A. sans palm trees. Narrow grass strips divided the thoroughfare, and every block or two stood a statue of a long-dead Virginian hero disinterring old myths and glories. "Still the best street in Richmond," Ted informed us. "Used to be, took tobacco money to live here. Mostly, nowadays, it's lawyers and doctors."

Jennie commented, "Darwinism."

Ted replied, "Whatism?" apparently missing this anthropological farce. What once gave wealth, prosperity, and optimism to Richmond's finer residents remained a meal ticket, and now it was lawyers and oncologists cashing in.

Ted swung hard to the right, hit the brakes, and we screeched to a sharp halt at the curb of a three-story townhouse. Clearly, Judge Barnes had not been without means. Actually, the guy was loaded. The house was tall, wide, and constructed of sturdy southern clay brick that had browned with age. From the looks of it, the house was circa 1920 or so, and in the architectural manner of that era, was austere, not garish or ostentatious, though still regal and impressive. The building's facade appeared well-kempt and tended, though the grass and shrubbery in front were overgrown and in need of loving care, evidence of a widow as the landlady.

Perhaps it was the darkness, but the judge's house struck me as slightly creepy and claustrophobic, a brooding gothic tableau awaiting a nightmare appropriate to its size and scale. But my imagination sometimes runs away with me.

Ted commented, "Whew—seven and a half minutes."

Jennie said, "Lucky you."

"Sheeit," said Ted, surely meaning, Yes, indeed, lucky me.

Two agents stood guard outside the door, and we clearly were expected, as one rushed forward and opened the rear door for Jennie. He informed her, "Mrs. Barnes is waiting in the home office. Incidentally, she goes by Margaret. I wouldn't suggest you call her Marge, or Maggie." He added, "Per orders, we haven't disclosed what this is about."

Jennie replied, "Good." She turned and said to me, "This is going to be delicate. If we upset her, she'll clam up. Let me handle it."

"You mean I can't just throttle her and ask how she raised a monster?"

"You cannot." She smiled. "Unless I get nowhere. Then she's all yours."

The agent pushed open the door and we three passed through the threshold with the sure knowledge we were about to ruin Margaret Barnes's night.

CHAPTER TWELVE

HE FIRST THING I NOTICED WAS THE SILVER TRAY ON A SMALL TABLE BY THE front door. I recalled a time when such trays were fixtures in the homes of senior officers, intended for visitors and guests to deposit business cards and thank-you notes. Agency people don't carry business cards, at least not real ones. And, after we finished with Mrs. Barnes, a thank-you note was probably out of the question.

But tradition has greater meaning in the South than the North, and the home we entered had the aura of a museum, or perhaps a mausoleum. We passed down a long, high-ceilinged hallway strewn with antique furniture and memorabilia that clearly meant something to the Barneses and looked like old junk to me.

A large living room was to our right, and to our left what is called a parlor, which has passed out of favor even in the South and never was in fashion in the less ceremonious North. I noticed that an elevator had been installed off the living room, perhaps the only nod to modernity in this house. Strewn there and about were paintings of the Barneses' ancestors, some women in antebellum gowns—only one real looker in the group—a few stout gentlemen in gray Civil War costumes and old-fashioned business suits, and so forth.

Above the living room mantel hung a more recent portrait of a man in a dark robe I assumed was Judge Calhoun Barnes, before he blew his brains out, I think.

The gent in the portrait was handsome in a florid, broad-faced manner, barrel-chested, silver-haired, with a long, noble nose, a tight, uncompromising mouth, and fiery eyes that seemed to bore not through, but at you. They were eyes that slammed you against a wall.

I felt an immediate jolt of sympathy for any lawyer who appeared before His Honor's bench. In Judge Barnes's features and facial creases, I observed no self-doubts, no sense of humor, no sympathy, no empathy—in fact, no hint of generosity or good-will. A very talented portrait artist had rendered this pose, and artists are called artists because of their license to interpret reality. But a painter cannot hide, disguise, or absolve the inner essence of his subject, and Calhoun Barnes's inner core was palpable. The man was a bully.

I mentioned to Jennie, after we'd browsed a little more, "This isn't a home. It's a history lesson."

She ignored this aside, and me. True to her craft, she was wandering around, immersing herself in the environment from which Jason Barnes was hatched. Having dealt with a few criminal profilers, I don't pretend to understand their skills, and it all sounds a bit psychobabbly, in my view. But they do put a lot of bad guys in the slammer, so I guess they're okay.

Anyway, we reached the end of the hallway, and where I expected the kitchen there was instead a small waiting room, through which we passed into a spacious, wood-paneled office. The agent who had escorted us inside and guided us through this maze of old furniture and dead Barneses stuck his head into the room and announced, "Special Agent Jennifer Margold is here." He backed out of the office without introducing me, and left us alone with our subject.

We walked to the middle of the room, where Mrs. Barnes remained seated—actually enveloped—inside a huge brown leather club chair with her legs resting comfortably on an overstuffed ottoman.

As I mentioned, Mrs. Barnes did not rise, nor did she offer her hand or proffer a greeting; she merely waved languidly in the direction of a long leather couch punctuated with buttons.

I glanced at our hostess as we sat—she seemed composed, almost smug, perhaps even expectant, as if we were here for her to interrogate us, rather than vice versa. Was she in for a big surprise.

Anyway, compared to Calhoun's portrait, Margaret Barnes was younger, by perhaps a decade, and at least physically, she and he were an interesting study in contrasts and contradictions. She was tiny and slender, frail actually, with a pallor that was unnaturally pale. In fact, her skin was nearly translucent, unlike so many southern ladies who looked like sunbaked prunes. Her features were beautiful and, were it not for the dark circles and deep crevices that surrounded her eyes and the sagging lines around her mouth, might even be considered youthful. Probably these were scars of grief, though they could be something more, something less immediate, something more intrinsically soul-sabotaging.

She looked at me and said, "I'm sorry . . . I didn't catch your name."

"Sean Drummond."

"Well, it's nice to meet you, Mr. Drummond. Are you also an agent?"

"No ma'am."

"Then what are you?"

"Well, I'm . . ." What was I?

"A consultant," Jennie cut in. "He's helping us close some old case files."

Mrs. Barnes smiled and said, "Oh . . . well, that's nice." She gathered her thoughts and added, "I don't understand why you chose to come at this late hour. Though as they say, better late than never."

In fact, there was no way Mrs. Barnes could understand why two federal agents were visiting her house after midnight, though she obviously had an idea, and that idea seemed not to trouble her. Jennie squeezed my leg, a gesture I understood to mean, Don't spook this lady.

Jennie withdrew a tape recorder from her pocketbook and held it up for Mrs. Barnes to observe. She explained, "I'm required to inform you that I'll be recording our conversation."

"I . . . is that necessary?"

"I'm afraid it is." She smiled reassuringly and added, "You're not suspected of any crimes, Mrs. Barnes. It's just a procedural formality."

Mrs. Barnes smiled at me. "I suppose as long as I'm not a suspect . . ."

I smiled back. "Completely harmless." A tape recorder in the hands of a federal agent is *never* harmless, incidentally.

After a moment, she said, "Goodness . . . my manners! Would either of you care for a drink? I know it's late . . . maybe an aperitif?"

I love the way southern women handle these common courtesies like a careless afterthought. I mean, they know it's phony, you know it's phony, and that just makes it more charming.

Margaret Barnes's accent, incidentally, like so much in this house, was a relic, what used to be called a plantation accent— a concoction of squashed vowels and expressive little midsentence bounces. I was sure a ton of Daddy's money went into finishing schools and Sweetbriar College perfecting her sugary tumble of intonations.

But in response to her kind offer, Jennie glanced at me and replied to Mrs. Barnes, "Thank you, we'll have to pass." She added, emphatically, "Hoover's law—federal officers never drink on duty."

I smiled at Mrs. Barnes. "Scotch, if you have it."

Jennie coughed into her hand.

Mrs. Barnes laughed. "'Course. My husband, Calhoun, adored a good scotch. Perhaps you'd be so good as to pour me a sherry as well?"

I got up and walked to the built-in bar across the room. Incidentally, the coda of southern gentility is hospitality, and I was a little surprised that she sent me to fetch the drinks, but happily, hospitality also means a well-stocked bar, and Judge Barnes was a thoughtful host. I poured myself a glass of Calhoun's Glenfiddich, and for Margaret I poured a glass of sherry I was sure Calhoun wouldn't be caught dead drinking.

I walked back and held her sherry slightly beyond her grasp, until it was apparent she could not slide forward and grab it, and it was apparent why. Margaret Barnes was a cripple. I said, "Excuse me," and placed the drink in her hands.

"That's quite all right." But I think she was a little peeved, because she diverted her eyes from me and toward Jennie. She said, "Well! So, to what do I owe this late-night visit . . . Jennifer? Or do you prefer Jennie?"

"I prefer Jennie. Could we begin with a few questions about your husband?"

"Oh . . . then this *does* concern Calhoun?"

"I'd like to begin there, yes."

Margaret Barnes did not bat an eye. She leaned back and her eyes shifted around the room, bringing transparency to why she had chosen to meet us here, in the back study, instead of the living room, or the front parlor, which probably was her custom.

Large and expansive walls surrounded us, and upon them hung the full and impressive regalia of Calhoun Barnes's long career and many accomplishments: his undergraduate and law degrees from the University of Virginia, framed documents ordaining him a city magistrate and then as a federal judge, an array of local awards, and a huge menagerie of photographs of the judge with famous personages.

I immediately ruled out self-esteem issues, frustrated narcissism, or excessive modesty as motives for Calhoun's suicide.

From the rogues' gallery, I picked out three former United States Presidents, a slew of Virginia governors and senators, and in the middle of this menagerie, where it could not be overlooked, a younger Judge Barnes sharing brandy and cigars with Saint J. Edgar Hoover, in this very same room, actually on the very same couch upon which Jennie and I sat. So there we were, so to speak, cheek-to-cheek with greatness.

Also, in the far left upper corner was an old black-and-white photograph of a very young Calhoun Barnes in fishing waders and a plaid shirt, with his arm around an equally young and considerably tinier Justice Phillip Fineberg, also in fishing gear. Interesting.

I met Margaret Barnes's eyes. I noted the obvious. "Your husband was very . . . successful."

"I suppose he was." She added, "I believe all men should have their private enclaves where they can view their triumphs. Don't you think that's so, Mr. Drummond?"

I nodded. "My many accomplishments hang on the wall over my toilet."

She forced a smile. I think my northern charm was wearing thin.

We were supposed to recognize, and we did recognize, that Calhoun Barnes had formed powerful alliances and connections, that his widow wasn't without resources, and that a federal power dance was out of the question. Jennie commented, "Your husband obviously had an extraordinarily successful career. Why did he . . . well—"

"Kill himself? I know what Calhoun did, Jennifer. He put a gun in his mouth, and he slipped a noose around his neck."

"All right. Why?"

But she appeared not to want to address this question yet. It was her intention to control this session, and she suggested, "Would I bore you if I went back a bit in time, to when Calhoun and I met?"

Beyond words. I replied, "Not at all, ma'am."

She took a long sip of sherry. She said, "I think it's important for you to know the Barneses are a venerable name in this city. Calhoun's great-grandfather owned a large and prosperous plantation in the tidewater area. His grandfather was an officer under Stonewall Jackson and was not without accomplishment on the battlefield. He turned to law after the war, moved the family here, and lawyering became their family vocation. In fact, Calhoun's daddy was also an attorney and became a highly regarded judge himself. There was even talk of his daddy ending up on the Supreme Court. I think, had not the Negro issue become so divisive and inflammatory, it likely would have happened."

Nobody spoke for a few moments as we sat and absorbed this tale. With southern aristocracy, family histories are like shadowboxing in a darkroom; you have to fine-tune a bit. In a nutshell, I understood her to say, Calhoun's family once owned a huge spread, big bucks, and mucho slaves, the Civil War came, the slaves hightailed it, the money dried up, the carpetbaggers elbowed in, the Barneses fled, became city folk, became professional, became successful, remained bigots, and history caught up with them. No wonder Faulkner had such a ball with these people.

That's the problem with the whole southern notion of family tradition and lineage; if the past is lily-white, it's okay, I guess—otherwise it's like being born with ten tons of shit on your back. The past is never the past with these people. Somehow this shaped Calhoun Barnes, and somehow this also shaped Jason Barnes.

Mrs. Barnes continued, "My family had a fine pedigree as well. Many thought Calhoun and I would make a good match."

Jennie commented, "He was a handsome man."

"Yes. Calhoun was many things, Jennifer. He played football at the University . . . Later, he became quite accomplished at tennis and golf. And brainy? At law school, he received a slew of offers from prestigious judges and firms from Atlanta to New York." She looked at Jennie and asked, "Are you a lawyer? I know many FBI agents are."

"No. I trained in psychiatry."

She sort of shrugged dismissively. "An interesting field also, I suppose."

Jennie nodded, and I wondered what was going through her mind.

Mrs. Barnes said, "A week after Calhoun passed the bar, he and I walked together down the aisle in the chapel at St. Christopher's, his prep school. This was 1965. He was regarded as quite the catch, and I was regarded as a very lucky woman. But Calhoun didn't want to work for an important judge, or at a big firm."

I asked, "Why not?"

"Well, I suppose we weren't inclined to depart this city for any amount of money."

It sounded like a lovely sentiment, and we both nodded in acknowledgment. Of course, all the money they wanted was in the city.

She added, "But I think Calhoun didn't want to go through the clerking or associate phase of law. He was a hungry man, ambitious and quite impatient. He decided that if he opened his own practice, he could jump ahead of everybody."

Hoping to get us out of this pit of nostalgia, I commented, "I would think he needed partners."

She looked at me a moment. "You're right, Mr. Drummond. And he knew just the right man . . . the top man of his law class, in fact."

I pointed in the direction of the framed picture. "Phillip Fineberg."

"Yes . . . Phillip."

"Good choice."

She did not acknowledge that judgment, and instead sipped from her sherry and studied the ceiling.

She remarked, "It was . . . well, an uneven relationship at first."

"Because Fineberg was Jewish?"

She nodded. "We were always more progressive than Selma, but it was . . . in those days, in this city, *complicated* to be Sephardic. A lot of business occurs on golf courses and at social events, and Phillip didn't— You understand, don't you?"

We understood. I also understood that a man with Calhoun's background and conservative leanings didn't partner with a social pariah to correct a racial injustice, or as an act of generosity.

Anyway, we listened as she prattled on about how Calhoun carried Fineberg on his strong back, the local boy with all the right stuff, schmoozing and boozing, roping in clients by the boatload. And it worked—Barnes and Fine, the title the partners delicately chose for their firm, became highly regarded, successful, and prosperous, in that order.

The chemistry between the founding partners was flawed, and often strained, but greed was the aphrodisiac. Calhoun hauled home the fish, and Fineberg gutted and filleted them, from the backroom, hidden behind his truncated name. The footwork, the research, the briefs, and court preparation fell on Fineberg's brilliant shoulders, and Calhoun was the courtroom shark, racking up victories, hammering witnesses, earning quite the local name as a brainy brawler. Interestingly, Fineberg never once set foot in a courtroom except to deliver a late filing or to help Calhoun haul his thick briefcases back and forth.

It was an intriguing tale with all the makings of a good tragedy, and you sensed where this might be going, but Mrs. Barnes suddenly looked up and said, slightly surprised, "Your glass appears empty, Mr. Drummond. Would you be so kind as to refill both our containers?"

So I did.

At the bar, I turned to her and asked, perhaps undiplomatically, "By the way, what happened to your legs?"

She glanced at me. "My legs are fine."

"I'm sorry. I thought—"

"You thought wrong. My back was broken."

"Oh, well, I'm sorry. How?"

"An automobile accident."

"I see."

I handed her the glass and she immediately took a long gulp of sherry. Eventually, she exhaled deeply and said, "I suppose you're wondering about the rumors?"

"Exactly." I had not a clue what she was talking about.

She stared into her drink and swirled it around a moment. "It's true that Calhoun drove that night. We never denied that."

Jennie tried to catch up and asked Mrs. Barnes, "Could we go back to the beginning?"

"The beginning? Yes . . . that would be spring, 1975, a few months after our son was born. I don't recall the evening overly well. But that sounds a little odd, doesn't it? I mean, you'd think . . ."

Whatever you'd think she let drift off. "We were at the country club," she continued, "celebrating with a client. Calhoun's firm had won a rather sizable settlement. We were driving home when it happened." She looked at me and added, I thought oddly, "But I've never blamed Calhoun."

Jennie asked, "The accident—the police investigated?"

"Calhoun found his way to a phone and he called the hospital and the police."

"And the police came?"

"Yes. An officer arrived shortly before the ambulance."

"And did he do an investigation?"

"There was no need for that, at all. The night was rainy, our car simply lost its traction and hit a tree. Nobody was injured. No property was damaged."

"*You* were injured."

She hesitated, then said, "The officer knew Calhoun. He spared us that indignity and inconvenience."

I noted, "Your insurance company wouldn't regard it as an indignity. The repairs . . . your medical treatments—who paid?"

"Us . . . of course." I suppose we both looked surprised by that revelation, because she explained, "My husband was highly principled, Mr. Drummond. It would have been improper to make somebody else pay for a mistake he regarded as entirely his own."

I wasn't sure how we got waylaid on this particular tangent, which appeared, on the surface, to have no bearing to our investigation. Yet some instinct told me it was relevant, possibly even important. Another instinct told me she was lying, or, at the least, withholding an important piece from this tale, and it wasn't hard to guess what it was. I said, "Mrs. Barnes, if your husband was intoxicated, he was a menace to the public, and his behavior was possibly criminal."

She looked at me a moment. "I did not say Calhoun was drunk."

"Was he?"

"Well, there was not such anxiety in those years about drinking and driving. It really wasn't—"

"Answer my question."

"Calhoun's frien— The officer recognized we had suffered enough. He—"

"Was or was not your husband intoxicated?"

"Calhoun *always* held his liquor well." She paused, then added tersely, "I have no idea why you're asking these questions. I hardly see how they pertain to what you're here to investigate."

I looked at Jennie. She turned to Mrs. Barnes, as if nothing amiss had been said, and asked, "This happened when? A few months after your son's birth? Right?"

"Yes. There were unfortunate complications . . . internal injuries, and . . . well, further babies became beyond our means."

An interesting way to put it. I mentioned, "That must've been difficult for you."

"Oh no, Mr. Drummond. I think our difficulties would have been magnified greatly with another baby."

"Because you were in a wheelchair?"

"I was bedridden for several years. More operations, rehabilitation clinics, and so forth. Then came the wheelchair."

Jennie said, "Yes. It would've been hard enough just raising . . . I apologize . . . your son's name?"

"Jason . . . Jason Nathan. Fortunately, Calhoun was an extraordinary father, very attentive, very active in Jason's life. They were exceedingly close."

Jennie commented, "That's unusual."

"Unusual?"

"A professional man raising an infant, in those years . . ."

Clearly we had tripped over some hidden wire in her psychic security system, because she raised an eyebrow and interrupted, "Why are you interested in that?"

"We're not," I insisted. "What happened to the firm?"

"I do not believe I'm ready to answer that." She looked at me and asked, "Exactly *what* are you two doing here?"

When neither of us responded, she said, "I assumed . . . at least, I expected . . ."

"Expected what?" Jennie asked.

"Well . . . the sabotage of my husband's reputation and . . . who caused Calhoun to kill himself . . . who exploited your Bureau . . . and . . . and who lied . . ."

I said, "Tell us about that."

Her head jerked up. "No . . . no, I don't believe I will. I believe I have already answered enough of your questions." She appeared confused, and suddenly upset, but she collected her wits enough to say, "You should leave my house. Right now, both of you."

I looked at Jennie. Clearly, the curtain had just collapsed on

Act One, and it was time to shift into Act Two, to give Margaret Barnes the proverbial knee in the balls. I said, "Mrs. Barnes, we were sent here by the Director of the FBI. We're not leaving."

"Oh, you are quite wrong about that. It's my home and—"

"Stop talking. Listen." I looked Mrs. Barnes in the eye and informed her, "At approximately 6:20 this morning, the White House Chief of Staff, his wife, and four Secret Service agents were murdered. This afternoon, the President's spokesman was murdered on the Washington beltway, as were seven entirely innocent people." She blinked in confusion, apparently not getting the connection, so to help her along I added, "Moments later, Phillip Fineberg—your husband's former partner—was blown in half as he opened his front door."

"Fineberg? I . . . I don't—"

"Yes . . . I think you do."

Jennie quickly added, "Agent Jason Barnes, your son, has been missing since he went off duty yesterday afternoon. We need your help to stop him before he kills more."

I looked at Margaret Barnes's stricken face and realized my earlier prediction had come true. We had just ruined her night, and very possibly we had also destroyed what was left of what I was now sure was an already miserable life.

CHAPTER THIRTEEN

MARGARET BARNES SAT QUIETLY IN A STATE OF MILD SHOCK. IN A FEW seconds, either she would go hysterical or fall headlong into a pit of incoherent despair. As a general rule in these situations, you have about three minutes to coax a subject into a chatty mood, or they aren't going to talk. Period.

I looked at Jennie, and we both knew what we had to do; further, we both knew *who* had to do what. I had no enthusiasm for this, but by temperaments and alpha factors, I was the obvious choice.

"Are you listening, Mrs. Barnes?" I leaned forward and informed her bluntly, "Your son *murdered* sixteen people."

She stared off into space, and appeared not to comprehend. I raised my voice and said, "The Belknap murder was an inside job—Jason was on his security team, he had the insight, and his footprints were placed at the scene at the time the crime occurred. We also have hard evidence showing Jason's access to the specialty munitions used to murder both the presidential spokesman and Justice Fineberg."

I paused to let this half-lie sink in, then threw in another half-lie. "We have evidence, we have opportunity, and at least the skeleton of a motive. In fact, Jason left a note announcing his intention to go on a killing spree." With a touch of theatrics, I paused, then added, "And lest I forget—he also intends to assassinate the President."

Margaret Barnes was starting to lose it. She appeared unfocused and woozy, and was gasping for breath. Jennie stood up. She walked over to Mrs. Barnes, knelt beside her chair, and said, "Can I get you something, Margaret? Water? Anything?"

She did not reply.

I said, "For Godsakes, you gave us the connection to Phillip Fineberg. But to tie this together we need to know more . . . and you're going to tell us more. Now."

She mumbled, "But . . . you lied, and I . . . you deceived me about—"

"No—we did not lie."

"Yes, you—"

"We identified ourselves as federal officers pursuing an official investigation." Following an instinct, I bluffed and said, "Knowing that, you still lied about the circumstances regarding your crippling. We can and will investigate your story, but we already know what we'll find, don't we, Mrs. Barnes? *You* lied to us—on tape." She gawked at the recorder as I informed her, "That's a prosecutable federal crime, if you're interested."

Jennie insisted, very softly, "It's true, Margaret. You did volunteer the information. And you weren't truthful, were you?"

"But, I . . . but, Jason couldn't . . . I mean— I think I'd like to speak to my—"

Before the L-word could slip out of her lips, I raised my voice and said, "In a few hours, your son will murder again. If you with-hold information that could help us stop him, I will arrest *you* for willful complicity in murder, for obstructing an investigation, and for willful concealment. I'll drag *you* out of this house in cuffs, and I'll put *you* in jail."

Mrs. Barnes turned her head and looked at Jennie. Jennie said, "Margaret . . . I'm sorry. I'm afraid we'd be left with no choice."

I said, "On tape, we already have you lying to federal officers. You'll be convicted. You'll go to prison, probably until you die."

In a way I was telling the truth, because any lie to a federal officer—even absent a Miranda warning—is a punishable of-fense. But as a lawyer, I was well aware that juries don't really ex-pect mothers to rat out their own kids. So this mild exaggeration was obviously not intended to be interpreted too literally.

But what mattered was not what I knew, what mattered was what she knew, and, judge's wife or not, apparently she didn't know enough. Tears were spilling down her cheeks, and she ap-peared to be on the verge of a complete meltdown. But she still wasn't talking, which was annoying and frustrating. You have to push the right button, and I still hadn't found it. I searched my mind for the soft spot and wasn't coming up with it.

Jennie raised an eyebrow at me and mentioned to Mrs. Barnes, somewhat sorrowfully, "This is terrible, Margaret. Your family, and your reputation will be ruined."

I got it.

Jennie got off her knees and sat on the arm of Margaret's chair. I walked toward Margaret and leaned over, getting three inches from her face. "But hey, Mrs. Barnes—imagine if your boy actually kills the President. Think about it—the President of the United States. You'll become overnight sensations. You'll be the modern equivalent of Mrs. John Wilkes Booth."

"No . . . it's not—"

"Wow—I mean, wow! What will that do for the glorious and esteemed Barnes name?" But in the event she couldn't piece it together in her muddled mental state, I spelled it out for her. "The Barnes name in all the history books, beside Sirhan Sirhan, Lee Harvey Oswald, and that loony Hinckley. There'll be books about you, your family, reporters crawling through everything, biopics of how you raised a sociopath, probably a Broadway play, some instant TV movies . . . Hey, who do you think they'll get to play you, Mrs. Barnes?"

"Stop it, Sean." Jennie looked at me and said, "Can't you see this is a huge shock for Margaret?"

"You're right. What was I thinking? Poor, poor Margaret Barnes. Why was I concerned about the wives, parents, and children of the sixteen people her son murdered today? How about Mr. Larry Elwood, Terrence Belknap's driver, who we found this morning, barbecued to a crisp, after Jason put a few slugs in his skull." Pause. "Or Agent June Lacy, one of Jason's partners, who would've been married next week—except Jason, this morning, put a bullet through her throat."

Margaret Barnes was shrinking into her seat. On her face you could see guilt, and in that guilt you could see that Jason's actions made sense to her, that something inside this family either had created or at least corrupted a human vessel capable of every wicked deed I had just described.

Jennie laid a hand on Mrs. Barnes's shoulder. She said, "Margaret, *we* need to find Jason." She confided, "By morning, he'll be the target of the largest manhunt in American history. *We're* the only hope of taking him alive."

I said to Jennie, "I hope she doesn't talk. Let them shoot the bastard."

"Sit down, Sean," Jennie ordered. "Just . . . sit down, and shut your mouth."

I sat.

Margaret Barnes was looking around the room, wide-eyed, and if she had a gun, a noose, and limbs that worked, I had not one doubt she would climb up onto a stool, slip the noose around her neck, and swallow a bullet herself. Actually, after what I'd just done to this poor lady, I felt ashamed enough to join her. Jennie said, "The human mind is a brittle thing, Margaret. We know Jason struggled to live a decent life . . . an honorable life. We also know he was fleeing something, some monster." She added, "Apparently, he did not run far enough."

Margaret Barnes looked at her, a little shocked by this insight. A good interrogator has to find common ground with the subject, of course. And the parent of a killer bears a special shame, and the mind of that parent searches for excuses, for solace, even absolution. Jennie said, "I don't blame you. Nobody should blame you. You shouldn't blame yourself."

"But you can't . . . It's not his fault."

"Whose fault is it, Margaret?"

She did not reply

"Margaret, help us understand."

Mrs. Barnes sipped from her sherry, and from her expression I wasn't sure *she* could piece it all together. She said, "He . . . his childhood . . ."

"Being robbed of his mother?"

"Yes. And my husband, he was very . . . he was quite strong-willed. And headstrong."

Jennie said, "I know this is difficult, Margaret. But Calhoun's dead. He can *never* hurt you again." She reached forward and she turned off the tape recorder. She said, "Whatever you tell us stays between us. I promise."

I knew why she did it, but turning off the recorder was, I thought, a bad move. But also, I realized in that instant that Jennie had picked up something I had missed entirely. Actually, she had picked up a lot I had missed, and I was curious to see what. Mrs. Barnes looked up at her. Jennie said, "It's going to come out. It can't stay hidden any longer. For your sake . . . for Jason's sake, tell us."

After a moment, Mrs. Barnes blubbered, "You can't imagine."

"Yes, well . . . I don't want to imagine. I need *you* to describe it. You'll feel better by telling us."

For a long moment, Margaret Barnes stared into Jennie's face, but it was not clear she understood a word. Jennie prompted, "Start with how he really broke your back."

With a distressed expression she recoiled back into her seat. "I don't want to talk about that."

"Yes . . . yes, you do. You've always wanted to talk about it. Haven't you?" She added, "For Jason. You owe him this."

In the past two minutes Margaret Barnes had learned her son was a homicidal maniac, that the two agents in her home had come to destroy her soul, that she was about to become the most shamed mother in the country, and possibly that she would spend the remainder of her years in prison. Interrogations are a tricky business, and every experienced interrogator will tell you there is a moment, not a crescendo necessarily, but a turning point after which the subject either blurts out everything or the lawyers take over. In fact, she looked at Jennie and asked, "Shouldn't I call my lawyer?"

Jennie glanced at me. I stood up and said, "Sure, Mrs. Barnes." To Jennie I said, "Hand me your cuffs." To Mrs. Barnes I ordered, "Put out your hands. After we've booked you, you can call your attorney from the holding cell of the nearest police station."

Margaret Barnes stared at the cuffs in my hand for a very

long time. Basically, a hardened criminal has been through the wringer a few times, and knows better than to talk to coppers under any circumstances. But ordinary people don't appreciate how the odds are stacked against them; they think they can bluff and outsmart cops, they think they can get away with a medley of half-truths and half-lies, and as first-timers, they still believe they have their untainted reputations to protect.

Some combination of all these thoughts went through Margaret Barnes's mind, and eventually she said, "All right. He . . . I mean, Calhoun . . . he beat me . . . and he threw me down the stairs. He was in a rage that night. He'd been . . . well, he'd been drinking . . . but he wasn't . . ." She stared at me and, as though to underscore the one irrelevant truth she'd told, insisted scornfully, "He wasn't *drunk.*"

Jennie said, "And afterward—together—you fabricated the car accident to conceal the truth."

Mrs. Barnes nodded.

Jennie said, "He threatened you, didn't he? He said it would ruin both your lives, and Jason's."

Again, she nodded. "I never lost consciousness. He . . . he hovered over me, and . . . and I couldn't move my body . . . and, so we both knew I was badly hurt and . . ." She tried to stifle a heavy sob. "He threatened to kill me, Jennifer. And he would— believe me, I had not a doubt he would. He . . . he could be brutishly violent."

Jennie allowed a moment to pass. She said, "I understand your decision, Margaret. I believe he might have killed you, and I'm sure he would've looked for a way to cover that up. But afterward . . . well, afterward, he controlled you, when you could go out, what you could do, when you could use the toilet, your feeding, your entertainment, and—"

She was nodding furiously. "I felt like . . . like an animal."

BRIAN HAIG

"He was a cruel man, wasn't he?"

"Beyond your imagination. He left the house every day, the good family man, the federal judge . . . you have no idea how normal . . . how charming he could be *outside* this house . . . how admired . . . how misjudged. But *inside* . . ."

"I do understand, Margaret. Calhoun was sick. He was addicted to control. He needed his partner to depend on him. He needed his wife to be subservient, and it may have been an accident, but probably he was satisfied when you ended up crippled and became absolutely dependent on him." Mrs. Barnes was still nodding as Jennie spoke, and Jennie paused and with exquisite timing suggested, "And from Jason, from his son, he *also* demanded absolute obedience, didn't he?"

Tears were now streaming down Margaret's face and she was intermittently sobbing and drawing short breaths. The first dark secret was out, and it was like plucking the cork on a dusty bottle of champagne.

"I . . . my son and I . . . we have no relationship. We haven't . . . well, we haven't spoken in years."

"We'll get to that. Tell me about your family."

And for the next ten minutes, Margaret related what it had been like to be a wife, to be a mother, and to be a son in the house of Calhoun Barnes, a greater monster than we had even imagined. Margaret Barnes, as Jennie said, did want to get it out, and it came like a torrent, a sobbing collection of endless nightmares for her, and for her son.

As I listened, I was struck that Jennie had also been surprisingly prescient back at Jason's townhouse; Calhoun had been a terrorizing, overbearing bully who whipped and beat his son to a pulp for the tiniest infractions, who demanded and enforced perfection in matters and habits large and small. The things that could trigger Calhoun's volcanic fury ranged from the trivial to the arbitrary. Little Jason once bought a turtle from a school classmate; Calhoun discovered the turtle, thrashed Jason with a belt, crushed the turtle under his foot, then forced Jason to clean up the squashed mess and, afterward, to wash his hands one hundred times. Adolescent Jason got into a schoolyard fight, which was fine, but he lost, which was not, and Calhoun thrashed him so badly he missed three days of school. And so forth, and so on.

Because the mother was equally terrorized, and because she was bedridden, and then handicapped, young Jason was forced to confront his monster alone, unprotected and vulnerable. But I think not even Jennie had anticipated the unremitting ferocity the father unleashed on his son. Margaret eventually commented, "But you know the oddest thing? Jason actually looked up to his father. He admired him, and he obeyed him, and wanted always to please him. The two of them were . . . unnaturally close. Jason idolized his father." She took a deep breath. "I did not lie about that." She inquired of her confessor, "Don't you find that peculiar?"

"I find it normal, Margaret. We see it sometimes in hostage situations. There's even a term for it—the Stockholm syndrome. The combination of applied terror and victim helplessness creates mental dependency, and, perversely, even affection and loyalty. For a young boy, trapped in the home of such an abusively dictatorial man, I'd be surprised to hear otherwise."

"I . . . yes, I could see how that explains it." In fact, she might—in her own way she probably had succumbed to the same bewitching phenomenon.

Jennie asked, "Did Jason ever learn the truth about your injury?"

"No. We . . . I kept it from him. I thought . . . a child . . . a son . . . should not have to bear such a terrible truth. Don't you think that's so?"

Jennie glanced at me, pointed at Margaret's glass, and I got her another refill. I was tempted to tell Margaret that whatever her intentions, she had made a serious, even fatal miscalculation. In truth, she had made many mistakes, starting with her marriage, but mistakes compound, and some are worse than others, and cumulatively they become a disaster. Had the boy understood his father's barbaric nature, he might have learned to despise, rather than admire and obey, the beast dominating his life.

In fact, the hour was very late, and I was tired and becoming increasingly impatient to learn exactly *what* had triggered Jason's rage—but Jennie continued her pursuit, methodically and patiently. Margaret's marriage to Calhoun had been a carnival of smoke and broken mirrors, and I was sure she had entertained strong visceral feelings, but she had never intellectualized or verbalized the causes and effects to others, or probably even to herself. Or perhaps she had, but with only the knowledge of how it had destroyed her life. Now she knew how it had destroyed her child's also, and she needed to rationalize the adjusted causes and effects.

For the next few minutes, alternating between a whispery intensity and hurt chokes and sobs, she detailed how Calhoun had estranged her from Jason, isolating him and isolating her. Daddy taught his boy to admire strength; Mommy was crippled, Mommy was weak, Mommy deserved contempt. Also, Mommy was physically incapable of caring for and protecting him, magnifying Jason's emotional enslavement to his father and his alienation from his mother. It struck me that young Jason might also have felt a sense of betrayal. Margaret had failed in nearly every sense, both practical and emotional, to be his mother, and a child is concerned not with cause but with effect.

Even I could understand that no child would emerge from such a malevolent and viciously manipulated environment healthy in mind, conscience, and soul. Jason's head was probably a shopping cart of pathologies, Oedipal guilts, and sexual confusion. No wonder the guy wasn't married yet. But Margaret finally paused to catch a breath, and Jennie, the good cop, asked her, "Another sherry?"

"Uh . . . if you'd be so kind."

Jennie handed me Margaret's glass. Being the bad cop carries its heavy burdens. I felt really bad about getting a witness liquored up and loose-lipped, but in murder investigations you do what works. As I got up, Jennie suggested to Margaret, "Now I think it's time to figure out what happened, why Jason has taken the course he's on."

Margaret thought a moment, then said, "I think . . . I suppose, his father."

"This was somehow related to the firm your husband and Phillip Fineberg started?"

"Oh . . . I believe most certainly it was."

"Can you explain what happened?"

Margaret waited for me to bring her the refill, then started, "As I mentioned, the fit between Calhoun and Phillip was never good or particularly healthy. Theirs was a partnership of convenience, at best. I think that with success and wealth, they needed each other less and disliked each other more."

"That's how it usually works," Jennie commented.

"Actually, I think Calhoun and Phillip were consummately jealous of each other." She paused for a moment before she added, "They grew to really hate one another."

"How long were they together?"

"Fifteen years. The last four or five were misery for them both. Calhoun complained viciously about Phillip. And I knew

Phillip thoroughly despised Calhoun as well. And of course, by the seventies, the opportunities in this city toward Jews had changed greatly. Phillip knew it, and so did Calhoun."

"Was there a blow-up?"

"Oh, nothing so reckless. They were both smart men, and quite greedy. They knew to manage their situation discreetly. Richmond is a small city, after all. They would invite unwanted scrutiny, and their legal competitors would have eaten them alive." She paused a moment, then said, "Phillip finally ended it."

"How?"

"In a most interesting manner. One day, he just never came back to work."

"He . . . what? He just quit?"

"In a manner of speaking. He accepted a position at Yale Law, teaching, I think, tort law. Calhoun learned afterward that, behind his back, Phillip had discussed partnerships with several of those large northern firms. That proved to be fruitless. Phillip's lack of courtroom experience completely disqualified him, and he wasn't willing to again start at the bottom. In the end, I'm sure he concluded, teaching was the only respectable escape. The pay was stingy, but with the money he had made at the firm, he could live quite comfortably."

"And he of course blamed this on Calhoun."

"Well, I'm sure he did." She nodded. "Rightly so, I suppose. Though I also think Phillip would have been a miserable litigator. The man was gifted with a gloriously brilliant mind—but had no tact or charm, or even the ability to manufacture charm, the trick Calhoun so readily mastered. To be frank, both were disgustingly arrogant men, but Calhoun could hide it."

I suggested, "But there's more, isn't there?"

"Between those two, there was always more, Mr. Drummond." She sipped from her sherry and said, "Do you believe that these two very smart lawyers failed to create an agreement for what would happen in the event their firm dissolved? Both men kept all their money invested in the firm, withdrawing what was needed for their personal expenses, and left the remainder sheltered from taxes. This was another of Phillip's brilliant ideas. Don't you find that ironic?"

She looked at Jennie and me to be sure we understood. "So Calhoun simply decided to keep all the money."

"And how did Phillip respond?" Jennie asked.

"In the way all lawyers respond."

"He sued."

"With great outrage. The matter was handled in a claims court here. Phillip represented himself, which was, I think, very naive on his part. But as I said, he had a very large ego, and I think he had always felt he could do better than Calhoun in court, if only given the chance. Of course, Calhoun tore him apart. He showed that Phillip had never taken a case to court and described him as nothing but a glorified clerk."

I commented, "That's why they always say lawyers should never represent themselves."

But she wasn't interested in my insights; she looked at Jennie and said, "Afterward, Phillip swore Calhoun had arranged to have the case handled by a judge he was friendly with. He also insisted that Calhoun had blocked him from getting access to the firm's records, and the founding document Calhoun showed the court had been doctored to indicate Phillip was never a full partner."

"He got nothing?" I asked.

"Oh . . . not nothing, Mr. Drummond. He asked for four million. He walked away with thirty thousand."

"And about the judge being a friend of Calhoun's—was he?"

"Well . . . I don't know that they were friends, exactly. They attended the same private school together, and were members of the same country club, and the same church." With a bemused half-smile she concluded, "I suppose they were . . . acquainted."

Jennie asked, "And what was Fineberg's response?"

"As a civil case, there was no appeal. But anyway, I think he concluded the game was rigged against him in this city. He left bitter, and we never heard from him again."

"And the firm?"

"For about six months, Calhoun tried going it alone. But without its legal mastermind, he began to lose large cases, and—"

"And he arranged a judgeship," I said.

"Yes, Mr. Drummond. And frankly, it better suited his natural talents and temperament. It was said that he ran the tightest courtroom in the Commonwealth. My husband worshipped law and order, as you might imagine. Felons did not get mercy before his bar."

"I'll bet." In fact, it was all beginning to make sense. But we needed to move this along, and I said, "So the years passed, and eventually Calhoun was notified he was under consideration for the Supreme Court. What happened?"

Of course, Jennie and I had already figured out what happened: Phillip Fineberg got his long-awaited revenge. Still, it was important to understand who else was involved, and how. In general terms, we now had a partial understanding of how one victim was connected to Jason Barnes. We needed to advance that understanding, and we needed to establish connections to the others, to piece together how a family spat became mass murder.

After a moment, Margaret said, "About seven months ago, Calhoun was asked to visit the Justice Department, where he met with a smart young lawyer from the White House and several senior Justice people. They notified him he was on the President's final list. It had come down to two final candidates; the President wanted a trial judge with a strict law-and-order pedigree, and Calhoun had the inside edge. They had reached the point of no return, the lawyer advised him. So he asked two questions—was there anything in Calhoun's background they should be aware of, and was he willing to expose himself to the scrutiny involved in these matters."

Jennie commented, "Was this notification a surprise for Calhoun?"

The sherry had gone to her head, and she giggled. "Goodness, no . . . he had plotted this moment for years. His father's failure to make the court was, I think, a burden his whole life. And when Phillip was brought onto the court ten years ago, it was, for Calhoun, as though he had been electrocuted. As I said, the two men were bitterly competitive."

I got up and took her glass, which was again empty, and went to retrieve another refill. Margaret looked exhausted and tipsy, and her speech was becoming slurred. Jennie asked her, "And what happened?"

"Apparently the White House circulated the list of candidates with the serving justices."

"I would've thought that was done earlier in the process," I commented.

"I would guess, Mr. Drummond, that it *was* done earlier."

Of course. Fineberg probably waved off on Calhoun's name in the early rounds, allowing him to become a finalist, allowing him to think the high court was within reach, and allowing his name to surface publicly. These two guys had long memories, and they played for keeps. The public humiliation of a federal judge is relevant only to his own jurisdiction, whereas a finalist for the Sacred Tribunal dances on the largest stage, and the fall from grace would be from an even loftier height. In fact, I wondered if it was Fineberg who found a way to introduce Barnes for consideration to the court in the first place. Margaret suggested she thought this was the case and added, "Phillip plotted his moment brilliantly. He began feeding damaging tales and insinuations about Calhoun, providing leads to the background investigators. Calhoun was recalled to Washington several times to offer his side of things."

"What kind of things?" Jennie asked.

"That as a lawyer, Calhoun had bribed some judges. That as a city magistrate he had done a few favors for the governor—a quid pro quo arrangement—in return for which the governor would assure Calhoun's elevation to the federal bench."

"Was there any truth to the charges?" Jennie asked.

"I . . . well, Calhoun insisted to me they were all blatant fabrications."

"But they weren't, were they?"

"No." She looked at Jennie. "I knew they were true. Calhoun, as I said, was very ambitious and calculating."

"And controlling," Jennie commented.

"Yes, and meticulous. It was not his way to leave things to chance."

Before anyone could come up with another adjective, I asked Margaret, "When did your husband learn Fineberg was behind this?"

"He knew—at least, he suspected Phillip immediately. And that truly infuriated him. But Calhoun was nothing if not willful. He was sure he could bull and lie his way through." She looked at us and added, "Unfortunately for Calhoun, Phillip proved smarter than him."

"How?" I asked.

She looked at me. "How do you think, Mr. Drummond?"

I considered it. "He kept evidence from their partnership.

Nothing implicating him—but something that proved Calhoun had violated the law."

"Very good. Phillip had three canceled checks, signed by Calhoun. All for very large sums, all to judges involved in important cases Calhoun took to trial."

Jennie gave me a funny look, then asked Mrs. Barnes, "He gave those checks to the Justice Department?"

"It was my understanding that he gave them to people in your Bureau who were performing the investigation on Calhoun's suitability. Your Director then carried everything over to the White House."

There was no need to ask what happened at the White House. She could only offer conjecture where we needed facts. But neither was it hard to piece together. Townsend took the disclosures to the President's legal counsel, together they took it to Terrence Belknap, the White House Chief of Staff, who accompanied them to see the President.

They stood around in the Oval Office and stared at those canceled checks and they realized Calhoun Barnes also needed to be canceled. At some point on the merry-go-round, Merrill Benedict, the White House spokesman, probably was instructed to quash the leaked reports about Barnes being a leading candidate, and perhaps to salt the ground with a few hints about Barnes's past, present, and maybe, about his future.

Margaret Barnes looked at me and held out her glass. I retrieved it and returned to the bar. Over my shoulder I asked her, "How did your husband learn his candidacy was in trouble?"

"He was recalled to Washington again, to meet with the Attorney General himself. Not only was Calhoun's nomination scratched, he was told he would also be charged. A task force had been created to investigate, though the evidence was already sufficient to ask Calhoun to resign from the federal bench immediately."

"And did he?"

"No . . . he . . . well, he was shocked and very upset. He asked to be allowed to think about it overnight, and was granted that wish."

Jennie suggested, "He then came home and he told you about all this?" Mrs. Barnes nodded, and Jennie asked, "What did you do, Margaret?"

After a long hesitation, she said, "Well . . . he was, as I said, upset . . . crushed, actually. I . . . I allowed him to vent. He cried . . . like a little child . . . he kept bawling. I told him I was heartbroken for him, that this was so unfair, that Phillip was a mean and spiteful bastard." She hesitated a moment, staring off into space. "I told him we'd get through this, and to go to bed. He . . . he said he wanted a nightcap, here . . . in the study, to think this out. I wish now . . . well, I wish I had talked him out of it." She stared at Jennie. She pointed up at a beamed rafter, and then at a short stool on rollers beside the bookshelf. "Right here . . . in this very room."

It was amazing, I thought, how good Jennie was at this, how falsely sensitive, and how blithely intuitive. I was aware that profilers are trained not only in developing sketches of killers but they are also masters of the art of interrogation. Yet, as in art and war, good training and practice only get you so far. Truly, Special Agent Margold was a prodigy. She placed a hand on Margaret Barnes's shoulder and said, not all that softly, "You're lying."

Margaret recoiled. "I . . . I don't understand what you mean?"

Jennie said, "You did not tell Calhoun it would be okay. You told Calhoun he had destroyed everything. You told him his career was over, ruined, that he had dishonored himself, and this family. And you suggested there was only one way out—only one way to short-circuit an investigation . . . one simple way to avoid the utter shame and disgrace that would follow. You planted the seed in his head, and you prayed he would do it. Didn't you?"

Margaret stared at Jennie a moment, a bit surprised and a lot shocked that her pal, the good cop, had suddenly become a bad cop and was not really her pal at all. She shook her head in denial. "No . . . I did not . . . I wouldn't—"

"In fact," Jennie continued, more harshly, "there was one thing you didn't tell him. You didn't describe how Phillip learned of his bribes, or where Phillip got those canceled checks."

Margaret Barnes was now staring into her sherry glass. Clearly Jennie Margold had penetrated a great deal further into this family's maelstrom of hatreds and treachery than she was meant to go.

After a moment, Jennie insisted, "You told us Phillip lost his case against Calhoun because he lacked access to the firm records. But aside from that, surely Calhoun was too sly to bribe judges with traceable checks from his firm's account. He would've used your private account. Copies of those checks are in the Bureau's possession—would you like me to make a call to verify which account they were drawn from? Perhaps you'd rather have me access your phone records during that month, to see if you and Phillip were in contact?"

Margaret wasn't going to confirm this charge, but neither did she try to deny it. Though, in fact, it didn't matter. We needed neither her confirmation nor her disavowal, and suggesting suicide to her husband—no matter how exquisitely timed—is not even a misdemeanor, much less a crime.

She continued to stare at Jennie, and in some weird way I thought Margaret Barnes was glad that we knew the whole truth. Her husband had crippled her, destroyed her life, alienated and corrupted her child, and in the end she had turned out not to be the numbingly passive lamb she appeared.

I looked at my watch. It was after two. I said, "Mrs. Barnes, when was the last time you heard from your son?"

"Not in years."

"Do you know where he is?"

"No, I do not."

"Can you give us the names of any of Calhoun's close friends, anybody who might know?"

"I don't know his close friends."

"If you hear from him, will you call?"

"Certainly." She was lying, of course.

I looked at Jennie. "Any more questions?"

"No."

We both stood. I asked Mrs. Barnes, "Do you need assistance getting to your bedroom?"

"No, I . . . I believe I will just sit here awhile."

We bid her good night, and left her cradling her sherry in the room where her former husband stored his greatest feats, and where she stored her greatest memory.

CHAPTER FOURTEEN

TED AWAITED US OUTSIDE, AND TED COULD KEEP WAITING. JENNIE AND I both walked halfway down the block, out of Ted's earshot and, in my case, far away from this house of fossilized horrors. We whipped out our cell phones, she called George and I called Phyllis.

Two hours learning about the Barnes family had put me in a foul mood. According to my watch the hour was quarter past two, and I actually looked forward to rousting Phyllis. But she was already awake and apparently she had caller ID, because on the first ring she answered, a little too jovially, "I'm glad to see you've learned your lesson about checking in, Drummond. Have you learned anything interesting?"

"I think it's interesting. Jason's our man."

"You're sure?"

"As close as we can get beyond beating a confession out of him."

"Tell me about it."

So I did. And three feet away Jennie told George about it, and, interestingly, we must have been synchronized because we finished and signed off at nearly the same instant.

Jennie looked at me and said, "George agrees we now have enough to take to a federal judge for an arrest warrant."

"Right."

"Jason's picture will be distributed to the Secret Service, the Bureau, local cops, and every major network and newspaper. Within an hour, the manhunt will be on."

"Good call."

"Thoughts . . . observations?"

I said, "For starters, turning off the recorder was a big mistake."

"Really?"

"No doubt about it. If Jason's caught, that part of the conversation—from his own mother's lips—any competent prosecutor would have put it to devastating use."

She regarded my face for a moment. "You think?"

"Well . . . I don't mean to nitpick."

She reached into her purse and withdrew the recorder. Then she reached into the side pocket of her jacket and took out a second recorder. She smiled. "Every veteran agent brings along a backup."

I stared at the second recorder. "Remind me never to cross you."

"I will. Frequently."

"Now, a question." I asked, "Why did she stay with him?"

"The usual reasons. Convention and practicality."

"Meaning?"

"Meaning, hers was a social class and a generation defined by a successful marriage and a successful husband. Calhoun was regarded as a prime marriageable specimen, and until the very end, he was . . . successful."

"He broke her back. 'Till death do you part' does not mean you part each other. Shouldn't it have occurred to her that theirs was a marriage with a few irreconcilable flaws?"

"I wouldn't expect a male to understand."

"Oh please."

"It's true. Biology dictates to women. It defines our life cycle, and it forms our choices. A divorced woman, bitter, crippled, and infertile, had no hope of attracting another mate. She had become completely dependent on Calhoun, financially and physically. Literally, she felt forced to sleep in the bed she made."

In my view, a life alone was better than the life she had. Yet Jennie was right—I probably couldn't understand. The choices of women from Margaret's generation made little sense to a male, and even less to a modern male, though maybe they made sense then. I said, "He must've been a real bastard."

"Would you like to hear the psychiatric explanation?"

"I . . . is there a Cliff's Notes version?"

She punched me in the stomach. "To start, these things run in families. Incest and spousal and child abuse are like inheritances. Behaviorally, they pass through the generations. Living in that house was to be inundated in the family tradition. Maybe you noticed that the heirlooms and paintings were all from *his* family?"

"I noticed that before Calhoun, all the Barnes men married dogs. Did you see the one with the crossed eyes and the wart on her nose?"

She rolled her eyes. "Why do I bother explaining these things to you?"

"You were saying?"

"From the sound of it, Calhoun's specific maladies were a

narcissistic disorder, extreme grandiosity, and a manic compulsion for control and order."

"Are we talking about a theory or a person?"

She concluded, correctly, that simpleminded Sean needed a less complicated explanation and brought it down a peg. "If you're interested, Adolf Hitler exhibited similar neuroses and dysfunctions. Think of the things Hitler did to shape what he considered the ideal society, the ideal race. Calhoun exuded the same fury and ferocity, but on a single target, his son." After a moment, she added, "I would also bet Calhoun's father exhibited similar disorders. Sons learn behavior from their fathers, regardless of their flaws."

"And Jason?"

"You're right. It's intriguing. The chain appears to be broken."

"But he's not married. He has no children. As a result, you can't be sure, can you?"

"Oh, I am sure."

"How? Why?"

"Because we've seen how he lives. Jason's an obsessive-compulsive personality. By definition, he should *never* have become submissive to his father. He would . . . well, he would vie and tilt with him. See the point?"

"Nope."

"As a child, Jason *did* become submissive."

"Why?"

"A survival mechanism. A chilling measure of Calhoun's brutality and manipulative skills—but the point is, Jason chose *not* to compete, as a child or, later, as an adult. He did not go into law, or even stay in Richmond. He deserted his father's game and his father's playing field, geographically and figuratively." She looked at me and said, "Got it? He fled."

"I don't get it."

Clearly my ignorance was testing Jennie's patience. I had cross-examined my share of shrinks on the stand. I recognized the warning signs.

The human brain. With any other organ in the body, the functions and dysfunctions are fairly objective and readily explainable. The heart is a pump, it shoves blood and oxygen through your arteries, and when it stops working, ditto for you. As it goes with kidneys, lungs, intestines, and so on. The brain is different, endlessly complex, mysterious, even weird. Even when functioning normally, in reality it can still be totally wrong.

It was Jennie's job to assign a rational explanation to perversely irrational behavior, and she was obviously very good at it. But Jason Barnes was a little twisted, even by her standards, and by my standards he was a dark labyrinth without so much as an entrance.

After a moment, Jennie said, "Here's my point. Margaret told us that Jason admired his father. Idolized him. Does that make sense to you?"

"No."

"Focus on that incongruity, Sean. In Jason's mind his father was a towering figure, a demigod. Much as the German people elevated Hitler to an almost supernatural plateau, so Jason felt about his father. He fled because he was convinced he couldn't compete with the overwhelming figure in his head."

She looked at me to be sure I understood. "It's curious that Jason has not fulfilled the destiny biology and family behavior ordained for him. You might say Jason is a prediction that should have happened, but didn't."

"People aren't programmed into defined paths, Jennie. We make choices."

"Sean, you had a normal upbringing, whatever that means.

You can't understand the monsters that inhabit a dark forest you never passed through."

"In the words of C. S. Lewis, 'evil is always man's doing, yet it is never his destiny.'"

"Spoken like a true lawyer. But all right, you explain it."

"Simple. According to Jason's bosses and teammates, he was a fairly normal guy and an exemplary agent. He made a choice to be the way he was, and he's making a choice now to be something different. We have to figure out why he made that choice."

"Actually, he was a time bomb placed in cold storage. Many psychopaths exhibit the *appearance* of normalcy. They interact socially, and even succeed professionally." She took my arm and added, "You could be sitting next to one, dating one, or even be married to one—you'd never know. Wives and neighbors are always shocked when they learn. In reality, Jason's mind has *always* been a cauldron of suppressed angers, confusions, and pathologies, awaiting a triggering event."

"Calhoun's suicide is that event?"

"No question about it. Recall Agent Kinney telling us that Jason's behavior became odd about six months ago. That coincides with his father's suicide, right?"

I stood a moment and thought about all this. It sounded like those Greek tragedies we were all forced to read and endure in college, where the hero always has some fatal flaw, like hubris or whatever, a brooding germ that lurks in remission until it eventually thaws and, like the Pac-Man, consumes all around it.

Jason's crimes were in the here and now, but the seeds were planted more than three decades before in a poisonous marriage, in a brutally claustrophobic household, and then richly fertilized by the hatred between two monumentally spiteful men.

I said, "Incidentally, you did a great job back there."

"As did you. Are you okay?"

"No, I feel awful."

She took my hand. "You should. You got carried away back there. That poor woman. You were really a bullying—"

"What the—"

"I mean, I hate to nitpick . . ." She laughed. "I'm joking. You were perfect. I couldn't have done it without you. I'll see if I can get you a merit badge."

I was just raising my eyebrow when a new thought struck me. "Holy shit!"

"What?"

I grabbed her arm and said, "Call your boss—now."

"Who do you think I was just talking to?"

"No—call Townsend."

"Why?"

"Because, probably, he's next."

She stared at me, and it took a moment before she put it together, and another moment before it registered. "Oh my God! You're right. He probably carried the news to the White House and the Attorney General."

"Right." While she called and informed Townsend that he was probably next on Jason's happy hit list, I wandered back to the car and Ted.

Ted saw me approach and said, "Get what you needed?"

It was none of Ted's business, so I diverted his attention to one of the statues and asked, "What great southern warrior is that?"

"Martin Luther King."

I must've looked a little surprised by that revelation.

He laughed. "Hey, times change, even down here."

"Right. Hey, Ted, you still single?"

"Yup."

"Good town for the ladies?"

Whereupon Ted launched into a lengthy dissertation about the quality of young women in Richmond, and apparently it was primo; he was really getting into it. I checked my watch a few times. Jennie was taking her sweet time with Townsend. The next act was about to unfold in Washington, and where I needed to be was not here but there. I mean, all Jennie had to say was, "Yo, boss, they're gunning for your ass. So, you know . . . think about investing in a Kevlar suit, rounding up a platoon of Army Rangers, and, incidentally, do not set foot outside your office for a week."

But eventually she finished and joined us. She said to me, "Sorry that took so long. I told the Director and George. We decided to get an authorization for surveillance and wiretaps on Mrs. Barnes. When she sobers up, I doubt she'll remain cooperative."

"Have no doubts."

She nodded. "There's more. They think we can do something with this. Something proactive."

I was afraid of this. "Bad idea."

"I know, I know. I advised against it also."

"No matter how good the protection, Jason and his pals could always get lucky."

She shrugged. "Yes, and that would be a shame. He's the best Director we've had in years."

Ted looked confused and asked, "What in the hell y'all talkin' about?"

In reply, Jennie looked at her watch and stressed, "Ted, you have exactly seven minutes to have us back at the chopper or I will ship your ass to Alaska."

"Sheeit," replied Ted, predictably.

CHAPTER FIFTEEN

WE SET DOWN IN THE PARKING LOT OF FERGUSON HOME SECURITY ELEC-
tronics at 4:45 A.M. The building was lit up like Macy's, no doubt
causing the neighbors to wonder if they were missing out on an
early-bird fire sale. At least—this being Washington—I'm sure
the one thought that never crossed anybody's mind was
whether some secretive government agency was operating this
building as a facade. How did I get involved with these people?

Phyllis awaited us in the parking lot. She handed a small
paper bag to Jennie, a small paper bag to me, and said, "Tooth-
brushes, toothpastes, and some baby wipes."

I said, "Thanks. This is very—"

"You'll be billed for it later," she informed me.

"I thought we would."

Her nose wrinkled and her eyes narrowed. "Drummond,
have you been drinking?"

Jennie dutifully came to my aid. "One . . . maybe two. Or three or four. All in the line of duty."

There was silence for a moment.

Eventually Phyllis said, "Whatever. In any regard, you two did a good job down in Richmond. We're quite pleased."

I wasn't sure who was included in "we," but I'd bet George Meany was not, whereas Mark Townsend, whose gilded tush we might have saved, probably was.

I mentioned to Phyllis, "Jennie made the breakthrough. You should be sure to mention that to her Director. She cracked Mrs. Barnes like a walnut . . . peanut . . . whatever."

Jennie immediately commented, "Sean's role was harder. He did the bad cop. He gave an amazing performance."

And back and forth awhile. We were both laying it on a bit thick. But finally Phyllis looked at me and commented, "I'm sure Drummond performed his part admirably. He brings certain authentic talents to the role."

I smiled. "Well, you know, old ladies are so easy."

Phyllis's lips were parting to say something when Jennie swiftly added, "Also, it was Sean who figured out Townsend could be the next target. It was brilliant deductive work. I missed the connection entirely."

Phyllis stared at me a moment, I'm sure thinking how pleased she was that she hired me. She finally said, "Both of you take a moment to pat each other on the back. Then get cleaned up and join us in the conference room."

Watching her back as she walked away, Jennie whispered to me, "Don't tangle with that lady, Sean. That's professional advice, if you're interested."

"Yeah, thanks. Let's see . . . don't mess with her . . . never screw with you . . . watch my ass around George—hey, with teamwork like this, why do you think we haven't caught these clowns yet?"

"Have you ever considered . . . ?"

"What?"

"These conflicts—if I'm getting too personal, let me know— but Sean, you have what we call authority issues."

"You mean this is my fault?"

"Look, I really like you . . ." She paused. "To be perfectly blunt, your career prospects would improve a lot if you stopped taunting your bosses."

"All right. You *are* getting too personal."

She apparently changed her mind about her promise, how- ever. She said, "In a way, you're like Jason Barnes. Predestination. I'll bet your father was also very strong-willed and overbearing. Transferral. Now you're taking it out on your bosses."

"I'm not . . . look—"

"You need to hear this."

"I do not."

"I'm offering you an insight into your own nature be- cause . . . because we're partners and . . . friends."

"Did it occur to you that partners and friends don't want to be psychoanalyzed?"

"Excuse me—I'm trying to be helpful." She stepped back and stared at me a moment. She asked, "Are we having a fight?"

I was too busy sulking to answer that.

She mentioned, "Because sometimes I *am* too nosy for my own good."

"Right. Drop the subject."

"Fine." After a moment she remarked, "We're both tired, wrung out, and irritable. We need showers, a decent meal, and sleep."

"Oh . . . you get less nosy and pushy when you're clean and well rested?"

"Watch it."

"Well . . . what do you suggest?"

"I thought, after we finish debriefing, we'd slip out for a few hours and get hotel rooms."

"I'm not sure that's—"

"There are hotels in Crystal City. Only five minutes from here. If needed, we'd be back in minutes."

I looked at Jennie. I did not get the sense there was anything more to this than was offered—a good meal, a warm shower, a little rest. But there could be more, and it was either an even better idea than it sounded or an invitation to real problems. Then I thought about Janet up in Boston, and I was sure there was a thick ream of forensics reports, intel updates, and witness statements on my desk waiting to be read. No, this just wasn't going to work. I didn't need the complications, emotional or otherwise.

I said, "Good idea."

She smiled. "Now, loosen up. The Bureau doesn't like it when you threaten our fearless leader. We'll get Barnes. Soon."

I nodded, and indeed, I hoped her confidence wasn't misplaced. But it's a truism that the best hopes don't always lead to the best outcomes. Also, something was gnawing at me, something missing I was sure was obvious, or should have been obvious. But what? I really needed a few hours of sleep. Jennie said, "Go brush your teeth. If Townsend sniffs your breath, he'll have you shot."

"I don't work for him."

"I know. Think he cares?"

Gee, I really missed the Army. There, you at least knew where you stood, and who could take you down. It's hard to mount your best defense when you don't know where the front is, and who's in your rear.

So into the building we both went, Jennie directly to the ladies' room, while I went directly into the men's room, where I dutifully brushed my teeth, and washed my face, and tried to cleanse my mind of naughty thoughts.

I'm sure I mentioned that Agent Margold was quite attractive. The thing is, the past few hours we'd been rubbing shoulders, brushing arms, all those annoying gestures two people usually do who can't wait to jump into the sack together. Unless I was misreading this, and she was just gracious and warm. And I was just horny.

The truth was we were partners and we had become friends. To move to the next level somebody has to make the next move, and somebody has to reciprocate, or not reciprocate, which gets a little sticky.

A stall door opened behind me and Director Mark Townsend walked out, began washing his hands and staring into the mirror.

I said, very nonchalantly, "Good morning, sir."

"Drummond."

I was making a retreat toward the exit, until he said, "Hold it."

Boy, good thing I brushed my teeth.

He walked to the dispenser, yanked out a paper towel, and began wiping his hands. He wore the same blue business suit and the same awful paisley tie from the day before. Remarkably, his suit still looked pressed, his white shirt appeared freshly starched, and there were no bags under his eyes, leading me to wonder if this man was born permapressed. He asked, not at all absently, "Agent Margold, you've worked with her for twenty-four hours now. What do you think of her?"

Had this question come from anybody but Townsend, I

would have replied it was none of his business and to go pound sand. But she was a vassal in his kingdom, so she was his business, and though I wasn't one of his vassals, I didn't want him to make me his business. While not often enough, there are occasions when I obey my survival instincts.

I therefore answered honestly, but selectively. "I find her highly competent, professional, and effective. Margaret Barnes was a hostile witness, a practiced liar, and totally confused. A few hours ago, I watched Agent Margold cut through thirty years of lies, evasions, and camouflage so dense the witness was lost in it. It was an impressive sight."

"Is that right?"

"Yes sir."

"And do you have any views regarding her overall management of this case?"

"I thought George Meany was managing this case."

"Meany is *in charge* of this case. But Agent Margold seems to have uncanny instincts for where to be, and when. De facto, *she* appears to be managing this case."

He looked me in the eye and said, "I ask, because I'm getting conflicting reports about her. Some sources are telling me she is not competent, nor is she a team player. This Bureau operates effectively only when it functions collectively, and unfortunately, my D.C. Field Office appears to be experiencing teamwork issues. Do you understand? At this moment, on this case, I cannot afford this problem. But the source of this problem is eluding me."

It wasn't hard to guess the source of the conflicting reports. George Meany has a lot of bad habits, an aversion to frontal assaults among them.

But generally speaking, I make it a practice not to rat out my peers, or even my bosses, to the bigger bosses. They get paid the big bucks because they're supposed to possess the intuition and insight to sort the sycophantic idiots from the nondescriptly competent. That's the theory. Of course, there is another theory, called the Peter Principle.

I did not think this applied here, however, and said, "Sir, I don't believe you got where you are by listening to subordinates tell you how to think. You should rely on your own instincts and judgment."

He changed the subject, sort of, and suggested, "Also, I think you and Agent Margold are becoming attached to one another. So perhaps I shouldn't be asking you. Perhaps you've developed an emotional bias in this matter."

I must have blushed, because he immediately commented, "Nothing wrong with it, Drummond. I met my own wife on a case. She was a forensics specialist, and I was the case agent. A murder and castration case, and the wife was our chief suspect." He ended this tale, saying, not for the first time, I'm sure, "You could say we fell in love over a pair of detached testicles."

"I thought that came after you said, 'I do.'"

He laughed. "Twenty-seven years . . . not once have I even considered cheating on my Joan."

"I'll bet."

He glanced at his watch, and this brief moment of bonding was over. He began walking to the door, then he stopped and faced me again. He asked, "Did you know George Meany prior to this case?"

"We worked a case together once."

He nodded, but did not amplify that thought. But it was apparent that George's whispered insights had not been limited to Agent Margold. Wouldn't it be interesting to know what George had to say about yours truly? Or maybe not.

CHAPTER SIXTEEN

At 5:00 A.M., Jennie was already seated at the table, thumbing through a clutch of papers, when I followed Townsend into the conference room. The only regulars missing from this gathering of greats were Director Peterson, still enjoying his prerogative to stay miles away from this thing, and Mr. Gene Halderman, who was enjoying a night's sleep, proving he wasn't a total idiot.

George, looking the worse for wear, opened the meeting. "Let's begin with a wrap-up of the progress we've made over the past six hours. Keep it brief." He pointed at his watch and added, as if we needed a reminder, "The morning witching hour is almost here."

He directed a finger at Jennie, who led off with an interesting, albeit slightly technical assessment of both Margaret and Jason Barnes's mental states, a concise summary of the Barnes family history, and a wrap-up of the connections that bound Calhoun Barnes to Phillip Fineberg and indirectly, to Jason Barnes.

At this point Phyllis raised her hand and asked a reasonable question. She said, "Why would he lift a finger to avenge a death I would have thought he celebrated?"

From the expressions around the table, everybody shared this same frame of inquiry. So Jennie offered an abbreviated version of the explanation she had earlier provided me. She let this sink in a moment, then advised us, "Love and hatred are the most intense and direct human emotions. When they become confused, the individual becomes a psychosexual mess."

I suggested, "So he's nuts?"

"I prefer the clinical expression," she replied. "Completely bonkers." Which got a few chuckles. She then cautioned all of us, "The point is, whatever wobbly equilibrium existed inside Jason's head is totally gone. In Jason's mind his father was a towering, monumental figure. He believes we drove and hounded him to death, and he now intends to punish us."

I'd heard enough about Jason Barnes's loopiness and, thankfully, nobody asked another question.

So Jennie brought us back to the present, saying, "But at this point, Sean and I were confronted with a number of holes. We were forced to make some educated guesses about what happened here—in Washington." She looked at Townsend. "Sir, it's very important to confirm some of those deductions."

He nodded.

Jennie asked, "Was it Phillip Fineberg who provided the canceled checks?"

"It was."

"Could you explain what circumstances led to that?"

"Yes . . . well, Fineberg had been feeding me charges for weeks. Usually over the phone, and he requested anonymity, which is fairly common in background checks. He had many disparaging things to say about Calhoun Barnes, some of which might be factual, and some of which sounded frivolous, even questionable. Eventually I told him we needed evidence to corroborate his charges."

"And how did he respond?"

"He promised to get back to me."

"And he did."

"At a cocktail party in Georgetown about a week later, he pulled me aside and gave me the canceled checks. I handed them over to your office."

"That was before my time. Who in my office, and how did my office respond?"

Townsend thought about it a moment. "John Fisk, your predecessor. First, John assigned some agents to verify the authenticity of the checks."

"And the checks were verified?"

"That's correct."

"And the checks were drawn from Calhoun's family account?"

"Also correct. And with that to go on, a second team was assigned to run down the three judges whose names were on the checks. Two were dead, from natural causes. The third was found in a retirement community in Florida. Advanced Alzheimer's. Completely senile."

"Then you carried the packet to the White House?"

"No. I carried the evidence to the Attorney General. Meade Everhill from his office was present. We reviewed what we'd gathered, and it was Everhill's legal judgment that we had enough to at least proceed with a criminal probe."

"Then the White House?"

"Only then."

"In addition to the President, the President's legal adviser, the White House Chief of Staff, the Attorney General, Meade Everhill, and presumably the White House spokesman, who else was involved?"

Townsend pointed at Mrs. Hooper. "Her."

Mrs. Hooper squirmed in her seat. She insisted, "But my presence would be known only to the other people in that meeting. I . . . Jason Barnes would have no reason to target me."

To which Townsend replied, "Don't presume that." Turning to Mr. Wardell, he asked, "Your people know who accesses the Oval Office. Correct?"

"Of course."

"Is a written log kept?"

"Always, for scheduled meetings. Of course, during the day certain favored staffers, like Mrs. Hooper, pop in and out spontaneously."

"There, you see—" Mrs. Hooper was saying.

"However," Wardell spoke over her, "in those instances, the agent at the President's door notifies the operations center. Those names are also entered into the log."

"I thought they might be," Townsend commented. "Could Jason Barnes have accessed that log?"

"I can't rule it out. He had an ops center pass and plenty of friends who work there. He could have seen the log himself, or a friend could have checked it for him."

I had the impression Director Townsend and Chuck Wardell did not particularly care for Mrs. Hooper, and this exchange was curious. When the big bosses clash, it's never a good idea to step in the middle. But Townsend did not strike me as small-minded or vindictive, and something seemed to be going on here. Jennie looked at me, and I raised my eyebrows. Jennie asked Townsend, "Could you explain how the decision was made, for our benefit?"

Townsend said, "All right. In my view, the evidence against

Calhoun Barnes was problematic and the case was flimsy. There were no living—at least no sensible—witnesses. There was no other physical evidence except the three canceled checks, and the personal word of Phillip Fineberg, who insisted he didn't witness the exchanges and only learned of them recently."

Asserting my lawyerliness I said, "To admit otherwise would make him a party to the crime." I then suggested, "I have the impression, sir, that you didn't trust Justice Fineberg."

"I did not. It was obvious he was carrying a bitter hatred toward Barnes. So I was . . . disturbed by his allegations."

"And about his motives?"

"In fact, yes. His initial claims were all over the map. Affairs with paralegals in their old firm, overbilling clients, and so on. It has been my experience with background checks, particularly for high-level positions, that some people use them as an opportunity to pursue private vendettas."

"So you thought Fineberg was trying to assassinate Barnes?"

"Well, only later did he assert that Barnes had bribed these three judges. I found that suspicious." He looked at our faces and added, "It makes sense now, but not then. Nor would he tell me how he came into possession of the checks, which created certain problems from a legal standpoint. There was the obvious chain of custody issues . . . but I suppose it was his motive that I questioned. So this was what I reported to the President."

Mrs. Hooper insisted, "There was enough there . . . Look, people, this is Washington. Reality check. Barnes was a big boy. He was warned he'd better be whistle-clean. Well . . . he wasn't."

We all guessed there had been an argument in front of the President, and Mrs. Hooper had argued for the safer course, to immediately throw Barnes to the sharks. But at this stage it didn't matter whether Calhoun Barnes oozed with corruption or had the soul of a saint, though we now knew the latter was out of the question. What mattered—all that mattered—as Jennie knew, was who else had been involved in the decision, who else might be on Jason's list, and who might need a heavy dose of special protection.

Townsend of course appreciated this point and said to Jennie, "So I think for your short list, you should include me, Mrs. Hooper, the Attorney General, the White House legal adviser, and Meade Everhill. Also, check your office records and see which agents were involved in the investigation."

Jennie nodded.

Thinking two steps ahead, Phyllis said to Townsend, "Mark, should we still be concerned about the bounty issue?"

Interestingly, he turned to Jennie, who said, "We can't rule it out. We've confirmed that Barnes was informed of the bounty the morning after we discovered it. He had at least forty-eight hours to apply before the Internet site was shut down."

I said, "But he's acting out of rage, not greed. Right?"

"That's true. But why not kill two birds with one stone?" She added, "Also, consider the possibility that he recruited his co-conspirators using the bounty. They're probably mercenaries, and this would certainly explain where he got at least the promise of money." She smiled at Phyllis and added, "I'm sorry. The Agency's not out of this thing yet."

Charles Wardell of the Secret Service announced, "I have to make some calls. The President and Attorney General are already apprised. But I didn't know about Clyde Burns—the legal adviser—or Everhill. Somebody better . . . check on them."

It was now 5:30 A.M. and we all wondered if the grim reaper had not already checked on Everhill and Burns. We'd been completely behind the curve, and it was a relief to play a little catch-up. In fact, the mood in the room had begun to shift, and everybody thought we might even be getting a step ahead of Jason: We knew why and we knew who. What could go wrong?

Again, I had this ominous foreboding that I—that all of us— were overlooking something important.

Wardell stepped out of the room to make his calls. Moving to the next order of business, Townsend turned to George and asked, "Where are we regarding the military munitions?"

George replied, "The lab reported back. Traces of Composition A5 were found on Fineberg's corpse. That's the same propellant used in the Bouncing Betty mine, and apparently, it's a distinctive trace. We're still waiting for confirmation about the antitank weapon." He paused a moment, then said, "We're assuming the weapons were stolen. Procedurally, the military has to report all domestic weapons and munitions thefts and losses to us. So we've accessed those files going back six months."

George paused again to look at the faces around the table. Like many self-important types, he had a lot of irritating habits, but we had to endure this moment of I-know-something-you-don't before he informed us, "There have been a total of sixty-eight reported cases of theft and loss over this six-month period. So I ordered our people to screen all unclosed cases that included the theft or loss of both Light Antitank Weapons and Bouncing Betty mines."

He then proceeded in laborious detail to describe this cross-examination, which was a curious waste of everybody's time, especially as it was George who had reminded the rest of us that we were running against the clock here. I began to wonder if he was running scared. Clearly, Jennie was the star of this show, and George was becoming like the supporting actor who speaks his lines a little too loud and overacts his limited scenes. Eventually, he wrapped it up, saying, "In the end, we found three possibilities. But unfortunately, our friends in the military don't work the same hours we do, so I haven't yet been able to question the Army's CID, that is, the Criminal Investigation Division."

Townsend looked a little exasperated. After a moment he asked George, "Did you make an official request to CID?"

"I . . . yes. I spoke with a night duty officer over in the Pentagon. A major named—"

"When? What time?"

"Uh . . . about two hours ago."

It suddenly became real quiet.

Phyllis looked at me and asked, "Sean, is there a better way to handle this?"

I avoided George's eyes and replied, truthfully, "CID does maintain a duty officer in the Pentagon. But CID headquarters is located at Fort Belvoir, Virginia. We should call Major General Daniel Tingle, the CID commander."

Phyllis looked at George, then at Townsend. She suggested, "Mark, it might be advisable to use Drummond on this."

Townsend looked at me. "You ever work with CID?"

I nodded.

"Then do it." He added, but I think not for my benefit, "Do I need to remind everybody that every hour lost can be counted in lives? We cannot . . . be sitting around . . . with our thumbs up our—"

"Up our noses," Phyllis helpfully interjected. "And you're absolutely right."

"I think I should go with Drummond," Jennie suggested.

Townsend looked at us both and asked, "Why are you still sitting here?"

And we weren't.

CHAPTER SEVENTEEN

WE TOOK THE SAME HELICOPTER, THOUGH THE PILOTS HAD CHANGED OUT while we were in the building. The new pilot jocularly informed us he was named Jimbo, the flight time to Fort Belvoir would be approximately twenty-five minutes, so we should sit back and enjoy the ride. A stewardess would be making the rounds after takeoff, offering a selection of fine wines, snacks, and reading materials.

I grabbed Jennie's gun and shot him. Just kidding.

About two minutes after takeoff, Jennie's cell phone went off. She answered, "Margold," then listened for a minute. "Yeah, good. Hold on." To me, she said, "It's Chuck Wardell. Meade Everhill was found at home, in bed, unharmed. They're moving him to FBI headquarters." She returned to her conversation with Wardell, and they began chatting about the protection screen being set up around Townsend.

It was a little odd that Wardell had called Jennie. But in

chaotic situations, people migrate toward competence, and through good luck, good timing, and, if I say so myself, a bit of deductive brilliance, Jennie and I were the heroes of the hour. I reminded myself that nothing has a shorter half-life than a hero.

I whipped out my cell, called the Pentagon switch, and asked the operator to put me through to the CID duty officer. She did and he answered, "Major Robbins. CID."

I identified myself and informed him I worked for the Director of the FBI, which was partly true and certainly more impressive than the whole truth. I said, "You've already gotten a request for assistance regarding some lost and stolen munitions. Right?"

"About two hours ago. An agent . . . uh, hold on"—he apparently checked his duty log—"Meany . . . George Meany, asked for assistance. He gave me a list of the purported thefts. I already faxed requests for assistance to the CID offices in the locations where the thefts occurred."

"He explained this was high priority?"

"Yes. I categorized them high priority."

"Well . . . explain what that means."

"It's SOP to code our requests. High priority means the receiving stations have seventy-two hours to respond."

"Seventy-two? . . . Is there a higher priority?"

"Of course. Urgent. You have twelve hours to respond."

The Army invented the word "procedures," and Major Robbins had done what he was asked, in a manner both timely and efficient—given his half-assed knowledge of what was going on here.

I didn't want to overwhelm Major Robbins with the facts, so I explained, "Perhaps Meany failed to emphasize the importance of this. So listen closely. We are dealing with a . . . *huge* . . . *fucking* . . . *emergency* here. Somebody's trying to murder the President with those weapons. If this President dies, his Vice

President is going to hunt down whoever failed to stop it and play croquet with their balls on the Rose Garden lawn. Major, do you understand?"

"Uh . . . got it."

"I'm in a helicopter, fifteen minutes out from Belvoir. During that fifteen minutes, you will call Major General Tingle. You will tell him to meet me in his office. You will tell him to have transportation meet me in the Post Exchange parking lot. You will tell him to round up whatever experts on these cases he needs. Got that?"

"Got all that."

"Repeat it back to me," and he did, word for word.

I pulled a pen out of my pocket. "Give me the case numbers of the thefts Meany gave you."

He did that, too, and I jotted them down on my palm. I thanked Major Robbins and punched off.

Jennie said to me, "You were pretty rough on that poor guy."

"Nonsense. Soldier talk."

"Define soldier talk."

"A simple statement of mission, basic steps to accomplish said mission, and the pain I will cause you if you fail."

She shook her head.

"Look, what if I had been all nice and polite? And what if he got it all wrong? Then I'd feel really bad."

She shrugged. "Well, you can't really blame George. To outsiders, the Army is a very foreign world."

"Exactly. That's why he should've called me and asked for help."

"Maybe if you had a more positive and nurturing relationship with George, he would have."

I was about to toss Agent Margold from the helicopter when I saw she was laughing.

For the remainder of the flight, she briefed me on the un-folding plan to use Director Townsend as a decoy to lure Jason Barnes out into the open. The concept, as I understood it, was to encase Townsend in three tons of body armor and have him move around in public all day, flanked and followed by a screen of handpicked agents, armed to the teeth with guns, bad atti-tudes, and Jason Barnes's photo. It sounded well put together, it probably was well put together, and try as I might, I thought of no more than ten things that could go completely wrong. But that wasn't my problem.

Two military police humvees with flashing blue lights awaited us on the tarmac when we set down. I regarded this as a good omen. I thanked Jimbo the pilot for not crashing, and informed him the in-flight movie sucked. He laughed.

Five minutes later we pulled up to the entrance of the head-quarters of the United States Army's Criminal Investigation Divi-sion. A CID officer in mufti awaited us. He escorted us swiftly inside, and down a hallway, and up a stairwell, then down an-other hall to the door of Major General Daniel Tingle, führer of the Army's equivalent of the Gestapo.

Understand that as a military lawyer, I worked with lots of criminal investigators, and when it comes to flatfoots, in my pro-fessional view, none are better. Most CID foot soldiers are former enlisted MPs promoted to the rank of warrant officer, a sort of halfway station between sergeants and commissioned officers, which affords them the best of both worlds. They are accorded the full privileges and respect of an officer, just none of the bull-shit. They can go to the NCO club—where the liquor's cheaper—or the officers' club, where young lieutenants' wives are usually cuter, lonelier, and more gullible. In general, CID types tend to be highly intelligent, arrogant, sneaky, diligent, treacherous, and disrespectful.

Essentially they are detectives, though, unlike their civilian counterparts, CID agents are highly trained in *all* arts and aspects of criminology and criminality, from interrogations through forensics, from rapes through murder, and with rare exceptions, they handle the A to Z of whatever case they're assigned.

Often their work takes them undercover. Arriving incognito, they report into a unit, they work hard to fit in, they create friendships and build strong bonds of trust, and then they bust everybody who farted outside the commode. It is this part of their duties, I think, that makes them beloved to the rest of the Army.

Guys and gals like this need strong adult supervision, and that odious task falls upon a corps of commissioned military police officers. General Tingle was the current top sneak, a guy the rest of the Army's generals try hard to get along with because he has the dirt on everybody.

So we entered the office where General Tingle was seated behind his desk, and he stayed seated behind his desk. On his left flank stood a large, heavyset black officer in battle dress uniform, the crossed pistols of an MP on one collar, the spread eagle of a full colonel on the other collar, and a nametag that read Johnson. On the general's right flank stood two middle-aged men in civilian clothes; from their sneaky faces, presumably both were senior agents. General Tingle, I noted, was attired in pale gray Army sweats, and although mostly bald, his few surviving strands were disheveled, nor had he shaved, nor was he smiling. Obviously he had been dragged out of bed, and from his expression he seemed to be pondering *why*, and by *whom*.

This might be a bad moment to mention my military rank, so I said, "Good morning, General. I'm Sean Drummond with the Central Intelligence Agency. This is Special Agent Jennifer Margold, the Senior Agent in Charge for National Security from the Washington office."

We stepped forward and shook his hand. He said, with remarkable prescience, "Well, I won't say it's nice to meet you. But would you care to sit?"

A pair of Rotarian chairs were in front of his desk, and we chose to sit. Without further ado, I informed him, "We're dealing with an emergency. I'll cut to the chase. I have bad news."

He smiled grimly. "Oh . . . I'm counting on that."

I did not smile back. "Perhaps you heard on the evening news that Merrill Benedict was murdered on the beltway. And a few minutes later, a Supreme Court justice was slain on his own doorstep."

"I heard. And the White House Chief of Staff was massacred in his house yesterday morning. The city's going nuts—I got it." He pointed at me and said, "What I don't get is what this has to do with Army CID."

"That would be the part you didn't hear on the news—Merrill Benedict was murdered with a LAW and Phillip Fineberg with a Bouncing Betty mine, modified into a command-detonated device."

Long silence. Eventually, the general said, "Shit."

"Enough to bury everybody. Don't worry about it."

But he obviously was worried about it. "You're positive these were U.S. military munitions? Russian and French hardware often find their way inside our borders. Both countries produce weapons analogous to the LAW and the Bouncing Betty."

"Traces of Composition A5 were on Fineberg's corpse—the distinctive propellant used with Bouncing Bettys." I allowed him a brief moment to mull that, then added, "As I hope your duty officer informed you, the killers vowed to assassinate the President. So you might say we're a little concerned about how they got these weapons, and about their access to other military munitions—types, quantities, and so forth."

General Tingle was a cool customer and took this understatement in stride. He stared at me. "All right. So this is . . . serious. Now, tell me why you—the CIA—are involved?"

"Because there's some chance this involves foreign terrorists."

He nodded. "Time line?"

"If they're true to their word, they'll try to kill the President within the next twenty-four hours."

"You believe this is credible?"

"They just filled two morgues. Don't you?"

He turned to Colonel Johnson. "Al, how long will it take you to scrub the files?"

But before Johnson could reply, I said, "Our FBI friends already did that. We have good reason to believe the weapons were acquired within the last six months, and our other assumptions are fairly obvious. There are three cases that meet our parameters."

I read the case file numbers and dates off my palm to Colonel Johnson, who left to gather the files. Apparently reading my mind, the general ordered coffee, and an aide left to scrounge a pot from the duty officer. The general looked at me and said, "Do you have military experience, Mr. Drummond?"

"I . . . yes, some."

"Then let me put this in perspective. Right now, we have two wars going on, Afghanistan and Iraq. The Army is shipping equipment and munitions at rates not seen since Vietnam. Visit the port at Galveston . . . it's like wandering through the aisles of some military Wal-Mart. Thousands of tons of artillery shells, main gun tank rounds, track pads, and spare parts pass out of that port every month."

"Meaning we . . . *you* have security problems?" I was having a little trouble with my pronouns.

"We have a security nightmare. Three-quarters of the Army's active, reserve, and National Guard MPs are in Iraq. Nearly all the Army's logistics specialists and security specialists are there, or Afghanistan. We're outsourcing security to civilian firms. They're hiring guys off the street, paying them $8.90 an hour, and begging them not to let their cousins walk through and filch a few M16s."

"But these are mines and LAWs," Jennie noted.

The general nodded. "Let me be frank. We don't really know how much is getting ripped off, or lost, or misplaced. And for obvious reasons we can't halt the train to find out. Sometimes, nobody discovers anything missing until the shipping container gets to Iraq or Afghanistan and it's opened and inventoried. Sometimes the guy doing the inventory arbitrarily decides it's just a bookkeeping error. Or he's lazy and doesn't feel like doing the paperwork to report the missing item. And when it's discovered missing overseas, there's always the questions of how, where it was stolen, and when—here, en route, or over there." He paused, and then added, "So what gets detected, and what gets reported to us, and what we choose to report to the FBI, could be a fraction of what's missing."

I traded glances with Jennie. Not good. The weapons could provide us a lead we desperately needed, and we definitely needed to learn what kind of nasty surprises Barnes might have in store. A lot of things go boom in the night, but some booms turn night into day.

But the general had another point to make. "During peacetime, our accountability, and our follow-up to thefts and losses, are exceptionally good. But what's seriously important in times of peace often becomes trivial when people are fighting and dying. So don't get your hopes up."

Incidentally, I found it both instructive and disconcerting to be on the other side of the table, observing the behavior of military officers through civilian eyes. The military is a brotherhood, or, these days, I guess, a brother-sisterhood. Even though most of the men in this room dressed like civilians, and even looked like civilians, they did not think or act like civilians. Jennie and I were here to stick our noses into an institutional embarrassment, and from their aloofness, shifty gazes, and occasional conversational hesitations, clearly we were not part of the tribe, nor were our efforts appreciated. Nobody was going to lie or deliberately misinform us, but getting the full truth could prove difficult.

I kicked Jennie under the table. She looked up at me, and I twirled my finger through the air. It took a moment before she got it. She reached into her pocket, withdrew her tape recorder, and placed it on the table. The officers all stared at it. She did not turn it on, but it sat there, a warning that only truth better be spoken inside this room.

Jennie smiled at them and said, "A completely harmless formality."

It didn't go over particularly well.

Anyway, we chitchatted a while about the murders, and I offered them a condensed version of the Jason Barnes story while we waited for Colonel Johnson to return with those three files. The coffee came and my mood brightened.

Despite his job title, General Tingle, it turned out, was a fairly amiable and even charming guy, with a good gift for gab, and he even tried out a few jokes on us, though his timing was off and they came off a little flat. You could tell he was a little unfocused and stressed, thinking ahead about how it was going to look for

Uncle Sam's Army when word got out that weapons intended to kill Al-Qaeda assholes and bad Iraqis had been used to exterminate important members of the U.S. executive and judiciary branches.

For some weird reason, I thought of the inscription on the side of the directional Claymore mine that reads, "Point this side toward the enemy." Yet in every conflict there is always the guy who's exhausted or nervous or hurrying, and the enemy moves into his sights, and he squeezes the triggering mechanism, and ten thousand tiny pellets fly up his own ass.

Despite the best precautions and the best intentions, sometimes shit just happens.

CHAPTER EIGHTEEN

COLONEL JOHNSON RETURNED, AND IN HIS BEEFY FISTS WERE THREE THICK files. General Tingle suggested we adjourn to the long conference table in the corner of his office. A general's wish is your command, and we got up and rearranged ourselves.

Tingle read each file first, then me, and I handed them to Jennie, who slid them down the table to Colonel Johnson. Having perused many CID files, Tingle and I raced through, whereas Jennie kept thumbing around, searching for the relevant pages and passages.

We were nearly halfway through when another gent wandered into the office. He wore a gray suit and was about twenty years younger than the other agents, nor did he look really sneaky, just slightly shifty. He walked directly to the far corner of the room, and Colonel Johnson left the table and the two of them engaged in a quick whispered conversation.

As I read, I learned that the M72 Light Antitank Weapon

comes stored in boxes of two, and the Bouncing Betty mine—the proper nomenclature being the M16A2 mine—comes stored in boxes of four. Thus it seemed a fair assumption that Jason and his pals had at least one more LAW, at least three more Bouncing Bettys, and, hopefully, no suitcase nukes or canisters of anthrax some idiot packed in the wrong box. But it happens.

One theft occurred from an arms storage bunker located at Fort Hood, Texas. The bunker was inventoried on November 16—everything on hand and shipshape—and was then reinventoried on December 16, a perfunctory monthly check done by a lieutenant detailed from a local infantry battalion. During the second inventory, the lieutenant noted that three containers of 81mm mortar rounds, two containers of LAWs, and three boxes of M16A2 mines that were present for duty at the first inventory were now AWOL, and he dutifully filed an appropriate Oh-Shit report.

The second open case was a bit more interesting, and from our perspective, more hair-raising. At 2:00 A.M. on the night of December 22, a flatbed truck pulled up to the Port of Galveston Pier 37 Roll-on, Roll-off Terminal. The driver dutifully showed the night guard a set of authorization documents and was allowed entry to the facility. Three bulk containers were loaded on board the truck's flatbed, and the vehicle and crew drove off into the steamy night. One container held forty boxes of LAWs, another held sixty containers of M16A2 mines, and the third held forty M16 automatic rifles. A routine check the next morning revealed that nobody in existence had dispatched the truck, and with the impressive clarity of hindsight it was swiftly concluded that the authorization documents were forgeries, and expert ones.

I truly hoped this wasn't the one. Jason and his pals could have enough stuff to turn D.C. into Baghdad.

On the other hand, the earmarks were there—superior organization, boldness, and cleverness. Not good.

The last theft was more ambiguous, more haphazard, and for its sheer brazenness, in a way the most ingenious. On February 9, also at Fort Hood, three different units engaged in marksmanship training on three different firing ranges reported the disappearance of munitions. An infantry unit at a LAW range reported two boxes of M72 LAWs mysteriously missing. Twenty minutes later, an engineer unit training at an explosives range reported that one box of M16A2 mines, a twenty-pound container of C4 plastic explosive, and two boxes of blasting caps were on the lam. And within minutes, a different infantry unit at a third range reported that twenty M203 grenades, as well as an M203 grenade launcher, were missing.

The reports rolled into the headquarters, the post commander went nuts, and a post-wide lockdown was immediately initiated. Within three hours, two range control inspectors were found, hog-tied with tent cord, in a small ravine beside a tank trail. Their unhappy story was that they had stopped on the trail to help a uniformed soldier who flagged them down, who then approached their humvee, suddenly whipped out a handheld Taser, and efficiently dispatched them both to la-la land. Their humvee and their range control armbands were stolen. The humvee turned up the next morning ditched beside another tank trail.

This theft was unsettling and curious, but of the three cases the one from Galveston had the ugliest possibilities. If Jason had that much stuff, an all-out assault on the White House was a possibility. Looking first at me, then at Jennie, General Tingle asked, "Well . . . any conclusions?"

I was sure the question was rhetorical. We didn't have a clue.

Tingle turned and requested the most recent arrival to join

us. Back to us, he explained, "Chief Warrant Eric Tanner, our resident expert in munitions and weapons security. One of our top investigators."

We all shook hands. Without any ado, Eric Tanner made a sweeping announcement, suggesting, "If international terrorists are behind these murders, you're wasting your time with all three of these cases."

Jennie glanced at me, and then informed him, "Our lead suspect is a Secret Service agent named Barnes. *If* there's a connection to foreign terrorists, it's only financial."

"Okay." He considered that a moment, then asked, "Accomplices?"

"Three we know of—possibly more. Barnes appears to be the mastermind. At least one woman is involved."

Eric raised an eyebrow but did not comment on that news.

I asked, "Why are you so sure these thefts didn't involve foreign terrorists?"

"Start with the first case at Fort Hood, the bunker theft. Here's what happened. The munitions bunker has a double lock system. It's electronically monitored whenever it's opened." He looked at me and said, "You get it, right?"

"The thefts occurred during an authorized entry."

From the corner of my eye I saw Tingle nod and Tanner continued, "The bunker was opened *only* once between the two monthly inventories, by a quartermaster team—a sergeant and three privates—delivering fifty containers of 5.56 ammo. It might interest you to know that this is our most common form of munitions thefts."

"I thought the case remained open."

"It is." Tingle again nodded, and Tanner explained, "We interrogated the four soldiers. Nobody confessed, though obviously at least one of them's lying. Nearly always in cases like this, it was a crime of opportunity. So now the thief has to locate a buyer, and we're watching all four of them."

I thought about that a moment. "Isn't that . . . a little passive?"

He gave me a sneaky smile. "Each of the four will soon be approached by a fat-cat arms merchant from the Middle East—one of our guys. He's already in Killeen, the town outside the base, casing his targets."

"I see."

"We know how to cover our asses, Mr. Drummond."

General Tingle coughed into his hand.

Eric Tanner shrugged, and continued, "The case at Galveston, on the other hand . . . well, you read the case file. These were professionals. They knew exactly when to arrive, where the containers were located, and had expert forgeries. The combination of the large quantity of the munitions and the level of criminal sophistication made us more concerned than usual."

"As it should."

"So after we reported it to the Bureau, we also notified your people at the Agency, Mr. Drummond."

Colonel Johnson got into the act, informing me, "About three weeks later, your people got word to us that a government military platoon in Colombia walked into a minefield and two soldiers were killed. The descriptions of the incident indicated the killing devices were Bouncing Bettys. They also reported a sharp step-up in vehicular ambushes by FARC rebel units using short-range rockets."

Eric surmised, "So we know where the weapons ended up."

"But not," General Tingle concluded, looking sharply at Tanner, "*who* orchestrated the theft." He turned back to me and asked, "Do you believe this Barnes is in some way connected to the Colombian FARC rebels?"

"No. Rule it out." So now we were down to the third and final case, the second theft at Fort Hood. These were all crafty men, and I doubted this was serendipity.

Colonel Johnson, who appeared to be Tingle's executive assistant, asked, "Anybody need a refill?"

While we refreshed our cups, Chief Tanner said, "Let's talk for a moment about what happened at Fort Hood on February 9."

Jennie glanced at her watch. "Let's do."

"But I'd like to precede that discussion with a little background. Around Fort Hood—around all our bases—are crime rings that feed off our troops, our families, and our equipment. Insurance fraud rings, phony mortgage and car loan setups, prostitution, and even burglary rings. Some of these parasites are strictly amateur hour. Others are incredibly shrewd. In those cases where the crimes cross boundaries between our bases and the surrounding communities, we work closely with local police forces, and often, with the FBI."

He paused to see if we had any questions. We didn't, and he continued, "At Fort Hood, we have a ring specializing in munitions and weapons thefts. Once or twice a year they pull off something. This has been going on for . . . about five years. A file cabinet in my office is crammed with various investigations we believe are all interrelated."

Jennie asked, "And you believe the February 9 incident and those cases are also related?"

"I'm sure of it." Becoming more animated, he bent forward and explained, "Here's what's interesting. This group never repeats the same thing twice. For a long time, nobody even realized we were dealing with a ring. The thefts were so different, and occurred so infrequently, you couldn't detect a common MO."

Colonel Johnson grabbed my left arm and confided, "Ignore his modesty. It was Eric who uncovered the common thread."

This compliment brought a happy beam to Tanner's face. Jennie leaned toward him and asked, "What is that common thread?"

"The very fact that no two thefts are alike. I'm sure that's by design. These are smart people with a certain flair for stagecraft, and a characteristic boldness I've come to regard as their calling card."

Jennie thought about that a moment. She said, "Interesting theory. Give us an example."

"Okay, take this February 9 incident. They probably came on post wearing uniforms, using forged military ID cards. Range control personnel are authority figures. They wear special armbands that allow them access to all ranges and license to poke around for safety violations, *and* to inspect and inventory munitions. So they hijack a range control vehicle, they show up at these three ranges, and they pilfer ammo while everybody thinks they're just doing their job."

I tried to picture this in my mind. In truth, it was a diabolically clever way to steal from the Army. Range control people tend to be mostly senior sergeants who, despite their lower rank, are feared by the young officers who run firing ranges, because, as Tanner mentioned, their mission involves hunting for safety and procedural problems, and if they find them, they have the clout to shut down the range and cite the young officers. This tends not to go down well with the officers' superiors. But neither does having weapons and ammunition stolen right under your nose, and I was sure that three young officers at Fort Hood were busily sending their résumés to career placement firms.

Tanner continued, "In fact, the thefts weren't even noticed

till the end of the day, as units were closing up the ranges and doing their final inventories. By then, these crooks are swigging beers at the Lone Star Bar and Grill, laughing at how stupid we are." After a moment, he reflected, "These people *really* have balls."

I sized up Eric Tanner for a moment. Clearly, this case was personal for him. That wasn't necessarily bad; neither was it necessarily good. It's healthy to feel some outrage over the crime. In the tough cases, that's what keeps you putting one foot in front of another to the end. But to get to the end, logic is the fuel, and emotion a poisonous indulgence.

As I said, Mr. Tanner was young, mid- to late twenties, I'd guess, and sort of baby-faced, so it was hard to pin down. Also, he was cocky, or at the least very sure of himself, if there's a difference. He spoke well, and presented his findings and his views in a linear, forceful fashion, which is sometimes the sign of a clear mind, and other times the trademark of a blowhard. But General Tingle, and Eric's peers, and Eric's superiors all thought highly of him, or he wouldn't have his responsibilities. For sure, he wouldn't have a seat at this table.

Still, as a prosecutor, I had a strong preference for older CID agents on the stand. Age implies wisdom and seasoning, whereas youth suggests greenness and impulsiveness, which make juries jittery. Physical impressions might be shallow or even misleading, but they are a factor, and they count. Eric Tanner should grow a mustache.

I looked at General Tingle and commented, "This was an inside job."

"Why do you say that?"

"Because Fort Hood's the largest base in the country. Because it contains hundreds of miles of range roads and many dozens of ranges. Because your perps understand how range management works, they're familiar with the tank trails, and because it looks like they knew which units were firing on which ranges that day."

"All good points."

"Come on, General. Don't tell me you missed this."

General Tingle found it amusing that some outside dunce could figure this out. He grinned at me and said, "Hold that thought."

Tanner added, "It might also interest you to know, Mr. Drummond, that the soldier who flagged down the range control vehicle was a woman."

"Oh. You got a description?"

"Better. Early thirties, slender, medium height, long blond hair wrapped in a tight bun. A looker, too—the witnesses all agreed on that point. In fact, we obtained reliable composite sketches of both her and her male accomplice from the hijacked range control crew, and from the witnesses at the ranges." Eric allowed us a moment to absorb that, and then suggested, "Off the top of my head, I think this case, and I think this ring, fits the parameters you're looking for."

"Because of the woman?"

He hesitated, and then leaned toward me. "Well—what if this same group is working with this guy Barnes?"

Jennie, however, looked at Eric and said, "Slow down, champ. You're driving way too fast."

I said to Jennie, "What bothers you?"

"Everything." She looked at the faces around the room. "Criminal Science 101—cases are connected by commonalities, not disparities." She fixed her chilly blue eyes on Eric. "You said you suspect a ring because no two thefts were alike. That kind of counterintuitive logic is the antithesis of sound police work."

From a technical and procedural standpoint, she was correct. Also, it was instructive to note from the expressions around the room that nobody really appreciated an outsider coming into the inner sanctum to announce that one of the fair-haired boys was full of crap. Least of all Eric, who responded, a bit defensively, "I know the science, Agent Margold. But there are times when you have to throw the manuals out the window."

"Do you?"

"Yes. After five years of weapons and munitions thefts, all targeting the same base, all showing unusual creativity, all evidenced by a strong awareness of base procedures and vulnerabilities . . . I'm *sure* these cases are connected."

Jennie did not immediately reply. She studied Eric, and then said, "I worked Behavioral Science at Quantico for five years before I got this job. You know what we hated?"

When nobody else pitched in, I said, "What?"

"A city gets ten unsolved female murders in a year. The detectives come under intolerable pressure to achieve a few closures. Pretty soon, somebody cleverly rationalizes that because it's the same crime, because of the common sex of the victims, because of the common province of the murders, they're all related, and some horrifying serial killer is behind it. So they notify us, and we jump through our ass, and fly out a team, and we spend weeks poring over everything. They get the heat off themselves by shifting it to us. Problem is, it's not one killer, it's a bunch of killers. Also a waste of time."

Everybody grew quiet. Jennie stared at Eric. "So I'd like to know more about how you tied this together."

Being the diplomatic type, I turned to Eric. "Give us an example of another theft."

"All right. Winter, two years ago. A unit was sending a two-and-a-half-ton truck filled with M16s off post to a depot facility to have the weapons reblued—that is, to have the exterior metal parts recoated with an antirust compound. Now, here's the first interesting fact. It's routine to send broken weapons to depot level to be repaired—*nonfunctioning* weapons that won't work till they're fixed—but the thieves targeted a vehicle filled with working weapons."

I commented, "Which would seem to imply inside knowledge."

"Yeah, exactly. The truck got about thirty miles outside Killeen, when a car roared up from behind and nearly sideswiped it. The car had apparently been following and waited until the truck reached a lightly trafficked back road. Then the car got just ahead, and one of the thieves tossed out a bunch of oversized tiretacks. Our lab later determined that the tacks had been specially manufactured for this hit. The thieves wore balaclava hoods, and were armed. They made off with forty M16s."

Jennie and I exchanged glances. I had no idea what she was thinking. She asked Eric, "How many people in the car?"

"Two."

"Was there a woman?"

"Maybe." But after a moment, he admitted, "Look, they were both built like men, and they moved like men. But as I said, they were masked, so the truck driver couldn't provide good descriptions. We know one man was extremely tall and lanky. Maybe six foot six or six foot seven."

Jennie asked, "Well . . . was a woman observed at any of the thefts you haven't described?"

"No. But there were no reliable witnesses to the other thefts."

"No . . . witnesses." She asked, "What about the tall guy?"

"Just at the hijack."

Jennie began tapping a pen on the table. "Yet you're *assum-*

ing all these people are part of the same ring, and you're assuming the female might have been present at other crimes?"

"I'm sure they're one team. And I'm sure she's part of the team. Sometimes she's involved, sometimes not."

"Did they kill anybody?"

"They planned well enough that they didn't have to."

Jennie leaned toward him. "Was that deliberate?"

"I'm sure it was."

"You're *sure*, Mr. Tanner? Seven times you've used that word. But, you're not . . . *sure*. You're manufacturing assumptions and guesses, and expressing them as facts. Right?"

"I—"

"Beyond the *possibility* of an inside source, I can't see any resemblance between the two thefts. You have witnesses to two of the crimes, yet none of the same perps were observed at both crime scenes. Correct?"

"Yes . . . but—"

"One crime was committed on base, employing masquerade, falsified documents, and a nonlethal weapon. The perps showed their faces and left witnesses. Have I described this accurately?"

"Yes, and I—"

"The earlier theft occurred off base. They used guns, they wore masks, and their technique was markedly less clever and less restrained. One theft showed complexity and finesse, the other was simple and coarse. One was a scam, the other your basic armed robbery." She leaned back into her chair and exhaled a long breath. "But maybe I'm just dense. Tell me again, what ties them together?"

Clearly, Eric had not been subjected to, nor had he anticipated, this kind of rigorous interrogation. He was becoming flustered, and it showed. He said, "Well, I see the differences, and . . . as I said, those differences are—"

"Those differences are enormous. How many weapons or munitions thefts and losses occurred at Fort Hood over the past five years?"

"Well . . . a lot."

"A *lot*?"

"It's our biggest base. Many dozens. Perhaps a hundred or so."

"Are they all interconnected? Applying your reasoning, the intent, the location, and the desired loot were the same."

"Look . . . we all know you can't—"

"That's right, Mr. Tanner—you can't. And now you're suggesting these same people—who aren't actually the same people—are working with Jason Barnes here in Washington. But how would Jason Barnes even know these people?"

"I . . . I don't know."

"You don't seem to know much." The room was completely still. General Tingle, Colonel Johnson, and the two older agents were mesmerized, watching their prize peacock getting his plumage ripped off by a pit bull.

I put a hand on Jennie's leg under the table and squeezed, a signal to back off. Jennie drew a breath. Speaking at Tanner, but clearly to me, she said, "I hope I'm not being too harsh on you, Mr. Tanner. We're investigating the most serious case in the land. Somebody assassinated three of our highest officials, and coldly murdered thirteen others. Now they are promising to murder our President. You've suggested a link to your case. We need to know if it's worth following. Understand?"

"Sure. And I—"

"Wouldn't you agree there's a compelling difference between this . . . this team of thieves you're hypothesizing, and a trio of expertly trained killers?"

"Well, I think—"

"What you should think—what you should *know*—there's a threshold in every criminal mind. You're describing thieves who tailor their schemes to avoid having to kill. They have a moral or pragmatic line in the sand."

"Crime is a stepladder, Miss Margold. Like dope—start with marijuana and eventually you're mainlining heroin."

Clearly, Jennie did not appreciate this lecture on criminology, and replied, "Boy . . . I sure wish I had your intuitive insights before I taught criminal motivation at Quantico for five years." She looked at me. Turning back to Eric, she said, "There has to be something you're withholding. Right?"

Eric's face was slightly pink. He was twisting his wedding band around his finger, I thought metaphorically, wishing he was wringing Jennie's neck. "No . . . unless you want to hear about the other thefts."

"I . . ." She looked at her watch and shook her head dismissively. "We don't really have time for that."

Jennie had made her point, but she had been really rough on the poor guy. He kept glancing at General Tingle, probably wondering if he still had a job. Actually, I felt sorry for Eric Tanner.

In a moment of uncharacteristic generosity, I turned to General Tingle and asked, "Earlier you asked me to hold that thought. What thought?"

He'd been so preoccupied watching Eric being bent over and Roto-Rooted that he needed a moment to come to his senses. "What? Oh, yes . . . right. I was going to say, when you raised the issue of an insider, Eric and the CID detachment at Fort Hood went through a painstaking process to try to pinpoint that source."

I nodded at Eric. It wouldn't hurt to get a few points back on the board, and I said, "Tell me about that."

Eric cleared his throat and recovered a little of his cockiness.

"Well, our people considered a number of variables. Soldiers are reassigned every two or three years, so we're *sure*— uh . . . we *think* we're dealing with a civilian employee, somebody with access to range control data, logistics information, information on MP security procedures, and certain other command information."

"Sounds reasonable."

"We narrowed it down to five civilian suspects."

"That's a workable number."

"Yeah, but that's when we hit a brick wall. They all looked good, and they all had discounting factors. So we sent this list to the Behavioral Science Unit, and we asked them to have a profiler assess our suspects and determine our most likely candidates."

Sounded like a smart move to me, but Jennie mumbled, "Good luck."

The general looked a little surprised. "What do you mean?"

"I mean, the BSU is up to its ass in serial killers, serial arsonists, serial rapists, and, these days, serial snipers." She turned to Eric and asked, "Have you gotten a response yet?"

"No."

"And you probably won't. Ever," Jennie informed him. "The BSU gets perhaps ten thousand requests a year, from the rest of the FBI, from every local and city police department in the country, and, these days, from police forces around the world who've heard of the unit and its unique abilities. The unit's very small and notoriously overworked. Your case is too vague and too trivial to merit their attention. It's probably near the bottom of the slush pile."

Jennie then turned to me. She pointed at her watch and said, "We *need* to be going."

I nodded. Everybody nodded, apparently agreeing that we should be going.

General Tingle stood, and we both stood. The general remarked to us, "I warned you that it might be difficult to isolate a particular case."

Jennie shrugged. "Elimination is as important as discovery. We've at least ruled out three cases that aren't hopeful."

In that light, I said, "However, General, you and your people should keep searching. It's possible the FBI screen missed some likely cases, and it's also possible the case was never reported to the FBI in the first place."

Tingle positioned himself between us, took our arms, and began speeding us along to the door. He couldn't get rid of us fast enough. "In an hour this headquarters will be swarming with investigators. I'll send a worldwide alert to all CID stations to review all lost and stolen weapons cases. I'll call if we get anything."

Eric Tanner looked particularly relieved as we bid our adieus and went back outside and climbed into the MP humvee for the drive back to the helicopter. Jennie was quiet and moody. Not a word was said during the ride.

Fortunately, Jimbo had somehow gotten his hands on a thermos of coffee and two mugs, and I suddenly saw him in a whole new light. You can run on adrenaline for only so long, after that it's all about caffeine.

The helicopter lifted off, and Jennie still said not a word. Eventually, she turned to me. "Was it your impression we got anything useful out of that?"

"Probably not."

She exhaled deeply. "I found that very . . . frustrating." After another moment she said, "That Tanner guy, he pissed me off."

"I thought you two hit it off really well."

"I'm serious. He got under my skin."

"Fooled me."

"He was so full of himself. I can't remember seeing shoddier police work. CID people . . . are they always that amateurish?"

"Now, that's unfair."

"Is it? If I brought a half-baked theory like that to my boss, I'd be fetching coffee and doughnuts for the bookkeepers."

"Goodness—did we get up on the wrong side of the bed this morning?"

"We never went to bed."

"Ah . . . that explains it."

"Would you get serious?" Apparently she *was* in a really foul mood, because she added, "I shouldn't have to remind you that every minute is precious. *That* was a complete waste of our time."

"Fine. That's what we'll report back."

"Fine." She stared out the window, and I stared out the other window.

I hadn't seen her like this, except at our first meeting, when the gun was really at her head. But as somebody wise and knowing once advised me, women speak two languages, one of which is verbal. Still, I thought I knew what was going on here. This wasn't about Eric Tanner, this was about George Meany. These two were playing for keeps. He had undermined her from day one, and now he was trying to deep-six her career, dropping dimes on her to Townsend, and who knew what else. Being her boss, George had lots of advantages he was not hesitating to use. Jennie's only chance was to bring home breakthroughs, not dead ends.

After a few minutes of silence, she grabbed my sleeve and pulled me toward her. She asked, "Am I being a bitch?"

Well, I do know when to keep my mouth shut.

She said, "I know I am."

"Well . . . actually—"

"Sorry. Lack of sleep. Lack of breakfast."

I did not reply to that either.

She said, "When we're done debriefing, let's get that hotel room."

And like that, the day was off to an interesting start.

CHAPTER NINETEEN

As WE CLIMBED OFF THE HELICOPTER AND WALKED ACROSS THE TARMAC, WE shook hands and agreed we would keep our debriefings short and be out in no time. In truth, I had felt fine until Jennie mentioned food and sleep, at which point Pavlov kicked in. My ass was really dragging.

But by coincidence, Mort Silverman was puffing on a big stogie outside the entrance as we made our way into the building. Between his plump physique, rumpled suit, and oversize cigar, the guy looked like Danny DeVito in front of a bad movie set. In fact, I had yet to observe a single CIA person who bore an even passing resemblance to James Bond. Most, like Mort or Phyllis, looked like somebody you'd run into in the produce section of the local Giant. Of course, it's not about how they *look*: It's about how they think. I introduced Mort to Jennie, and Jennie to Mort, and they exchanged a few pleasantries.

Incidentally, I noticed that Mort was standing on my left foot,

234

which I interpreted as a subtle way of telling me not to go anywhere. Jennie had to check her phone messages, and eventually she departed, leaving us alone.

Mort drew a heavy puff from his cigar and asked, "Got a minute?"

"For you, Mort, two minutes."

"Two things. You want the good news first or last?"

"How about the kick in the ass first."

He laughed. "Yeah, well . . . you know a guy named George?"

"Why? Has he been shot? Tell me it's so."

"You should wish. He called Phyllis while I was in there. Not for nothin', watch your ass around him."

"And what was George's issue?"

"I couldn't hear much. But I caught enough to know he was pissing all over you."

"Thanks. I owe you one."

"Yeah, you do. Now you're about to owe me two." He asked, "You know what Carnivore is?"

"Sort of like an Internet search service, right?"

"Like King Kong is sort of a monkey. It belongs to the FBI, and NSA's got another version that works internationally. You cue it for . . . like, certain words and phrases, and it sweeps through the world's telephone and e-mail conversations. If one of these phrases pops up, say, in a conversation, it gets collected."

Perhaps recalling that I was a technological dimwit, Mort searched my face to be sure I understood before he continued. "Phyllis had Peterson order NSA to look for the phrase 'one hundred million bucks,' or variations thereof."

"Good thinking. They get anything?"

"A lot of hits, from banks, security houses, and the U.S. Congress." He paused a moment and sucked on his cigar. "But somebody's shoving a block of a hundred million bucks pretty quickly through a bunch of banks."

"Explain that."

"This basket of money's gone through . . . like, six banks, just in the past twelve hours."

"Okay. Why would somebody do that?"

"You tell me."

I thought about it a moment. "Laundering?"

"Well, I called some sources over at Treasury. Good guys . . . they're into this money shit, right? Not laundered . . . hidden."

"And there's a distinction?"

He laughed. "That's what I said. Sometimes tax dodgers, they shift their money around a lot. It creates a long chain, and tax authorities lose the thread."

"Okay."

"I said, so if you had to make an illegal payment of, like, a hundred million sometime in the near future, would you do that? They said that's exactly what you'd do. The money loses its identity. Cycle it a few times through Swiss banks, the Caymans, a few little Pacific islands—places with liberal-to-no reporting procedures—pretty soon, you wouldn't have a clue where the money originated."

"But would you know where it comes out?"

"*If* it stays in a single block. But if, at some point, they break it up, like into a bunch of five- or ten-million packets, and wire it sequentially, you could lose visibility of it."

I nodded, and he said, "If these guys are any good, they'll do just that."

"So what do we do about that?"

"Phyllis is on the phone right now with NSA and Treasury. They say, if they can catch it at just the right moment, NSA can put tracers on it, like a thousand little cookies. Then, no matter what the meatheads try, we'll know."

Interesting. Only one problem. "But—"

"Yeah . . . you got it." Mort looked down at his shoes a moment. "We catch them *after* the President's already dead."

So anyway, Mort asked what I'd been up to. He'd been open and straight with me, so I was open and straight with him, and I told him about Margaret and Jason, and we both agreed that the Barneses were one screwy family. It's all about reciprocation.

Phyllis was still chatting on the phone when I entered her office. I stood perfectly still in front of her desk for about thirty seconds. Unfortunately, patience is really not my strong suit. I began wandering around, pawing her pictures, pulling out her books and checking titles, playing with the few personal items on her desk. I hate it when people do that.

She eventually got the message, and she put a hand over the phone's mouthpiece. "Drummond, if you don't take your hands off my property, sit down, and behave, I'll boil you alive."

Goodness. I set down her teacup, sat at the conference table, and behaved perfectly, while loudly drumming my fingers and tapping my foot. Two out of three is really good for me.

Whoever Phyllis was chatting with apparently was bellyaching about how much trouble and expense it would be to follow, say, a hundred packets of wired money, if the bad guys chose to break it up. I mean, somebody just murdered three of our highest officials, they've threatened to assassinate the President, and this bureaucrat's worried about his overtime account. Typical. But Phyllis knew the drill and remained patient, though firm and insistent.

Eventually, she hung up and focused on me. "Well? Anything worthwhile turn up from our CID friends?"

"The one lead that looked good turned out not to be good."

"That happens. Still you have to go through the process. You know about—?"

"I know. I ran into Mort."

"Fine. Now I'll update you on our other progress." And for the next two minutes she did. Apparently, the world had now been informed that Jason Barnes was the killer and the manhunt was in full froth. With its usual anal efficiency, the Bureau had released and distributed not only Jason's official photograph but a sort of facsimile gallery of this-asshole-could-look-like-this sketches—Jason with a mustache, with glasses, a beard, bald, as a blond cross-dresser, whatever. The gallery would be printed on the front page of the *Washington Post*. This way, in the morning Jason would know what disguise not to wear.

The Bureau had to go through the paces, but sometimes the right thing to do is also the stupid thing to do. Not that I had a better suggestion. In fact, as Phyllis elaborated more of the steps and precautions—setting up checkpoints at strategic locations, screening Jason's charge card purchases to see where he liked to hang out, his phone records to see who he hung out with, etcetera—it struck me that hunting this guy down was going to be a bitch. I mean, there are people without Jason's brains, experience, and inside edges who spent ten years on the FBI's most wanted list. But Jason had lived in D.C. for three years, he knew the streets, he knew how to get around, and he knew what the police could do and what the police could not do.

Also, Jason's accomplices, in the parlance of the Bureau, remained UnSubs. Without the slightest tick of recognition, they could go out, retrieve groceries, scope out the checkpoints, and surveil the targets, while Jason hung around his hidey-hole and hatched his nefarious plans and plots. But enough unbridled optimism.

Eventually, Phyllis wrapped it up by asking me, "Anything you can think of we should be doing but aren't?"

"Not a thing."

"Do you think he'll go after Mark Townsend?"

"I think, if he's half as good as he's been so far, he'll detect the security coverage and look elsewhere."

She nodded. "It's not a good posture, is it?"

"It's a terrible posture. Basically, we're waiting for him to make the next move, and praying he makes the kind of mistake he hasn't made yet."

"My read also." She added, "Let's hope his next move's not too awful."

"If you're the target," I noted, "it *will* be awful."

"Of course. Speaking of awful, you look terrible."

Well, I should. I was trying to look terrible. I had scruffed up my hair and I sank a little lower in my seat. I yawned. "Well . . . I'm fine, boss . . . a little . . . tired . . . hungry . . . filthy . . . but—"

"Go get cleaned up and take a nap, Drummond. You're no good to anybody if you can't think. Lord knows what might develop later today."

I stood. "I . . . if you insist."

She looked at me curiously. "I'm certainly not . . . insisting."

I fast-stepped toward the exit, before she had a change of heart. She said, as I went out the door, "Just be sure to leave your number with the comm center in the event—"

I shut the door.

Elizabeth sat at her station outside Jennie's office door, and she smiled at me as I approached. She appeared to like me for some reason. As I said, women are rotten judges of men. I smiled back and said, "Good morning, Elizabeth. Is her majesty ready to depart?"

"On the phone at the moment."

I leaned against Elizabeth's desk and waited. We chatted amiably for a few moments, then, totally out of the blue, she mentioned, "I think she likes you."

I ordinarily don't like nosy, gossipy women sticking their noses in my business. But this was okay. "Oh . . . well, you know, we're just partners . . . maybe friends—"

"I don't think so. She thinks you're very attractive . . . and sexy."

"She never mentioned smart?"

Elizabeth laughed. She then paused, as gabbers do, contemplating how much to disclose. Eventually she stated, "She needs a man. She should have children by now. Have you ever been married?"

"Nope."

"Never? How old are you, Major?"

It could only go downhill from here, so I pointed at her ring. "Well . . . how long have you been married?"

"Twenty-seven wonderful years. Seven kids. Three girls and four boys. Just had our first grandchild."

"Wow! That's a lot of—"

"Children. Yes, I know. Don't you want children?"

"Can't I just borrow them?"

"How many?"

I was on the verge of killing either her or myself when fortunately the red blinker on Elizabeth's phone stopped blinking. Before Elizabeth could say another word, I said, "I'd better catch her while she's free." I popped my head into Jennie's office. "Still up for this?"

"Yes . . . I think."

She looked doubtful, however, and I suggested, "Maybe we shouldn't."

"With everything going on, you're probably right."

So we both weighed the choice between lounging around our cramped offices and waiting for something to happen or a nice breakfast, shower, and a nap, or perhaps something more than a nap. I said, "Bring your cell phone."

She grabbed her purse and mentioned, "That was George."

"What's he doing?"

"He's assumed direct control of the security around Townsend."

"Smart boy. Take care of the boss, and the boss takes care of you."

She smiled. "He's not as smart as we are."

I smiled back.

CHAPTER TWENTY

WE PARKED IN THE UNDERGROUND GARAGE, AND VIA THE ELEVATOR AScended up to ground level. It is in the strange nature of females to always plan ahead, and Jennie informed me she had already called and booked us at the Hyatt Regency on Jefferson Davis Highway, which, as you might expect, had a lobby the size of a pro basketball court filled with la-di-da furnishings. A long line of overnighters and businesspeople gripping their briefcases were nonchalantly waiting to check out and shove off for the next town while we waited to check in.

It took a while to reach the head of the line, and we passed our time the way two people do who are on the cusp of first-time sex, or at least seriously thinking about it—a little shy, nervously flirtatious, laughing a little too hard, but at least we weren't panting.

But it could be I was misreading the signals here. It could be that Ms. Margold was just giddy from relief to be away from the hubbub of the investigation and from George. Women are confusing.

Jennie gave her name to the clerk, who punched it into the bowels of her computer. After a moment she looked up, first at Jennie, then at me. She clarified, "Two rooms, right?"

Jennie looked at me and asked the clerk, "Do you have a room with two double beds?"

"Of course."

Back to me, Jennie asked, "Do you mind?"

Did I? "Well . . . considering the federal debt . . ."

"I was thinking it would keep either of us from oversleeping." Jennie looked at the clerk. "One room will be fine."

She passed her Bureau charge card across the counter, and while the desk clerk made the necessary adjustments, I stood and contemplated the meaning of this. Two rooms definitely meant breakfast and a nap. One room could mean breakfast and no nap. Alternatively, one room could also mean breakfast, a cold shower, and a nap. I wasn't really sure what I was getting into, or if this was a good idea for either of us.

The magnetic passkey and charge card were passed across the counter, and Jennie informed the clerk, "We're federal agents. We're here on government business. Call the room in four hours, would you?"

I smiled at the young lady, who smiled back, I'm sure thinking how very fortunate our republic was to have such thrift-minded public servants.

We walked across the lobby and entered the elevator without exchanging a word, or even eye contact. Inside the elevator, Jennie said, "Ninth floor," and pushed what I hoped was the appropriate button.

I said, "Nice day, isn't it?"

"Seasonably warm," replied Jennie, staring straight ahead.

Well, this didn't sound like precoital banter.

We left the elevator and found the room with the same number on the door as the number on the envelope the clerk had given her. This was a good start. Jennie stuffed the magnetic keycard in the slot and the door opened.

We stepped inside. The room was expansive, I noted, with two comfy beds, the usual array of chairs, TV, side tables, and an overpowering aura of nervous uncertainty. I walked across the room, removing my coat and tie, which I threw into a messy heap on a chair. Jennie went to the other side of the room, removing her jacket, which she neatly folded and hung carefully on the other chair. I pointed at the Glock and holster on her hip. "I don't think you'll be needing that."

She smiled. "Won't I?"

Interesting. But she removed her holster and pistol and placed them dead center on the writing desk.

I sat on the bed, picked up the phone, and punched the button for room service. I ordered a six-egg western omelet for me, a large dish of fries, a side order of bacon, extra catsup, a pot of coffee, and a pot of tea for the lady. I asked Jennie what she wanted to eat.

"Fruit platter and two strawberry yogurts."

We obviously had different concepts of food, but I passed it along and hung up. I informed Jennie, "Fifteen minutes." I pointed toward the bathroom. "Ladies before gents."

"Oh . . . there's a gentleman around?" She was casually unbuttoning her blouse and moving toward the bathroom when she added, "I'll be quick. Don't fall asleep," which was also interesting.

I put on the TV and switched to Fox News, which offers only "News that is fair and balanced" which somehow is different from "All the news that's fit to print," whatever that means. A commercial was running, and some old guy I thought I recognized was talking about erectile dysfunction, which at that moment was not really my problem. I could hear the shower running and Jennie humming.

It was funny, I thought, how much first-time sex and battle have in common, the same air of tension and anxiety, where everybody's uncertain about the outcome or even whether they really want to be there.

The bathroom door opened, and out stepped Jennie wearing no more than a fluffy white towel and her birthday suit. She walked straight to a window, turned her back to me, and stared down at the street as she used a second towel to dry her hair.

Being a perfect gentleman, I naturally turned my head and averted my eyes, at least until the instant she had her back turned. Then I peeked. In fact Agent Margold was the pride of the FBI gym, had nicer legs than I had imagined, wider shoulders, and not an ounce of flab I could see. Her skin was creamy white, although I noted a number of small scars on her arms and legs, some of which appeared to be burn marks, others were abrasions. But all in all, Jennie had nothing to be ashamed of, and I felt a strange tingling sensation in my stomach, or perhaps a little lower. She looked over her shoulder and mentioned, "I left the water running for you." She threw the towel she'd used to dry her hair in my face. "Hurry."

I went into the bathroom, stripped out of my shoes, socks, ridiculously expensive Brooks Brothers dress shirt and pants, and stepped into the shower. A minute later, I was all lathered up when I heard the door open. Through the glass I saw Jennie step into the bathroom. I don't really like showering alone and said, "Can you do my back?"

She laughed. "The food's at the door. My wallet's in here."

"Then I'll do my own back."

"Maybe another time." She left with her wallet. Goodness.

I emerged from the bathroom three minutes later, with a towel wrapped around my midsection. Jennie was seated on the far bed, stripping the skin off a banana, which is always a little suggestive, and was still wearing no more than a towel, which is better yet.

The cart was parked between the two double beds, and I sat on the other bed and poured myself a cup of coffee. So there we were, two mostly naked people in a hotel room with four hours to kill, separated by nothing more than three feet, a foodcart and, possibly, differing intentions. But truly there is a Maslow's Hierarchy of Needs, and food is higher on the list than sex, though not always.

Jennie pointed at the TV. "Did you see any updates about the murders?"

"I saw some guy talking about something called sexual dysfunction."

"Is that a problem for you?"

"Absolutely not."

"You're sure?"

"I have the other problem."

She smiled. "I meant a problem with commercials about sexual dysfunction, contraceptives, or feminine hygiene products?"

I smiled and dug into the fries.

She asked, "Does it make you nervous to talk about sex?"

I replied, "Have you seen any good movies lately?"

"It's a perfectly healthy topic, you know. Men can be a little strange about it. Adults should be open about these things."

"My thoughts exactly. So . . . are you a Democrat or a Republican?"

"You're weird."

She reached over and turned on the radio, moved the dial

around a while, and settled on a station playing a romantic ballad by Pete Seeger.

I finished my omelet.

She said, "I love this song." She stretched and added, "I need to lay down."

So she lay back on her bed, I polished off the fries, and I lay back on mine. After a moment, I asked her, "Where did all those scars come from?"

"I was quite the tomboy when I was younger."

"You should've stuck to skirts and dolls."

"Yeah, well, you should see the other guy."

"Right."

Silence.

Eventually, Jennie said, "This is . . . a little uncomfortable, isn't it? Should we have gotten two rooms?"

"Well, what can I say? We're partners."

"I don't often do this . . . even with partners."

"I hope not."

Silence.

I said, "Why aren't you married?"

"Why should I be?"

"Elizabeth thinks you should be married. Elizabeth thinks you should have a house in a burb, and ten kids screaming in the back of a red stretch minivan."

"Elizabeth should mind her own business." After a moment she asked, "What about you?"

"Ask Elizabeth."

She laughed.

She turned on her side and faced me. "Look, I enjoy you as a partner. You're very smart and very quick. I also think we've become friends."

"Right. I think—"

"Shut up. Let me finish. We've only known each other a day. It's been a very long and tense day, and . . . both our emotions are running high. If we . . . well, if we take the next step . . . and I'll admit I'm thinking about it, too . . . Sean, I don't do this casually."

"That's not what Elizabeth told me."

A strawberry bounced off my forehead. "Cut it out."

"I always send flowers."

She smiled. I thought we were on the cusp of something. Maybe. So far, I had been the perfect gentleman. I had put down the toilet seat, and even taken the other bed. I don't believe in throwing myself at women, and she was telling me she didn't believe in throwing herself at men, which meant one of us had to get over it and make the first move, or we'd both walk out of here with our beliefs intact. So, going where no man had gone before—or I hoped very few—I stood up and took a step toward her bed.

Suddenly we both heard a loud bleeping sound.

We looked into each other's eyes a moment. She said, "It's mine."

"No—they're both going off."

"Shit." We raced back to our clothes and scrambled around for our cell phones. Jennie found hers first. "Margold."

I got mine. "Drummond."

Phyllis was on the line. "Where are you?" she asked.

"I'm . . . nearby."

"They . . . they struck again. It's very bad, Sean."

I had assumed so from her tone. In fact, her voice sounded shaky, and I thought she had been crying. "Tell me about it."

"Well, we . . . we should have considered . . . but we didn't. It's the one thing we weren't guarding against."

It suddenly hit me. "The families."

Phyllis said nothing, which said everything.

"Whose?"

"It's . . . they . . . Mark Townsend's wife."

"Shit." I felt really stupid. Worse, I felt terrible. Why hadn't I figured this out before?

Phyllis said, "Please, get there right away. It's important for Mark to know, at this moment, that we in the Agency . . . that we . . ."

A long silence ensued while Phyllis discovered what she wanted to say. Eventually, she informed me, "I've known Mark and Joan nearly two decades. They have a daughter in college . . . Janice. I've . . . well, we're very . . ."

"I'm on my way. I *will* find these people, Phyllis."

"Do that. I mean it." She hung up.

I began dressing. Jennie was pulling up her pants with one hand, and with the other she held the phone to her ear and listened to the details of what had happened, and where.

I already knew what had happened. Literally and figuratively, we'd been caught with our pants down. Too late, I realized what had been gnawing at me. For Jason Barnes, this was a vendetta—both personal and borderless—like the Hatfields and McCoys, a blood feud with lines of vengeance that radiated beyond the government officials he believed had wronged his father. Barnes was a man of faith, a fundamentalist par excellence; he would subscribe to a biblical retribution, an eye for an eye and a tooth for a tooth; a mother for a father and a parent for an angry son.

CHAPTER TWENTY-ONE

THE AFTERMATH OF A BOMBING IS MORE TERRIFYING AND MORE HORRIBLE than any other form of murder. When I was an infantry officer, I once helped clear a bombed barracks in the Middle East. I have never erased the sights, nor the distinctive smells of seared flesh, blood, and internal organs from my mind.

Joan Townsend was a former FBI agent. Once a Fibbie, always a Fibbie. She remained admirably disciplined, a creature of habits wholesome and predictable—church every Sunday morning, a stop at the dry cleaners every Wednesday, grocery shopping on Tuesdays and Thursdays, and an efficient cardio workout every Monday, Wednesday, and Friday morning at the Gold's Gym located at Tysons Corner.

Twenty minutes of pumping light weights, ten minutes on the stairstep, finished off with twenty minutes on the running machine, a quick shower, and a fast dash out to the parking lot for the drive home. She was dedicated and she was fit, and at sixty years old she still wore a size four. She had just settled her firm and svelte butt into the leather seat of her gray Crown Victoria, and was probably in the process of buckling her seat belt when she blew right into the roof and windshield.

Three unfortunate souls were getting out of the car parked beside Joan Townsend's and also were obliterated. A few limbs were scattered around, and I noted some viscera hanging from the handicapped parking sign.

When it's the boss's wife, word spreads both efficiently and fast. It appeared that half the FBI had rushed to the scene. Three fire trucks were parked alongside the curb as the firemen were rolling up hoses and putting away their equipment. Yellow crime scene tape was already strung, and forensics experts were combing the scene, picking through body scraps and car parts, bagging and tagging. Also, I noted, a few TV vans had made it to the scene, and three or four reporters were scrambling to get their mikes and camera crews into broadcast mode. The circus had started: It was going to be a three-ringer. But a large and expanding crowd of people who mostly dressed and looked distinctively alike were congregating outside the black-and-yellow tape, staring numbly and unhappily at what was left of their chief's mate.

You can bet they all had big knots in their stomachs. Right under their noses, the first lady of the Bureau had been blown to bits. Jason Barnes had chosen a spectacular and, I thought, horribly personal way to stick a finger in their eye. Also this was a spectacular exhibition to show Washington how utterly helpless it was against his incandescent ruthlessness.

On the drive over, Jennie and I argued fiercely about which of us had been the most stupid and the most blind. It was a tough proposition. Her position was that as an experienced profiler, she was trained and conditioned to put together the schematic pieces, and she—more than anybody—should have appreciated that Joan Townsend was a victim in the wings. She was right. My position was that I had allowed a combination of exhaustion and lust to deaden my instincts. I was equally right.

Agent Mark Butterman was in charge of this mess, and he stood with a group of agents interrogating witnesses. Away from the crowd I saw George Meany, off by himself, shoulders slumped, experiencing a quiet fit of depression and frustration. Jason Barnes had outsmarted us all, and for sure, there would be enough blame to go around. But, ultimately, George was in charge, and rank conveys not just enviable privileges and advantages, but also responsibility. When this was over, George would be lucky to be handing out towels at the FBI gym.

Jennie got us past the crime tape, and we approached Mark Butterman, who stepped away from the witnesses and guided us to a quiet spot. Without pleasantries, Jennie asked, "What have you got?"

"It went down like a mob hit. Joan got into the car, and boom."

"Was the bomb rigged to the ignition?"

"Doubtful. Her keys were found in the backseat."

I said, "Then we're assuming it was command detonated?"

"That's our working assumption. The underside of her car's still too hot to touch. After it cools, we'll know."

"Type of explosive?"

"That we *are* sure of; C4."

I glanced at Jennie.

Butterman continued, "The field tests have confirmed that, and trace samples are on the way to the lab at headquarters. In a few hours, they'll know the type, the manufacturer, and who it was shipped to."

Jennie said, "I want to know as soon as you know."

"Got it, boss."

She asked, "Anything from the witnesses?"

He looked over his shoulder at the agents doing the interrogation. "Bombings are always a bitch. Nobody really pays attention till the boom, then they're all fixated on the blast. So far, it's useless."

I observed the local surroundings. The gym was situated in a strip mall that abutted a busy highway, and directly across the road and to the left, I noted two more strip malls with large, heavily trafficked parking lots. Basically, within a five-hundred-yard radius were hundreds of places where the killer could perch, hunched down in the seat of a car or leaning casually against a shop front, finger poised on a toggle switch or listening to a cell phone, observing the entrance to the gym, and waiting for Joan Townsend so he could blow her to pieces.

Jennie continued to pepper Mark Butterman with questions, but I had stopped engaging and I had stopped listening. In fact, I was experiencing a delayed reaction to something Butterman had said, and my stomach was in knots. I waited for a pause in their conversation before I took Jennie's arm and said, "Let's have a word. Now."

"Of course."

Butterman returned to the witnesses, and Jennie and I moved a few yards to another isolated spot where we couldn't be overheard. I said, "We blew it. We really—"

She released a large breath. "Don't rehash it. I should've known about Joan. You should've known about Joan. We all should've put this—"

"Not that—the C4."

"What about it?"

"The theft at Fort Hood. The range thefts—Bouncing Bettys,

LAWs, and C4 explosive were stolen." I added, "Tanner was right. These *are* the same people."

"You can't be certain of that."

"Come on, Jennie. We have an exact munitions match. In a few hours, your lab will confirm that the C4 was military grade." I stared at her and said, "Eric Tanner, maybe for all the wrong reasons, came to the right conclusion."

She turned away and surveyed the destruction in front of the gym. Not looking at me, she replied, "I'm not ruling it out. I never ruled it out with Tanner."

"Yes you—"

"I did not. Don't put words into my mouth."

"But you—"

"I merely pointed out that his investigation was sloppy and his conclusions were nonpersuasive. I *never* said it wasn't *possible*."

She was splitting hairs and mincing words, and that pissed me off. "Bullshit."

"Excuse me."

"You tore the guy to pieces. You ripped him and his theory to shreds."

"His fault, not mine. He did shoddy work and misrepresented his findings. I did my job."

"You steamrolled him."

Her eyes turned really cold. "You were right beside me. I don't remember hearing you object or coming to his defense then. And I don't appreciate your accusation now."

Of course, she was right. More to the point, she knew she was right. After a moment she advised me, "Cool off."

But I wasn't ready to cool off yet. "Doesn't this bother you in the least, Jennie? Tanner handed it to us, and we ignored him."

She touched my arm. "Post facto, Sean, everything always

looks clearer. This isn't a court of law, where everything's a review of the past. This is police work. It's happening now. It's part of our business."

Right. I still felt like crap.

She continued, "Ask yourself—what difference would it have made? Tanner couldn't identify the culprits. He had no idea of the target. Right? Even if we reacted to his theory, it wouldn't have saved Joan's life."

I said nothing.

"So now we both feel guilty. We made a mistake. Let's not compound that with a bigger mistake."

"Meaning what?"

"Don't exaggerate what we know."

"I'm no longer sure we know anything."

"Well . . . focus on what we don't know. This does *not* prove the people who stole the munitions are involved in this. But I'll grant that Barnes—perhaps somebody working *with* Barnes— might have somehow gotten the munitions from them, either directly or indirectly."

"And what won't you grant?"

"I don't see how Jason Barnes knew these people, I don't see how he convinced them to join him, and I don't understand why they would escalate from thievery and blackmarketing to murder."

Those were all good and pertinent questions and I had a reasonable answer for none of them. On the other hand, having written off Tanner's theory, we had not pursued the possible leads, which gave me an idea. I excused myself, stepped off to the side, and called Charles Wardell.

I identified myself and he said, "Jesus . . . you hear what happened to Townsend's wife?"

"I'm staring at the pieces—yeah, awful. Now, quick, I need to know if Barnes ever went near Fort Hood, or Killeen . . . yeah, Texas." I punched off and waited for Wardell to call somebody on another line and have them check their travel records. After a while he called back and he gave me the answer. I said, "Uh-huh . . . right—well, when?"

I put the phone back into my pocket and approached Jennie. I told her, "Barnes was at Fort Hood. Twice. He was on the security detail for a vice presidential trip . . . also he was there for three weeks as part of the backup when the President was vacationing at his ranch."

"When?"

"With the Veep, nearly two years ago. The last time was last summer."

"It doesn't fit. Two years ago, even last summer, he had no conception he wanted to do this."

"But he was there."

"I'm . . . Look, I'm not ruling it out. Not again."

"Then let's go with that a moment. Could he have learned about the weapons thefts at Hood?"

"Possibly. In fact, the Secret Service coordinates these visits with the local police. The advance team gets thorough briefings on local threats, nuts, and crime rings." She looked at me and said, "You're right."

"Could he have been briefed by CID?"

"I would expect he was briefed by CID. So he knew there was a ring and he may even have known the names of the suspects." She thought about it a moment then said, "I wish Tanner had been more convincing."

After a further moment of contemplation I said, "What else did we miss?"

She and I mulled that question together for a moment. When you make one big screwup, it's time to look back over your shoulder to see what else you may have left in your path. So we both sort of mentally ran backward for a moment, the theme of this review being that Jason Barnes was smarter than we assumed, and we were not as smart as we thought. Finally she said, "In retrospect, Jason would assume his disappearance would make him a prime suspect. Right?"

"Right. And he would probably presume we investigated his background, and eventually, that led us to his mother."

Jennie nodded. "He would assume we now have our arms around his motive, and from that we would compile a list of predictable targets. We underestimated him, Sean. Jason may be mentally scrambled, but he *is* a genius."

"So we believed we were getting a step on him, and he knew he was ten yards ahead of us."

"Well, I wouldn't . . . Yes." Then her jaw dropped and she suddenly pointed at a lone figure standing off to the side of the investigators. "Oh God . . . *he* shouldn't be here."

I followed her finger, and about thirty feet from us stood Mark Townsend wearing the same blue suit, the same ugly paisley tie, hands in his pockets, dumbstruck as he watched his people go about their tasks.

On instinct, we both walked over to him. His eyes were riveted on the burned, upright corpse in the Crown Vic, and he ignored us. We ended up about two feet from him, and we both stood, very awkwardly, neither of us sure what to say to this poor man silently surveying the wreckage of his car, his wife, and possibly his life. I could not remember feeling worse than I did at that moment. I was at a complete loss for words.

But somebody had to break the searing silence, and finally I said, "Our deepest condolences, sir."

Jennie said, "This was . . . I mean, this is . . . it's terrible."

He did not look at us, or even reply for a long time. He mumbled, "Joan was . . . she had no idea . . ." Then he sobbed and lost whatever words he had planned to say.

I put a hand on his arm. "Sir, this is not the right place for you. Please . . . allow me to escort you back to your car."

He still did not look at me. "I . . . I've . . ." I followed his eyes, and we both watched an agent bent over something on the ground. He picked it up and studied it. I noted it was a woman's hand, detached cleanly at the wrist. We all three silently watched the agent, oblivious to his audience, drop it into a plastic Baggie.

I said, "Come with me." I pulled on Mark Townsend's arm and guided him toward the crowd of local gawkers and Bureau agents loitering outside the crime scene tape. They saw us and began parting, and we moved through the sea of stricken and mawkish faces. Two TV cameras located us, and I saw the reporters speaking rapidly into their mikes, following our progress, Director Townsend stumbling forward until his legs grew weak and I was holding him up. He was mumbling incoherently, a stream of incomprehensible words intermittently broken up by choked sobs. Mark Townsend was in a state of shock and falling deeper and deeper into that long, dark pit.

I saw a dark blue sedan, and at nearly the same instant Jennie noticed it and signaled the two bodyguards who loitered beside it to join us. I guided Townsend as quickly as I could to his car. The bodyguards approached, and one immediately grabbed the Director's other arm. Jennie asked him, very sharply, "What were you thinking? Why did you let him come here?"

The man answered, "He . . . I mean, we knew . . . he *ordered* us to bring him. We—"

"You're idiots. You should never . . ." She drew a few breaths and got herself under control. "Take him home. Use your radio. Find out which college his daughter's at, and have the Bureau dispatch a plane to retrieve her. Also, locate the Townsend family priest. Have somebody rush him to Director Townsend's house. Don't let him into the house, and don't leave him alone till the pastor arrives. Do you understand me?"

"Yes ma'am."

"Repeat it back to me." And he did, almost word for word.

Regardless, it was too late, the damage was done. No amount of postmortem deftness was going to ameliorate it. Mark Townsend had witnessed what no man or woman should ever see.

I maneuvered him into the backseat of his sedan, and I bent over and belted him in, a silly gesture, but I felt genuine concern for this man. The crowd and the TV cameras gathered and watched the Director of the vaunted and recently feared FBI being driven away, a man so thoroughly crushed and defeated he could only stare numbly at his shoes.

I tried to think of a manner in which Jason Barnes could have choreographed this to more theatrical effect. I couldn't. I just couldn't.

In the porn industry, when the moment of ejaculation is caught on film it's called the money shot. Jason had just achieved a million-dollar money shot, and it was hard to see how he could possibly outdo this one.

But perhaps I was underestimating him again. I reminded myself to stop doing that.

CHAPTER TWENTY-TWO

Jennie and I walked together over to George Meany, who had budged not an inch from the spot where we first observed him. Clearly his mind was going through some kind of self-reflection, and his body was in a frozen trance. He looked at us, blinked a few times, and asked Jennie, "Was that Townsend?"

"Yeah. Not in good shape."

"He's going to need a long vacation," I added. "You should call headquarters and tell the Deputy Director it's his turn at bat."

George looked like *he'd* rather have the long vacation, but he nodded.

I pointed at the TV crews and said, "In a few minutes, this is going to be a camera farm. Appoint somebody like Butterman to speak to them and spin it as best he can."

The enormity of this thing was finally piercing the density of George's self-pity. "I . . . good idea. Maybe I'll—"

I said, "By the way, we have a lead."

"What are you talking about?"

I proceeded to give George a quick rundown about the range thefts at Fort Hood, and he listened intently, with no change in facial expression, and initially, at least, without comment.

When I finished, he rolled it around his brain for a moment. He looked at Jennie and observed, "You accompanied Drummond to the CID headquarters?"

"Yes."

"And you heard about this theft?"

"I did."

"Why didn't you report this lead to me?"

"Because I felt it lacked plausibility."

George stared at her a moment. "That was your professional judgment?"

Before George made a big case out of this, I interrupted to say, "It was a reasonable assessment at that moment. CID's case had big holes and wasn't fleshed out. Had we known Barnes possessed C4 and blasting caps, we obviously would've thought differently."

George looked at me and replied, "By the same token, had *we* known about this group, we would've *known* they had C4, and we would've instituted proper precautions. However . . . you two blinded us to the possibility."

"Joan Townsend was never on our protection list," I pointed out.

"She would've been, had we known."

"Ridiculous."

George ignored me, looked at Jennie, and said, "By noon, I want a statement on my desk. I'm referring this to the review board to decide if you executed your duties competently. Understood?"

Needless to say, what was going on here wasn't hard to figure out. George needed to throw somebody to the wolves and I had just shoved Jennie in the path.

Jennie informed him, very coolly, "I'm formally requesting an extension until five o'clock. It would be poor judgment to interrupt the flow of this investigation over paperwork."

"Fine." Apparently the twofer of sidestepping the blame and burning Jennie put George in a more magnanimous frame of mind.

I said to Jennie, a bit tersely, "Excuse us a moment."

"I'm not going anywhere. I can handle this myself."

To my surprise, George ordered, "Leave us alone."

She looked a little pissed, but George was her superior, as he had just reminded her. We said nothing as she walked off.

George turned to me, shaking his head and smiling. "Looks like you picked the losing team, Drummond. Don't say I didn't warn you."

"This is not working for me, George. If you want my ass, go for it. She stays out of it."

"You're asking for favors now? Well . . . you're not groveling hard enough."

"George, people are dying. She's trying her best. This is not helping the process."

This seemed to amuse George. He said, "Let me be frank, Drummond. You're making my day. I don't like you, and the thought of getting rid of her and pissing you off . . . that's sort of irresistible, isn't it?"

"You're a small-minded prick, George."

"And you're out of your league, Drummond. You always were, you just didn't realize it. So let me close with this thought—fuck you." He looked off in the direction of the TV vans and said whimsically, "You know, I'd better go issue a statement myself. You can't trust anybody these days."

I said, "Break a leg . . . a neck, whatever," and I really meant it. He smiled, and off he went, a little too much bounce in his step, and I gave serious thought to whooping his ass in front of all those cameras.

I found Jennie studying the front of Gold's Gym. At first she was lost in thought, but finally she said, "What a guy."

"Give me your Glock. I'm going to blow his brains out."

"He doesn't have brains."

"Then I'll blow out my brains."

She resisted the urge to tell me I don't have brains either, but only because her cell phone suddenly went crazy.

I moved away from her and watched George gather the cameras around for an impromptu press conference. Despite my feelings toward this guy, he was no idiot, and I was sure he would do a terrifically creative job of putting this incident, and himself, in the best light. Actually George was a pretty good agent—smart, diligent, and even resourceful. His problem was that he always put himself first.

I felt really lousy. I had developed great respect, even affection, for Mark Townsend. I had let him down. As a criminal lawyer I made my living tying pieces of crimes together, but this time I had failed. Failed when it most counted, failed when the stakes weren't guilt or innocence, but survival.

"Sean?"

I turned, and Jennie had walked over and was about a foot away. She lowered her voice and confided, "This is . . . really strange. The Bureau hotline just got a call."

"About what?"

"They—listen to this—they want a deal."

"They?"

She pointed at the still smoking Crown Vic. *"Them."*

I pointed at the TV vans. "Word's out, Jennie. A lot of people and groups will be lining up to claim credit."

"Tell me about it. The hotline's logged hundreds of calls." After a moment she added, "But the caller said that June Lacy got a bullet in the throat. Also that Merrill Benedict was wearing a brown checked suit when the rocket tore through his car."

That detail about Lacy had not been released to the press, nor, for that matter, had Benedict's sartorial selection as he was blown in half been regarded as news fit to print. But tapes of Merrill Benedict's final press conference were being replayed constantly on the tube—a befitting testimonial to a world-class bullshitter—so what he wore that day was public knowledge. And certainly enough people were in the know about what happened in the Hawk's house that it would be foolish to rule out a leak, or even an insider trying to exploit a bad situation. I commented, "Not strong enough."

"No? Well, how about this? The caller also mentioned he was willing to forgo the chance for a hundred million in exchange for a sure fifty million. Sean, this is a very interesting development. The caller said he would call back in one hour."

"Don't expect it to pan out."

"Well, here's another thing I should mention. The caller insisted he would only deal with you, or with me. He knew our names. The ops officer thought it sounded legitimate and gave him our cell numbers."

I sort of stared at her a moment.

She said, "I know, I know. It *could* imply an inside source." She quickly added, "But more likely Barnes had his mother's house watched, or she somehow found a way to communicate with her son after we left."

I shook my head. "One hour."

"He's running us silly."

She was right. Jason Barnes was so far ahead of us he knew where we were going before we knew where we'd been.

But this development was a bit beyond our pay grade, and where we needed to be at that moment was no longer here but with the rest of the task force. We walked back to Jennie's car and departed.

As we were driving a fresh thought hit me, and I used my cell to call General Tingle's office. His secretary answered, I identified myself and told her to break into whatever meeting he was in.

Twenty seconds later, Tingle's voice said, "Jesus, I hope you're not calling to inform me Joan Townsend was blown up with C4."

Apparently his TV was on. I tried to think up a good zinger, but I wasn't really in the mood, nor would he be in another moment. I said, "It was. Though the FBI lab hasn't yet discovered its provenance."

I heard a quiet curse on the other end. Eventually, he concluded the obvious. "Tanner was right."

"Probably. About the source of the munitions anyway. The rest remains speculative."

But it didn't need to stay speculative, and I quickly went over what Tingle and his command needed to accomplish. Basically, the plan was to screen Tanner's list of insider suspects, and the question was: Where were those five employees at that moment? Tingle heard me out and mumbled, "Outside shot."

"And do you have an inside shot to offer? You need to do this, General. You left toys in the sandbox, and it's time to get them back."

Tingle did not enjoy my metaphor, but got the point and assured me he could get an answer fairly quickly. I gave him my cell number.

Jennie glanced at me and said, "That's cunning. I never even considered that thread."

"Had we followed that thread a few hours ago, *that* would've been cunning."

"Stop looking backward."

I replied, "Look, about George, I'm sorry. I gave him the perfect shot at your ass."

She did not contradict me, but she did say, "The *only* important thing at this moment is stopping Jason Barnes." After another moment she observed, "He's playing mind games with us, Sean. He's very good at it."

I knew exactly what she meant, but I wanted to hear her thoughts on the matter. "Explain that."

"He knows how we work and how the bureaucracy functions. These quick, unexpected hammer blows are meant to keep us off balance and at each other's throats. He's aware of our individual and institutional propensity to cover our own asses."

True enough. Still, it was strange, I thought, how shrewdly Barnes was playing his hand. I said to Jennie, "I really underestimated this clown. Nothing in his background suggests this level of deviousness."

She squeezed my arm. "With a father like his, he grew up hiding his feelings and disguising his strengths and weaknesses. This is a remarkably conflicted individual, religious yet murderous, a servant of the government who's now out to destroy that government, a man sworn to protect the same President he now vows to kill. Jason Barnes is a severely fractured personality. When he looks in the mirror, I doubt he recognizes himself."

Jennie called the ops center, informed the duty officer we

were en route, and ordered an emergency all-hands call for a very important meeting.

I commented, "Can I get out of this blamefest—I mean, meeting?"

"No." She looked at her watch and punched the gas.

I leaned my head back and closed my eyes. Once again, a nagging intuition was telling me something was very wrong.

CHAPTER TWENTY-THREE

MARK TOWNSEND WASN'T GOING TO SHOW UP.

Nor George Meany, who remained at the bomb scene, having generously volunteered to act as the on-site commander and public spokesman. Consequently, Meany's fingerprints would not be on whatever decision we made, a thought that I'm sure crossed his mind.

Anyway, before we entered the conference room, Jennie arranged for the Bureau to acquire both of our cell phone frequencies, essentially by calling each other, allowing some homing device to get our footprint.

Quick reaction teams were scrambling into position around the city, and five helicopters filled with sharpshooters were in the air. The idea was, the moment the bad guys called, the Bureau would get a fix on them, the quick reaction teams would swoop, and game over.

But the mood in the room, far from festive, was dispirited and edgy, though at least not panicky.

Everybody knew it was only a matter of time before we were stuffing shivs in one another's backs at the Senate inquest. It's a little hard to strike a chord of amity when everybody's busy covering their butt. There were a lot of forced smiles.

By dint of seniority, Phyllis assumed the chair at the end of the table and took responsibility for this nightmare. Roger Hammersly, Deputy Director of the FBI, had been duly notified he was the acting chief, but he was in Seattle, at least six hours from Washington and about two thousand miles from the blameline. Lucky him. Somebody was having a happy day.

We were all standing around, chatting aimlessly as we waited for the last important personage to appear. Eventually the door opened, and Mrs. Nancy Hooper entered. Outside the door I saw a large gaggle of Secret Service agents sort of standing stiffly against the walls, that way they do.

Mrs. Hooper, I noted, had added a bulletproof vest to her wardrobe and a nasty scowl to her face.

Everybody moved to their seats, and Phyllis brought the meeting to order, saying, "A number of us in this room knew Joan Townsend. Nearly everybody here has now lost a friend. I'm sure we are all deeply affected. So I will remind you, this is a time for clear and unemotional thinking."

Everybody nodded. Great advice—if I recalled correctly, the exact words the captain of the *Titanic* advised his crew.

Phyllis then said, "I should begin with an update on my activities. Some of you may know that we've been tracking a hundred-million-dollar block of money flowing very quickly through the international banking system."

Aside from me, this was news to this crowd, who all craned forward and looked intensely interested. I also leaned forward, curious to hear how this turned out. Phyllis shrugged and then informed us, "Unfortunately, this lead has not panned out. The money belongs to another of those Russian oil barons trying to hide his money from the taxman. However, we'll keep looking, and who knows what might turn up."

This brought no sighs of relief.

Turning to Mr. Halderman, Phyllis said, "Gene is now going to offer us his department's assessment of the state of the nation."

So far, Mr. Halderman and his Department of Homeland Security had contributed nothing, and said nothing, so this was a nod to smart politics. You never know who you might need at the next crisis, only that there will be a next one, and it always pays to debruise hurt egos. One does not get to be an old hand in this business, like Phyllis, by overlooking the small things.

Gene gathered some papers in his hand and stood. I noticed he had switched out of his Armani suit and into some conservatively cut rags from Joe Bank. He at least appeared to be getting the cultural message, but the rest of us were baggy-eyed, wrinkled, smelly, and unkempt, whereas Gene looked well rested, freshly shaved, and somebody was wearing a really bad aftershave. The guy looked like he had just stepped out of the latest edition of *Grooming for Success*. Why did none of us take this guy seriously?

He coughed into his hand and collected his thoughts. He said, "The department has raised the national threat level to orange. This is a recognition of where we're at, tempered by the fact that the threat is internal. In our lingo, that means we still regard it as a domestic issue."

People were yawning.

"I know a lot of you have been too busy to watch the news," Gene continued. "The American people are stunned . . . shocked . . . almost convulsed. It's not quite at 9/11 intensity, but close . . ." Gene went on with his spiel, talking about the number of news hits and Internet mentions the murders had gleaned. It appeared that some channels were providing endless updates every fifteen minutes, so the public could keep score. I began to wonder what in the hell the Homeland Security Department did. When this was over, maybe I should apply for a job there. I pictured the rest of my career seated around TVs and computer screens, munching doughnuts and popcorn, logging mentions. I mean, the worst that could happen was a paper cut, or hot coffee spilling in my lap.

Next came a rundown of all the measures his department had implemented regarding air- and seaports, none of which had the slightest fucking thing to do with the threat we faced. On the other hand, nothing we'd done seemed to be working either. Eventually Phyllis saw that this clown was wasting our time and our limited attention and she stood up and interrupted, "Thank you, Gene."

He was in the midst of describing the increase in port security. "I . . . excuse me?"

Phyllis said, "Thank you for your update. Sit down, Gene."

He looked a little crushed, but he shut up and he sat. Phyllis summarized for Gene, informing us, "If you haven't been paying attention, Gene's point is, these killings have hugely upset the entire country. We are in a national crisis."

Mrs. Hooper saw her opening and amplified on that thought. "I just left the President. He is . . . enraged. He released a taped statement this morning—before Joan Townsend's murder—telling the country to calm down, that our law enforcement is the best in the world, our officials will be protected, and these people will be caught."

She paused to allow us to consider how ironic, or perhaps

idiotic, that statement looked, a mere two hours later. Like all of us, apparently the Prez had been a bit too optimistic.

Mrs. Hooper continued, "We just canceled the President's southern sweep." She glanced in the direction of an unsmiling Mr. Charles Wardell. "This could cost him the election, but the Secret Service insists that the risks are simply too great. Congress has granted itself a three-day holiday. The President and the Vice President are now quarantined in separate and secure locations. Also, the Secretary of State and the Secretary of Defense were dispatched early this morning on separate overseas trips. So, even if the worst happens . . ."

As she droned on, not for nothing, I again recalled that cold war nuclear evacuation plan. This sounded exactly like what was going on here, and a chill actually went down my spine. In only two short days, Jason Barnes had become a ten-megaton asshole.

Anyway, Mrs. Hooper's mood was testy, and essentially, she informed us that we shouldn't get too smug about the President's earlier words, because the White House now regarded us as incompetent fools, the nation had lost all respect for us, Jason Barnes was running circles around us, and so on. This wasn't exactly news, nor even particularly helpful, especially since we all knew it to be true.

I mean, all our careers were probably in the crapper, the clock was ticking, we were tired and demoralized, and this browbeating wasn't helping. I finally got a little hot under the collar and stood up. "Mrs. Hooper . . ."

She looked at me, and I said, "If you're through rubbing our faces in shit, we have important and timely issues to consider. Sit down and shut up."

I had caught her completely off guard, and for a moment there was a stunned silence in the room. In fact, her lips were parting to say something when Phyllis said to me, "You have the nuance of a jackhammer." She turned to Mrs. Hooper. "However regrettably worded, Drummond's point is valid. Mrs. Hooper, you may sit, or you may leave, and we'll find somebody else in the White House to deal with."

Mrs. Hooper had to get her own growl in and replied, "I'm not about to leave. I've sat through all these meetings. I have notes. I know who did what."

Phyllis stared at her. "At a later time I'm sure that will be . . . useful. But now"—she looked at her watch—"we have less than fifteen minutes before Sean or Jennie gets a call. A productive use of that time might be to consider how to verify the callers, and how we should respond in the face of this offer."

Nobody objected. What was there to object to?

Jennie jumped in and said, "Sean and I viewed nearly all the murder scenes. It won't be difficult to confirm their authenticity."

Phyllis nodded, then posed the question on all our minds. "Why would they want a deal at this stage?"

Why indeed.

Jennie had already considered this question and said, "The logical conclusion would be because Barnes has largely achieved what he wants. Retribution was his goal, and he has certainly exacted a lot of that. Maybe he has satiated his fury and is ready to move on."

"But you seem to be implying there's another conclusion," Phyllis stated, or asked.

"In fact, I believe there is. I think his partners are in it for the money. Now he needs money."

I took the big risk of overintellectualizing this and suggested, "I think it stinks."

"Why?" Phyllis asked.

"Because Barnes is on an emotional rampage. The grim

reaper." For want of a better way to express this, I asked, "Why would he . . . you know, stop reaping?"

"In fact, Sean makes a good point," Jennie informed us. "So allow me to speculate. As I said, his partners want money. They know the noose is tightening. It's the inherent weakness of all criminal conspiracies—conflicting motives. They never shared Barnes's emotional objective, it's all about the money for them, and in a sense, he could be experiencing a mutiny. They're probably putting unbearable pressure on Barnes to cut a deal now."

"To forgo a hundred for fifty million?" I asked skeptically.

"I hope you're not suggesting that's chump change." Jennie then looked at Mr. Wardell and added, "The President's their hardest target. We know he's in their crosshairs, and they know we're taking extraordinary precautions."

In that light, Phyllis asked Mr. Wardell, "How do you regard your odds?"

"Considering that Barnes was one of us, we've altered our normal procedures. Also, we're keeping the President in a room in the White House we've never used before and we've tripled our coverage. Getting in and out is next to impossible."

"But not impossible?" Jennie asked.

Chuck squirmed a little. "That word's not in our lexicon. Could he get through? His first year, he worked in the White House. He has intimate knowledge of the physical setup. Could he and his people penetrate our defenses? They would have to be damned good." He looked at all our faces and asked, "Are they that good?"

Nobody touched that one. But Jennie said, "Consider this also—the caller asked to speak with me or with Sean."

In line with her background, Phyllis naturally observed, "By *name* . . . Yes, that is odd. Neither of you have been in the news. One wonders if perhaps Barnes has a friend on the inside."

Jennie replied, "It's much likelier he learned about us through our visit to Mrs. Barnes. But yes. We have to consider the possibility that somebody on the inside is leaking information to Barnes."

So that unhappy thought was batted back and forth a bit. If Barnes had an inside source, it would explain some of his success. If not, he was just smarter than us. Actually, those competing thoughts weren't necessarily mutually exclusive. Either way, or both ways, we weren't going to learn the answer anytime soon. Phyllis very wisely made this point, suggesting, "Assume the worst. Barnes has somebody well positioned to keep him abreast of what we're doing. So there's that additional element of risk to be factored."

Jennie said, "From this moment on, we'll need to compartmentalize our decisions."

Phyllis turned back to Mrs. Hooper and raised the issue we should've discussed from the beginning. She said, "The decision to pay them off is a political issue. We in the bureaucracy can recommend . . . However, the decision rests with your boss."

For a moment I thought Mrs. Hooper was reconsidering her decision about whether to stay or go. Hers had been a free ride until this moment, but now the buck was passed. After a pained hesitation she replied, "Absolutely not. You all know our national policy. We never negotiate with terrorists."

Jennie said, "One, these aren't terrorists. Two, all policies are malleable. It all depends on the size of the gun pointed at our heads. We have negotiated with terrorists in the past, and we surely will in the future. Think Iran/contra."

"I don't need a lecture from any of you. The cost of paying off murderers would be politically catastrophic in the midst of an election."

I mentioned, "Good point," and she nodded in my direction.

I added, "Boy—think what it will do for the election if your boss is dead."

And at just that instant, my cell phone went off. Everyone stopped staring at me and stared at *it*.

It beeped a second time, and a third. I cleared my throat, lifted it up, and said, "Drummond."

The voice was male, and he said, "Eureka."

"I . . . who is this?"

"Tingle. Remember, I owe you a call." He added, "We ran the check you requested."

Six sets of eyes were fixed on my lips. Nobody was even breathing. I put my hand over the phone. "Relax." I said to Tingle, "Tell me about it."

"Okay. Of the five suspects, three are at work. The fourth has been on leave for the past two weeks. Thank God he left an address. We found him at his lakehouse in Utah. Fishing."

"And the fifth?"

"Name's Clyde Wizner. He quit about seven weeks ago. His supervisor was very surprised. He was very good at his job, there were no signs he was unhappy, or—"

I said, "General, we've got the fucking roof falling on top of us here. Speed it up."

"Uh . . . fine. Wizner has prior military service. Used to be an EOD specialist. That's—"

I already knew EOD specialists were experts in defusing and exploding bombs and mines. "Got it—move on."

For a moment there was silence. Then he said, "Don't push me, Major. That's right . . . I checked on you, too. Later, you and I will discuss passing yourself off as a civilian."

As I said, these guys are really sneaky. "At the appropriate time, I look forward to that talk, sir."

"Well—you shouldn't. Now, regarding Wizner, give me a number and we'll fax over his service record and his civilian record."

I asked Jennie for help, and she read the number off the fax machine in the far corner of the room. I relayed it to Tingle, who closed saying, "Wizner has the technical training and know-how to be the bomber. I have ten agents backgrounding him. We'll know a lot more soon. I'll call when I—"

"Thank you, sir."

I punched off.

Almost simultaneously the fax machine started spewing out sheets.

I looked at Jennie and pointed at my watch. Maybe five minutes. Time was really short. Jennie looked around and asked, "Well? Do Sean and I have permission to say yes, or is it no?"

All eyes shifted back to Mrs. Hooper.

She said, "You may negotiate, but not commit." Typical politician.

Jennie said, "That won't do. They'll insist on a firm answer. Yes or no?"

Mrs. Hooper replied, "I've given you permission to negotiate. That's more than enough."

Seconding Jennie, I said, "It's not. Don't assume these people are stupid, Mrs. Hooper. We know they're not—right?"

She looked at Jennie, and then me. "Deal with it."

My phone rang again. Thinking it was Tingle again, I lifted it up and said, "Look, I know you're pissed, but we're a little busy over here."

I heard a harsh laugh. A voice said, "I'll bet you're busy as all hell, son." The voice was male and middle-aged, with a smoker's rasp, the accent was Texan, and the tone sounded folksy and condescending, like he held all the cards, which wasn't at all presumptuous. The man on the other end of the line was not

Tingle. But neither did he sound like Jason Barnes, which was a bit disappointing.

I waved my arm, and in a tone as good-humored as I could manufacture, I asked, "Is this who I think it is?"

"You ain't got a fuckin' clue who I am. Let's not pretend otherwise."

"I do know you've really caused us a lot of trouble."

"Well, hey . . . this ain't good news, I'm sure, but you ain't seen shit yet."

Jennie had dashed around the table and now stood beside me, bent over, her face brushing mine, straining to overhear his words.

"Neither have you, pal. Seriously. The President's hidden inside a deep hole, somewhere up in, I think, Alaska. He's at the bottom of an old missile silo surrounded by a regiment of pissed-off Army Rangers. You won't get him, but we will get you."

He chuckled. "Who gives a shit where you got him hid. Never actually said we're gonna git *him*, did we?"

"I . . . what?"

"Well, sheeit, boy, read the note. We never said we were gonna kill that sonuvabitch. Jus' said he's history. Think about it."

Before I could reply, he said, "Hey, tell you what. Fifty million's the price and it ain't open to debate. You pay . . . we'll quit fuckin' with you. You don't . . . the next one'll really suck. Simple deal. Call you back in a minute."

The line suddenly went dead.

I said, "Shit."

Jennie said, "He's changing cell phones. He's using throwaways, so we can't get a fix."

In fact, an agent slipped into the conference room, shook his head, and said, "Too fast," then slipped back out.

Jennie informed the rest of the task force, "We've been looking in the wrong direction. He says they may not want to kill the President."

Proving that all politics is local, Chuck Wardell slid back into his chair and commented, "Thank God."

Mrs. Hooper asked, "Then what do they have in mind?"

I informed her, "Not what—*who.*"

The phone rang and I again answered, "Drummond."

"Hey. Well, you got an answer for me, boy?"

"Look, we've got a small problem here."

He laughed, "You got a lot a problems, none of which are small."

Asshole. "Okay, for starters . . . how do we know you're the real McCoy? We're a little deluged with assholes calling and claiming credit. How do I know you're the *right* asshole?"

"I like that." He laughed again. "For a stupid butthead who's run hisself silly the past two days, it's real good you still got a sense of humor." He stopped laughing. "But don't fuck with me, son. Maybe I'll put a Bouncin' Betty up yer ass, too."

Jennie overheard this exchange and whispered, "Stay cool."

I drew a long breath. "A lot of people know Fineberg got it with a mine."

"Yeah? Hey, guess that's right . . . news gits 'round, don't it?" He laughed again. "Now tell me, how many of them folks know how them three jerkoffs in Belknap's basement got it? I did the little gal at the commo console myself. Three shots straight into her right side, *boom-boom-boom.* You shoulda seen that gal's body twitch and bounce, Drummond. One of my partners did the other two, the asshole who was sleepin' and the idiot in the chair."

"Fuck you."

He laughed. "Aw hell . . . don't go all pissy on me. You asked for proof, I try to be helpful, and now you go actin' like a porky-pine with a burr up its ass. Yer hard to please. Hey . . . call you back in a minute."

The line went dead again. Everyone began chattering at once.

Jennie said, "Don't let him goad you, Sean. Stay cool. This is just business."

Mrs. Hooper ordered, "Negotiate, Drummond. Find out what they have in mind next."

Mr. Halderman advised, "Emphasize that all the sea- and airports are completely covered. Tell him they should give up—they'll never make it out of this country alive."

I nearly got up and walked out. But I knew they had the best intentions. I tried to think. I glanced at my watch. Thirty more seconds. It was important to take away the initiative, but nothing was coming to me.

Jennie clearly understood this and announced to all concerned, "We have to set up a deal with these people. We need to buy time."

Mrs. Hooper kept shaking her head.

Jennie and I exchanged glances. Not good.

The phone rang. I lifted it up, and the voice said, "Okay, Drummond, here's the deal. You ain't got the brass to make this decision, so probably you got a bunch of important assholes sittin' 'round you. Tell 'em I got a target in my sights. All I gotta do is push this teeny button, and boom, this President's got one less high-level asshole. Got that?"

"Yeah, and—"

"What're you waitin' for, boy? Do it."

I put my hand over the phone and explained our predicament.

I put the phone back to my mouth. "Done."

"Okeydokey. Now, what's the answer? Fifty million, or you gonna try playin' dick-around with me?"

Something in his tone sounded wrong. I slapped my hand over the phone again and yelled, "Right now—he wants an answer."

We all looked at Mrs. Hooper. This was developing really quickly. Mrs. Hooper kept shaking her head.

Looking at her, I said, "He's serious. Yes or no?"

She stared at the tabletop for about ten seconds. She said nothing.

Then, through the earphone, I heard a loud blast. The line went dead again.

I put down the phone. "Shit. He just murdered somebody."

Mrs. Hooper avoided my eyes and asked, "Who?"

"How the hell would I know?"

We all looked at one another. For once, nobody said a word until the phone rang again. I picked it up and demanded, "Who did you just murder?"

"That? Aw, jus' the head of the Republican National Committee. Hey, you believe he's got a mistress over by Dupont Circle? Married man, too. What'n the hell's this world comin' to, huh? Y'know, all this shit goin' on . . . and that horny bastard jus' had to sneak off and get a little afternoon poon." He added, "By the way, cash, used fifties and hunnerds. Oh, and none of that sneaky shit them Treasury assholes like to try. We'll look, we know what to look for, and if we find something, it's gonna really suck for you."

I put my hand over the phone and informed everybody that the RNC just got a job opening. Mrs. Hooper's eyes shot wide open. She said, "Danny Carter . . . he . . . oh God . . . he . . ." Then she suddenly started crying.

I no longer needed, nor did I wait, for a consensus or permission. I said, "Deal."

"Well, yee-haw. Good call, boy."

"But murder one more person, it's off. Understand? Kill one more soul, and you're dead. We'll hunt you down, and we'll find you. I'll personally cut out your guts."

He laughed. "That's the spirit. By the by, yer gonna be the delivery boy. Hey, call you back in an hour."

"No, you'll call in two hours. We have a lot of work to do to get the money."

There was silence for a few seconds. Eventually, he said, "Now listen up—the next asshole gets it in two hours and ten minutes. Don't fuck nothin' up. Keep yer phone battery charged, 'cause you and me, we gonna powwow in two hours."

The line went dead.

CHAPTER TWENTY-FOUR

MRS. HOOPER SAT PERFECTLY STILL, CRYING AND SOBBING. SHE SAID, "HE killed Danny. I . . . what could I . . ." A chorus of racking sobs began belching up from her stomach.

Jennie looked at Mrs. Hooper and said, "We warned you."

Mrs. Hooper bounced in her seat like somebody had just shot a ten-thousand-volt bolt up her fanny. "I . . . I . . ."

Phyllis stood up and snapped, "That's enough!" She looked at all our faces and said, "No more finger-pointing." She stared at Jennie. "Understood?"

Clearly, Special Agent Jennifer Margold, who had been so compulsively rational since the start of this thing, was experiencing a rare emotional outburst. It was a human response, and I, for one, was glad to see it, glad to see that the raw pathos had gotten under her skin, and glad to see I wasn't falling for an ice queen.

More selfishly, I was now on the hook for agreeing to a deal, and I was out on a limb all by myself. Somebody needed to make Mrs. Hooper understand that what was happening here was far beyond the calculus of presidential vanity and the pornography of electoral politics. This was a choice with human consequences, life or death. Eventually, Jennie said to Phyllis, "You're right."

She turned to Mrs. Hooper, who was slumped in her chair, staring at her knuckles, experiencing a sort of Pontius Pilate epiphany.

Jennie said, "That was . . . unforgivable. Was Danny Carter a friend?"

"Yes."

"Was he married?"

"He and . . . well, he and Terry . . . have two kids, and I . . . I've known them over twenty years." She looked around at our faces. "I got him this job. Danny was so energetic, so brilliant, so . . . so loyal." Which apparently reminded her, and she looked at Jennie and asked, "Who's going to notify Terry Carter?"

There was an awkward stillness in the room while we jointly considered the baffling dilemma of how you inform a wife that she's now a widow, and, by the way, her husband died in the arms of somebody other than her, and incidentally, in a few minutes, that revolting revelation was going to be all over the tube. "When we get confirmation he's dead, I'll assign an agent to handle it," Jennie informed her.

Mrs. Hooper looked more than a little relieved.

Jennie turned to Phyllis and said, "With this bargain, the Agency no longer has any justification for involvement. It's gone purely domestic." As if we needed to be reminded, she cautioned us, "Everything we do is going to undergo congressional and maybe public scrutiny."

I won't say Phyllis also looked relieved, but without sounding at all reluctant, she replied, "Of course."

Which put Jennie in the driver's seat and in charge of this mess. She said, "Mrs. Hooper, you need to call the President for permission to proceed."

Mrs. Hooper returned to studying the tabletop. "He's not going to pay them off. In any event, as his political adviser I still have to advise against it."

I said, "Why?"

She looked up at me. "Because nobody in this country will vote for a man who pays off murderers. But I know him. He'll say that's irrelevant. He'll say that indulging murderers is morally wrong and begets more murders and more murderers. He tends to be practical that way."

Jennie looked at me. I shrugged.

Mr. Wardell chose this moment to make an interesting observation. "Incidentally, Danny Carter was not one of our suspected targets. How in the hell was he involved in this Barnes thing?"

Jennie said, "He wasn't. He was a message."

"What message?" Mrs. Hooper asked.

"This confirms my speculation. It's no longer about revenge. They're now concerned only with money and making their escape. They're telling us they'll murder whoever they please, until their demands are met."

We all pondered that fresh insight a moment.

I noted the obvious. "We've lost our only advantage. We can't even guess who they're targeting."

"That's right. We can't," Jennie observed. She turned back to Mrs. Hooper. "Listen . . . I think there might be a way out of this for us and the President."

"What are you talking about?"

"Simple. We use the money to lure Barnes and his people into a trap."

Everybody thought about that proposal a moment.

Phyllis was the first to speak up. "I don't like it."

"Why not?"

"It will be expected. These are not stupid people, Jennifer. They'll take precautions."

"I'm sure they will. Entrapments are always a gamble. We have to outthink them."

Recognizing the thought that was running through all our minds, Jennie added, "The past doesn't always have to be a prelude to the future. Right?" She turned to Mrs. Hooper and suggested, "If this works, the President's a bold leader who rolled the dice. If it fails, his intentions were honorable, and we screwed up the execution."

I still wasn't sure this was such a good idea. On the other hand, I had really gotten myself into a box. I was the one who agreed to the deal.

Chuck Wardell was nodding, and Mrs. Hooper also began nodding. It was dawning on them that this wasn't a perfect solution, but there were no perfect solutions, and it satisfied everybody's needs, egos, and moral/political equations.

Actually, not quite everybody's.

Jennie knew it, too, because she turned to me and said, "Sean, the final vote is yours. They selected you as the courier."

"Right. Why?"

"Who knows? Perhaps because you're a lawyer, not a law enforcement professional. Perhaps they regard you as the least threatening option. But I doubt they'll accept a replacement. If it were possible, believe me, I would do this myself."

Everybody at the table was now avoiding my eyes.

Jennie assured me, "It won't be as risky as it sounds. We do this all the time, usually with kidnappers. We have experts in this field. You'll have the best professionals in the world backing you up."

Very persuasive. So I thought about it a little more. I thought about June Lacy and about Joan Townsend. I really wanted to get physically close to Jason Barnes. I had an almost burning need to put my hands around his throat. Also, if we didn't take this chance, every additional death would be on my shoulders, my conscience, my watch. Could I live with that?

Then again, I'd be an idiot to say yes. It was a desperate gamble and, like all reckless choices, was too obvious, too predictable, too transparent. Jason Barnes, a former Secret Service agent, would expect this; he would know the tricks, and as Phyllis noted, he would have safeguards and precautions. Also, up to this point, I was on the losing team, they were the winning team, and the underlying reasons for that hadn't changed.

When I was young and idealistic, brimming with youthful naïveté, I would have regarded this as Sean Drummond's God-given duty in the eternal battle of good versus evil. But I had become too old and too worldly to subscribe to the facile conceit that the good guys always win, or even that the good guys always *have* to win. The truth is, it can be enough to just make the bad guys go away. Somewhere down in Brazil, I'm convinced, there's a quaint ville populated by smug assholes who gather in the bars every evening and regale one another with tales about how *they* got away with it. Fine. As long as they weren't still getting away with it.

So I looked Jennie straight in the eye and I said, "Great idea."

Jennie squeezed my shoulder. To Mrs. Hooper she said, "Please call the White House and get authorization." To Mr. Wardell, "Call your old bosses at Treasury. We need fifty million in clean, used bills here in one hour."

CHAPTER TWENTY-FIVE

IN NO TIME, THE ROOM CLEARED, AND BUREAU EXPERTS OF VARIOUS VIN-tages and types began pouring in, including a heavyset Hispanic lady named Rita Sanchez. Jennie introduced us and informed me that Special Agent Sanchez was the FBI's expert in ransom and hostage extremis situations, whatever that means. I was really hoping she was here for her expertise in the former, not the latter.

Rita studied me a moment, then said, "So . . . you're the sucker, huh?"

I must've looked a little upset by that remark, because she laughed and said, "Hey, loosen up. You're gonna be fine. Payoffs are a cakewalk. Hostages are the bitch. I've lost only"—she paused and counted her fingers—"only three couriers in my career." She laughed. "The other guy still sends me Christmas gifts."

For some reason, Jennie also found this really funny.

288

Personally, I thought Rita Sanchez's bedside manner could stand a little work.

Jennie then smoothly backed off and allowed Rita and me to chitchat about inconsequential nonsense for about five minutes. The manual calls this establishing rapport and developing a personal connection. Con men call it sizing up the mark.

Rita was very good at this, and in no time we bonded, were exchanging home addresses, and planning a future vacation together. Not really.

Anyway, Rita Sanchez had a slight Spanish accent, and was a bit plump for an agent, but it has been my experience that in image-conscious organizations that accentuate fitness and trimness—like the Army—exceptions get made for the prodigies. She was not particularly polished, but she struck me as street-smart and savvy.

Agent Sanchez pointed at a chair and said, "Sit. Now we're gonna go over a few things. Listen real close to every word. Seriously. Do everything I tell you, and the Bureau will buy you a nice steak dinner tonight."

Golden words. I sat.

"Let me tell you what could happen," she said. "Then I'll tell you what I think's gonna happen."

"Could we start with what I want to happen?"

She glanced at Jennie and commented, "Hey, he's funny."

Jennie replied, "When he's stressed, he responds with sarcasm." She then lifted a hand to her ear and asked, "By the way, Rita, are those your knees I hear knocking?"

Yuck-yuck.

"All right," Rita informed me, "for starters, they might run you around a bit. Probably inside the city, maybe around some built-up suburbs. This way they can blend into the environment and watch for tails."

I nodded.

She continued, "I've seen cases where they ran the courier seven or eight hours. Sometimes they'll run you by the same site three or four times. The smarter ones are trying to draw us to that site. The dumb ones actually use that site for the drop-off. Haw-haw—you wouldn't believe how stupid some of these people are." She turned to Jennie and advised, "He's gotta have a phone jack in the car for his cell phone. Two or three spare batteries, too, some sandwiches and sodas. And make sure the car tank's topped off."

Jennie turned to an agent standing beside the door and said, "Handle that now."

He collected my cell phone and departed.

Rita asked me, "You know D.C.?"

"Where? Oh . . . that big place across the river."

Jennie said, "Ignore him. He knows it well enough."

"Right." Rita looked a little worried, however, and said, "We'll make sure a map's in the car. Point is, stay cool. They jerk you around, that's a good sign. The pros know the car's gonna have a tracker on it, you're tagged, and it don't really make a damn whether they run you back and forth to Phoenix." She paused to be sure I understood.

"Got it."

"Sometimes, they send you straight to the drop-off. That's usually a bad sign for us."

"Why?"

"Then you're gonna become a hostage. We don't like that. See, the smarter ones, they reverse the process. They'll have their own vehicle, and usually they'll try to make you get in. Got it?"

"Right."

"They'll try all kinds of gimmicks and tricks. Car switches,

usually done inside parking garages or tunnels. That kind of shit."
She looked at Jennie and said, "Case they get nervous or pissed
off, we need to make sure they got another number to call other
than his."

"They already have mine," Jennie assured her.

I didn't like the sound of this.

I asked, "Nervous or pissed off about *what*?"

She turned back to me and, I noted, did not specifically address this question. She said, "But I have to tell you, taking
hostages, that's rare. Most criminals are bush league. They think
they can outsmart us and they're wrong."

Great. "My question was, in case they get pissed off about
what?"

Rita and Jennie exchanged quick glances. Jennie commented, "Sean, we know these people are experienced in killing,
and possibly weapons thefts. But expertise in kidnapping is a
whole different skillset with a whole different set of risks and
rules."

I was being reassured to death and getting a little tired of it.
I looked at Jennie, no longer sure whose side she was on. I said,
"You and I, we're still watching each other's butts, right?"

She squeezed my shoulder and smiled.

It couldn't hurt to ask, so I looked at Rita. "Ever have a case
where they just whacked the courier?"

I saw that evasive look again. "There's no upside in that.
Once they get the money, you got no value dead. It only com-
plicates things for them. If they make you a hostage, you only got
value alive and kicking. See how that works?" She paused for a
moment before she noted, "Unless . . . well, now, I gotta ask . . .
you done anything to piss these people off?"

Had I? Well, I had tried to put all their murderous asses into the electric chair. But that hadn't worked out obviously. I shook my head.

"Good. Don't. Stay real polite and respectful. These people are gonna be nervous and strung out. Agitating them would be a really dumb idea. Remember . . . polite and respectful."

Jennie shook her head and commented, "That's not really his strong suit."

Hah-hah. This went on a while longer, the two of them keeping it lighthearted, like this was just a big lark that stupid little Sean really shouldn't worry about. Then Rita began relating anecdotes from past cases she thought might be illustrative and instructive. Of course, they all had happy endings.

Then phase one—called, I think, "Motivating and Instructing the Idiot"—ended, and three new agents hustled into the conference room.

Rita introduced her colleagues, whose names I immediately forgot. One studied me a moment, then reached into a big bag, withdrew a flak jacket, and handed it to me. Rita said, "Try it on. Just a precaution."

Jennie chose this moment to inform me, "We can't give you a weapon, Sean. You're not a federal agent. Also, if Barnes's people discover a gun it would cause major problems."

I very reasonably pointed out, "Not having a gun could pose bigger problems."

Rita Sanchez had obviously been through all this before, because she brushed my objection aside and informed me, "Now it's time to show our bag of tricks. You'll be driving a Suburban—that's your weapon. It's a special model with a nitrous oxide–charged 450-horsepower engine, it's bulletproof, and nearly bombproof. Curb weight's four tons, enough to bash aside anything that gets in your path. So if this goes to shit, push the nitrous oxide button, hit the pedal, and scoot."

"I'd rather have the gun, thank you."

She smiled at me, turned to one of her assistants, and said, "Get the suppository."

The agent opened a small briefcase, peeked inside, and then withdrew a tiny metal cylinder, which he held up for me to examine.

"Wait a minute—You're not sticking that up my butt."

Rita thought this was very funny. She said, "We used to do that. But I got tired of looking up people's asses, so I begged the Bureau to find something else. This is the ingestible form." I'm sure the relief on my face was palpable as she held it in front of my eyes to inspect. "As you probably guessed, it's a tracking device. In this case, developed by our friends at the Agency. Spooks tend to be real cautious, and they use wands to detect transmitting devices. These days anyone can buy those wands on eBay, so this little baby stays inactive till we signal it to transmit. We turn it on and off intermittently. Range of fifty miles, and it stays in your tummy till your next bowel movement. We'll activate it only if you become a hostage."

And more of the same. Basically, the plan was that I would go wherever Jason sent me, would rise to unexplored heights of courteousness and civility, and would deliver the package, which turned out to be not one package but fifteen oversized Samsonite suitcases stuffed with fifty million in used cash.

Option A was to unload the suitcases at the location of their choice and then depart, Sean's ass intact. Under option B, Sean would end up escorting the money containers a little longer than anticipated.

Nobody wanted to dwell much on option B. This was not a particularly good sign.

About twenty minutes into this, Jennie took a call from Mrs.

Hooper, who informed her the President said it was a go and personally wished me luck and Godspeed.

Great—my final chance for a reprieve just flew out the window. But if this thing worked out okay, maybe I could ask *him* for a job. Of course, if it didn't work out, I wouldn't have a job problem and his would just be starting.

Rita and Jennie reassured me three dozen times that everything was going to work out fine. A tribe of agents would be following my every move. A fleet of helicopters would darken the skies. The District of Columbia police commissioner had been brought into the act, and at that moment was maneuvering blocking units into position to close every major and even insignificant artery out of the city.

But it would never come to that, Rita assured me. In the unlikely event I became a hostage, and the completely unlikely event the bad guys gave them the slip, Rita would flip on the little transmitter and I'd be in broadcast mode. Once I made face-to-face contact with the perps, their minutes were numbered.

The Army has a saying: Prior planning prevents piss-poor execution. I knew Agent Rita Sanchez and her crew had been through this drill before, they sounded like they understood the odds and possibilities, they appeared confident, and they were making the proper preparations. Yet it did not escape my attention that we weren't the only ones planning. The opposition probably had schemed and prepared for this moment for months.

A very long day had become an eternity.

CHAPTER TWENTY-SIX

EVENTUALLY THE PREPARATION PHASE ENDED AND WE SHIFTED INTO PHASE two, titled, I think, "Don't Let the Idiot Think About It."

Somebody wheeled a television into the conference room, and we sipped coffee, shared a tray of stale tuna sandwiches, observed the news coverage, and tried to act cool and relaxed.

Jennie informed us she had calls to make and important coordination to accomplish, and she stepped out, leaving me with Rita, who for the next thirty minutes tried to thread that fine line between impressing me with her sharpness and keeping my head in the clouds. Eventually, Jennie returned.

It did not escape my attention that Jennie and Rita were isolating me from the preparations occurring outside this room. Occasionally, agents poked their heads into the room, and either Rita or Jennie stepped outside to confer for a few moments.

At one point, Jennie informed Rita, "Did you know Sean was a former infantry officer? Special Forces, in fact. He survived some really tough scrapes." Rita looked suitably impressed and commented, "Great. Barnes and his pals won't give a certified badass like him the slightest problem."

I was sure this routine came straight from the Bureau manual chapter called "Preparing the Happy Lamb for the Slaughter."

Nor did it escape my notice that Jennifer Margold, with whom I had nearly played a round of hide-the-willie, had suddenly cooled considerably toward yours truly. She had become distanced, and almost clinical, bordering on manipulative. I was sure she was legitimately concerned for me. Still, I found it annoying to go from being the object of her sweaty obsession to Sean the idiot.

In a way, I was delighted she had her head in the game. In a larger way, I really wasn't.

Eventually I asked Rita, "Why do they want cash?"

"It's why bad guys do the things they do."

"I mean—"

"I know what you mean. You thought crooks all had numbered accounts in some overseas bank they want you to wire money to."

"Don't they?"

"Lots do want it done electronically. These days, the more sophisticated ones don't."

"Why not?"

"We now have the ability to put electronic tracers on it. Don't matter how many times they move it, we'll still be waiting at the end, when they try to get it out of the bank."

Intermittently, George appeared on the tube creating what I thought was a splendid illusion of professional confidence, ballooning into optimism. A few pesky reporters weren't buying this act and kept trying to worm embarrassing or insightful information from him, which George parried with wonderfully vague responses and his perpetual I-know-something-you-don't smirk. I usually found that expression annoying. This was the exception. The public would be scared shitless if it knew the amount of vacuous space behind that smirk.

Eventually, Jennie went to the fax machine and retrieved the files CID had zipped over regarding our newest suspect, Mr. Clyde Wizner. She tried to struggle through them, but they made little sense to her, and she slid them across the table at me. "Tell me about this guy."

In one way or another, Clyde Wizner might soon be enjoying a very big role in my life, so this was the first useful diversion. Anyway, military files tend to be somewhat one-dimensional and impersonal. They tell you things like where a soldier's from, where he/she has been assigned, how he/she's been trained, and what to do with him/her after they're dead. In short, a great deal about the person and nothing about the personality.

So here's the deal. Clyde Wizner was forty-nine years old, originally from Killeen, the town outside Fort Hood. He had entered the Army at the age of twenty-two in the year 1977, a high school graduate, no college, and had a GT score—roughly comparable to an IQ—of 135. So Clyde was bright and was selected to become an Army engineer, with a subspecialty in EOD, or Explosive Ordnance Disposal—an expertise that takes nerves of steel, a wonderful memory for tiny details and textbook procedures, and a large reliable life insurance policy.

After basic training and a few specialty training courses, Clyde spent three years at Fort Hood, followed by three years in Germany, a year in Korea, three more years at Hood, and then out. Interspersed between those assignments, he attended plenty of additional training, a few leadership courses and a few bombs and mines things to keep him current on the latest battlefield nasties. He remained single and presumably unattached.

He made it to the rank of staff sergeant, and I guess his service was honorable, because I saw no evidence of blemishes, and he was immediately accepted for civilian employment at Fort Hood.

The interesting fact was that Clyde Wizner spent almost seventeen years performing civilian service before he mysteriously walked into his boss's office and quit. He was only three short years from grabbing the golden ring of lifetime monthly checks and half-assed medical benefits. A cynical mind might suspect Clyde had found a better deal. I'm good at cynical.

I glanced inside his thick civilian personnel file and saw exactly what drew Mr. Eric Tanner to this guy. At Fort Hood, Mr. Wizner had worked in the Office of Post Operations, the nerve center of all that did and did not happen across the sprawling base. As long as he cloaked his nosiness, Clyde could access everything from range operations data to weapons shipments, to military police training activities.

I summarized this for Jennie, who commented, "Do you think it was Wizner who made the call?"

"Texan accent . . . right age . . . same crappy civilian employee attitude all soldiers know and love. Possibly."

She and Rita exchanged glances again. Rita looked at me and commented, "Whatever you do, do *not* let on that you know or even *suspect* his identity. Understand?"

Jennie said, "She's right, Sean. It would be like putting a gun to your own head."

I drew a zipper across my lips.

"I'm serious. He'll kill you." Jennie added, "But, if the chance comes up, try to get a confirmation. Look and listen for hints or clues to his background and identity."

"Don't worry. Subtlety is my forte."

Nobody seemed to buy that for some reason. Jennie explained, "This could be a huge break, Sean. Even if they some-how get away, it would give us a valuable trail to follow."

"I understand."

The phone rang.

It didn't matter that we were expecting, even anticipating it. Literally, we all three ended up on our feet, staring down at the little cell phone lying on the long shiny conference table like a poisoned chalice. Rita smiled at me and said, "Last chance. You sure you wanta put your head in the lion's mouth?"

I was not at all sure. The phone rang again. I lifted it up, cleared my throat, and said, "Drummond."

"You got my money? All of it?" It was the same raspy bass voice, the same in-your-face tone.

"Fifteen suitcases full. But it's not yours yet, pal."

"Used and unmarked, right, boy?"

I looked at Jennie, who nodded. "I'm assured the money's clean and untraceable."

"Yer friends better be playin' you straight. If not, somebody's gonna be dead."

"Hey, they're federal employees. You can trust them."

He laughed. "Okay . . . what're you drivin'?"

"A big blue Suburban."

"Got it. Now, here's the way this goes down. There's a park-ing garage on 13th and L Street. Third deck down. Fifteen min-utes. Not a second later. Comprendo? Say it back to me."

I repeated it, and he hung up.

I shoved back my chair and sprinted for the exit, and Jennie and Rita trotted alongside me. Rita gave me a big cotton-candy smile and assured me, "We'll have five units inside that garage long before you get there. They'll never get out."

We were out in the parking lot, where a dark blue Suburban with the driver's door opened was parked and idling. The back cargo area was loaded to the roof with large gray suitcases. I jumped into the driver's seat and took a moment to familiarize myself with the controls. Rita pointed at a little button by the gearshift. "Push that to get the nitrous oxide to kick in."

"Got it."

Jennie grabbed my arm. I turned and looked at her. She informed me, "Rita and I will be in a command-and-control van a few blocks from you." She leaned inside and kissed my cheek. She whispered, "Trust me. I'll get you out of this. No matter what."

"If you don't, I'll never forgive you."

She laughed. It wasn't a joke.

I closed the door and sped off. I glanced at my watch and noted it was 3:00 P.M., not yet rush hour, though this was a city of government servants, who have a habit of knocking off a wee bit early. The traffic was not sparse, but neither was it overly heavy. I floored it and made good time to I-395, then the 14th Street Bridge, crossed over the muddy brown Potomac, and entered the District, where I was promptly stopped by a red light.

I pounded on the horn, and in return got angry stares and a few middle fingers. In the words of John F. Kennedy, Washington truly is a city with southern efficiency and northern charm. I honked again; nobody budged. I looked at my watch and began to wonder if the green light was broken. Then I glanced down and saw that some smart person had placed a blue bubble light on the floor by the passenger seat. I opened my window, stuck the light to the roof, and then studied the dash until I located a small toggle switch. I flipped it, a siren went off, and the cars ahead of me began scooting up onto the curbs, making a narrow passage. I moved ahead, cautiously looked both ways at the red light, and then pushed the nitrous oxide button and shot through the intersection like a rocket.

I should have been wearing a cape. Actually I should have been wearing a straitjacket. I proceeded north a few blocks, went right, and then left, and ended up on 13th, heading north toward L Street. I detected nobody following me, nobody to my flanks, nobody ahead. But if I took Rita at her word, every other person I saw was a Fed, and every third car was packed with flatfeet, armed, dangerous, and dedicated solely to the preservation of yours truly.

Directly ahead, I picked out the sign for L Street. I reached forward and flipped a switch, and the siren fizzled out. I saw a garage, and then . . . directly across the street, a *second* garage. It struck me that we might have a big problem here.

I looked left and right, and indeed, there were two garages. Definitely, both were on 13th and L; one had a sign reading "Partially Full," whatever that means, but neither had a sign reading "Assholes in here."

I had a sudden vision of being stuck down on the lower deck of the wrong parking garage, as Jason and his pals blew down the Treasury Building or something.

Less than two minutes left, according to my watch. It was a fifty-fifty chance. In fact, I was halfway through eeny-meeny-miney-moe when my phone rang.

I put it to my ear. A female voice said, "Damn. Confusin', ain't it, Drummond?"

I didn't recognize the voice, but the shitkicker accent was familiar, as was the shitty attitude and the superior undertone, or overtone, or whatever. "Who's this?"

"Shut up. Jus' do what I tell ya. Keep drivin'."

The phone remained at my ear as I drove. I could hear her breathing. Shit—again, I reminded myself to stop underestimating Jason Barnes. Back at 13th and L were two garages crawling with Bureau undercover types. Also, because I was being kept on the phone, I was out of contact with Jennie and Rita, who were probably experiencing heart attacks. A little late, it struck me that somebody should have thought about adding a second cell phone to my arsenal of goodies. The voice said, "Go left on M."

Ahead I saw the sign for M Street, and I noted beside the entry another sign that indicated it was a one-way street. She either sensed or prejudged my hesitancy and said, "Jus' friggin' do it."

Left it was. No oncoming traffic was headed in my direction, which was fortunate, as this big behemoth would have rolled over anything in its path.

About halfway down the block, she said, "On your right . . . pull into that alley."

I turned into the passageway; it was narrow, essentially one-way, and I saw, about halfway down the alley, the rear of a parked gray cargo van. "I can't make it through," I informed her. "The path is blocked."

"No shit. Put all them suitcases in the van. Hurry your ass."

I pulled to a stop some three feet behind the van, stepped out, and quickly surveyed my environment. The van was a stretched-out Ford Econoline, designed for hauling cargo, with a completely enclosed back, and at the rear and on both sides the windows were darkly tinted.

I left my phone on the driver's seat, dashed to the rear of the Suburban, and began yanking out suitcases crammed with money. Money, at least a lot of money, can be very heavy. My own money, for some reason, is always ridiculously light. Anyway, I was reduced to lugging one case at a time, requiring about three minutes to complete the task.

I looked around again and saw nobody. Not a soul. Still, I had that eerie feeling of being watched.

I felt a wash of relief, and at the same time, to be frank, a little let down. I had really gotten myself psyched up for this escapade, pumped up with good intentions and adrenaline. Now it was over, finis, end of story. I had thought my part was going to be more dramatic, or perhaps climactic, than a simple transfer from one vehicle to another. But Mother Luck seemed to be smiling upon Sean Drummond. The worst case hadn't materialized, I wasn't a hostage, I was still alive, I was free to go on my way.

Returning to the phone in the Suburban, I informed the lady, "I'm done."

"No you ain't."

"I'm . . . what?"

"What are you waitin' for, moron? Go drive the van."

Well, it did seem too easy. I walked the driver's side, opened the door, and noted that the key was in the ignition. I climbed in, started it up, and pulled forward. I got to the end of the alleyway and she said, "Go left, then take a left on 14th."

As the lady ordered, I went left, then left.

After a moment, she said, "Hey, somethin' I forgot to tell ya. Drive real safe, now. No accidents, and be sure to avoid any big potholes, y'hear." She giggled. After a moment she added, "Thing is, remember when we said we had somebody lined up for the next kill?"

"In fact, I was thinking you could do us all a favor and kill yourself. What do you think?"

"Shut up, asshole. Guess what? Ten pounds of C4 and thirty sticks of dynamite are hardwired to the gas tank of that van. Point is . . . you're the man, Drummond. We push a button and klablewie."

"You . . . Listen, lady, that would be really stupid. I've got the money."

303

"No, you're stupid. It's federal money. Plenty more where that came from."

Shit. "I . . . I understand."

"You better. Now call yer friends. If all the helicopters ain't outta the sky, and all the cop cars followin' you ain't gone in three minutes, you're toast."

She hung up.

I speed-dialed Jennie, who recognized my number and answered, "How you holding up, Sean?"

"We've . . . I mean . . . I've got a, uh . . . a *big* problem."

In a very reassuring tone, she said, "No you don't, Sean. Remember, trust me. We observed the switch. You're now in a gray 2003 Ford cargo van driving south on 14th. Relax. You're tailed and covered."

"Well . . . you should probably inform those tails to back off a bit. See, I'm now driving around with ten pounds of C4 and thirty sticks of dynamite wired to a full gas tank. I really wouldn't want anybody to get . . . you know, hurt."

For a moment there was silence. But my attempt at sarcasm apparently struck home, because it took a moment before Jennie said, "Remain calm."

"Ten pounds of C4 are under my ass, and that's your best advice? Do better, Jennie. Tell me how I'm going to get out of this."

When she didn't answer I said, "Incidentally, you have less than three minutes to get all the helicopters out of the sky and all the trail cars away from me, or I'm hamburger." I added, "Now assure me that you and Sanchez have a plan for this."

But Jennie had apparently handed the phone to Rita, who informed me, "Jennie's getting rid of the cars and helicopters. Just don't sweat it. We'll disperse our ground coverage."

"Don't disperse it—get rid of it."

"I understand."

"You've had cases like this before, right?"

Apparently Rita had to think about that. She said, "No two cases are ever identical. There are always new twists and curves."

"Uh-huh. Tell me about the contingency where the courier becomes a bomb."

"I'll . . . Give me a little time to think about that."

"Wrong answer. Wrong, wrong answer." I punched off.

My blood pressure had just shot up about a hundred points. Barnes and his merry shitkickers would think nothing of vaporizing me, or even the fifty million disposable bucks in the back of this van. Then out of the blue, a truly disturbing thought popped into my brain. What if this was a dry run? Like an object lesson for Barnes to show the Feds not to try any funny business next time? How do I get myself into these things?

My phone rang. I said, "You've got my attention. Now what?"

But it was Jennie again, who said, "Sean, I'm sorry. We didn't expect this. We're thinking furiously back here. Whatever you do, don't try jumping out of the van. Your seat could be hardwired to the C4. In fact, our technicians consider that . . . well, very likely."

"I already thought of that. Tell me something useful."

She said, "We thought we should warn you." But in the event I didn't get the moral of her warning, she added, "There's no way to get you extracted. Do everything they say." She punched off.

So there I was on a gloriously beautiful spring afternoon, driving down 15th Street in my favorite city in the whole world, in the very lopsided state of having fifty million bucks in the backseat of my car and a big bomb strapped to my ass.

God looks after fools and scoundrels, but I wasn't sure whether that applied to idiots.

CHAPTER TWENTY-SEVEN

THE NEXT CALL CAME ABOUT TWO MINUTES LATER, FROM RITA, WHO IN-formed me, "The coverage is off," and abruptly hung up.

Why didn't I feel relieved? This really sucked. A minute later the phone rang and I said, "Relax, lady. The coverage's all gone."

She replied, "Better be. Pull over at the curb."

A moment later I said, "I'm here. What now?"

"Now you strip and throw yer clothes out the window. Shoes, everything."

"Look, I'm wearing a really expensive suit, and—"

"You ain't naked in one minute, yer very nice suit's gonna be confetti."

Before she could punch off I said, "Wait!"

"What?"

"Is there a pressure switch under the driver's seat?"

"Yeah."

"Then . . . how—"

"Figure it out, Drummond." After a moment, she added, "'Course you ain't been all that bright so far. So if I hear a big boom and see a bunch of yer guts flyin' through the air, I'll know you fucked up." She laughed and punched off.

I ordinarily like a woman with a hearty sense of humor. I definitely didn't like her. I wondered for a moment if she was the one who did June Lacy.

Anyway, the tie and shirt came off almost effortlessly. Then, one at a time, I brought my feet up to the dash and, one shoe and one sock at a time, dispensed with my footwear without a hitch. Obviously, the pants posed the really tricky challenge, and had I not practiced this drill a few times as a teenager in the backseat of Papa Drummond's '71 Buick, Mama Drummond wouldn't have to worry about a Christmas gift for me anymore. But trust me, it's a very different pressure, wriggling out of your trousers to get laid and trying to keep your ass connected to your torso. I was down to my undershorts and I decided, as a matter of pride, practicality, and modesty, that this was it. No mas.

I dialed Jennie, who answered, "What are you *doing*? Clothes are flying out of that van."

"How do you— Hey, are you still covering me?"

"I'm . . . yes."

"But Rita said—"

"Rita lied."

"Get rid of the escorts."

"I can't. I'm sorry."

"Yes . . . you *can*—my ass is on the line here."

For a moment she did not respond. Eventually, she said, "Sean, you're driving around our capital in a large explosive device. Did you really believe we were going to eliminate all coverage?"

"I'm sorry. Didn't you say I should trust you?"

I think she put her hand over the phone, because I dimly overheard her speaking with somebody in the background. Then she said, "We did not predict this. The White House and the D.C. police are going nuts on us right now. I've lost some authority and a lot of flexibility here. Understand?"

I didn't really want to hear this. I had become a lobotomized pawn in a game being played between Jennie and Barnes, and now even the federal government was in the act. Everyone had a piece of me but me.

I drew a few deep breaths and tried to get myself under control. I said, "Incidentally, the woman on the phone has to be nearby. She said that if I blow up, pieces of Sean Drummond would splatter her windshield."

"An interesting way to put it."

"Tell me about it."

"She's two blocks over. Heading south, like you."

"Why didn't you tell me?"

"You didn't ask."

"Is *she* under observation, too?"

"Don't be such an optimist. Your last call, she stayed on too long. But it was a moving signal. We only got her basic proximity."

"All right. What next?"

"This phase is a head game. They want to isolate you from us, geographically and psychologically. They're trying to exert their control and trying to throw us off balance." To reassure me that this wasn't a one-way street, I guess, Jennie added, "We're gaming it as we go along. Expect them to try a switch of some sort."

I thought about it a moment. I said, "Who's the optimist now?"

"What's that mean?"

"Maybe they'll order me to drive to the White House and then blow me up."

"I . . . We're alert to that possibility."

"I see."

"We just ordered all federal facilities to put into effect their barrier plans. You won't get through."

"I'll be sure to pass that along."

"Do just that. They need to know it's not an option."

What she diplomatically failed to mention, I was sure, was the Feds also had a more proactive plan in place. If I moved within two blocks of the White House, a SWAT sharpshooter would put ten slugs through the driver of this van. "Jennie?"

"What?"

"Whose side are you on?"

"Don't even ask that."

"Sorry. I'm . . . Well, my day's not really going all that well."

"I've had better days, too. Remember, you may feel alone, but you're not."

"Oh . . . you've got sticks of TNT under your ass, too?"

She ignored that and said, "Listen, somebody's trying to reach me and Barnes may be trying to reach you." She hung up.

So I sat for a moment in my undershorts, feeling stupid, humiliated, and vulnerable. I tried to think through my options. It was a brief moment. I had none.

The phone rang, and I said, "Drummond."

"Hey, asshole, you're not completely naked," the woman informed me.

"Give me a break. I'm down to my underpants."

"Get rid of 'em."

"No."

"*No?* Hey, don't fuck with me, pal."

"Up yours."

"I'll push this little button."

"Lady, I'm tired, I'm frustrated, and I'm in a really foul mood. If you want to spread me and fifty million bucks across thirty blocks over a pair of undershorts, do it. I'm going out in my underpants."

I closed my eyes, held my breath, and waited to be turned into pasta paste. You have to draw the line somewhere.

Eventually, she said, "Feisty, aren't you?"

"Just pissed."

"Uh-huh. Well, this one's no-shit nonnegotiable. Open the glove box." So I did. She said, "Take out the phone and throw yers out the window. We don't want no trackin' devices, do we?"

I reached into the glove box, withdrew the cell phone, and tossed mine out the window. The new cell phone rang. She said, "Don't even *think* of callin' the Feds again. I'll know, and it'll be your last call. Now drive to Rosslyn, through Georgetown, and I'll call you. Try anything stupid, they'll be scrapin' you off the sides of buildings." She punched off.

I put the car in gear, began to pull out—then slammed on the brakes. What the . . . how had she known I was in my underpants? I looked carefully at the cars around me and carefully at the pedestrians on the sidewalk. Though I saw no one looking back at me, there had to be a spotter.

Then it hit me. I began a visual inspection of the cab and the rear of the van. Well I'll be—clipped to the shade visor on the passenger side was a miniature camera, directed at me, broadcasting my every move. Somewhere else, I was sure, would be a microphone. Obviously, they had seen and probably heard everything.

I looked dead into the camera, lifted up my left hand, and stuck up my middle finger.

Fortunately, there was no big boom, however, the phone

rang again. It was her, and she said, "That reminds me, Drummond. Git rid of that watch, too."

Shit.

But rush hour was getting into full swing, and without my helpful blue light it took me twenty minutes to get to Georgetown, and another ten to crawl down the length of heavily congested M Street and go left onto Key Bridge.

As I stared ahead at the glass towers of Rosslyn, it struck me, and I'm sure it also struck Jennie and Rita, that moving me out of the District was another shrewd move. Our whole two hours of preparation had been spent coordinating and rehearsing with the D.C. Police Department. An institution accustomed to being bossed around by the Feds. An institution that exerted monolithic control over everything inside the District's boundaries. The Virginia side of the river was bureaucratic chaos. The police departments were balkanized by county, and coordination between the Bureau and the corresponding local departments would be a hopeless mess.

As Rita Sanchez had said, I knew it to be true that most bad guys aren't particularly clever. In fact, most are annoyingly stupid. I had spent part of my career defending them, and I was frequently astounded, often appalled, and occasionally overwhelmed by the monumentally idiotic things they did. The plea bargain was contrived on the very premise that most criminals are just too mortally ignorant to even waste a trial over.

Regardless of what had shaped or perverted Jason Barnes's character, he was different. As far as we knew, he came to the arts of larceny and murder a stone-cold virgin. Yet he had come so far, so fast. His were crimes of passion, yet exhibited none of the telltale rashness, disorder, or carelessness that nearly always define that criminal breed. He had made none of the usual beginner's mistakes, or even a mistake one might expect from a hardened veteran. Up against the very best American law enforcement had to offer—the best coppers the world had to offer—he was running circles around them.

Unbelievable.

I wondered what Jason had up his sleeve for his next move. I couldn't even guess. But if—as Jennie was convinced—a man's past is the chronicle to his future, it was going to be something else.

I was about to find out.

CHAPTER TWENTY-EIGHT

Halfway across Key Bridge, she called and said, "Go straight to Seven Corners."

"And you go straight to hell." Assuming she was observing me on Candid Camera, for good measure, I gave her another bird.

"Yeah? Well, who's the one drivin' 'round in his undershorts with a bomb under his ass?"

Good point. "Hey, I've got an idea, lady. Give yourself up. I'm a lawyer—maybe I'll keep your ass from frying in an electric chair."

"Shut up, or you'll get to hell first." She sounded really indignant, and hung up. Obviously, I needed to be careful here. The electric chair is sort of a hot-button topic with criminals. Also, women can be really touchy, and you never know when it's that time of the month.

With that sexist thought in mind, I smiled into the camera, hoping she'd see I was a good sport.

Anyway, I knew how to get to Seven Corners, was aware it was both a location and a shopping center, and I even knew how it got its name. It was in the county of Fairfax, a mile or so south of Falls Church, perched at the strategic junction of seven major arteries. It was a perfect example of what happens when urban planning boards are idiots—a congested maze of shopping malls, small roads, and substantial highways, surrounded by densely built-up suburbs with myriad side streets.

There were so many roads, large and small, leading into and out of Seven Corners it would take an entire field army to block them all off. In short, the perfect place for a shuffle, and somehow, I was sure, this was the decisive ground and the decisive moment.

So off I sped, straight through the steel-and-concrete corridors of Rosslyn, to the Route 50 exit, and then toward Seven Corners. I considered calling Jennie to forewarn her, and even more quickly concluded it would be both stupid and superfluous. With all the people watching, listening, and electronically tracking me, I felt like I was on one of those TV reality shows, this one called *How to Save—or Not—Your Own Ass.*

After another twenty minutes, I ended up at a stoplight, and to my right were two large strip malls, and ahead, off to my left, the lower parking lot for the Seven Corners Shopping Center, a two-level extravaganza, long and rectangular, half a million square feet of the best the capitalist world had to offer, where you could scratch virtually any materialistic itch and gratify any spending impulse. I love America.

In addition to all else, there had to be a tracking device in the van, because she called and said, "Now, straight to the intersection of Route 50 and Route 7, hang a left, and go to the upper parkin' lot of the shopping center. Keep the phone to yer ear."

I could hear the tension in her voice, and my heart began to race. The upper parking lot was around the other side of the shopping center, a mere few yards from the crossroads of four major highways running east, west, north, and south, the most options for egress. Clearly we had a major problem. Barnes had thought this through with frightening cleverness.

I hoped Jennie and Rita knew I was here, and I hoped they recognized what an ideal spot this was.

I wheeled into the north end of the upper parking lot, a long and narrow patch of black tarmac, approximately sixty yards in depth by about three hundred yards in length. She said, "Pull to the curb right next to the shoppin' center."

So I did.

"Now, keep going . . . little further . . . little more—now, stop."

It struck me that we had a big problem here. The parking spaces in the lot were filled with the usual mix of cars, SUVs, and minivans, and more cars were circling around and waiting for a space to open. Sated shoppers were coming out of the shopping center, toting bags of loot and dragging their kiddies, even as large numbers of hungry shoppers were crossing the lot and heading inside. Also, while the shopping center was as large as most malls, it wasn't enclosed—and thus wasn't labeled a mall—but instead had open walkways under overhangs where throngs of shoppers strolled and noodled.

If this thing went south, a lot of innocent people could get caught in the crossfire. If Jason's friend got nervous and ignited the little device wired to this van, we would have a major disaster, mostly moms and kiddies who would never know what hit them, not to mention moi.

But I didn't care what happened to me any longer. I rolled down the window, stuck my head out, and yelled, "This car has a bomb in it! Everybody run! Get away from here, now! . . . Run!"

People were just focusing on the nut screaming scary things when a bunch of small gray canisters came flying through the air from the covered space inside the shopping center. The canisters struck the black tarmac around the van and rolled around, at least a dozen of them.

Nobody else did, but I recognized them instantly—Army smoke grenades.

They all started popping off, spitting and spewing thick clouds of green, red, and gray smoke into the air. Within seconds, the clouds became impenetrable; I could see nothing through my windshield but my own dazed reflection. Then my car door was jerked opened and a large and powerful hand got a grip on the back of my neck and pulled me out of the seat and onto the tarmac, where I landed with a loud *oompf* on my fifth point of contact.

My first thought was surprise that I could still have a thought. No bomb went off in the van. My second thought was to wonder if Jennie and Rita had somehow beaten me here, if all this smoke was to cover their assault and apprehension plan.

Alas, I had again committed the unpardonable sin of optimism. When I looked up, through the dense smoke and haze I observed a towering figure in blue jeans and a dark top looming above me. I was just starting to say something when the pointy end of a cowboy boot came slashing through the air, directly into my solar plexus.

I made a sound like a popped balloon. I rolled backward and immediately vomited up the tuna salad lunch I had shared with Rita and Jennie. I rolled around, gasped for breath, and mumbled a quick prayer to the god of hopeless causes—*"Don't let that damn suppository be in that mess."*

I tried to force air into my lungs, and I tried to get upright, but a hand shoved me back onto my butt. Over the noise of screaming people I heard the sounds of heavy grunting and of suitcases thumping onto metal. More smoke grenades were ignited, and I found myself coughing and sputtering from the irritation to my throat.

Then I heard the sound of a loud whoosh, followed instantly by a boom. A moment later, the sounds were repeated—*Whoosh . . . Boom!* I recognized the sound—Light Antitank Weapons were being fired, presumably into the parking lot.

I knew what Barnes was doing and I knew it was brilliant. The smoke was hiding the transfer of the suitcases into some other vehicle, and the rockets were fired into the parking lot to create a diversion. All police forces live by the credo Protect and Serve, in that order. Protection of the public trumps apprehension, and assuming Bureau agents were at the scene, they had their hands full protecting the innocents from the flying missiles.

A pair of powerful hands jerked me to my feet. The same big guy moved in front of me, and an electronic wand was swiftly waved over the length of my body. Apparently I wasn't in broadcast mode, which was either really good or really bad news for me. He spun me around and began shoving me toward the shopping center. I had about ten feet and three seconds to consider my options.

Option one—whirl around, kick the big guy, and haul ass. He was, as I said, large and strong, but he wasn't expecting it, and I owed him a kick in the nuts at the very least. Also, once I got a few feet away, I would be obscured by smoke and it would take a remarkably lucky shot to put a bullet in my back. My day hadn't been lucky so far, but you never know.

Option two—remain with these people, hoping my tracking device wasn't in a pile of vomit, hoping they had some unfathomable reason to keep me alive, and hoping the Feds rose to a level of competence they hadn't yet shown.

Option one meant they would probably escape, but coincidentally, so would I. Option two contained the most hopes, and I had just sworn off optimism.

Through the smoke I observed two people shoving a rolling metal cargo cart loaded with gray suitcases into the shopping center's elevator.

In that instant, it struck me that they had outsmarted the cops; they were going to get away with it. The Feds would be rushing to block the escape routes accessible from the upper lot. Unobserved, Jason's crew would slip down the elevator to the lower level, making their escape out the other side of the shopping center, on different highways.

Either I was propelled by a noble impulse or I procrastinated too long, because suddenly I had no options. I was shoved with great force into the elevator, five more smoke grenades were tossed out, the doors slid closed, and we began our descent.

CHAPTER TWENTY-NINE

THERE WERE THREE OF THEM IN THE ELEVATOR. NOBODY SAID A WORD. WE were all winded, breathing heavily, and, for different reasons, consumed with our own thoughts and fears.

I used the descent to take stock of my new companions. They were dressed regularly—if shitkicker haberdashery can be termed regular—with black balaclava hoods over their heads, so I couldn't observe their fiendish faces, just their soulless eyes.

The one to my right, who maintained a vise grip on my arm, was square-shouldered, lanky, and extremely tall, perhaps six foot six or six foot seven. He smelled a little rank, or these days, I guess, "hygienically challenged."

The one to my left—specifically, the one holding the Glock pistol at my ear—had a feminine physique, slender where it counted, curvy where it counted, with a pair of huge rockets where it counted more. I assumed this was the same lady who had jerked me around on the phone.

The third member of their party had positioned himself in front of the elevator control panel. About my size, just shy of six feet, roughly 190 pounds, which coincided neatly with the descriptive data in Clyde Wizner's personnel files.

In fact, sexually, physically, and morally, these three were a cold match for Eric Tanner's hypothetical ring.

Not present in this gathering of murderers was the fourth party in their conspiracy, the brains of this outfit, Mr. Jason Barnes. Not really surprising, considering that his picture was in every newspaper in the country.

The elevator doors slid open. We were now on the ground level of the shopping center, and mirroring the upper level, there were no walls enclosing the shops; only a narrow covered walkway separated us from the lower parking lot. The cart and I were shoved out of the elevator, then straight toward the curb, where there were two Texas Cadillacs, i.e., beat-up Ford pickups, one red in color, one black, cabs empty, engines idling.

The guy who appeared to be Clyde Wizner said to the woman, "Get yers. Hurry," and off she loped, bouncing and jiggling.

He said to me, "You kin help load these cases, or you kin stand with yer thumb up yer butt and I'll blow yer brains out."

Time to be the perfect guest. I lifted the first suitcase and set it gently in the back of the black pickup.

Then the three of us were tossing suitcases into the beds of the red and black pickup trucks. There were no bags or luggage in any of the trucks, indicating, I thought, the possibility of a nearby hiding place. The license plates on both vehicles were Virginian, though presumably they were stolen, as was the fifty million, as was Sean Drummond.

In less than thirty seconds, the lady rolled up in her pickup, a yellow one, and the last four suitcases were thrown into the bed. The tall guy ran down the line and drew canvases over the cases, and there was their haul—fifty million in clean, untraceable cash divided not quite equally three ways, plus indivisible me.

The lady tossed me her keys and said, "Yer drivin' mine. Git in."

To clear up my apparent hesitation, she allowed me to examine how clean she kept the bore of her Glock pistol. She said, "I'd jus' as soon kill you. Move it, asshole."

And like that, I was in the mood for a drive.

The other two pickups sped off in different directions, as she and I climbed into the cab of her yellow Ford. Fastidiousness and nutritional fussiness were not among her faults; the floor was covered with crushed Bud cans and balled-up candy wrappers, and the lady appeared to own a bald dog, because tiny gray hairs were matted everywhere. Also, on the dash, directly in front of the steering wheel, was mounted a small video screen, presumably the one she had used to observe me inside the van.

Her right hand kept her pistol leveled at me, and with the other she removed her black balaclava hood and shook out her blond hair. As Chief Eric Tanner's witnesses attested, this was a lady who could spin a few heads; a little past thirty, cool blue eyes, tanned skin just turning wrinkly, pouty lips, and a firm chin. She was quite pretty, though a little slutty. Definitely not the type of girl Mom dreamed you'd bring home, but I think Pop would've enjoyed her. Except this lady had no heart and the black soul of a murderess.

Obeying perhaps her only law of the day, she buckled her seat belt. She said to me, "Don't buckle yers. Try crashin' this truck, yer goin' through the windshield, not me." She waved her pistol in front of my nose. "What'n the hell you lookin' at? Move it."

I pulled forward, and she directed me toward the far end of the parking lot. We sat on a long bench seat, and, showing sound survival skills, she scooted up against the passenger door and faced me. She said, "Don't speed, neither. Git back on Route 50, toward D.C."

After a moment, I commented, "You lied."

"I lie all the time. What's yer point?"

"There was no bomb."

"Oh . . . yeah." She looked around to see if any cops were in the vicinity. Unfortunately, they were all attending a convention on the other side of the mall, and it was smooth sailing. She looked at me and giggled. "Now, don't you feel like a stupid ass? Law degree and all that . . . still, I bullshitted you down to yer underpants. You were shittin' yer drawers."

"I never believed you in the first place."

"Liar." She laughed. "I saw yer face through the camera, and heard you tell the FBI. Like hell you din't believe me."

I laughed, too. "It did kind of suck."

I kept my eyes on the road, but after a moment I said to her, "You know, every cop in the entire world is going to come after you. Forever. You murdered a lot of important people. They'll never forget. Never. Eventually, they'll get you."

"Shut up."

"I just thought you should know they're really pissed."

"So what? They ain't impressed me yet."

That was probably true. After another moment I said, "What should I call you?"

"Don't call me nothin'. Shut up and drive."

"Come on. Give me a name. You're going to kill me anyway. Think about it . . . What will it hurt?"

She seemed to consider this. Obviously, she had removed her balaclava because in this era of terrorphobia people get a little stressed when they see hooded people riding around town. Yet allowing me to see her face was bad news for me. In fact, I was clueless as to why they hadn't already whacked me. Somehow, I fit into their agenda. Probably it suited their purposes to keep a hostage until they were free and clear, not a second longer. In any event, her failure to contradict my assertion confirmed that I didn't have to worry about my dinner plans. She said, "Mary-Lou."

Why do all these people from Texas sound like country singers? I said, "Pretty name."

"Don't try that shit. We ain't gonna be friends."

I looked at her. "You're right, MaryLou, we'll never be friends. I'd just like my last few hours to pass pleasantly. Okay with you?"

We could hear, off in the distance, the screams of sirens, and again she twisted around and looked to be sure there weren't any flashing lights on our tail. No such luck.

I mentioned, "Anyway, it doesn't matter. The Bureau already knows about you."

"Yeah, right—nice try. They don't got a clue about me."

"Well . . . look, I hate to be the harbinger of bad news here . . . but yeah . . . they really do."

"Bullshit. They don't—"

"They know you're from Killeen, they know you've been pilfering weapons, and they know all about your pal Clyde Wizner."

As intended, this disclosure got a big jolt out of her. She sort of recoiled backward, the pistol dipped a little, and her eyes went wide.

"Investigators are running all over Killeen," I continued. "What I'll bet is somebody will remember seeing you and Clyde together." I added, "With your looks . . . the boys do take notice, don't they?"

"I . . . when . . . I mean, how—"

"Hey . . . you should see the composite of you they're flashing around. From that range theft—the day you ran around Fort Hood in the range control getup. Those guys on the range sure remembered you. In fact, seeing you in the flesh—wow, it's *you* . . . a dead ringer." I glanced at her and said, "Hey . . . you seem a little tense . . . upset. Should I be telling you this?"

"Jus' . . . fuck— Jus' shut up."

"Fine. I'll just, you know, drive."

I stared straight ahead. MaryLou was apparently not one of those people who accepts bad news gracefully. Neither am I.

I was thinking on my feet, looking for an angle, trying to get a bead on this lady. Having grown up in Army bases in the South, I knew girls who at least looked and sounded like MaryLou— rednecky, bred on the wrong side of the tracks, and willing to do anything to get to the right side. Mentally underendowed, but overendowed with great looks, great knockers, and the drives and instincts of a true carnivore.

Okay, I was constructing an overused stereotype, but stereotypes have their uses, and often even have roots in some useful and telling truths. For instance, I guessed that MaryLou probably was a little insecure about her background, resentful toward authority figures, and probably had a history with the coppers. Like most people from hardscrabble backgrounds, she was perhaps prone to believe that every piece of good fortune comes wrapped in a shitty lining.

Motive was also a factor. I would guess MaryLou beat the odds of early disaster, and now the shadow of long-term failure loomed; she was too old and carried too much baggage to impress a rich boy, her good looks were getting wrinkly, and a forklift was required to keep her boobs aloft. For MaryLou, it had become all or nothing, which was not really happy news for me.

As I suspected she might, she waved her pistol and asked, "Hey, you. What else the cops know?"

"MaryLou, it's not what they know *now*—it's what they'll soon know. You born and raised in Killeen?"

"So?"

I shook my head. "So, that's unfortunate for you. For the cops, it's one-stop/one-shop. The thing with cops is, they may get off to a slow start, but they're resilient and very persistent." I added, "By nightfall, they'll know your name, your history, even your shoe size."

Actually, from the molds taken at the Hawk's place, they already had her shoe size, width, an estimate of her weight, and even her shoe type. Under the circumstances, however, it probably was best not to bring that up. I suggested, "But maybe you don't have a problem."

"How's that?"

"Well, I'm sure you've got a good disguise and a fake passport to get out of the country. Right?"

"Nope. I know where I can git one, though."

"Killeen?"

"So?"

"What do you think?"

"Too hot, huh?"

I allowed her to think about that. She didn't strike me as overly bright, but I would be foolish to underestimate her. At least given our brief history together, there was no risk she would overestimate me. I suggested, "I'm not saying you're going to get caught, but I don't really see how you're not."

From her expression, these thoughts were disturbing for her. Actually, I was a little astonished. These people had thought out everything; why not a reasonable escape plan? Then again, success breeds overconfidence, and we all know where that lands you: sloppy.

Eventually she said, "Maybe yer not as smart as you think, Drummond."

"Maybe. I know this; once the cops ID you, you'll be as recognizable as Madonna. As will your partners. You murdered some very important people, MaryLou, and you painted a bull's-eye on the President's ass. They're calling this the crime of the century."

"I kin still get away."

"Maybe. But what if you don't?"

"What's that mean?"

"A smart person considers the alternatives."

"Yeah?"

"Sometimes shit happens, MaryLou. But it doesn't have to happen to you."

"I'm listenin'."

"We're talking multiple counts of murder in the first degree, extortion, and conspiracy to commit murder . . ." I looked at her and explained, accurately, "The government will have to ask for capital punishment. At least a couple of you will fry." I paused to allow that reality to register, and then suggested, "But I'll bet one of you won't."

I directed my eyes back to the road, though I could sense her studying me. Eventually she said, "Look, asshole, I got maybe twelve million comin' to me. Now yer tryin' to jerk me around, like *I* got a problem."

"Don't you?"

"Turn there, on Glebe." She added, "Way I see it, only problem I got's how to spend all that cash."

"Fine. Good luck."

"Yeah? Well, nobody kin prove shit on me."

"Except your partners." I smiled.

She raised her pistol and pointed it at my head. With a quick glance I saw that her trigger finger was white with pressure and her pupils were dilated with anger. Uh-oh. She said, "I think I'll jus' blow yer friggin' brains out."

"Boy, is that my thanks for trying to help you out here?"

Her fingers tightened a little more, and she was about a millimeter short of ending this conversation. "Don't, MaryLou. I'm driving, we'll crash, the cops will come, and you might have a little trouble explaining those suitcases in the truck bed." I very reasonably added, "Take a deep breath. Forget everything I said."

She obviously couldn't, however. She said, "Clyde's smarterin' you anyway."

"Probably."

"He thinks things through."

"Sure does. I'll bet he knows exactly what he's going to do if you're apprehended."

"What's that mean?"

"Think about it."

"Yer tryin' to fuck with my head."

Exactly. "No, I'm simply suggesting that if you're apprehended, your reality changes. Maybe you and Clyde are as close as brother and sister. Or maybe you're not."

"Clyde always played me square."

"And the big guy?"

"Hank? Well, he's a little slow. Stupid, actually."

"You see . . . that's exactly what I'm talking about. If you're caught, somebody's going to squeal. They always do. The Feds will separate you, sweat you a little, and then offer you each one chance to live. First to squeal gets the deal. Maybe it'll be the smart guy who thinks ahead, or maybe the dumbass who can't think two seconds ahead."

She appeared to be pondering which of her partners, Hank or Clyde, would be the first to rat her out. I added, "The thought of ten thousand volts popping your eyeballs out of your skull . . . your teeth exploding . . . smoke curling out your hairtips and pouring out your ears . . . Some people . . . well, you know, they go all squirmy just thinking about it."

A little revolting imagery is always sobering. We were still headed west on Glebe Road, and she had cooled off a bit and was cradling her gun in her lap. Off to the left was a turn into a large and slightly run-down complex of red-brick townhouses and apartment buildings. She pointed at a turn into the complex and said, "Go past that. Circle 'round a bit."

"Fine." I now knew where we were going to end up.

After a moment, she said, "All right, Mr. Smartass Lawyer, say I git caught. What am I supposed to do?"

"First, don't hesitate. Like that game show . . . you know, *Jeopardy*, that Alex guy asks the question and whoever hits the buzzer first gets first shot."

"What's that mean? First shot?"

"Well, I didn't say it was automatic, did I?"

"No?"

"No. Maybe Hank, or maybe Clyde, or maybe both, will also jump at the deal." I shook my head. "You wouldn't believe how often that happens."

"I thought you said first to squeal gets the deal."

"Didn't I also say that somebody has got to fry?"

She nodded.

"See the problem here? The prosecutor's going to tell the cops the quota's for one. Only one. Whoever games it best gets the deal."

"Uh-huh. How's that work?"

"Well, it weighs on what they call extenuating factors. Like . . . for instance, who murdered the most people?"

"Uh . . . well, that would be Clyde and Hank, for damned sure. I only did . . . like two. Uh . . . maybe three."

"Which three? The lady at the door at Belknap's?"

She nodded. "Uh-huh."

My grip on the steering wheel got a little tighter. "Belknap's driver?"

Another nod.

"And was it you who planted the mine beside Justice Fineberg's door?"

"Nah. Clyde did that. He's really into bombs and shit. He don't let nobody near 'em. I jus' pushed the button that blew the ol' fart in half."

"That it?"

She had to think about it a moment. This was surreal. "Maybe one more," she said after a hesitation.

"*Maybe?*"

"Okay, one more . . . Belknap's old lady." She looked at me and said, petulantly, "Clyde and Hank did like . . . I don't know . . . like maybe *ten* people."

It's always amazing, not to mention dismaying, when you talk to killers and discover what idiots they are, and how shockingly little remorse or even guilt they feel. I shook my head.

"What? You got a problem with that?"

"No, but you will. MaryLou, you need something else to offer the Feds. Exactly *how* dumb is Hank?"

"*Real* dumb. Clyde and I got all the brains. We'd get the targets, and plan 'em out." She laughed. "Ol' Hank, you tell him to stick his head up a cow's butt, he don't even think about it. That boy's stupider'n dirt."

"Well, that's not good."

She stopped laughing. "What ain't good?"

"You have to understand, the law gives idiots all the breaks. Like, the stupider you are, the less guilt you bear. You've got to balance that out."

"Yeah? How?"

"Maybe show you had a stab of conscience. Do something good to outweigh the bad. Remember, you only have to look slightly better in comparison to them." I added, quite sincerely, "That's not hard, is it?"

She studied me a moment. She said, "Like I should let you live? That's what yer edgin' at, right?"

"Not at all." After a moment, I added, "Well, obviously it wouldn't hurt."

"Uh-huh. And you'd say nice things about me?"

"It's a little late to make you sound like a saint. I'd be as complimentary as circumstances allow."

She said, "Go back to that turn I showed you."

"Sure." I asked, "Well, what do you think?"

"Don't know yet. Gotta think about it."

Neither she nor I said a word the rest of our way. I had planted the seed, and either it would sprout or I was screwed.

I made the turn into the complex, then two rights and then a left, and we ended up in a tight cul-de-sac, where I pulled into a space right beside Hank's red pickup. Clyde's black pickup was nowhere in sight.

MaryLou hung a cloth over her pistol and ordered me out of the truck. We looked a little suspicious walking up the sidewalk, me in my underpants, her three paces behind me with her right arm locked. But the neighborhood was run-down and decrepit, and neighbors probably tended to mind their own business.

We entered a two-floored colonial-style townhouse, and I was directed down a narrow hallway that led into the sparsely furnished living room. I observed a small TV, a foldable card table, and some plastic outdoor furniture; otherwise, the place was bare. Martha Stewart would have a fit.

Hank stood off to our left, in the efficiency kitchen. He was a bit older than I expected, maybe fifty, dark-haired, slack-jawed, sugar-sabotaged teeth, and there was sullen dullness in his dark eyes, like somebody forgot to turn on the lights inside his skull. He was just knocking off a Bud; he tipped it at MaryLou and said, "Hey."

"Hey," she replied.

"Him?" he commented, directing the beer can at me.

"Him," replied MaryLou, which seemed to end their monosyllabic discussion.

Incidentally, seated in a chair in the middle of the living room was a guy with his hands tied behind his back, with a black gag taped around his mouth, and with a face I instantly recognized: Jason Barnes.

CHAPTER THIRTY

HANK PUT DOWN HIS BEER, GRABBED A KNIFE AND COIL OF ROPE OFF THE counter, approached me, and swiftly tied my hands behind my back. Next he drew black tape across my lips, as MaryLou pushed another outdoor chair into the center of the living room. Without a hint of gentleness, Hank shoved me toward and then into it. He then tied the rope around my hands to a rear chair leg, and my feet to a front leg.

Hank was quick and strong, with a sailor's dexterity with knots. Probably he had worked with cattle at some point in his life, and it showed. The bonds were so tight I would have gangrene within the hour.

But it was interesting, I thought, that MaryLou failed to inform him that their identities were now known to the cops, or that her, his, and Clyde's asses might be a little exposed.

Maybe she was worried that Hank might fly off the handle.

Or maybe she didn't care what Hank thought. Or maybe Mary-Lou did care and was preserving her edge.

I noted Jason's gray eyes following me throughout this drill. I was surprised to observe that he did not look at all like a crazed dog or even a schizoid nut. In fact, he looked like a perfectly ordinary guy in an utterly helpless state, a little afraid, monumentally befuddled, and more than a little curious about the new guest.

It further struck me that Jennie had been right about what was happening here—as she had been right about so many other matters in this convoluted case.

As they are wont to do, the thieves had had a falling-out. The Texans wanted their money now, Jason still frothed for blood, and the odd man found himself out, with a mutiny on his hands. I wondered, though, why the captain of this ship hadn't been forced to walk the gangplank in the venerable tradition. Why keep this guy alive? The Texans had the money, the killing was over—or nearly over, I reminded myself—and I couldn't see how Jason was still useful to them.

Then I recalled MaryLou informing me that her cut was about twelve million. Divide fifty million four ways, and it sounded like Jason was still getting his share. Honor among thieves? Why was I having trouble believing that?

MaryLou said to Hank, "C'mon, let's git packed and ready to split."

"Okay."

For the next fifteen minutes I could hear the sounds of Hank and MaryLou opening closets and drawers and throwing clothes into suitcases. Jason sat quietly beside me, breathing easily, apparently bored out of his mind.

Then the front door opened and a guy walked in. He was

about my size, dark hair sprinkled with gray, a broad, hard-looking face, thick nose, and mean eyes.

He looked at Jason, then at me, and yelled, "Hey, what the hell we got here? MaryLou, you sneakin' men in here behind my back?"

From the bedroom, MaryLou yelled, "Damn it, Big Daddy, you took yer damned time."

"Traffic," he yelled. "Seems like some crooked people did a bad thing somewheres, and the cops shut down a buncha roads." He laughed. "Ain't that some bullshit?"

Dressed in only her panties and bra, MaryLou came traipsing down the hallway, straight toward Clyde, then into his arms. He lifted her off the floor with his hands on her butt and they kissed for a long time. Uh-oh. Maybe she and Clyde were closer than she'd let on.

Clyde said to her, "Well, baby, you'n me are now rich as shit. What'd I tell ya, huh?"

"You said it jus' right, Big Daddy."

He laughed. "Tol' you we should take the deal."

She leaned away from him and said, "Only we got a big problem we din't figure on."

"How's that?"

She pointed at me and said, "That asshole there. Said the cops got you ID'd already. Said they know all about the weapons we stole." Shit. I was hearing the sounds of my best-laid plans falling apart. Actually, my only plans.

Clyde asked, "He said that?"

"Yep. Also said a buncha cops are runnin' 'round Killeen diggin' up our histories."

Clyde stared at her a moment. He appeared at first astonished, then his mood shifted and his face turned dark. He looked at me. "Yer sure he wasn't jus' bullshittin' ya? MaryLou—y'know all them lawyers lie."

She laughed.

He said, "Seriously, baby."

"It ain't bullshit, Clyde. He knew *way* too much."

Clyde crossed the floor. He ended up directly to my front, sort of looking down and studying me. He said to MaryLou, "I don't like the sound of this, baby. We shoulda learned about that."

She crossed her arms and said, "You got it. That's what I'm wonderin'."

I was really interested in this conversation, and Clyde had his lips open to say something I was sure was going to be really interesting, but before he got a word out, the front door blew right off the hinges with a loud boom. At almost the same instant, the glass doors to the porch exploded inward, showering us with glass.

MaryLou screamed. For a fraction of an instant, she and Clyde stared at each other, mesmerized. Then they came to their senses and immediately spun and dashed for the bedrooms.

Instinctively I tipped my chair sideways and toppled over, ending up on the floor. The room filled with smoke and dust and stunk of cordite. Then, through the smoke I saw a squad of men in dark pants, dark shirts, bulletproof armor, and black helmets rushing from the front door, and more pouring through the now gaping rear porch entrance. Hopefully somebody had remembered to brief the cavalry that we weren't all Indians in here.

But it looked like somebody with a body heat sensor was directing the traffic, because they ignored me, and they ignored Jason, and they sped right past us, straight for the bedrooms.

In an instant, I heard shots being fired and men yelling. I looked at the front door again, and through the haze and smoke

I saw another figure, and after a moment I made out Agent Jennifer Margold, in her blue FBI windbreaker, with her blue FBI ballcap, in the shooter's crouch, scanning the room, pointing her FBI pistol directly at me. I saw her face, and I saw it tighten, and then the barrel shifted slightly upward and went off.

I heard the first bullet strike tissue, make a soft thudding sound, and even through his gag, Jason Barnes emitted a sort of muffled groan. I tried yelling through my gag and I tried kicking his chair over, but I was too late. *Bang, bang*—Jennie fired two more shots—his chair flew backward, and Barnes ended up on his back.

Jennie kept her arms straight and her pistol up, just as they teach at the FBI Academy, and she rushed toward me. More shots and loud cursing were coming from the back bedrooms, where the Texans were apparently making their last stand.

Jennie tore the black tape off my mouth, then rushed behind me, bent down, and untied the ropes. She asked, "You okay?"

"I'm . . . yes."

"We kept turning your tracker off and on. You were still moving. We had to wait till you stopped."

I was free of the restraints and I stood up and rubbed my wrists, which would be sore for a week. I pointed at Jason's body. "Why did you do *that*?"

"To keep him from shooting you."

"The guy was tied up, Jennie."

Jennie looked down at the body. She studied Jason Barnes for a moment, and then looked at me, her eyes wide, her mouth hanging open. "I . . . oh, Jesus. Sean, I . . . I had no idea. Through the smoke, I saw you . . . on the floor . . . then . . . and then him. I thought he was . . . was standing over you, and I thought . . ."

I regarded Jason's corpse. One shot had entered his mid-chest, and two had punched into his forehead and gone straight through, blowing his brains across the room. His eyes were locked open, his pupils rolled upward—as though he had tried to watch the bullets pass through.

From down the hall, by the bedrooms, came a really loud boom—we both recoiled from the shock. Another percussion or stun grenade went off, followed by more yells and more shots. A real battle was going on back there.

"Come on." Jennie took my arm and pulled me along. I followed, a little dumbstruck. Outside and about fifty yards from the townhouse were parked two armored trucks, and we sprinted down the sidewalk and ended up taking cover behind the nearest one.

We stood for a moment, winded, a little unsteady. Then Jennie reached over and touched my face. Actually, not touched, she wiped. She said, "You're bleeding a lot."

Until that moment, I hadn't realized that glass splinters from the porch door had sprayed me. Blood was streaming into my face from my scalp, and a quick visual inspection revealed a number of cuts on my chest, my arms, even my legs. Now that I realized they were there, they hurt like hell.

An agent dressed in an urban commando getup, a flak vest, and a royally pissed-off expression approached. He walked straight to Jennie, got two inches from her face, and barked, "What in the hell were you doing?"

"Getting my man out."

"I told you, Agent, nobody enters till the Hostage Rescue Team gives the all-clear."

"I recall that."

"This was an outrageous breach of procedures. I could care less if you're a supervisor. I'm gonna report this."

Jennie looked at him, not giving an inch. "Go ahead. I told my hostage I'd guarantee his safety. I meant it."

Mr. Macho saw this was going nowhere, apparently remembered he had a firefight on his hands, and stomped off in a nasty huff.

Did I suddenly feel bad, or what? I said, "You were coming in to get me?"

She did not reply.

I squeezed her hand. "Thank you."

She looked very unhappy, distracted even, and I thought I knew what was going on here.

After a moment, I asked her, "Jason was your first kill. Right?"

"Yeah. My first kill. A man with his hands tied behind his back. I . . . well, I . . ." Her eyes became misty.

"It happens, Jennie. You couldn't know his hands were *tied* behind his back. For all you knew, he had a weapon. Through the smoke and dust, that's what your eye saw, and what your mind registered. In the heat of action, the eye overrules the mind, and the finger on the trigger doesn't discriminate."

She looked at me and said nothing.

CHAPTER THIRTY-ONE

WITHIN THREE MINUTES, THE HOSTAGE RESCUE TEAM LEADER MUST'VE radioed out that the deed was done, because everybody suddenly relaxed. Actually that might be overstating it, but a few agents lit up cigarettes, and a few people wandered out into the open from behind the vans.

A forensics team was sent into the townhouse, followed closely by four teams of medical technicians bearing stretchers. Then lots of unmarked sedans filled with Johnny-come-latelies began pouring down the street. On their heels followed the ubiquitous TV news vans, prenotified, I guess, so the public could witness this effervescent moment in FBI history. But I wasn't being judgmental—the Feds had bled and suffered for this one. What little credit was due, they deserved.

Somebody with bad manners in a gray suit kept ordering me into an ambulance. I insisted I was fine, and swore I could and would swagger out of here on my own two feet. It was all macho posturing from big bad Sean, of course. I get a little weird standing around in public in my undershorts.

Also, Jennie remained very hurt and uptight, staring off into space, absorbed in her own thoughts. I held her hand and I figured—no matter how silly—that I was helping her hold it together.

But the FBI has a lot of rules, and rule number one is follow all the rules. So somebody went and found the commander of the HRT, who approached me and said, "Drummond, right?"

"No. He's the tall, good-looking guy wearing all his clothes."

"One of those splinters fly into your brain or something?"

I checked my groin. "Nope."

He laughed. "I heard you were crazy as hell. Listen, you did a good job. We appreciate it."

"Aw, any dumbass could've done it."

"My thoughts exactly." He stopped smiling. "Now, are you getting into that ambulance or do I put your ass in?"

Through the corner of my eye I saw a few TV cameramen taking shots, and one was about ten feet away and just starting a sweep in our direction. Before I made *Five O'Clock Live* in my present condition, I stepped into the back of the ambulance.

I even got a ride in a wheelchair once we arrived at Arlington General and was hustled toward the operating room. A pair of young docs had a field day, digging shards of glass out of my skin and stitching me up. One even offered me the fragments, suggesting they would make a very memorable stained-glass mosaic. Another noted the scars from my old war wounds and remarked upon what a terrifically popular person I must be. They were very funny. Seriously.

I swallowed three aspirins, and one of the docs told me to wait thirty minutes for observation, in the event I had a sudden attack of common sense, unlikely as that might be. I was given a set of genuine surgeon's scrubs to wear, which was pretty cool. I was assured it would be on my bill of course.

I was allowed to walk on my own out to the waiting room, and I found a chair off in the corner, where, for the first time in two days, I was alone and could think.

Starting from when Jennie picked me up at the George Bush Center for Intelligence, the past forty-eight hours had been like some Hollywood action movie at 78 rpm, a blur of gore, emotional chaos, and frantic confusion. I had seen enough death and misery for a lifetime, and those images were imprinted on my brain. I had set up four people to die, and I had a few misgivings about that. I had a lot to contemplate.

But there happened to be a TV perched on a nearby wall bracket, the evening news was on, and the shootout was the story of the hour, the day, and probably the month. I leaned back into my chair, put my feet up, and started watching, when a voice inside my head screamed, Hey idiot, you haven't slept in two days.

Then somebody was shaking my shoulder, asking, "Hey—you all right?"

I saw Agent Rita Sanchez, holding two steaming cups of coffee, bless her heart. I had not a clue how long I had slept, nor was there a way to tell. In hospitals there is no day and no night.

Rita fell into the seat beside me. She handed me a cup, and I took a long sip. She informed me, "Jennie said you might need a ride home. She's real busy right now."

"I'll bet."

"How you doing?"

I could answer that two ways—honestly or not. So I lied. "Fine. Glad it's over, glad the good guys won . . ."

She smiled knowingly. "You got postpartem blues. All that

adrenaline gets pumped into you, then it just goes, like a petered-out balloon. I see it all the time."

"You don't see it this time."

"I think I do."

"I think you don't. The knights slew the dragons, I'm glad."

"Sure you are." After a moment she added, "We're gonna need a statement. You're the only person who actually spent time with these people."

"The only one who survived."

"Same thing."

"No, it's not the same thing."

Rita detected that I was in a queer mood and decided not to press it. Changing the subject, she said, "They put up a hell of a battle at the end. The HRT guys said they fought like wildcats. The woman went down last. She ran out of the bedroom spraying her M16."

"In fact, I was wondering about that."

"About what?"

I looked Rita in the eyes. "Correct me if I'm wrong. It was my impression that the proper procedure in hostage rescue situations is to first warn the suspects they are surrounded, then offer to negotiate, and only if that fails . . . then assault by force."

"There are times when we do it that way."

"Why wasn't it done that way *this* time?"

"Tactical judgment."

"I see. Well . . . what made this assault so different that it was decided to deviate from procedure?"

She matter-of-factly replied, "We have a standard template for making these calls. Assessment of the criminal mindset, prior experience with the perps, an evaluation of risk regarding our hostage—all these factors are carefully weighed and considered.

That last point is always preeminent. The hostage is always our priority."

I think she knew where I was going with this, and I don't think she liked it. I informed her, "I can see where an undeclared assault might be justified, but here's where I get confused. The Hostage Rescue Team managed to physically separate the hostage from the kidnappers. The Texans left me and Barnes behind and fled to the bedrooms. Yet the assault continued unabated. Why?"

After a moment, Rita said, "I make it a practice to never second-guess the decision of the team leader in contact. You should do the same. Those people saved your ass."

"And I'm not ungrateful. But you see, Rita, I was surprised when the team rushed right past me. Nobody paused to check on me, untie me, or even evacuate me. Jason Barnes was equally ignored."

She sort of shrugged. "I'm sure the team felt you were safe and the prisoner was secured. As I said, hostage safety is priority number one, followed by apprehension of the suspects."

"What were the team's orders?"

"What I stated. Secure the hostage, neutralize, then apprehend the suspects."

"Their rules of engagement?"

"Use reasonable force. But this was an extremis situation, obviously. The killers were heavily armed, and I shouldn't have to remind you of all people, they were vicious murderers. If you're implying we sent that team in to assassinate those people, you're wrong."

"Good." I examined Rita's face. "I'd really be bothered to learn the team was sent in on a mission of vengeance."

She did not reply to that point.

I continued, "Joan Townsend's death doesn't sit well with

me. I'm sure it sat even less well with the men and women of the Bureau. I believe down to my soul that Hank, MaryLou, and Clyde deserved to die. But they deserved to end their lives on an electric chair after attempting to lie their way out of it, the God-given right of every American." I paused for emphasis and added, "I would not like to believe I was no better than Jason Barnes, that I was part of a vendetta."

She turned and looked at the far wall for a moment. Eventually she said, "Well, shit happens. You know what they say."

"No, Rita, what do they say?"

"Live by the sword, die by the sword."

After a moment I asked, "Is Jennie's ass hanging out?"

"Not at all. She made a procedural error, running in there that way. But she put only *herself* at risk. The Bureau makes allowances for these things."

This was news to me.

Rita continued, "She swore an oath to a volunteer hostage and risked her life to honor it. Actually, she's a big hero now. She saved your ass, and our bacon. The Bureau don't forget those things."

"What about shooting Jason?"

"Yeah, there'll obviously be an investigation on that. But with all the smoke and dust from the blast, Jennie said she couldn't clearly observe her target. The HRT guys already gave statements that confirm how hard it was to see. The team leader said the thermal sensors were the only things that saved them from the same mistake. She just saw his face peering at her through the smoke and confusion, and she fired."

"If you need another statement to support that, let me know."

Rita nodded. "Come on. I'll give you a ride home."

I stood up and we began walking.

She said, "I never worked with Margold before. But you know what? She's pretty good, a straight shooter."

"Bad word choice."

She laughed. "Right."

CHAPTER THIRTY-TWO

As you'd expect, the case dominated the headlines for the next week. A lot of good people were dead, and a lot of important people needed to be buried with ceremonies appropriate to their fame and station in life. The city, and the entire country, had been caught in an emotional vise, and the aftershock was a huge sigh of relief, accompanied by the usual wave of prurient exposure.

So the Bureau dished out the story in dribs and drabs, a smorgasbord of the good with the bad; of course it was hard to recognize the bad after all the verbs, pronouns, and facts were adjusted and twisted a bit. It's true that knowledge is power, especially when dispensed selectively.

I tend to be cynical about these things, for some reason.

On a happier note, my name and my role in the affair were kept out of it. When you sign on with the Agency—even as a loaner—you are guaranteed complete, ironclad anonymity. This works really well if you owe a lot of people money.

As you might further expect, the White House did its part to make this thing smell less like feces and more like roses. I particularly enjoyed watching Mrs. Hooper on one of those cable news talk shows, like Fox, I think. She recounted the unremitting pressure the President was under as the murderous toll mounted, and his overwhelming sadness since several of the dead were people he knew intimately, friends and colleagues. She described in tender detail how he reached out to their families and so forth. This part was both moving and touching. Maybe this part was even true.

Then, in all sincerity, she said to the anchor, "So the President pulled me into his office. This was the morning Mrs. Townsend was murdered. I'd . . . well, I'd never seen the President so calm . . . so committed . . . so . . . presidential. He said the killers had to be stopped. The American people *had* to be protected, no matter how drastic the action, no matter the cost to him politically. He told me to suggest to the FBI something entirely unorthodox. He said we had to arrange a trap." And so on.

Not exactly how I remembered it. On the other hand, it sounded better than the truth.

I was a little unhappy when the President's approval rating bounced up ten points, for, as I mentioned, I'm not his biggest fan. On the other hand, the guy going after his job looked like an even bigger putz, so maybe it was a wash.

Anyway, the President never called to thank me, and Rita never bought me the promised steak dinner. See how quickly they forget.

I should add that Phyllis gave me a week off, for mental recovery, she said. In fact, her final words to me were, "But I don't mean that literally. I don't really want you returning *exactly* the way you were. Understand?"

I understood.

So I lounged around my apartment for a week, read a few trashy novels, bought some new underpants, cheated my way through a bunch of *Times* crossword puzzles, threw water balloons off my porch, and got bored out of my wits. Mostly, I waited for Jennie to call. She never did.

For some reason, I didn't call her either.

Okay, I called her office, three times. Elizabeth promised to give her the messages, but Jennie never returned my calls. Maybe she failed to get my messages. Maybe not.

So there I was, at the end of the week, walking through the entrance of Ferguson Home Security, mentally rested, physically healed, emotionally a wreck.

Lila was seated behind her desk, wearing a hot pink sweater that showed great cleavage. I didn't even peek, or at least, I didn't get caught. She smiled at me and said, "Welcome back. You're late."

I wasn't in a smiley mood. "I wouldn't be here at all if I hadn't run out of coffee at home."

"Nice suit, incidentally."

"Thank you."

"No, I mean it. You look really . . . good in a suit."

What the . . . ? Following her eyes to the far corner of the room, there hung a life-size blow-up of an idiot in nothing but his Hanes briefs standing beside an armored van. Attached was a banner reading, "Major Underpants Strikes Again." Somebody had a sense of humor.

I smiled at Lila.

She smiled back.

I looked Lila in the eye and said, "Get rid of that picture."

"On eBay . . . tonight." She added, "By the way, three guests are waiting for you in the conference room."

So off I went to the conference room, where indeed, three men in blue and gray suits and Phyllis with a pissed-off expression awaited. Phyllis tapped her watch and said, "You're late."

"Punctuality is the habit of the weak-minded."

"I think you mean punctuality is the habit of those who want to keep their jobs."

"Exactly."

She introduced me to the three gentlemen, named Larry, Moe, and Shemp. Or perhaps they were named Larry, Bob, and Bill. I wasn't in a particularly charitable mood.

Larry flashed an FBI shield and beamed a pseudo-smile. Bill and Bob shuffled their feet. Nobody mentioned it, but something in their shifty manner suggested they were from the Bureau's equivalent of internal investigations.

This was better than a congressional subcommittee, but not much.

Larry appeared to be the ringleader—he invited me to sit, and he informed me that his team was cleaning up some loose ends and probing a few unresolved matters.

Nobody read me my rights, which is always a good sign. Larry glanced at Bob, and Bob put a tape recorder on the table. Bill reached forward and turned on the recorder. I'm not making this up.

Larry informed me, "This is an official testimony. Be accurate and truthful, as best you can. Speak clearly. Now recount for us your involvement in the case involving Jason Barnes."

So I did.

About two dozen times, Larry, or Bob, or Bill interrupted to ask me to clarify a certain point or elaborate on some event. Three times Bob changed tapes, and Bill turned the recorder on and off each time. Seriously, I'm not making this up. But they were good listeners, and they had done their homework and seemed to be up to speed on what occurred, because they knew the right questions to ask and didn't waste too much of my time.

They seemed particularly interested in who killed whom, so I related what MaryLou told me and I hypothesized that—by process of elimination—the rest were murdered by Clyde or Hank. I shared my view that I didn't think Jason pulled any triggers himself.

Bob confided that in fact, ballistics comparisons from the weapons found on the bodies at the townhouse confirmed this guess. Yet there remained open questions about who fired the LAW on the beltway and who pushed the button that exploded the bomb that killed Joan Townsend, as though it really mattered.

But these people wrote reports for a living, and their lives were dedicated to leaving no blank spaces on any form. So they batted around a few theories, and I listened politely, without comment, until we got down to the nutcutting, which turned out to be not an inappropriate metaphor.

Larry said to me, "So when you arrived at the townhouse, only the red pickup was present. Correct?"

"No, the yellow pickup was also present. I was driving it."

Larry didn't like being corrected and snapped, "That's what I meant."

"Then say what you mean." I didn't like Larry very much.

Bob asked me, "Do you know where the black pickup was? The one driven by Clyde Barnes?"

"Why?"

"If you don't mind, we'll ask the questions."

"Bob, I do mind. If you want me to keep answering your questions, you'll answer my questions."

Bob leaned toward me and said, "I'm not here to cure your curiosity, Major. We can always compel your testimony."

"How, Bob?"

"What?"

"I don't work at your Bureau. How will you compel my testimony?"

"We have our ways. Answer my question," Bob insisted. Incidentally, I didn't really like Bob either.

Larry again asked if I knew where the black pickup went after we departed the shopping center and before Clyde returned to the townhouse.

I replied, "Larry, I'm developing a serious memory lapse."

Bill appeared to be the designated good cop. He said, very amiably, "All right, Sean. Some of the money seems to be missing."

"*Seems* to be missing?"

Bill smiled unctuously. "Hey . . . you got me there, didn't you? All right—it *is* missing."

"How much is missing, Bill?"

Time for Bob, and he said, "None of your business."

"It is now."

Larry felt the need to assert himself. "Drummond, I don't like your attitude. I'll remind you again, this is an official investigation."

When that didn't seem to work, Larry turned to Phyllis and said, "Reason with him."

Phyllis smiled at Larry and replied, "I've tried from the day he started working here. The only advice I can offer is to answer his questions. He sometimes responds well to reciprocity."

Larry, Bob, and Bill looked a little baffled by this insight. I'm sure Bureau employees were scared out of their wits by these guys. I'm sure Larry, Bob, and Bill asked, and everybody popped out answers. I was just as sure I'd be an idiot to answer another question without knowing what this was about.

It was Bill's turn again. He said, "About twelve million is missing."

"About?"

He smiled again. "Twelve and a half, to be precise."

I remarked, "Precision is always good, right, Bill? I mean, what if you guys had identified yourselves as internal investigations or whatever you are, and what if I had been distrustful of you right from the start. What if I knew this was an interrogation, not a debriefing. That wouldn't have been good, would it, Bill?"

Bob said, "You'd be well-advised to can the sarcasm, Drummond."

Phyllis interjected, "He can't. It's like Tourette's syndrome. It just spills from his lips, an uncontrollable river."

I smiled at Phyllis. She smiled back. I really liked her. I think she was getting used to me.

Bob and Larry thought Bill had the best chance with me, and he took over. But I didn't really like Bill either, to be honest. He was the sneaky type. Bill said, "Help us determine where the money went. You told us it was loaded in the back of Clyde Wizner's truck when he departed the shopping center. Between our discussions with Agent Sanchez and with you, we've managed to time out approximately how long it took each pickup to arrive at the townhouse. You arrived with MaryLou Johnson, you said, perhaps ten to twelve minutes behind Hank Mercer. Correct?"

Bill examined my face for confirmation. I stared back at him, sort of blankly.

Eventually Bill said, "We know for sure that Clyde Wizner arrived at least thirty minutes later. What did you and MaryLou Johnson talk about during the nearly forty-five minutes you were alone together?"

"Mostly, Bill, we argued about where my cut was to be delivered." Obviously this was a joke. Right? I should work on my comic timing.

Bill did not laugh, or even smile. Bob examined me more closely.

Larry decided I was kidding. He was sharp. He leaned toward me and said, "When Clyde Wizner first called, he specified that you had to be the courier. Why you? And how did he know you?"

"Ask him."

After a moment, Bob also leaned forward and informed me, "The Army would not allow us to view your military records, which they said are classified and sealed. However, the Office of the Judge Advocate cooperated with our request for information. We were informed that although you were never actually stationed at Fort Hood, on three different occasions you were there on temporary duty, once for over two months. Isn't it possible that during those months you might have met Clyde Wizner?"

"Of course, Bob. It's possible."

Larry saw that Bob wasn't doing well, and said, "Here's another thing we find interesting. Agent Sanchez informed us that you initially refused to take the tracking device."

"She called it a suppository. I don't like people looking up my ass. I was joking."

"Yes. That's what she thought at first—a perfectly innocuous misunderstanding. She then assured you it was taken orally, and your excuse disappeared."

"Sounds right."

Bob hit his hand on the table and pointed out, "However, a pool of vomit was found beside the van at the shopping center."

"Hank kicked me in the stomach. I blew lunch. It's in my oral statement. So what?"

"So maybe you were trying to dislodge the tracking device. Maybe you stuck your finger down your throat, initiating an involuntary gag."

"I still had the tracking device, Bob."

Larry stopped using conditionals and switched to straightforward accusations. He said, "But you didn't know that. Through the dense smoke you couldn't see whether it came out or not. And considering the hectic circumstances, you were in too much of a hurry to dig through your vomit to be sure it was gone."

Bob wanted back into the action and said, "Nor was there a bomb in the van, as you informed Sanchez and Margold. We've listened to the transcripts of all your phone conversations with the control van. You demanded they remove all coverage, and you threw a fit when you discovered the tails were still on you."

I think Bill was tired of playing the good cop, which wasn't a particularly comfortable fit for him anyway. Ticking off fingers, he said, "As we reviewed the activities of that day, Drummond, you're the sore thumb. Wizner asked for you, and you eagerly volunteered. You tried to refuse a tracking device. Later you tried to get rid of it. You lied about the bomb and tried to get the coverage eliminated." He paused and then, with half-assed melodrama, pointed a finger at my chest. "Where's the money, Drummond?"

Larry, Bob, and Bill sat back in their chairs and studied me. Now I knew what they thought, and I knew why they thought it. Nor did it escape my notice that they hadn't read me my rights or formally charged me. Ergo, they lacked evidence. They had a strong suspicion backed up by a strong circumstantial construction. Period.

Also they suspected that the moment they initiated the rights process, I would clam up and demand representation, and around and around we would go. Smart guys.

So I looked at Larry, Bob, and Bill and, speaking clearly into their recorder, I said, "Sean Drummond has the right to remain silent . . ." and they sat quietly and watched dumbly as I gave myself a Miranda warning.

When I finished, Bill, with a disappointed pout, said, "That's not helpful."

"It's very helpful, Bill. If I had twelve and a half million bucks salted away, would I confess?"

Bob said, "We know it's not in your possession yet."

"How?"

Nobody answered. Nobody needed to answer. They had staked out my apartment, probably tapped my phones, and surely accessed my minuscule checking and savings account. That meant they had a court order, and that meant I had at least one foot in the crapper.

No further good was going to come from this conversation, so I stood and, directing my words at Larry, announced, "Unless you have a warrant, I'm outta here."

Larry replied, "We don't have a warrant—yet."

Phyllis said to the three gentlemen, "Actually, he works here, and he's not leaving. You are."

Larry nodded. He reached into his pocket, withdrew a business card, and flipped it at me. He said, "If you rediscover your conscience, give me a call." Then Larry and Bob and Bill collected their notepads and recorder, and with nasty expressions filed out the door.

The door closed and there was a moment of silence. Phyllis finally said, "Sean, look me in the eye and tell me you don't have the money."

I looked Phyllis in the eye. "It's mine, all mine. You're not getting a dime of it."

I thought I heard a sigh of relief.

She said, "It's preposterous. I assigned you this case. How could you have arranged this when you had no intimation you would become involved?" She confessed, "I now feel a certain burden of guilt for involving you in this."

I made no reply to that. However, I did make a note in my mental chitpad that she thought she owed me one. I said, "Well . . . I'm not worried."

"You should worry."

"I'd be very worried if they made me meet them across the river, rather than here. I'm a lawyer, Phyllis. Trust me."

She did not comment on that oxymoron. She said, "They presented a very convincing case, Sean."

"A pile of dough's missing, and the accountants in the basement are demanding a pass from internal investigations. Standard procedure. They have to shake the bushes."

"You're missing something."

"Am I?"

"George Meany. He was fired this week. Of course, 'fired' wasn't the expression used, because it seldom is. But you know how it works. A lot of people are dead, and somebody had to take the blame. It was announced that George is the new assistant to the Bureau's spokesperson."

This was news to me. "I had nothing to do with it. George was in charge, and rank and responsibility are a double-edged sword. And at the end he chose to be in the wrong place, at the wrong time, and ended up without any helpings of glory."

"I believe that what matters is not what you think, what matters is what Meany thinks."

Good point. She continued, "He has a vindictive streak, Sean, and he's not without connections within the Bureau." She added, "Incidentally, Mark Townsend submitted his resignation as Director this morning. The President is going to accept it.

Also, your friend Jennie is now the acting ADIC, and I hear there's a good chance that'll be made permanent."

"She earned it. I'm sorry about Townsend."

"Me too. And about Margold, yes, she did earn it. She did better on this case than anybody." After a moment she added, "As did you."

I had turned toward the door, and I spun around and faced Phyllis. Had I been seated this unexpected praise would've caused me to fall out of my chair. "Thank you."

"Think nothing of it." She added, "I'll give you two days to get your professional and personal affairs sorted out. The Agency doesn't need this messiness, nor do you. Fix it."

"Yes ma'am."

Actually, I did have a big problem. It was even possible I had two big problems, one personal and one professional. Worse, there was a chance my personal problems were my professional problems. But I wasn't ready to say that yet.

CHAPTER THIRTY-THREE

THE FBI's WASHINGTON METROPOLITAN FIELD OFFICE IS AMONG THE four largest and busiest field offices in the country.

I located a place to park near the corner of 4th Street, NW, crossed the street, and passed through the surprisingly nondescript entrance. I flashed my CIA credentials and was allowed by the nice front-desk guard to sign a form and wiggle through the metal detector directly into the inner sanctum. His directions were good and I had no trouble locating the office with the plaque that read, "Senior Agent in Charge, National Security." At least, very little.

I opened the door and entered the office, which turned out to be an outer office with a door leading to the boss's office. Elizabeth, Jennie's nosy, chatty executive assistant, looked up and was surprised, though not delighted, to see me. She said, a little uncertainly, "It's nice to see you again, Mr. Drummond."

I smiled back. "Nice to see you, too, Elizabeth. That's a . . . lovely dress you're wearing."

"Oh . . . well . . ." Actually, her dress was surprisingly ugly, a pink paisley top with a bright red skirt, and I wondered if Elizabeth was color-blind, or, these days, I guess, "chromatically challenged." She giggled self-consciously and confessed, "I made it myself."

"Well . . . who would ever have guessed?"

"Do you think?"

"I think you should open a business . . . start a line. You'll be the talk of Washington in no time," I informed her with some insight. "So is her ladyship in?"

"I'm . . . well, you should have called ahead. She's in a meeting downtown."

"I see." Actually, only forty minutes before I *had* called ahead, though Elizabeth could be forgiven for her faulty recall, as I think I might have been a little confused and identified myself incorrectly. So I knew that Jennie had left the building twenty minutes before, and I knew she would not return till one, which was fine. I said, "I wanted to surprise her. Take her to lunch." I leaned against Elizabeth's desk and complained, "Now that the case is over, we're experiencing a little trouble connecting. Her schedule . . . my schedule . . ."

Apparently something on Elizabeth's computer screen suddenly became very absorbing, because she avoided my eyes. "Yes, it's certainly gotten . . . hectic . . . around here. Miss Margold is now carrying two very demanding jobs." Just in the event her boss's butt wasn't covered enough, she pointed at a stack of message slips and added, "She doesn't even have time to return her calls."

"Of course. I just wanted to be sure she's okay. Considering what's going on."

"She's fine. Very busy, as I said."

"Good. I'm glad the internal investigation's not weighing on her. I mean, if I had something like that hanging over my head, I'd be a wreck . . . I couldn't sleep or—"

"Investigation?"

"Yeah . . . about the missing money."

"I don't think I know what you're talking about."

I withdrew from my pocket Larry Boswell's business card, which I displayed for Elizabeth's benefit. "This guy dropped by to see me this morning. What nonsense. Twelve million in bounty money's missing. Do you believe they suspect Jennie has it?"

Oops, there I went again, getting my identities confused. The thing is, this lady was very protective of Jennie and, given the sensitive nature of this office, was not likely to be forthcoming with me. Sometimes it takes a lie to get truth; the point is, I needed to know if Jennie had spoken with Larry, and I needed to know whose side she was on.

Elizabeth eyed the name on the card, and I detected a note of recognition. I said, "I mean, in the event Jennie didn't know they were interviewing people behind her back, I thought . . . you know, I'd give her a heads-up."

"I . . . well, I think she must already know."

"You think?"

She hesitated momentarily before she pointed at the card. "He's been here. Last week. Several times, with two other agents."

This was the last thing I wanted to hear, though I obviously wouldn't be going through this charade had I not suspected something. Of course, the topic Larry came to discuss with Jennie was not her, but me. So I could now put a motive behind Jennie's repeated failures to return my calls. Either she had a guilty conscience because she had dumped on me to Larry, or Larry had ordered her to withhold contact until I was cleared—or on my way to Leavenworth. Oh, there was, I suppose, a third possibility, but being irresistible, I completely ruled that out. The point is, my personal problems were becoming my professional problems.

Regarding me, I was sure Jennie told Larry to piss off, that Sean Drummond was one of the good guys, pure in mind, body, and soul, that obviously I had nothing to do with the disappearance of the money. Partners help each other out in a jam, right? But by the same token, don't partners also call each other when somebody's ass is hanging out?

Elizabeth misinterpreted the worried expression on my face and asked, "Do you think this is serious? Is she in trouble?"

"Nah. A waste of everybody's time. She's a hero."

Elizabeth was proud of her boss and said, "She is amazing. Her intuition is extraordinary. I sometimes think she can read minds and predict the future."

"Well . . . I wouldn't go that far."

"Oh, I would. Do you know that three months ago, she studied our file on that Jason Barnes character? Almost as if she foresaw this coming."

I looked at Elizabeth.

She said, "What were the chances of that?"

What *were* the chances of that? "Elizabeth . . . *what* file?"

"Jason Barnes's clearance packet. As I recall, Barnes's Top Secret clearance was nearly five years old. They expire at that point. A complete new background investigation had to be completed."

"I think you're mistaken."

"Oh, no, I'm not mistaken. So many clearance requests come through here, I'm sure I wouldn't remember, except . . . well, afterward, Miss Margold asked me to retrieve another file . . . a background investigation on Jason Barnes's father."

I was staring at Elizabeth, or perhaps past her.

"It was quite sensitive. I had to go through a lot of trouble to get my hands on it."

Elizabeth was now looking at me a little oddly. She said, "Are you all right?"

Was I? No—I was two beats short of a heart attack. I could not keep the shock and amazement from my face. I felt a numbness beginning in my chest, working its way up to my throat.

"Can I get you some water?" Elizabeth asked, peering at me closely.

"No . . . I'm . . . I just remembered . . ."

"Remembered what, Mr. Drummond?"

It was none of Elizabeth's business what I remembered. Without another word, I left.

CHAPTER THIRTY-FOUR

A QUICK CALL TO PHYLLIS DISCLOSED THE ADDRESS AND DIRECTIONS TO Mark Townsend's home in Vienna, a stone's throw from where Joan was blown to pieces at Tysons Corner.

I slid the radio dial to a golden oldies station and listened to Fleetwood Mac and Heart, zoned out the whole way.

Townsend's home was on Bois Avenue, a French word, I believe, for "woods." True to the appellation, the neighborhood was filled with tall, leafy oaks and well-manicured, unostentatious middle-class homes. I pulled into the driveway, parked, and made my way to a front door neatly wreathed in black velvet. I pushed the buzzer, and after a moment a young lady opened the door.

I said, "Good afternoon. My name's Drummond. You must be . . . ?"

"Janice Townsend."

Obviously this was the daughter we rushed home from college. She was quite pretty, petite, and thin, and I assumed the good looks and svelteness came from Joan. I said, "I'm very sorry about your mother, Janice. I worked with your father. Is he in?"

"Is this important?"

"I'm afraid it is."

"All right. Follow me."

So I did. The house was not at all stiff and formal like its master, probably reflecting the taste of its mistress; it was homey and furnished fairly tastefully, which is as much as you can hope for on Uncle Sam's paychecks. We passed by a living room on the right, a dining room and kitchen on the left, and she and I ended up at a small study in the rear. Janice asked me to wait, then pushed open the door and entered alone. She emerged a moment later, stepped aside, and I went in.

Her father sat leadenly in a heavily worn leather chair beside a small fireplace, with a fire roaring, and the newspaper resting in his lap was unopened and unread. I was surprised to note that Mark Townsend, a man who probably slept in starched PJs, was unshaven, uncombed, and sloppily dressed in jeans and a T-shirt. He had aged at least ten years.

I said, "Good afternoon, sir. Allow me to start with my condolences."

"Yes . . . thank you." He said, sort of absently, "Would you . . . uh . . ."

I thought he was offering me a seat, and I fell into the cozy cloth easy chair directly across from him, uncomfortably aware that this was probably Joan's chair, and this was probably the room where Mark and Joan had spent their Sunday mornings, and I was intruding on his reveries.

As I mentioned, Mr. Townsend looked awful, and, less charitably, I thought, a little out of it. The eyes that were once unblinkingly laserlike now flitted epileptically, and his pupils appeared glassy and dilated. I presumed he had been prescribed some form of medication, which was better than drowning his grief in booze, and probably cheaper.

One of us had to speak, but I had rushed over here in a mental blur, and I wasn't exactly sure how to start this, much less where I wanted to take it, or definitely where it would end. Fortunately, he looked at me and said, "I heard about your role in catching these . . . Well, you took a big chance. I thank you."

I nodded.

After a moment he asked me, "What were they like?"

I knew why he asked, and I wanted to tell him the people who murdered his wife were worthy foes, that our collective failure to get them before the ax fell had nothing to do with our ineptitude, it had everything to do with their staggering genius. But he deserved the truth.

I took a deep breath. "I spent considerable time with the woman, MaryLou. She was wild and trampy, viscerally cunning and treacherous. I observed Hank for only a few moments. A large man, physically powerful, though a hair's breadth from a moron. Wizner had more brains than the others, and certainly he had impressive technological skills."

"He was the ringleader?"

"I think he planned the killings—the single acts themselves. But he had neither the talent nor the background to construct the overarching plot, to arrange the environment, to track the targets, or to design the complexities that surrounded each of the murders."

"What about what he and his ring accomplished at Fort Hood? Some of those thefts showed impressive ingenuity and boldness."

"That was Fort Hood, where he spent much of his life, and where he was on the inside. Also those were thefts committed against a community that had no idea he was preying on them and failed to take proper precautions. This was Washington, our turf. We were aware he was here, we were aware what he was doing, and we did our best to take him down."

He contemplated this, and me, a moment. He said, "I hadn't realized they were so utterly dependent on Barnes. All this, over . . . over what? Family shame." He added, "In thirty-two years in the Bureau, I went up against all types. It's dismaying to see the shades of evil that reside in some people's hearts." He stared at his hands a moment, and I knew this was a deeply troubled man who had spent his professional life fighting crime, and, in the end, it landed on his own doorstep in the most horrible way imaginable. He was struggling to understand why, but the truth was why no longer mattered.

After a moment he looked up at me and said, "I believe that most of us have the capacity to kill, but it is the rare few with the capacity to murder. Don't you think that's so?"

"Certainly that has been my experience. I served with men in combat who killed without hesitation or the slightest remorse. But if you told them to commit murder, to kill for self-gain or for a cause that was immoral, illegal, or trivial, you'd better be able to run fast."

He said, "We come from different worlds, yet not all that different."

"No, not all that different."

"Well, it's over." He looked at me and asked, "Are you a religious man?"

"I am."

"We buried Joan last week. At least I had the satisfaction of standing at her grave and telling her the people who murdered her are all in hell."

I nodded. Though I was no longer so sure of it.

In fact, the time had come to find out, and I said, "If you don't mind, I have a few questions."

"You've earned that right."

"Perhaps not." I asked, "A few months back, you appointed a new SAC for National Security at the D.C. Metro Office. How was that decision made?"

The swift change in topic momentarily confused him. "What's this about?"

"I'm not ready to answer that. Please."

"All right. Well . . . Andy Sinclair retired from the job about seven months ago. Our board that manages sensitive selections put two names before me, John Fisk and Jennifer Margold. John's qualifications were, in my view, more impressive than Jennifer's. She had some brick time and she did well. But essentially she was an ace profiler without Washington or high-level bureaucratic experience, which is important for that sensitive job."

"So you chose Fisk?"

He nodded. "Damned shame what happened to him. John was a good and able man."

"He was killed three months ago?"

"Murdered. Yes . . . though closer to four months, I think."

"Did Jennie at any point make it known to you, or to others, that she didn't want the job?"

"I'm unaware of it. But it was my practice not to discuss personnel decisions with others, and certainly not with candidates. The FBI is not a democracy."

"Of course. Then John Fisk was murdered, and you appointed her?"

"That's right."

"Maybe she mentioned then that she wasn't interested."

"No. She was quite pleased. Why?"

"One more question . . . please." I was stretching his patience. But I saw a reluctant nod and before his mind changed, I asked, "Why Jennie in the first place?"

"Her record at Quantico."

"She was good?"

"Good is inadequate, Drummond. From a technical standpoint, she was a virtuoso. You're familiar with the program down there?"

"Essentially."

"They are our seers into the minds of our society's most serious criminals. A lot of science and fact-based study goes into their craft, but the best of them, like Jennifer, seem to have an uncanny instinct, almost a sixth sense for it."

He got up and placed another log in the fireplace. It was April, so the room was already stuffy and overheated, though I think his medication left him immune. Sweat was running down my forehead, and I felt like I was smothering. He said, "Jennifer's genius was recognized early. We paid for her advanced degrees. She was assigned some of our most difficult cases. Believe me, she helped stop some of the worst monsters you can imagine."

Either it was the stifling heat or something else, but I suddenly felt ill. Truly ill. Ideas were popping off in my head, little firecrackers, and I was reeling. I abruptly stood and said, "Sir, thank you . . . for your time . . . I . . . but I have to leave."

"And I'd like you to tell me what the hell this is about."

"It might be about nothing."

But Mark Townsend was a smart man, with a lifelong cop's read on people. He looked annoyed and said, "Don't try that on me. Why are you here?"

I looked him in the eye and said, "I'm not sure I understand why I'm here. But I'll know shortly, and you'll be the first to hear."

He examined me a moment. "I suppose that will have to be good enough."

"In fact, sir, it will."

"I see. Well, thank you for stopping by."

"Again . . . my deepest condolences."

I walked out of Mark Townsend's office and his home. I could see his daughter, Janice, observing me through the living room window blinds as I made my way down the steps and across their driveway. I sat down in the car and drew a few heavy breaths. I tried to gather my thoughts, and after a few moments, I dialed the office of Major General Daniel Tingle.

His secretary answered and I identified myself. The general came on a moment later, and unfortunately, he remembered me and said, "Drummond, don't you and I have an appointment for a small talk?"

"And at the appropriate moment, General, I'll be there, ass in hand, and you may gnaw to your heart's content."

"Well, I'll be damned." He laughed.

"But first, I need you to do something. I need you to do it very badly, and I need you to do it very fast."

He said, "Does this have to do with—"

"General, I need you—not an assistant—you, personally, to call the Behavioral Science Unit at Quantico. I need *you* to ask what happened to Tanner's request for assistance on that Fort Hood case. This is very fucking important."

I gave him my cell number, and he agreed to call as soon as he had a response.

Sometimes that which should be plain and obvious is too obvious. Fact: Jennifer Margold was a renowned criminologist—in Townsend's words, a prodigy in the foggy art of comprehending the criminal mind, criminal behavior, and criminal techniques. I could barely bring myself to think it, but who more than she had the know-how, opportunity, and means to put this together?

The Secret Service's background checks flowed like a river through her office. She could pluck fish from that stream and apply her particular wizardry to decide whom among those mostly normal men and women best met her need, best fit her notional construct of a homicidal maniac.

She had feigned complete ignorance when Townsend first raised the connection between Jason and his father. Yet I now knew Jennie had read the file on Jason Barnes, had read it months before—noted his father's name—put two and two together, and asked Elizabeth to retrieve Calhoun's background report.

As a profiler and a trained psychiatrist, she would put Jason under her peculiar microscope and unmask—even contrive and embellish—a web of connections and aberrations ordinary investigators would never guess or imagine. With a little more patient digging, she would understand the unique pathologies of Jason Barnes's family. She would be confident of her ability to create an intoxicating illusion around Jason and, through guile and cleverness, persuade the rest of us that an ugly seed in Jason Barnes's soul had metastasized into a bloodlust.

I conjured a mental picture of Jason Barnes in the moments before his death, seated in the chair beside me, inert, confused, fearful, helpless. He had absolutely no clue what he was doing, hog-tied to a chair in that room. He was not a killer. Possibly, he was forged to become a killer, but Jason Barnes, by finding refuge in his better self and in the higher callings of his God and country, eluded whatever destiny intended for him.

I thought back over the frantic two days Jennie and I had shared, from the moment we entered Terry Belknap's house to the final shootout. She had led me, and she had led the rest of the task force, down the road of leads and breaks, of miscues and misdirections that marked and marred the handling of this case.

It was Jennie who insisted that we interview Belknap's Secret Service detail. She knew Jason had been kidnapped the day before, and she drew our attention to him. His running shoes were lifted from his townhouse, worn probably by Clyde Wizner at Belknap's house, and then returned to his closet. Jennie made sure we found that damning clue, and afterward, it was a simple matter of following Jason's trail, as Jennie filled in the colors and contours of a paint-by-numbers portrait of a tortured soul, enraged and conflicted, punishing us for the sins of his monstrous father.

The phone rang. It was Tingle, and he said, "Drummond, I think Agent Margold was right."

"Right about *what*?"

"The folks at Quantico tried to find that file. It disappeared."

"But . . ." *Think*, Drummond. "Don't they have a logging . . . a tracking system . . . something?"

"Of course. The request was logged in six months ago. When it arrived, it was assigned a lower priority and placed in a sort of hold status. Just as Agent Margold said, their procedure is to work emergency and higher-profile cases first, then the hold cases as they get to them."

"They have no idea *how* it disappeared?"

"They have *an* idea." After a moment he explained, "There's only one way it could have happened. Somebody who works at the unit removed the file and carelessly failed to log it out."

That was exactly what happened, I was sure, and carelessness had nothing to do with it. I now knew what I needed to know, and I bid the general farewell.

As she had with Jason, Jennie had probably sifted through hundreds of opened cases before she located Clyde, MaryLou, and Hank, who, individually and collectively, personified the résumé for her plan. Or maybe not—maybe it was vice versa. Thinking back, the murders were tailored to fit their peculiar skills, each mirroring in some way their crimes at Fort Hood. As Jennie knew, practice makes perfect in crime, as in most human endeavors.

She gave them intimate insights into the defenses they needed to breach, and into the vulnerabilities and mindset of their victims, and their victims' defenders. After all, Jennie's office reviewed and provided physical support for the Secret Service and Supreme Court protection plans—she knew which victims were accessible, how, and when. As the task force responded to the wave of killings, as we adjusted our strategies and defenses, she adjusted hers, shifting from the most protected targets to the most careless, like horny Danny Carter, or to the most clueless, like poor Joan Townsend.

It now *looked* so obvious I couldn't believe we never even suspected it. But it wasn't at all obvious. In fact, it was the most stunning fakery I had ever seen. Only one piece, in fact, could not have been more apparent.

We should all have noticed the intensely psychological nature of the campaign waged against us, a psychic blitzkrieg. We awoke one morning to a disaster, behind the power curve, gripped with desperation, and the relentless fusillade of ensuing murders ground us down—left us sleepless, demoralized, frantic, clawing at one another's throats, and, in the end, so myopically focused on the facts that we missed the overall pattern.

The Army has an entire branch dedicated to the pursuit of psychological warfare, an art intended not to kill and maim, but to incubate panic, fear, and confusion, to create division, and ultimately, to cause defeat. Jennie directed the campaign from the outside, and from the inside, she worked on our brittle psyches, selfish impulses, and frayed egos.

I got out of my car and walked slowly back to Mark Townsend's door. I rang the bell again, and pretty young Janice answered again. I walked back down the hallway to the office and sat down with Mr. Townsend and told him everything I knew.

CHAPTER THIRTY-FIVE

Using Mr. Townsend's phone, I called Larry, who rushed over with his apostles, Bob and Bill. They were anticipating a confession and looked a little demoralized when that turned out not to be the case.

Also, I called Chief Eric Tanner, who arrived alone.

Any cop will tell you the hardest part of the job is narrowing the suspects. Once you know *who*, the whats, whens, and hows come fairly easily. Once you know *who*, you wonder what took you so long.

Jennie's plan relied on misdirection. She led the dogs as we chased the fox, and we never once thought to sniff her tail. She was confident we wouldn't, and as I mentioned previously, we all know what overconfidence breeds: sloppiness. The trail of breadcrumbs she left in her wake was long and reckless.

Within a few short hours, Larry obtained her record of travel five months earlier, the three-day round trip to Killeen, the hotel she stayed in, the meals she charged, the rental car she used, and so forth. It wasn't hard, really. It was all there on her Bureau Visa card.

Bob obtained her cell phone records from the week of the killings. What those records revealed were Jennie's repeated calls to several cell phones registered under the name Chester Upyers, though billed to a guy named Clyde Wizner. That Clyde, what a wicked sense of humor. Who would've guessed?

Bill worked on becoming my buddy again. Fat chance.

Eric Tanner really didn't need to be there, but he had earned a front-row seat at the endgame, and I wanted him to have it. And to justify his presence, he updated us on what the CID gumshoes at Fort Hood had learned about Clyde Wizner, about MaryLou Johnson, and about Hank Mercer.

There's always something, and in Clyde's case it was a voracious gambling problem. He was a high roller on a low roller's dime, and from accounts at various casinos he had visited, Clyde didn't know how or when to push away from the table. His only winnings from Vegas were frequent flyer miles and, according to a scrub of his medical records, two cases of clap. As Mom, in her more ruminative moments, used to warn me, one vice always begets another. Also, interviews with his neighbors and some talkative regulars at a local redneck dive indicated Clyde and MaryLou were a hot item and had been for years.

Regarding MaryLou, she had a record: three counts of prostitution, two for passing bad checks, and sundry lesser offenses. Born and bred in a dilapidated trailer park on the western outskirts of Killeen, she never came close to the American dream. Also, people who lived there a long time remembered that MaryLou's mother, who never married, many years before used to date a guy named Clyde something-or-other, a soldier at Fort Hood, if they recalled rightly. The possibility here was fairly ugly and, we all agreed, more than we needed, and a lot more than we wanted to know.

Hank lived three apartments down the hall from MaryLou, had twice been institutionalized, and had an IQ of 72. Neighbors in the apartment complex were shocked and dismayed to learn that he was an infamous thief and murderer. He was widely recalled as a gentle giant, helpful and compliant, a playful guy who liked to horse around with the little kiddies on the playground.

Eric Tanner had another interesting tidbit to pass on. Two of the civilian employees on his list of suspects at Fort Hood recalled being interviewed some five months earlier by a lady agent from the FBI. No, they didn't remember her name, but she was a looker and they'd know her if they ever saw her again.

So day turned into evening, and we gathered together in Mr. Townsend's tiny, overheated study. We were all, I think, shocked and thoroughly depressed. Larry said to Townsend, "What we have, sir, is damning . . . but not damning enough. We can justify an arrest for conspiracy. Unfortunately nothing we have ties her directly to the most serious crimes, murder and extortion."

Bob seconded that view and further advised, "We could get a warrant, but an arrest would be premature at this point. We'll dig all night, but we shouldn't jeopardize our chances of a conviction."

Bill nodded agreeably. Bill was everybody's pal. Bill would probably smile and nod even if I said we should just forget the whole thing. For the record, I preferred Larry over Bill. With Larry, you saw it coming, at least.

Mr. Townsend for some reason looked at me. He asked, "What do you think?"

"Arrest her right *now.*"

"Why?"

"Because she's brilliant. Because she's smarter than us, and offered the slightest chance she'll outwit us. Because she has access to twelve and a half million bucks, and we have no idea what might spook her."

Mark Townsend's pupils, I noted, were no longer dilated or unfocused. The fish stare was back in full force, and after a moment he said, "You're a lawyer. Could you get a conviction?"

As he well knew, no experienced criminal attorney, no matter how rich the vein of evidence or how persuasive the case, ever promises a conviction. But he also knew that Jennifer Margold had ordered the murder of his wife. I replied, "I'll guarantee you this—if she gets away, we'll never see her again."

He told Larry, "Pick her up now."

In retrospect, Mr. Townsend's decisiveness was timely and providential.

It seemed Jennie departed her office early that day, complaining of an upset stomach. The onset of her illness came only moments after she spoke with Elizabeth, her gabby secretary, who disclosed both my unexpected visit and my interest regarding *her* early interest in Jason and his father.

So, the good news. Like her now departed colleagues, Jennie had made no real preparations to escape. I don't think it ever dawned on her that she would lose, and in fact, until that moment, she had every reason to believe she had won it all. The bad news was that it took the FBI two hours to find her name on the manifest of a United Airways flight, high above the Atlantic, three-quarters of the way to Paris, and freedom.

But when you murder the wife of the FBI Director, the wheels of justice do not want for grease. Townsend made a few calls, the pilot turned the plane around, the onboard air marshal changed seats, and he and Jennie became acquainted.

We stayed at the house, swilled coffee, monitored our phones, and traded theories about Jennie, none of which made the slightest bit of sense. At 1:30 A.M., Larry's phone rang; the plane had landed at Dulles International, and the air marshal handed over custody of his prisoner to a team of FBI agents on the tarmac. Jennie was being sped to a federal facility, where she would be photographed, fingerprinted, and our collective hope was she would do everybody a favor and confess to everything. I was sure she wouldn't, but my job was done. I went home.

I went back to work the following morning. Unfortunately I don't wear bad moods well, and within an hour people began avoiding me, which made me happy. Phyllis tried hard to keep me busy, flooding my in-box with memos and wasting my time with unimportant meetings. I don't handle that well under the best of circumstances.

I was haunted by feelings of guilt that I had missed it. I had been right beside Jennie as she ordered those deaths, and had I not allowed myself to become enamored with her, had I kept my eyes open and paid better attention, some of those people might be alive.

Two days after Jennie's arrest, I looked up and Phyllis was standing over my desk. She said, with some insight, "You're useless to me."

"Thank you. I try my best."

"It wasn't your fault."

"No? Who's fault was it?"

"We all missed it."

"You have an excuse. I was with her the whole time."

"By the same token, proximity can be blinding." After a moment she observed, "I worked with Aldrich Ames for years. We often lunched together. I never saw it coming."

"Did you nearly sleep with Aldrich Ames?"

"Oh . . . well, no . . . of course not." She examined me a moment, then said, "By the way, we have a very intriguing development in our Oman embassy. A most valuable source of ours was murdered. Our station chief suspects it may have been the result of an in-house betrayal. A team is being sent over to investigate. We need somebody to head that team."

"Sounds interesting."

"I'm sure it will be. Are *you* interested?"

"Not in the least."

"I think you should be."

"I've been to Oman. It's hot and dusty, there's no booze, the women wear veils, and they don't sleep with Christians."

She ignored this comment. "When you fall off the horse, you have to get back on."

"No . . . you learn to walk or drive." In case she wasn't getting the message, I reminded her, "Not interested."

"Have I mistakenly given you the impression I was looking for a volunteer?" She threw something on my desk that looked amazingly like an airline ticket. "Depart from Dulles Saturday afternoon. Mort will familiarize you with the details in the interim. Do a good job or I'll make your life miserable."

I hate women who think they know what's good for you.

On the third day after Jennie's dramatic midflight apprehension Larry called, which was an unhappy surprise.

As I mentioned, once you know *who*, you quickly figure out the whats, whens, and hows—it's the *why* that often remains elusive. Larry told me they had sweated Jennie for three days and nights without puncturing her shield of sanctity. He said, "You know our problem here? She was a profiler. She helped write the manual on interrogations."

"Then get creative."

He replied, a little dumbly, "We threw away the manual two days ago. Nothing's working. I've got two interrogators experiencing nervous breakdowns."

"Then get new ones. Wear her down."

"I'm talking about the fourth team we've thrown at her. Each day, she just hardens."

"No new evidence?"

"None. If she's got the money, we can't find it."

"Is her lawyer in the act?"

"Says she doesn't need one."

"Because she's completely innocent."

"She swears it. She's making it really hard on us."

"Alibis?"

"She doesn't know who called Clyde Wizner. Says it wasn't her. Sometimes her cell phone was left lying around, and anybody could've used it. Says she stopped her interviews at Fort Hood after the first two suspects didn't pan out, a more important case came up, and she left. Swears she never met Clyde."

"And the Paris thing?"

"You'll love this. The pressure of the case and the crushing burden of her new responsibilities put her on the verge of a nervous breakdown. She had an anxiety attack only French cuisine could cure."

"So she's introducing reasonable doubt, and you have no proof, no evidence. Nothing to convince a jury she did these things *beyond* a reasonable doubt."

Larry agreed this was so, and added that the Justice Department believed the odds of a conviction for conspiracy were dropping fast, and the chance of convicting her for murder had nowhere to drop as it was already nil. At best, she'd get five years, maybe less. And Jennie's cocky obstinance indicated she was aware of it. He finally came to the point of this call and informed me, "She says she wants to see you."

"I don't want to see her. Tell her no."

"Just hear me out."

"I'm very busy, Larry. I'm going to—"

"You were the one who talked Townsend into the arrest. You can at least hear what I've got to say."

"Fine. Why does she want to meet with me?"

"You tell me why."

"I haven't got a clue, Larry." Though he and I both knew it was a lie.

But sometimes, Larry explained, recalcitrant witnesses soften up in the presence of people with whom they feel a strong emotional connection. I informed Larry that my emotional attachment with Jennie Margold was the same as a fish to a hook. He laughed. I don't know why; it wasn't a joke.

So we went back and forth for a while, Larry trying to tell me why it was a good idea, me trying to tell him to piss off.

Because on one level, I thought it was a lousy idea, and on another, more personal level, I did not want to ever see Jennie again. I still had not the vaguest idea why she did what she did. I did not want to know.

But back to that first level, whatever romantic sparks had flown between us were hot and deluded on my part, and on her part, a calculated pretense. Jennie suckered me, intellectually and emotionally—she knew it, and I knew it. I was an aching, self-pitying Lothario, Jennie would know this, and Jennie would find a way to exploit it. Putting me in a cage with her was like throwing red meat to a lioness.

Back to that second level, I recalled a warning Jennie once gave me. If you haven't passed through the darkest forest, you cannot imagine the ghoulies and monsters that inhabit the back shelves inside people's minds. She was right. I had prosecuted and even defended individuals whose crimes seemed to be the progeny of madness, but on closer inspection, always the roots of those sins were sunk in more ordinary, proletarian muck: greed, lust, or some other idiosyncrasy of human selfishness.

Jennie was most certainly different. For all her outward sanity, I was sure she was utterly insane, whatever that means these days. Some stew of demons had mortgaged her soul, and I did not want even a peek at them.

But Larry was persistent. He said, "Come on, Drummond. This might be our last chance." After a moment, he added, "Incidentally, Townsend asked me to pass on that he would regard this as a huge favor to him."

Well, what could I say? So Larry and I batted around a few ideas, and I agreed to meet with Jennie—conditionally—though not until the next morning, and only after I had had a chance to run down one small detail.

Which was how I ended up pacing in a tiny courtyard tightly enclosed in chain-link and barbed wire, experiencing a quiet claustrophobic fit. Jennie insisted that we would meet out here, or nothing. Probably she was just tired of being ogled by prying eyes through two-way mirrors. Or maybe she thought the outdoor setting would level the playing field a bit. Or maybe both. Nothing was arbitrary with this lady.

Jennie was led to the doorway by a hefty matron, who backed away and allowed her to shuffle into the courtyard alone. The day was warm, though off in the distance dark clouds were gathering, which seemed fitting somehow. She stopped about two yards from me.

We avoided each other's faces and eyes, and the silence grew uncomfortable. I knew she was forcing me to make the first move. I said, "Would the prisoner like a cigarette?"

"The prisoner does not smoke. Neither do you."

"Well, one acquires bad habits on death row. Never too early to get a head start."

She ignored this barb and asked, "Are you wired?"

"No. Are you?"

"Liar."

"Spare me, Jennie."

She finally looked up at me. Sounding hurt and annoyed, she said, "I'm sorry . . . I'm having a little trouble trusting you these days. The deal, as I remember it, was you'd watch my ass."

"The deal turned out to be too open-ended."

"Did it? I saved your life."

"Did you?"

Jennie reached up and grabbed my chin. She said, "Look at me. Look at what you did."

So I did. She did look dreadful. She was dressed, appropriately, in a baggy gray hopsack muumuu with matching foot and hand manacles, and white slippers. Her hair was dirty, stringy, and matted and hung in oily clumps and strands. Dark pits were under her eyes, and her shoulders slumped with fatigue. She was still very pretty, but like a rag doll after a playdate with the family rottweiler. In an accusing tone, she said, "Now they want you to finish what you started. Right?"

"I'm here because you wanted to see me."

She acknowledged this truth with an ambiguous shrug. "And how do you feel now that you see me? Proud? Guilty? Disgusted?"

I knew she was trying to put me on the defensive, and if I let her, I knew I'd never get out of the pit. "I feel sorry for you."

She laughed. "You should. I'm innocent."

I replied, truthfully, "In a way, Jennie, I believe you are."

She looked a little surprised by this admission, and I was sure she wondered why I felt this way. In an irony run amok, the profilers at Quantico had taken a deep and incisive look at the woman who had walked among them not so long ago, one of their top guns. Employing their queer skills, they had cast a net far and wide into her past and dragged back a number of revelations that in hindsight were illuminating, breathtaking, and, mostly, quite saddening.

In preparation for this meeting, I had been provided that file, which I read closely.

As Jennie once told me, she was an only child, and in fact, her parents did die when she was only thirteen, though not in a car crash, as she expressed; they were roasted in a fast-burning house fire in the middle of the night. The neighbors told the investigating officer that Mr. Terry Margold was a heavy drinker, a brown-fingered chain-smoker, an abusive husband, and a father whose cruelty was nearly boundless. Jennie's mother, Mrs. Anne Margold, was meek, timid, and overpowered, or as a neighbor described to a police officer after the fire, "Old man Margold ruled that house and beat the . . . well, the dickens outta everybody. You'd always hear howls and screams comin' from that place. I got chills just walkin' past it. Good riddance to 'em, I say. Nicer neighborhood now."

And from other neighbors, more of the same. Essentially, people who knew Jennie and her family in those early years universally recalled a monstrous man, and a childhood of Dickensian horror, a poor little girl born into pathetically harsh circumstances, molded by brutality and terror.

A few pages later I found this interview, conducted with Mrs. Jessica Parker, Jennie's eighth-grade English comp teacher: "She was an odd girl, brilliant, highly competitive, though I thought, insular and utterly stressed. I . . . actually, several of us . . . we often saw horrible bruises, and scrapes, and scabs. Once she had a cast on her leg. Several times I asked how she got these wounds. She claimed through roughhousing on the playground. She would even make up elaborate alibis about her wounds. She could be terribly deceptive and utterly convincing. I knew she lived in mortal dread of her father. Really—I felt awfully sorry for her."

I recalled the scars and burns on Jennie's body, and I understood, as I suspected Jessica Parker had understood, that some scars go more than skin-deep, straight to the soul.

On the night of her parents' roast, according to the police report, Jennie had had the rare good fortune to be at a sleepover at a friend's house, only three blocks and a short walk through the woods from her own home. No arson inspectors were brought in to sift through the ashes, as there was no evident cause for suspicion, the house was small and wooden, and the local fire department found traces of cigarette butts sprinkled around the bed of Terry Margold, a known drunk and careless slob.

Beyond the age of adoption, Jennie was shuttled into the foster home system. Twice, she had to be relocated after accusations of sexual abuse that were never proven, though a medical examination—conducted when she was only thirteen and first entered the child welfare system—revealed that Jennie's virginity was a long and distant memory. Her cervix was unnaturally enlarged with unusual erosion, indicating extensive and painful sexual activity with adult-sized male organs.

Reading through the thick ream of reports from various Ohio State Child Welfare Agency officials, over the years Jennie displayed none of the classic symptoms of abused childhoods— she remained well behaved, no trouble with the authorities, no truancy, no drugs, no alcohol, and no transparent personality disorders. Jennie Margold, in fact, was regarded as a shining exemplar of the welfare system's healing vitality and success. She remained a top student, popular, brilliant, talented, and driven.

I wasn't judging the hardworking welfare officials of that

very fine state, nor did I doubt Jennie's precocious flair for deception. Yet somebody should have had enough sense to know that, contrary to all outward appearances, no child spawned in such a shower of horrors could emerge internally intact. In effect, the more normal she appeared the less normal she probably was.

In an analysis of possible motives regarding the recent murders, some anonymous investigator wrote:

> Jennifer Margold would benefit from the administration murders in two very striking ways. She would exploit her knowledge to humiliate and professionally eliminate George Meany and maneuver herself into position as his replacement. She would also end up with a private fortune, estimated at some twelve and a half million dollars.

No kidding. These were the correct rational motives, but reason and logic had nothing to do with why Jennie killed.

Near the back of the report I found an attachment from a profiler named Terry Higgens with this more insightful description:

> Serial killers are either internalizers or externalizers. The internalizer likes distance, likes to create separation between him/herself and the victim, and conceivably the crime. Most internalizers are predatory bombers or arsonists. Internalizers are cowardly and normally choose victims who are smaller or weaker, as a fair match is the last thing they want. There are exceptions, however. And when they tackle larger, more powerful victims they unleash a frenzied assault, a blitzkrieg of ferocity in an attempt to overwhelm and neutralize the victim.

It wasn't hard to see what led Terry Higgens to lump Jennie in this particular pool. In all likelihood, Jennie's first crime was murder through arson, and her MO in these more recent murders was a variation on the theme, killing anonymously, from a distance, through surrogates. Also, no prey is more powerful than the United States government. Just as Terry Higgens diagnosed, Jennie had unleashed an assault that was fierce, unrelenting, and punishing, a frenzy of killing with such centrifugal impact it squashed our ability to react. Her diagnosis went on to say:

> It should be further noted that many sociopathic individuals, particularly psychopathic serial killers, have a perverse fascination with police work. They attempt to get and stay near the police, hanging around cop bars, shooting ranges, places where the police tend to congregate. In fact, some have been known to attempt to become police.
>
> As a final note, we would point out that pyschopaths are lifelong killers. They start with small crimes, they improve through experience, and they evolve higher-level skills. Recurring success breeds a psychosexual need to escalate their violence and achieve satisfaction by committing ever more heinous crimes.

I thought these observations sounded too clinical and detached to put any human face on. Certainly they did not sound like the Jennie I knew. I had never observed her revealing even a twinge of satisfaction or pleasure at the sight of her victims. Like the rest of us, Jennie appeared horrified and appalled, though it was now clear that the Jennie you saw and the Jennie you got were very different species.

But as I thought about it, the ingredients of this foul casserole—an internalizer, a psychopath, a need to escalate the violence—clearly linked the perpetrator to the crime, nor was there the slightest doubt who choreographed this carnival of slaughter. Still, there's a wide gap between knowing it and proving it beyond a reasonable doubt in a court of law.

Likewise, I thought Jennie's background and Terry Higgens's prognosis explained *why* Jennie plucked poor Jason Barnes from the immense and varied pool of government servants undergoing background checks. Essentially, Jennie hunted for herself, at least a reasonable mirror of herself, a psychological doppelganger she could knowingly bring into sharp focus for the rest of us, because, really, Jennie was describing someone she knew intimately: herself.

Ergo, Jennie was self-aware enough to know who she was, and how she got there. I knew that if I talked with psychiatrists they would tell me that for most, self-knowledge is the first step on the road to salvation and self-perfection. Yet for others, I think, it is the direct path to self-resignation. For whatever reasons, Jennie chose not to fight her inner demons; she chose to feed their terrible urges.

Perversely, it was probably this same self-awareness that drew Jennie to the study of psychology—as girls of the sixties used to say, to *find* herself—just as it gave her the extraordinary acuity to understand other twisted minds. Recalling her words when we discussed Jason, she insisted that he was a victim of his past, that predestination grasped and led him, just as it guides us all. I think, looking back on it, that Jennie wasn't talking about Jason; she was offering me her Jungian rationalization for her own state of being.

But crazy as she might be, an insanity plea was out of the question. She knew right from wrong, and she knew that what she had done was in every moral sense wrong, because she went to such fierce and imaginative lengths to escape detection.

In fact, Jason was a shadow of her own sad history in almost every way, except one—Jason eluded the conscription of fate. Jennie did not.

But in Larry's words, the Bureau now had a problem of Holy Shit proportions flopping around its plate. The scale, sophistication, and difficulty of the recent murders suggested a killer with long practice and varied experience. There *had* to be a long treadmill of escalation in Jennie's past. The Behavioral Science Unit now had to sift through every case Jennie ever worked—particularly her most notable successes—to determine whether the investigator might also have been the predator. Scary thought. But I had my own big problem.

As though reading my mind, Jennie interrupted my musings and asked, "So are we here to talk about your problems, or about mine?"

"You are my problem."

"Oh . . . Poor little Sean got his feelings hurt."

We were getting nowhere. Which was exactly where Jennie's taunts were meant to land us. But this was her idea, so somehow I was on her agenda. I thought I knew why and suggested, "You must be wondering how I knew."

"Why would I wonder? You made lots of blunders and misjudgments. You've made another."

"Have I?"

"Don't kid yourself. Look, a few months ago, I might have seen Jason Barnes's file. Maybe I even saw his father's file. Thousands of files roll across my desk. They certainly never stuck in my mind."

"You know, Jennie, I wish I could believe you. But you lied about your background, you lied throughout the case, and you're still lying. It's too late for the truth to set you free, but it can keep fifty thousand volts from ruining your hairdo."

She stared at me a moment. "I had a reason for that."

"For what?"

"Misleading you about my background."

Apparently this topic was sensitive for her. "Tell me about it."

"It's simple. Every time I tell people, I get this look, and they say, 'Oh, you poor little thing.' I find pity disgusting."

"And I thought you were just trying to hide a bad memory."

"You're a bad memory. You're here."

She was beginning to annoy me, and I decided to annoy her back. "I'm curious, Jennie. Did you stand outside and watch your parents roast? Did you peek inside the window and watch their skin bubble and fry?"

"That's sick. Stop it."

"Did you listen to their screams and howls? Did you sniff the air and relish the odor of their burning flesh? Tell me, Jennie. How did it smell?"

A flash of anger showed in Jennie's eyes. She started to speak, and I said, "Share it with me, Jennie. I want to hear. How did it feel to murder your own parents? This is a new one for me—I am sincerely curious."

But she knew where I was going with this, and she smiled and said, "The shock and awe's not working, Sean." She added, in a tone that was surprisingly nonchalant, "Read the police report. It was an accident. My father smoked. We always warned him it would be bad for his health."

As she said, this wasn't working so I changed the topic and informed her, "They'll get you on conspiracy, at a minimum."

"Will they? Where's the proof I called Clyde? Where's the proof I knew Clyde?"

"As your lawyer will eventually advise you, Jennie, in court not everything has to be proved. All cases have elements of circumstantial construction."

"Yes, and all winning cases are built on evidence and facts. Not conjecture," she pointed out.

"Good point. In fact, I thought it might be enlightening for you to learn how much we do know."

As I expected she might, Jennie liked this suggestion. "It would be very interesting to hear what you *think* you know. Please proceed."

After a moment I said, "Well, you'll recall that I spent a lot of time with MaryLou, and later, a little time with Clyde."

"Don't hold that against me. *You* should recall that you volunteered for that."

"No, you volunteered me. You told Clyde to pick me."

"Conjecture again."

I ignored her and said, "You should know that I informed MaryLou that the Feds knew about Clyde, and that in short order they would know about her."

Jennie looked a little annoyed by this news. "Didn't we tell you not to do that? Didn't we warn you it was dangerous?"

"Very emphatically." I added, "Jennie, I have to tell you, Mary-Lou did not take this news well. She became very . . . agitated. An interesting verb, don't you think?"

Jennie gave no indication that the word was interesting.

"She never mentioned your name," I admitted, "but she talked at some length about the scheme, starting with you going to Fort Hood and tracking down Clyde." This wasn't the complete truth, but true enough.

"How? How did I find Clyde and meet with him?"

"I don't know how."

"Then you're in a difficult position. You can't prove I met Clyde. Nor will you ever, because I never did."

After a moment, I said, "But it's not hard to guess. He was the third suspect you looked into, and the moment you laid your profiler's eyes on him, you knew. So you shook him up good and then offered him salvation. Kill for you . . . and he walks, scot-free, with a boatload of money. Otherwise, he and his pals are going into the slammer until their grandkids' teeth rot."

"Is that how it'll be presented in court, Sean? A guess."

I said, "At first, MaryLou thought it was a bad deal and a worse idea. Right? Until Clyde assured her that their new friend would do more than provide information . . . their new friend would actually head up the effort to stop them. Wow—what a deal. What could go wrong?"

Jennie said, "Complete nonsense. I always agreed they might have an inside source. But it wasn't me."

"But let's assume for a moment it was you."

"This is silly."

No, this was surreal. In every way she seemed to be the same Jennie I knew, yet she wasn't in any sense the same Jennie. The Jennie I knew was brave, noble, and resourceful. This Jennie was a lying, conniving, murderous bitch. I said, "For this to work, first you had to eliminate the man who took your job. Clyde was an expert marksman in the Army, a lifelong gun nut, and poor John Fisk had not a clue he was being hunted. Boom, boom—Fisk was maggot meat, and Jennifer Margold has his desk and his mantle."

Her face remained perfectly composed, as though we were talking about some other Jennie. "Ridiculous."

"Should I go on?"

"You're very clever, Sean. This is almost comically entertaining. By all means."

"Only one problem—how to ensure these killings ended up on your desk. There are like . . . what? . . . four, five SACs in the D.C. Metro Field Office?"

"Four."

"Thank you. The problem is, if it's plain and simple murder, the SAC with homicide on his slate gets the crack at it. So about a month before this thing kicks into gear, you slap up a Web site and put a bounty on the President. You tip the Al Jazeera network to be sure it's advertised, and we learn about it. As the honcho for national security in D.C., you were in the loop when the bounty was detected. Right?"

"I was informed, yes."

"Why did you deny that when I asked?"

"It was compartmentalized knowledge, Sean. The government has this crazy idea that sharing state secrets with strange men I've just met is taboo. Silly, isn't it?"

"Oh, please. The cat was already out of the bag. Phyllis informed the whole group."

"And did that give me authorization to discuss it with you?"

Obviously she had an answer for everything. I said, "Anyway, suddenly it looks like assassinations with national security overtones, and it's yours."

She laughed. "You're concocting a plot so convoluted it will sound outrageous to any jury."

"You're right. It's completely outrageous. Do you mind if I jump ahead to the endgame?"

She rolled her eyes. "Why not?"

"Let's begin with a little setting. I'm in the townhouse with the bad guys, MaryLou's scared that she might get caught, and Clyde's bitching about how his source screwed him. So now I know they've got an inside source and I ask myself, Hey, don't these idiots know I've got a transmitter in my intestines? I'm a cop magnet. Haven't they been warned?"

"Go on."

"Well, I've got a gag over my mouth so I can't ask."

"And if you did ask, they would've killed you and run."

"There was that, too."

"Did you ever think they didn't know because I wasn't their source? Let me remind you, I knew about the transmitter."

"And your lawyer should make exactly that argument to the jury. I would." I added, "But you knew they'd been compromised. And you knew that if any of those three were captured alive . . . Well, that's always the problem with a conspiracy. Someone always turns stoolie."

"Is that a fact?"

"Cut the crap, Jennie. It's beneath you."

"Go on."

"Ergo it was time to improvise. It's not complicated. The secret had to go to the grave."

"And how would I arrange that?"

"You tell me."

She was shaking her head. "You know what I think, Sean?"

"Jennie, I haven't got a clue *how* you think, much less what you think."

My outburst seemed to amuse her. She chuckled, and after a moment she said, "We'll get to what I think in a moment. Finish telling me what you think."

"Well . . . where was I?"

"You were with Clyde and MaryLou." She pointed out, "I believe I was about to save your life."

"You mean *spare* my life. After all, had I not uncovered Clyde—as you know—the initial plan was to kill me the instant I handed over the money."

She appeared to be confused and said, "You seem to be implying that I told Clyde to keep you alive." After a moment of pretending to think this through, she chuckled. "Oh . . . I suppose you're thinking I wanted you alive to draw us to them."

"It was . . . a brilliant betrayal. You advised Clyde that if the cops found them, they would need barter. Just be sure I'm electronically sterile, and in the event of a turn for the worse, I was their way out."

She thought about that a moment. She said, "More nonsense. They had you as a hostage, yet there was no negotiation."

"No, but you knew there wouldn't be. In fact, that's why you had them murder Joan Townsend. She wasn't on the original kill list, was she?"

Jennie looked at me curiously. In her worst nightmare, she was probably sure nobody would ever put this together.

"As you surely told Clyde," I continued, "things were heating up, and all the good targets were too heavily protected. But Joan was soft, unsuspecting, and vulnerable. Poor Clyde was too ignorant to know that wasting the wife of the FBI Director was tantamount to putting a gun to his own head. Feds are still cops and all cops hate cop killers. Cops really hate killers who murder cop families—and to murder the top cop's wife in such a public, in-your-face fashion was a humiliation on top of an insult. There would be no negotiations, and Clyde and his pals had no chance of surviving a shootout."

"Sean, listen to yourself. You're accusing the Bureau of executing those three. I sure hope you don't intend to repeat that in court."

She was right, of course. Though it didn't really matter. I said, "So we're at the point where the HRT guys are crashing into the room, lusting for blood, you're right behind them . . . and you . . . Well, there sat the final loose end, poor Jason Barnes."

Jennie shook her head. "I was cleared in Barnes's death three days after the shooting. It's public record, Sean. You gave a statement to that effect yourself." With a look of staged anguish, she said, "All that smoke and confusion . . . it was . . . a terrible mistake. I regret it, of course . . . but we can't change the past, can we?" She asked me, "Incidentally, aren't the investigation findings admissible evidence?"

I nodded.

"Thank you for pointing that out. They exonerate me. In fact, I'll suggest to my lawyer to make sure it's entered as evidence."

We stared at each other a moment. Clearly I was losing this battle of wits and wills. She knew it and I knew it. From that very first murder scene at Belknap's house, I now knew, Jennie had chosen me. I had impressed her with my bright deductions and pissed her off with my cockiness, and Jennie had decided I was the one to beat. She would cozy up to me, she would partner with me, we would share intimacies and grow close, perhaps she would even fuck me. And then she would kill me.

Recalling the look on her face at the instant before she blew Jason's brains out of his head, I was sure she toyed with the idea of popping us both. Had she thought she could fabricate an excuse, had she thought she could get away with it, I wouldn't be in this prison yard, I'd be a chalk outline. She was now settling that belated score by letting me know she was smarter than me, she would get away with these murders, she would win.

In fact, Jennie said, "But neither Clyde nor MaryLou ever mentioned my name, did they?"

"No . . . they never did."

"Nor can you prove that I met Clyde, or that I ever called him."

"There are no surviving witnesses."

"I've already offered perfectly plausible explanations for the evidence you have, haven't I?"

"Plausible enough."

She nodded. "You don't see the fatal problem with your fantasy, Sean?"

"Tell me."

"They never mentioned my name because I wasn't their source. There are no witnesses . . . there is no evidence, because it wasn't me." She sounded sincere, without a wrinkle of dishonesty on her face or even a hint of insincerity in her blue eyes. In fact she was so utterly convincing, no jury in the world would disbelieve her. She stepped toward me and took my hands. She smiled. "I'm afraid you're going to make a lousy witness."

"Am I?"

"Were you falling for me, Sean?"

I wasn't going to answer that.

Of course she already knew the answer. "Because you're obviously brokenhearted and embittered. You're allowing your hurt and anger to cloud your judgment."

"Is that right?"

"Look, it's time to be honest with yourself. You were a decent partner and mildly entertaining company, Sean. That's all there ever was. I'm sorry if you thought there was more." She squeezed my hand and added, "There wasn't."

"I know."

"I hope you do know." We stared at each other for a long moment. Endgame. She had gloated at her victory and was administering her coup de grâce. She looked at me long enough to be sure I knew she had won before she glanced at her watch and said, "Oh my, look how the time flies. My exercise period starts in only two minutes. You don't mind, do you?"

"Not at all."

I turned and started to walk away. About ten feet from Jennie, I turned back around and faced her. I said, "Back at the townhouse, you nearly killed me, didn't you? You thought about it, didn't you?"

She shrugged, a gesture of complete neutrality. Yet, given the nature of the question, anything but neutral. In that moment Jennie wanted me to know, wanted me to fully appreciate that I was, in her mind, entirely disposable. She could kill me or not; I was that irrelevant.

I informed her, "Not killing me was the one mistake you made."

"And why would that be, Sean?"

"Because yesterday I remembered something. The Bureau was so focused on the killings up here, it's the one thing they . . . actually, the one lead we all overlooked."

Though she clearly knew this was not going to be good news, she did not bat an eye. "Go on."

"I asked Eric Tanner to have his people conduct a second search of Clyde's house in Killeen. I told him to use jackhammers this time, tear it to pieces, right down to the foundation." When she did not respond, I informed her, "They found it in the basement, behind a false wall."

"Found what?"

"Knowing Clyde, as you surely do, he had a great fondness for weapons. Apparently, the idea of discarding one—even one he used for murder—it was simply too much for him. A military surplus M14 rifle with a long-range scope was found behind that wall. The ballistics match with the bullet that killed John Fisk was made this morning."

For the briefest instant, Jennie's scrupulous composure left her, and I saw in her eyes a flicker of fear, of anger, and something I've never seen in any human eye . . . something indescribable I was sure was madness. As fast as it appeared, it disappeared, replaced by an expression of chilling complacence. But she surely understood the game was truly over. She understood that the rifle tied Clyde Wizner to John Fisk's murder, and it tied Jennifer Margold to Clyde Wizner, and as she herself had underscored throughout this conversation, once that connection was made, she was toast.

Also, Jennie had guessed right, I was wired. On that signal the door was shoved open, and two large matrons and Larry emerged. The matrons took Jennie's arms and tried to lead her back inside. She said, "Wait . . . I'm not ready—just give me a minute. Please."

The matrons appeared confused and looked to Larry for guidance. He signaled with his arm for them to release her.

Then Jennie did the strangest thing. She walked straight to me, bent forward, and kissed me. Then she spun around and left with her two matrons in tow, leaving me alone with Larry.

I knew Jennie would not be going to her exercise period. She would be brought to another interrogation room, where two fresh faces she had not yet defeated would take another whack at her. Larry and the interrogation experts had predicted that the emotional shock of this damning new evidence would crack Jennie wide open. They would go back to the textbook, using one lie to expose the next, and would elicit, if not contrition, at least a partial confession.

I was certain they were wrong. And I was certain it no longer mattered.

I watched the door close behind her.

Larry watched, too, then said to me, "Great job, Drummond. You really rattled her."

"But she never confessed," I pointed out.

"She didn't have to. The rifle is the prybar. We'll get it out of her."

Since I was sure he was wrong, I offered no reply.

He looked at me and said, "You okay?"

"No. I'm not."

"Forget about her. She was bad news, Drummond."

"She was beyond bad news, Larry." After a moment I asked him, "What's your best federal prison?"

"I don't . . . Well, I guess . . . probably Leavenworth."

"Put her there. Give Jennie her own cell in her own wing. Keep her in complete isolation. Throw away the key. Pray she never gets out."

"If she ever did, I wouldn't want to be you."

I did not respond because Larry's observation required no response.

The kiss—it is the most universal gesture and, thereby, easily the most misread. In America it signifies affection, or lust, or even love, whereas in other cultures, and in other societies, its meaning can stretch from a modest greeting to a fraternal gesture, to a mark of revenge or even a promise of death.

Jennie made her own rules, and I knew that her kiss was no ordinary gesture, and that, in any normal sense, it defied a simple or innocent classification. She was a trapped animal and that kiss was her last feral growl. As a rancher brands a cow or, I think, more uniquely, as a dog marks a tree, Jennie's kiss was both territorial and an implicit promise that she was not through with me, and this was not over.

CHAPTER THIRTY-SIX

THE RAIN WAS COMING DOWN IN HEAVY SHEETS AS THE GOVERNMENT sedan took Phyllis and me to Dulles International Airport for the afternoon flight to Oman. She had insisted on accompanying me for some reason. We said very little at first. I think Phyllis was happy to be rid of me, happy to have me out of her hair, and she came along to be sure I climbed on the plane and left.

I must not have been paying attention because when I looked out the window, we had left the GW Parkway and were three-quarters up the exit ramp for Rosslyn. I bent forward toward the driver. "Hey pal, Dulles is back that way."

Phyllis said, "He knows where Dulles is."

"But—"

"Sit back and relax."

"Where are we going?"

"You'll see."

"I want to know now."

"I knew you'd say that."

So I sat back into the seat and watched the gleaming high-rises and people rushing around as we drove through Rosslyn, and off to our left I saw the Iwo Jima monument, where five Marines and a Navy corpsman were straining to stuff the stars and stripes into the pinnacle of Mount Suribachi. We entered the north gate of Fort Myer. We drove up a large hill and took a left and ended up at the tidy, red-brick post chapel. Phyllis grabbed an umbrella and said to me, "Come along."

She came around the car to meet me with her umbrella, and she took my arm. For the next five minutes we walked without exchanging a word, her guiding, me following, through the entrance into Arlington National Cemetery, and then down a long hill, through the long, neat rows of white stones with crosses and stars, memorials to the dead. The skies were dark, and a few hardy souls were wandering through the markers. Here and there, I saw people placing a wreath on a grave.

Still walking, Phyllis pointed toward a white stone on our left. "Harry Rostow. I dated Harry in high school. A fine boy. The best athlete in the class. He was on his way to Harvard when the war broke out. Poor Harry got it at Anzio, had his legs blown off and died horribly."

She turned and pointed at another marker, about ten crosses in. "Jackson Byler. The best man at my wedding. Jackson was killed at Pork Chop Hill in Korea. Left behind a wife and two babies."

I too had friends buried here, and relatives. In fact, I had last been here the year before burying a dear friend. Like all soldiers, I could not tread this hillside without getting a dullness in my chest and a lump in my throat. Among all the vast fields and prairies that are in America, these few acres are special and unique, a pasture of dead soldiers, the resting place of both heroes and simple men and women who did their best when it was needed. There is a wonderful gentleness to the place, the serenity of the dead, and more than a few haunting memories. I pointed over Phyllis's left shoulder. "My uncle Jerry's over there. Vietnam, class of '68. The Tet offensive. My father was in country at the same time. Missed his own brother's funeral."

"I imagine you've attended lots of funerals here."

"I'll bet not as many as you." After a moment, I asked, "Phyllis, why are we here?"

She ignored my question. "Oblige me."

Anyway, as we continued to walk, my mind wandered back to the day I entered the Army, like all new soldiers filled with optimism and lofty purpose, the noble knight donning his armor to go forth and slay the dragons. The task ahead was simple and uncomplicated—to battle all enemies, foreign and domestic, black versus white, good versus evil, noble people combating ignoble people, and indeed, God was, is, and always will be on our side. But the years pass. You learn it is never so clean, so pure, so chaste. God hedges and takes everybody's side. You fight the battles to the best of your ability, but each battle has its own cost, if not of the flesh, always there are new chips on your soul.

We reached the bottom of the hill, and Phyllis went left and led me about ten stones in. We stopped, and I looked at the particular cross Phyllis was gazing at: "Alexander Carney, Major, USMC."

"Your husband?"

"I try to come here every April 17th." She fell silent, watching the cross, sharing some kind of silent reverie with the dead. But also, I thought, at Phyllis's age, she surely was aware that the shadows were lengthening, it wouldn't be long before there would be a cross with her name etched on it, and I wondered if she was reflecting on her own mortality.

Eventually she said, "All these fine people . . . how much they would give to live another day, another hour, another minute."

Remembering my biblical verses, I whispered, "The Lord giveth, and the Lord taketh away."

She commented, though I suspect not with relation to anybody on this hillside, "But he taketh away more from some than others."

Indeed he does. I recalled a photograph of Jennifer Margold from the Bureau's background file, taken when she was about ten years old, still innocent, still pure, not yet in the grip of the malignant demons who would infest her soul.

The picture was lifted from a yearbook, perhaps, with twenty little boys and girls gathered in two rows, standing and staring brightly into the camera. They were all smiling happily and innocently, but for one; fourth from the left, in the second row, one little girl appeared sullen and distant, not looking at the camera but into an empty space, as though already aware she was soiled and impure and did not belong in this group.

The world can try men's souls, but truly, children should not have to witness and bear its horrors before their time. I think we create our own monsters, and then we wonder in amazement how they failed us, when it was we who failed them.

Phyllis took my arm again, and we began our long walk back up the hill.